P9-DUD-432

RISE OF THE
DEMON

DIANA ROWLAND

DAW

Copyright © 2022 by Diana Rowland.

All Rights Reserved.

Cover illustration by Kieran Yanner.

Cover design by Adam Auerbach.

Edited by Betsy Wollheim.

DAW Book Collectors No. 1934.

DAW Books
An Imprint of Astra Publishing House
www.dawbooks.com
DAW Books and its logo are registered
trademarks of Astra Publishing House.

All characters and events in this book are fictitious.
Any resemblance to persons living or dead is strictly coincidental.

If you purchased this book without a cover you should be aware that this book may
have been stolen property and reported as "unsold and destroyed" to the publisher.
In such case neither the author nor the publisher has received any payment for this
"stripped book."

The scanning, uploading, and distribution of this book via the Internet or via any
other means without the permission of the publisher is illegal, and punishable by law.
Please purchase only authorized electronic editions, and do not participate in or
encourage the electronic piracy of copyrighted materials. Your support of the author's
rights is appreciated.

Nearly all the designs and trade names in this book are registered trademarks. All
that are still in commercial use are protected by United States and international
trademark law.

ISBN 9780756408282 (mass market) | ISBN 9781101608913 (ebook)

First Printing, November 2022
1 2 3 4 5 6 7 8 9

DAW TRADEMARK REGISTERED
U.S. PAT. AND TM. OFF. AND FOREIGN COUNTRIES
—MARCA REGISTRADA
HECHO EN U.S.A.

PRINTED IN THE U.S.A.

JAN 18 2023

BROADVIEW LIBRARY

NO LONGER PROPERTY OF
SEATTLE PUBLIC LIBRARY

Raves for Diana Rowland's Kara Gillian Novels:

"A nifty combination of police procedural and urban fantasy. Not too many detectives summon demons in their basement for the fun of it, but Kara Gillian is not your average law enforcement officer."

—Charlaine Harris, *New York Times*–bestselling author

"Rowland's world of arcane magic and demons is fresh and original . . . [and her] characters are well-developed and distinct . . . Dark, fast-paced, and gripping." —SciFiChick

"A fascinating mixture of a hard-boiled police procedural and gritty yet other-worldly urban fantasy. Diana Rowland's professional background as both a street cop and forensic assistant not only shows through but gives the book a realism sadly lacking in all too many urban fantasy 'crime' novels."

—L. E. Modesitt, Jr., author of the *Saga of Recluse*

"I was awestruck at the twists and turns and the, 'Oh man, why didn't I see that before!' . . . This series is top-notch in the genre."

—Felicia Day, author of
You're Never Weird on the Internet (Almost)

"Rowland once again writes the perfect blend of police procedural and paranormal fantasy." —Night Owl Paranormal

"Phenomenal world building, a tough yet vulnerable heroine, a captivating love triangle, and an increasingly compelling metanarrative that just gets juicier with each book. . . . Blows most other urban fantasies out of the park." —All Things Urban Fantasy

"I would say [the series] just keeps getting better—but it was already so good that I'm not sure that's even possible."

—Fangs for the Fantasy

"*Mark of the Demon* crosses police procedure with weird magic. Diana Rowland's background makes her an expert in the former, and her writing convinces me she's also an expert in the latter in this fast-paced story that ends with a bang."

—Carrie Vaughn, *New York Times*–bestselling author

Also by Diana Rowland:

MARK OF THE DEMON[†]
BLOOD OF THE DEMON[†]
SECRETS OF THE DEMON
SINS OF THE DEMON
TOUCH OF THE DEMON
FURY OF THE DEMON
VENGEANCE OF THE DEMON
LEGACY OF THE DEMON
RISE OF THE DEMON

* * *

MY LIFE AS A WHITE TRASH ZOMBIE
EVEN WHITE TRASH ZOMBIES GET THE BLUES
WHITE TRASH ZOMBIE APOCALYPSE
HOW THE WHITE TRASH ZOMBIE GOT HER GROOVE
BACK
WHITE TRASH ZOMBIE GONE WILD
WHITE TRASH ZOMBIE UNCHAINED

[†] Available from Bantam

RECAP OF THE DEMON

THE BEGINNING: EKIRI

Twelve thousand years ago, a non-corporeal, immortal race of telepathic beings—the Ekiri collective—arrived on a planet that came to be known as the demon realm. Their overarching goal and drive was to "enlighten" emerging species then move on to a new destination. To that end, they observed for centuries before most took on demon forms and fully immersed in the cultures and ambience of the world. After a few millennia, some shifted to an Ekiri corporeal form and openly became mentors of the native demons—Jontari.

Xhan, Khatur, and Vsuhl emerged as the Ekiri's most promising students and mastered the ways of the arcane.

Unbeknownst to all, an interdimensional conduit connected the demon realm to Earth, and the Ekiri presence drew potency, gradually depleting Earth while engorging the demon realm.

EKIRI AND EARTH

After the discovery of the conduit and Earth, a handful of Ekiri, led by Zakaar, traveled there and took human form to integrate with and guide the natives. For two thousand years, their offspring were fully human, as expected. Then, for the first time in their existence, the Ekiri produced true hybrids. Eleven of them.

The hybrids lacked the experience and skill to control their arcane and mental abilities. This caused instability on Earth, and so the Ekiri parents (demahnk) abruptly abducted their offspring—ranging in age from still-in-the-womb to mid-twenties—and moved them to the demon realm.

To control the hybrids, the demahnk formed mental "ptarl" bonds and stripped their memories of Earth and the parental relationships. When the bonds proved insufficient, they implanted mental strictures to curb many of the hybrids' natural abilities, which included shape-changing and telepathy with one another.

RAKKUHR, EXODUS, AND THE LORDS

However, the demon realm soon reached critical mass with potency drawn from Earth. Core potency—rakkuhr—erupted to the surface and proved toxic to the Ekiri. In desperation, they severed the conduit to Earth, but that only served to trap the potency on the demon realm side with no chance to equalize.

All Ekiri abandoned the planet except for the eleven demahnk parents and a neutral caretaker, Xharbek—and these twelve were charged with stabilizing the planets and offspring. The Ekiri would return in the far future to judge their progress and decide then whether to allow the demahnk to rejoin the collective—or not.

The demahnk installed the hybrids as qaztahl (lords), each with their own realm, and tasked them with constant monitoring and stabilization of potency in the demon realm.

MITIGATION, DISASTER, AND CONSEQUENCES

The demahnk created Earthgates in each lord's realm, both to allow excess potency to escape and to give humans access to the demon realm. Humans and lords mingled, but when women became pregnant by the lords, the demahnk returned them to Earth and erased their memories of the demon realm. The lords' memories were then adjusted to exclude knowledge of the pregnancies.

After several centuries, the Earthgates collapsed. The demahnk Rho, parent of Szerain, merged with the planet's core to stabilize it, and manifested as the sentient demon realm "groves." Xharbek stepped in as Szerain's ptarl—wiping Szerain's memory of Rho in the process.

To help achieve arcane balance between the worlds, Zakaar developed an interdimensional valve system. During this time, Helori tracked the descendants of the lord-human hybrids on Earth and selected one to be the first summoner.

For reasons yet unknown, Mzatal imprisoned Khatur, Xhan, and Vsuhl, and split their essences and psyches between gimkrahs and blades. The gimkrahs were hidden away, and Mzatal, Rhyzkahl, and Szerain—the oldest and most powerful demonic lords—became the bearers of these essence blades.

A couple thousand years after the collapse of the Earthgates, Szerain, along with the summoner Elinor Bayliss, tried to raise his defunct gate. The ritual went horribly awry and, on the verge of Elinor's demise, Szerain managed to encapsulate and preserve her essence.

The failed ritual caused the collapse of the valve system, resulting in a century-long, planetwide cataclysm whose effects still linger. The ways between the worlds closed, and summoning became impossible. Rhyzkahl vowed vengeance on Szerain for endangering his beloved Elinor—even though Elinor's heart belonged to another.

RESTITUTION, ROWAN, AND REOPENING

For over two hundred years, Szerain and Helori labored to stabilize and heal the interdimensional ruptures and distortions. During his research and experimentation, Szerain crafted an "arcane A.I." dubbed Rowan, which was meant to exemplify the ultimate summoner. However, he intended it to be a learning and testing tool only, never an overlay for a human.

In 1908, Szerain and Helori managed to reopen an arcane valve, restoring a thread of connection between the worlds. Fifteen years later, Isumo Katashi, a gifted young summoner, performed the first summoning in centuries.

SUMMONERS AND MACHINATIONS

Katashi became the key mentor and trainer to summoners over the next decades, though the demahnk had their own agenda. The Ekiri collective would be returning sooner rather than later, and the demahnk were desperate to rejoin, as it had become tortuous to be bound in corporeal form and separated from their kind. But the balance between the worlds was still unstable, and they had the legitimate fear that, with the demon realm in its current state, the collective would deny them re-entry. A few of them, led by Xharbek, started hatching more drastic and desperate plans.

Xharbek worked through Katashi to ruthlessly acquire, control, and groom summoners, often via telepathic manipulation and murder.

Tessa Pazhel trained under Katashi, and also spent time in the demon realm in a relationship with Rhyzkahl. When she became pregnant, she was whisked back to Earth. Rhyzkahl's memory of her was tweaked, and Xharbek altered Tessa's memories to forget the demon realm and believe her pregnancy and stillborn baby was the result of a fling with a human. In truth, Xharbek stole the infant (Idris Palatino) to be fostered and groomed.

Shortly after Kara was born, Szerain surreptitiously transferred Elinor's essence to her for safekeeping, as she was a good match. Kara lost her mother at an early age, and a few years later, Xharbek engineered her dad's fatal "accident" to ensure Kara would become the ward of Tessa (her aunt.) He encouraged and manipulated Tessa to train Kara only in the rudiments of summoning, as he only needed a functional summoner, not a *good* summoner, for his schemes.

Szerain had a conflict with Xharbek (his ptarl) and managed to scatter him, breaking his essence into a billion pieces that would take time to recoalesce. As punishment and to contain him, Szerain was brutally submerged within the construct of FBI agent Ryan Kristoff and banished to Earth to live as a human. Zakaar, posing as Agent Zack Garner, acted as both his protector and jailer, and did his best to keep Szerain from going mad in submersion.

KARA, TREACHERY, AND MZATAL

Kara became a police officer and summoned demons in her basement summoning chamber. She accidentally summoned Rhyzkahl, who sensed the Elinor essence hidden within Kara. Wanting control of both, he seduced Kara and convinced her to become his sworn summoner.

She worked homicide cases with Ryan and Zack—and began to develop feelings for Ryan. She soon learned he was actually Szerain, though the Ryan consciousness didn't know this. Meanwhile, her best friend, Jill Faciane, started dating Zack and became pregnant by him. Zack eventually confessed his true nature.

Suspecting treachery from Rhyzkahl, Mzatal and his summoner student Idris repeatedly tried to summon Kara to the demon realm, and eventually succeeded. Kara escaped to Rhyz-kahl's realm, discovering in the process that she had an affinity for and connection to the groves (Rho).

The Xharbek-aligned Mraztur—Rhyzkahl, Jesral, Amkir and, to a far lesser extent, Kadir—stole and perverted Szerain's Rowan construct, with the intention of transforming Kara into a super-powerful thrall. During a horrific torture ritual, Rhyzkahl carved a sigil for each of the eleven lords—plus a twelfth "unifier" sigil—into her torso with his essence blade, Xhan. Mzatal managed to rescue her right before the ritual was finalized.

Mzatal trained her in the arcane, and they eventually developed a deep relationship. Kara learned that Elinor's essence was attached to her own.

DESPERATE MEASURES

The Mraztur and Katashi captured Idris and took him to Earth, where they murdered his sister in a brutal ritual designed to sub-jugate him as well as activate Kara's sigil scars to make her Rowan. They also attempted to use the valve system to travel between the planets but caused rampant instability.

To counter their machinations, Mzatal came to Earth with Kara and, while investigating valves, saved a young hacker (Paul Ortiz) and his bodyguard (Bryce Thatcher/Taggart) from asso-ciates of J.M. Farouche—a deeply crooked businessman and accomplice of the Mraztur.

Kara and her allies battled the Mraztur at the Farouche plan-tation. Unable to abide Rhyzkahl's behavior any longer, Zakaar broke his ptarl bond with him—grievously shattering both while turning the tide of the battle in Kara's favor. However, Idris was badly injured, and Mzatal released an arcane flare that nearly killed Paul. Kadir severed his already-loose ties with the Mraz-tur due to their utter disregard for interdimensional stability.

NO REST FOR THE WEARY

The battle was won, but the remaining Mraztur and Katashi con-tinued their perversion of the valves in order to fulfill Xharbek's drastic plan to rebalance potency levels regardless of the cost to Earth.

At the same time, the Mraztur's ritual was gradually succeeding in activating Kara's sigil scars. In a desperate and brilliant move, Szerain altered the twelfth "unifier" sigil—linking it to Jill and Zakaar's unborn child—and allowed Kara to be briefly overtaken by the Rowan construct. He then stabbed her with his essence blade, withdrawing it just in time to remove Rowan but not kill Kara.

Kara learned that her aunt Tessa had lied to her and betrayed her in order to keep Kara under the control of Katashi and the Mraztur.

While trying to stop Katashi, Kara was attacked by Angus McDunn, who had the talent to enhance or diminish arcane abilities. He drained hers to near nothing but inexplicably (to Kara) left a fragment behind so she had a chance of recovering.

GROUND ZERO AND KATASHI'S DEFEAT

Katashi prepared to set off an arcane explosion in a valve in downtown Beaulac. Kara and her allies were trying—and failing—to stop them when Jill's near-term baby (Ashava) *teleported out of Jill* in baby-dragon form and managed to keep the explosion localized rather than world-shattering, though mutagen from the ruptured valve still contaminated the area. Idris killed Katashi. Zakaar and Ryan/Szerain appeared and stole Ashava away to keep her safe from Xharbek. Jill was not pleased.

During the upheaval, Mzatal tethered Rhyzkahl to Kara's nexus. This imprisonment allowed her to tap Rhyzkahl's lordpowers, recover her own arcane abilities, and gain deep arcane insight—as well as come to terms with his ritual brutalization of her.

RIFTS AND COMPLICATIONS

When Jontari demons began forming rifts between the worlds and attacking Earth, Kara became the Arcane Commander of DIRT—Demonic Incursion Retaliation and Tactics.

Kara found out Xharbek held the living body of Elinor (sans essence) at a federal facility. Elinor's lover, Giovanni, who was presumed killed along with her, also appeared on Earth and was brought to Kara. Meanwhile, some people who were exposed to the mutagen at ground zero began inexplicably sweating red goo before becoming encased in impenetrable pods.

During this time, Kara received upsetting and confusing intel that implied Tessa might have been manipulated and perhaps had not willingly betrayed Kara.

KARA'S DEMONIC PACT AND XHARBEK'S FURY

To rescue Elinor from Xharbek, Kara decided to summon Dekkak—a powerful Jontari Imperator demon. Xharbek tried to convince Dekkak to kill Kara, but Seretis offered himself to Dekkak as prisoner and slave in order to spare Kara's life. Dekkak and Kara struck a deal: Dekkak would rescue Elinor and, in exchange, Kara had only a few months to recover the three essence blades and return them to the Jontari, or her life would be forfeit.

Kara made the pact. One of the compound guards, Bubba Suarez, volunteered to go with Dekkak as a hostage. After Elinor was rescued and her essence restored, Xharbek reacted with fury, intending to flood the Earth with rakkuhr. Kara and her allies managed to defeat Xharbek, and Mzatal, using two essence blades, scattered his essence, reducing him to a non-threat for the foreseeable future.

However, Mzatal was being controlled more and more by his ptarl, Ilana, who'd been allied with Xharbek and was just as desperate to return to the Ekiri collective.

RESPITE

Zakaar, debilitated from breaking the ptarl bond with Rhyzkahl, was too weak to hold a physical form any longer. With Szerain's help, he went non-corporeal and sequestered himself within Szerain, for his own recovery and protection.

The pod people emerged, mutated in strange yet beneficial ways. The kittens Squig and Fillion transform into winged cats after exposure to ground zero mutagen. Ashava, as the only unfettered demonic lord, shape-changed to playfully fly with them. Kara, Szerain, and the others knew there was still a hard road ahead of them but began to have hope for the future.

Chapter 1

Mzatal stood facing away from me, hands clasped behind his back, and framed by the glass wall of his solarium. Beyond, demons wheeled and sparred above the restless, sunlit sea, their bellows clear and resonant.

Surely if I didn't move, didn't breathe, I could hold on to this moment.

"Zharkat," he murmured. *Beloved.*

My resolve evaporated. I wrapped my arms around him, rested my cheek against his back, breathed in his familiar scent—like petrichor with the faintest whiff of sulfur. I would take whatever moments I could get.

"Boss." My term of affection for him, our private joke—one I thought I might never have a chance to speak again.

He turned in my arms and cradled me to his chest. I sighed into the comfort of the embrace, relaxed for the first time in ages. The deep thud of his heart amplified into a rumble of thunder, a perfect complement to our communion. After a time, he eased back and laid his palm against my cheek. The demons were gone, and lightning streaked through roiling clouds. Warmth filled eyes the color of the storm, and a flicker of a smile touched his lips. "I miss you."

My throat tightened. "Miss you, too." I wiped a trickle of blood from his temple. "I'm so worried about you. About what Ilana has done to—"

He held a finger to his lips. With his shushing exhale, the solarium phosphoresced, flowed away. Stars shimmered in a moonless sky, crickets rasped, and a soft breeze carried the fragrance of rain and pines. We sat on the back steps of my house, his arm around me. Weedy grass stretched unbroken to the surrounding trees, and deer grazed near a trail leading into the woods.

Home. My haven and retreat. Like it used to be. Before it became a militarized compound.

Mzatal tightened his arm around me. "Do not worry for me, beloved."

"How can I not?" I tugged his braid and found it bound so tightly it felt like steel cable. "I just wish I knew how to fix the worlds. How to free you."

"It would seem impossible."

"Doing the impossible is in our job description. Together we can do anything."

"Even if we aren't together." A smile I felt to my core lit his eyes as he echoed my thought from what seemed like an age ago.

"I'm just so tired of it all." I buried my face against his neck, sensed the arcane flare of my sigil on his chest—the scar he had sculpted to remind him of our connection. Of himself. "Oh! I have a ring for you. Made from—"

"Not here. Not yet." The intensity in his voice set the earth shaking.

A reyza bellowed, and an icy vortex sucked away the peace of home and deposited us back in the solarium.

Mzatal gripped my shoulders, eyes flint-hard on mine. "Worlds are breaking." The demon-glass wall shattered into a billion iridescent shards that reminded me of something I couldn't place. Wind whipped at my hair, and a flight of reyza—somehow merely the size of geese—swarmed in, screaming profanities. Their aerial antics toppled a *gimkrah* from its pedestal, scattered scrolls, and sent a portrait of demonic lord Seretis crashing to the floor.

"Could you *not*?" I snarled.

But they shouted louder—"No no no no no! Watch out!"—drowning out Mzatal's words. I tried to read his lips, his thoughts, but—

I jerked awake to a crash and David Nguyen yelling in the back yard. "Dammit, Prikahn. I told you to hold the rope steady. You almost killed me!"

"I am not beholden to you, tailless *chekkunden*." No mistaking the threat in the demon's growling tone toward the compound's arborist.

I scrambled up from the desk and flung open my office window, letting in a wave of frigid air. The Jontari reyza Prikahn loomed over Nguyen and his two assistants, wings spread and lips pulled back from fangs as long as my hand. A branchless pine lay downed between them. Nguyen held an idling chainsaw that had zero chance of injuring the demon should violence commence, while Dagor—a reyza half the height of his comrade at a mere nine feet—crouched nearby, a red pulsing orb of *rakkuhr* gathered in his clawed hand, ready for a strike. Bryce Taggart, head of security, and three of his team stood a debatably safe distance away, monitoring the uncertain situation.

"Prikahn!" I hollered. "You're sure as hell beholden to *me*. Don't make me come out there!"

The warlord pivoted my way, sinuous tail thrashing. "I will not abide disrespect from this unscarred weakling, Kara Gillian." He thrust a wicked claw in Nguyen's direction.

I packed every lick of arcane potency I could muster behind my words. "You and Dagor damaged the tree, my property— against our agreement—and you will *abide* by whatever Nguyen says needs to be done to clear it." I paused to reinforce potency. "Are we in accord?"

Prikahn spread his wings wide, threw back his head, and let out a roaring bellow that rattled windows and sent birds flying.

"Yeah, yeah, yeah. You're a serious badass," I muttered, then counted to three to honor his dominance display. "Are we in accord?"

Nguyen scrambled back as the warlord hefted the tree—surely a strain even for a demon as massive as Prikahn.

"Kri, Kara Gillian. We . . . Are . . . In . . . Accord." The demon snarled each word through clenched teeth, but folded his wings, a signal of acquiescence.

Prikahn loped off east with the tree, but Dagor went still, eyes locked on Nguyen. Only the tip of his tail twitched, and the gathered orb of rakkuhr throbbed like a beating heart in his hand. Shit. Sunlight struck him as clouds shifted. His battle-scarred skin glistened rich burgundy, and adornments of gold glinted on his arms, ears, wings, and horns. Dagor didn't appear as formidable as Prikahn, but I wasn't fooled for an instant. He was wicked-fast, a master of the arcane, and could more than hold his own in a fight with the larger warlord.

"Dagor!" I called. "Enough! It's over. Stand down."

He paid me no heed other than to issue a deep growl I felt more than heard.

Double shit.

Bryce's voice crackled through the desk comms speaker. "*Kara . . . SkeeterCheater's ready.*"

My focus didn't leave Dagor as I fumbled my comms earpiece into place. "And I'm building potency for bindings, but hold on." Deploying the cannon-fired graphene net would probably snare the demon, but it would piss him off royally, making him triply dangerous, and no doubt bring Prikahn right back. Dagor was waiting for something, but what?

He was riveted on Nguyen, who was holding—

"Nguyen, you got comms on?"

Nguyen nodded just enough for me to see.

"Okay, listen." I kept my voice calm and confident, even though my gut churned and flipped. "You need to rev the chainsaw, wave it over your head, and give the biggest baddest war cry you can muster."

"*Kara,*" Bryce said in a voice filled with *what-the-fuck.*

Nguyen didn't move, but his two assistants edged back toward Bryce's position.

"Nguyen. Trust me." I hoped beyond hope I wasn't misreading the situation. "It's demon social behavior. Dagor's waiting for you to show you're either as weak as Prikahn said, or that you're fearless and worthy. That's what you want to show him. Pretend you're Prikahn. Badass. Scared of nothing. *Do it.*"

Dagor stood from his crouch, and the rakkuhr flared.

Nguyen remained frozen in place.

Time for Plan B. Net. Potency. Deal with the fallout later.

"Bryce, SkeeterCheater on three . . . two . . ."

The chainsaw roared. Nguyen swung it over his head and yelled, "I AM THE ONE AND ONLY DAVID NGUYEN! NO ONE FUCKS WITH ME! I DON'T HAVE A FUCKING TAIL, BUT I'VE GOT SCARS OF MY OWN AND THE CHAINSAW OF DOOM!" He followed up with a bloodcurdling bellow that was an impressive cross between a mountain lion and a gorilla.

I remained poised to act, but I'd spotted the demon's telltale flick of his tail. "Bryce, I think we're good."

Bryce didn't seem so certain. Dagor raised his hand, and crimson wreathed in black blasted the ground where the tree had been, sending up a plume of dirt and smoke, and leaving a two-foot crater.

To his credit, Nguyen staggered back but kept the Chainsaw

of Doom revved and swinging. Dagor bugled, a piercing but non-menacing cry, and launched into flight.

Nguyen stopped the chainsaw and sagged to one knee. Bryce hurried over to crouch beside him. *"We'll take care of Nguyen and mop up, Kara."*

I gave a shaky laugh. "That's why I let you have all that juicy responsibility." I eased my hold on the potency I'd gathered, released it. "We got lucky."

"You made a good call. We get through this one minute at a time."

Neither of us addressed the elephant—or demon—in the room. We didn't have to. We lived with it 24/7. Though the four Jontari demons—Ambassadors? Observers? Foreign Exchange Students?—were oathbound not to harm, maim, or kill, one vexed flick of a reyza's tail could end a human—and they were getting surlier by the day. This incident had come closer to a bad outcome than ever before. Logically, I couldn't blame them for not being beacons of positivity. We were all stir-crazy and feeling the effects of the constant stress, and the demons had the added stress of being away from their home world. Yet understanding and empathy wouldn't make a lick of difference if it all blew up in my face.

These four warlords were here as a condition of the agreement I made a few months ago with the ancient Jontari Imperator Dekkak: her eyes and ears on Earth. But it was the two reyza—Prikahn and Dagor—who were my big headaches, both of them sick of Earth and chafing at restrictions.

They could be stuck here for a while, though. Dekkak had fulfilled her part of the bargain by rescuing Elinor from Xharbek, but I had yet to fulfill mine—acquire and relinquish to Dekkak all three essence blades, each the arcane prison for a millennia-old Jontari elder: Xhan, Vsuhl, and Khatur. Problem was, the demonic lord Szerain held Vsuhl, and a very closed-off and dangerous Mzatal possessed the other two. Piece of cake! The only bright spot was that I still had over two months until the agreed upon deadline.

I shut the window before returning to my desk—or rather tried to shut it, letting out a barrage of filthy words when it jammed open with an inch to go. After a brief and fruitless struggle, I gave up and left the window to think about its life choices. Hell, maybe the crisp January air would help me stay awake since, as always,

I had a buttload of work still to do. That said, if there was a chance in hell a nap would take me back to dream-Mzatal's arms, I'd snuggle into the recliner in the corner and snooze the day away. To hell with obligations. But dreams didn't cooperate that way, dammit.

I stroked my thumb over the ring on the middle finger of my left hand. Mzatal's ring, which I'd someday be able to give to him. Beside it, on my fourth finger, rested its mate, both re-forged from a ring he'd given me what seemed a lifetime ago, though it was barely over a year.

Pushing down the emotion that threatened to swamp me, I collapsed into the desk chair and slapped the spacebar of my laptop to wake it up. The yard beyond the window was nothing like the peaceful refuge of the dream. Instead of an expanse of grass to the tree line, my nexus—an arcane circular slab of obsidian—dominated the center, flanked by a rift to the demon realm on the right and a white-trunked demon-grove tree on the left. The tree was a sentient extension of Rho, the demahnk-Ekiri entity who had merged with the demon realm planet millennia ago in order to stabilize it. Beyond it, portable buildings crowded the woods' edge: workspaces, barracks for the security team, along with equipment and weapons storage.

Cory Crawford—my former sergeant from when I was a detective with Beaulac PD, and who was now known as Krawkor—emerged from the communications building and glide-walked toward the front gate, his trio of tails working in oddly harmonious conjunction with his prosthetic right leg. He'd lost his leg during the chaos and destruction of the ground zero valve explosion the previous July. Moreover, he was one of several humans who'd been affected by the mutagen flowing from that valve. It had triggered a bizarre podding process that involved merging with a demon—one of the mysterious and fog-like ilius—and he'd subsequently metamorphosed into . . . well, he was still definitely the same person on the inside, but now his skin was a constantly shifting canvas of brilliant color. Then there were the three prehensile tails. They not only helped him with balance and mobility, but also served as tentacle-like extra hands. Even better, he'd gained two valuable skills: a keen sense of the arcane, and the ability to counteract the constant and frustrating arcane interference that plagued our comms systems—a talent that I suspected was influenced by his prior expertise as a ham radio operator. Within a week of emerging from the demon pod, he'd overhauled and upgraded our system, and now carried a compact sound deck slung across his body like a purse, which he used to control and adjust pretty much everything related to compound communications.

A shadowy form wavered along behind him: the zhurn Sloosh, another of the Jontari warlords. Sloosh had hit it off with Krawkor—maybe because Krawkor was kinda sorta part demon now?—and also seemed to seek out humans for games and simple company, unlike the other three more standoffish warlords.

The fourth warlord perched atop the security office, silently observing everything with sharp eyes set in a face akin to a Chinese dragon. Weyix was a kehza, and though far smaller than the two reyza, he was a clever and dangerous fighter, as I'd learned from seeing him spar the other warlords. Every. Single. Day.

Weyix's gaze tracked Turek as the ancient savik made his way across the yard, translucent scales gleaming on his seven-foot-long reptilian torso. The only non-Jontari demon at the compound—and Szerain's essence-bond mate—Turek was well-liked and exchanged friendly greetings with every human he passed as they bustled back and forth, carrying out their duties of the moment.

Duties. Fuck. I scrolled through my to-do list. Everybody and their grandma wanted something, from reports to interviews to testimony. I'd returned only last night from a Congressional grilling in D.C., and my calendar was crammed with obligations. As the Arcane Commander of DIRT—Demonic Incursion Retaliation and Tactics—I carried the burden of responsibility for damn near everything demon-related, along with oversight of personnel, safety, tactics, and intel. Since making the "ceasefire" agreement with Dekkak, rift activity and demon attacks had decreased by about eighty percent, with the remaining twenty percent instigated by Jontari clans outside of Dekkak's authority. Yet that simply meant we could keep up—for the most part—rather than be overwhelmed. A DIRT response still happened a couple times per week somewhere on the planet.

My cellphone rang, caller ID reading, *UGHLuschkaLackey*. I let it go to voicemail. I already had my landline calls going straight to voicemail, but this Sergeant Cox apparently couldn't take a hint, considering this was his fifth call in an hour. His boss's boss, Colonel Hanna Luschka, was the aide de camp for DIRT's General Starr, and both were members of the U.S. contingent of the IDTF—International Demon Task Force—along with three other bigwigs. She was demanding a high-priority-to-her requisition revision, which happened to be Number Thirty-One on my to-do list.

Before I could even open the file for Number One on the list, my cell rang again. I snatched it up. "Six calls? Really? I told you I'd have the requisition crap as soon as—"

"Kara!"

A jolt went through me. That was my aunt Tessa's voice.

"Listen . . ." A sea of garbled static obliterated her words. "Don't . . . I'm . . ."

"Tessa? I can't understand a word you're saying." Couldn't even tell what her tone was. Frantic? Excited? Angry? Didn't help that my heart was pounding a mile a minute. The mega static told me she was in a location where potency distorted her unshielded phone. That narrowed it down to basically the entire damn world.

"Kara—" The line went dead. Shit. The ID was "Unknown" so no way to try calling her back. If I even wanted to. Did I?

I yanked open the desk drawer and scrabbled through crap to retrieve a battered, soot-smudged letter—an apology from Tessa for her monumental betrayal and a plea to meet with her because "she needed me." It had arrived in early October, a week *after* the proposed meeting date, so I'd dodged having to make a decision on whether or not to go. My trust was thinner than graphene fiber, and for damn good reason. Maybe. The whole betrayed-by-Tessa situation was weirdly complicated, and I wasn't sure of anything anymore. I'd read the letter dozens of times, fury gradually displaced by an aching need to know the *truth*, no matter what it was. And now, I read it again. And again.

And again.

"Sonny!" I called out.

The office door opened, and Sonny Hernandez entered, a steaming mug of coffee in hand. "Thought you could use this. And judging by the shout, my timing was impeccable."

"I'd wonder who'd taken over your body if it wasn't." Even as I reached for the proffered coffee, I drank in his welcome aura of ultra-calm: a subtle but mega-handy superpower that had made him a prize acquisition for J.M. Farouche—a powerful businessman who'd basically enslaved Sonny for well over a decade to be his personal hitman and kidnapper. I drew a deep breath, and the anxiety triggered by Tessa's call slipped away.

His gaze flicked from the letter to my face. "You okay?"

"Better now." I shoved the letter back in the drawer and gave him a rundown of the Tessa call. "Let Bryce know, please. No clue what her game is, but best to keep our eyes and ears open."

"On it," he said, already tapping out a text on his phone. Not long after the Dekkak truce, Bryce insisted I have an aide de camp of my own to help manage day to day business. I *miiiight* have been losing my mind a teensy bit. Sonny stepped into the role and had since proven indispensable. "You have messages waiting from the Dalai Lama and Oprah Winfrey. The China Sea inquiry was postponed until next week, but the Arctic Summit has been moved up to Saturday." He winced and gave an apologetic shrug at my look of dismay. "And Sergeant Cox has called three times this morning. I tried to pry a meaningful message out of him, but he just says Colonel Luschka wants to hear back from you ASAP."

"Got you beat. He's called my cell five times." I took a sip of perfectly cream-and-sugared coffee. "Just because they can't comprehend why the compound needs actual paved roads and a second tractor and a solar power array and an upgraded septic system and a new well dug, they want more paperwork. I already have a billion more important things on my plate than getting umpteen redundant cost estimates, so I guess I'd better return Cox's call and deploy some serious get-off-my-back tactics."

"I have a contact who could help with the justifications and cost estimates. You could let Cox know we'll have something to the Colonel by tomorrow morning."

"Are you sure you're not a deity of some sort? Because I'm ready to start worshipping you."

"Gotta earn my keep!" He hooked a thumb toward the door. "Scott's waiting to see you."

My grin dropped away. "Oh hell no. We've been through this already."

"I'll tell him you're tied up."

I massaged my temples. As enticing as Sonny's suggestion was, Scott deserved better. "No. Ask Bryce to meet Scott and me in the war room. We'll get this settled once and for all."

Chapter 2

I paused outside the dining-room-turned-conference-room to get a feel for the situation. Scott Glassman, a self-proclaimed good ol' boy, paced the video wall with its various muted news streams, manila folder clutched in one hand. A maroon DIRT-issued knit hat hid his bald head, and his face seemed ruddier than usual, whether due to the chilly weather or the topic on his mind. He'd been a street cop for years and had sworn he'd be on the street 'til he died. No desk job for him. A move to patrol sergeant and trainer several years back had suited him well—until the Demon Wars subverted that career path. Now, as corporal of DIRT's Alpha Team, he was still on patrol, but for demon interlopers rather than street perps.

Dammit. I didn't have the bandwidth for this, but Scott had been my teammate when I was a street cop and more than deserved a few minutes of my time. It sucked that I was going to disappoint him yet again.

Bryce leaned against the wall on the far side of the room, focused on his cell phone, made clunky by its arcane-shielding case. A distinctive triple *ding-dop-ding* tone issued from the device, and the corners of his mouth twitched in a satisfied and self-indulgent smile. He'd just recruited an ally—a dinoslug or porkerpie or ubiquitous slimer—in Pro Krasta Nation, the hottest new game craze to take over the world. The stupid thing even had me hooked. When life's a hellscape, what's not to like about teaming up with horrifically adorbs critters to build exotic treehouses and farm fictional fruit? Like most of us at the compound, Bryce didn't get a lot of downtime, so I couldn't blame him one bit for cleansing his brain with some PKN while waiting for me.

Bryce wasn't a member of DIRT, but he carried himself with an undeniable paramilitary air—dressed in well-worn but tidy forest camo fatigues, his Sig Sauer P227 and a no-nonsense tactical knife on his belt. No telling how many other weapons he had concealed on his person, though at least one was sure to be his backup Glock 26.

I swept into the room and clunked my mug down on the table. Almost two months ago, we'd stored my grandparents' dining furniture and replaced it with a sturdy five-by-ten-foot conference table and a dozen chairs, better suited for intense daily use. Occupying the center of the table were three landline phones, an intercom, a bank of four walkie-talkies on their charger, as well as remotes for the numerous TVs on the wall. A computer station networked to the compound servers sat at the far end, along with a platter containing nothing but cinnamon roll crumbs.

Bryce tucked the phone away and folded his arms, expression now unreadable. I shot him a look I hoped conveyed absolute solidarity in the matter at hand.

"Scott, have a seat." I dropped into a chair opposite the one he chose. Even as he opened his mouth to speak, I cut right to the chase. "The answer is still no. I'm sorry. I really am, but we have an essential-personnel-only rule for good reasons."

"Yeah yeah. Inherent danger and stonewalling nosy authorities. But please just hear me out."

Bryce grimaced. "You made your case yesterday. And the day before."

"And both times y'all said no after thirty seconds!"

I tugged my hands through my hair. "Because we've been slammed, and that's all the time we needed to see your request was going nowhere. Nothing has changed."

The "case" was a plea for us to give sanctuary to one Walter Harrison, a reclusive octogenarian, and Scott's long-time neighbor. Though Scott now lived at the compound along with the rest of Alpha Squad, a couple of days ago he'd returned to his old house—in a hot zone not more than a hundred yards from an active rift—to collect a few personal items. Scott had found Walter back at home even though he'd been mandatorily evacuated weeks before, and Walter flat out refused to budge despite the danger posed by the nearby rift. *No family. No place else I want to be.* Scott, being an all-around decent guy, took it upon himself to look out for his neighbor.

"But the situation *has* changed!" he said. "The rift—"

I held up my hand. "Rift-67a belched at four a.m., and there are worflings and ratos everywhere within a quarter mile radius." Rifts occasionally glitched and gave Earth-access to demon-realm fauna—some benign, some not so much. Either way, if nutria, kudzu, and Formosan termites had taught Louisianans anything, it was that the last thing we needed was a *demon* invasive species establishing itself. "It's time to do what we should have done two days ago. Bryce, please notify the Sheriff's evac response team that there's a civvie holed up in the area so they don't go crazy firebombing the infestation until they evacuate him."

"Wait!" Desperation tinged Scott's voice. "He'll resist and end up dead—or as good as."

I softened my tone. "Scott, listen to yourself. You're asking us to take in a man who would rather die than simply be evacuated to a safe location."

"I know how it sounds, but he built the damn house. It's all he has left. Can you blame him for not wanting to be carted off again to some holding facility where they treat him like an invalid just because of his age? He's *not* an invalid, and he's set on staying." Before I could offer a counter argument for why a stubborn solo-player wasn't a good fit for our compound—even if we didn't have a personnel-only rule—he forged on. "Like this house. Your grandfather built it. Maintained it. Now, you have it. You wouldn't want to leave."

"You're right. I love this house and plan on growing old here, but if I needed to evacuate for a good reason, I'd go and—" I narrowed my eyes at Scott. "Wait. If he's so damned determined to stay in his house, what's the point of having this conversation?"

"I, uh, I'm *sure* I can convince him to leave if I tell him he's needed here."

"But even if we made an exception and allowed him in, he's *not* needed."

Scott shot to his feet. "You don't know that!" He looked away and said in a quieter voice, "You don't know that."

My peripheral vision caught Bryce's step forward, and I gave my head a slight shake to stall him.

"I know we're not lacking personnel in any particular area at the moment," I said quietly. "I also know that having an elderly civilian on the property is a risk for everyone."

Scott sank into his chair, blanketed in an air of defeat. "This will probably come across like some emo overreaction, but I swear it's not." He stared down at the manila folder. "My current enlistment is up at the end of the month. I . . . I won't be re-upping." The words came out rough and tortured. "I gotta go take care of Walter."

If he'd stripped naked, jumped on the table, and started singing Baby Shark at the top of his lungs, I'd have been less gobsmacked than by this proclamation. "Scott—"

"Kara, I'm sorry. I don't want to do this, but I *have* to."

My brain whirled through the facts of the situation. There was a hole in the story—one big enough to have Scott be willing to resign from a job he loved and where he was needed—and "being a good neighbor" wasn't filling the gap by a long shot. I leaned forward and said softly, "Who's Walter to you, Scott?"

At first I thought he wasn't going to answer, leaving me feeling as if I'd asked to be let into a private area of his life. But after a moment, he cleared his throat.

"Walter's been more of a father to me than my own dad ever was. I don't talk much about him, mainly because I'm not proud of my role in how things turned out."

I nodded for him to continue.

"Walter founded Harrison Engineering about fifty years ago, and my dad became a partner not long before I was born. Well, my dad threw everything into work—and I mean *everything*. He wasn't abusive, just absent. I basically didn't have a dad at all. Then when I was fourteen or so, Mom ran off with a guy she knew from her hometown, and I started getting into trouble. Shoplifting. Vandalism. Fighting. That sort of thing. Walter had always been around and supportive, but he really stepped up to the plate then. Despite having just as much work as my dad, he made time for me. Helped me find solid footing again."

Boy did that sound familiar. Much like what Tessa had done for me when I was a confused teen.

"I was a senior in high school when Walter transferred most of his company shares to my dad—for *my* future, which I didn't realize back then. After my dad died of a massive heart attack a year later, I jumped at the offer from a foreign investor to buy the stock. My nineteen-year-old self didn't want anything to do with the company I blamed for my dad's indifference, and I didn't have the wisdom to look at the big picture." He scrubbed a hand over his face. "Long story short, Walter got run out of his own company with virtually nothing, and he was never the same. Reclusive for near twenty years, now. But he's always been there for me. I gotta be there for him now."

"Thanks for sharing that." I fell silent while I pondered this new information—and Scott's ultimatum. I had to admit I'd likely do the same in his situation. Wouldn't I? In an alternate universe where Tessa hadn't betrayed me, surely I'd be willing to quit a beloved job in order to keep her safe. *And what about in* this *universe?* I shifted in my seat, uncomfortable with the direction of my thoughts. "All right, Scott. We need you here, and I want to do right by you if we can figure something out." I drummed my fingers on the table. "He's an engineer?"

"Architectural." Scott slid the manila folder across the table. "I was going to bring it up today, but we kinda hit the 'NO' wall again before I could get to it."

I flipped the folder open and perused the images of buildings and houses, then paused on cabinetry and woodwork labeled as being from Walter's own home. Though the style was different, the workmanship reminded me of Bubba Suarez, the compound's construction specialist and all-round handyman. Unfortunately, Bubba had volunteered to be Dekkak's hostage in the demon realm until the terms of our agreement were met. I tapped the last photo. "Does Walter still do this sort of thing?"

"Yep. He's in his workshop day and night."

"Bryce, I'm thinking that with Bubba stuck in the demon realm for the foreseeable future, Walter might be able to fill that skill set for the time being." Not that I really expected an eighty-something-year-old to take up the slack for the strapping Bubba, but the pretense would make Scott happy.

Bryce was clearly on my wavelength as far as the pretense went, and gave a single, thoughtful nod. "Bringing him in as an official new hire would simplify matters and uphold the rules."

Scott slapped the table, beaming. "That's all I was hoping for!"

"Excellent. Glad we could sort it out before I made a complete ass of myself *and* lost you. Now, all you have to—"

The intercom on the table beeped an alert tone in unison with the radio on my shoulder.

Main Gate tower to Compound. Level 3 alert.

A rush of adrenaline hit me, warranted or not. Months of living on the edge had conditioned my body to be ready for critical action at a moment's notice. A compound-wide level 3 alert didn't indicate imminent danger, but it wasn't a "howdy y'all, the field kitchen opens in ten minutes" message, either.

Vehicle in the north ditch, east of main gate. Low-speed veer.

Not surprising. Patches of black ice from two days of sub-freezing temps plus intermittent sleet made the asphalt treacherous, and Louisianans were the worst winter drivers in the known universe. Wouldn't warrant a level 3 alert, though.

Low-grade arcane flicker. Continuous.

That would. A minor flicker was unlikely to be anything more than residual charge from driving through a random arcane dust devil—common enough given the number of open rifts within a fifty-mile radius. But we responded to all arcane incidents as if they were known top tier threats. We'd learned the hard way: take "unlikely" for granted, and that sonovabitch would burn the crap out of you.

Bryce snapped crisp orders via comms. "Gamma Strategy response. Unit one to the gate and tower. Two, secure central personnel. Three, motor pool. Four, livestock." He caught my eye. "No one approaches the vehicle until Kara assesses."

I stood and stretched until my back cracked with a satisfying pop. "You read my mind."

"That's my job. See you out there." And he was off.

"Scott, scramble Alpha Squad."

"No rollers, just boots on the ground, right?" he said, expression impish.

I snorted. "Nice try, smartass." Though deploying the combat vehicles meant more work for the squad, we both knew it was better to have and not need than need and not have.

He let out an exaggerated groan even as he headed off at a jog. "Rollin' rollin' rollin'! Yeeee haw!"

"Go get Walter once we're clear," I called after him. "And be discreet!"

I could only pray this whole Walter situation wouldn't bite me in the ass.

Chapter 3

A quick weapons check, and I was good to go. I hustled into the hallway—and crashed headlong into Szerain as he bounded up from his basement lair.

I recovered with something almost resembling grace. "Going to the party?"

"Someone has to chaperone you kids."

I slugged him in the arm. "Let's do this."

Wintry air struck me as we exited, and I yanked a DIRT knit cap from my jacket pocket and crammed it onto my head. A couple of four-wheeler All-Terrain Vehicles were parked on the drive by the porch steps, and a third rumbled toward us from the east road, driven by Jill Faciane—my best friend and compound manager extraordinaire—returning to the safety of the warded house in response to the alert.

Szerain took advantage of my split-second distraction to beat me to the driver's seat of the nearest ATV. I climbed on to ride pillion as Jill parked beside us, a padded crate of freshly collected eggs strapped to the back of her vehicle. "Hey, Jill, where's Ashava?"

"She insisted on getting Cookie and Flufftail into the shed and will pop back as soon as she's done." She glanced at her watch. "Or in thirty-two seconds. Whichever comes first. *Or else.*"

I grinned. "Gotcha. No way is she gonna risk mama bear's 'or else,' even for the sake of the cows."

"Damn straight!"

Szerain took off, and I grabbed hold of his waist to keep from tumbling off the back of the ATV.

"Y'all be careful!" Jill called.

We barreled down the new asphalt-paved road that cut straight through the woods to the front gate. Though I loved my winding gravel drive for sentimental and aesthetic reasons, it took more than twice the time and didn't offer a line of sight from the house to the gate.

ATVs and Utility Task Vehicles were commonplace on the compound these days, invaluable for making runs around the hundred and fifty acres we now owned. With dire and unpredictable dangers in the area, land was pennies on the dollar, and we hadn't been shy about taking advantage of the circumstances. In addition to my original ten acres, we'd acquired forty acres to the east three months back and developed it: motor pool, mess hall, DIRT Alpha Squad barracks, non-DIRT personnel housing, infirmary, rec center, fields for crops, and even a barn and some pasture for poultry, goats, pigs, and the two milk cows.

Jill tried several times to acquire the property to the west, a fancy hundred-acre horse farm with full facilities. It matched her vision of adding to our livestock resources, and mine of housing the horses *and* riders of the DIRT 1st Calvary Unit within our arcanely protected perimeter. But, despite grim warnings from both local officials and us, the owner had been adamant about staying, certain this "demon nonsense" would blow over and leave her unscathed. It wasn't until two months ago, when a pair of rogue kzak—large dog-like quasi-reptilian demons—killed half a dozen horses and scared the bejeesus out of her that she finally decided to cut her losses and get the hell out of Louisiana, taking most of her remaining stock and abandoning the property. Technically, under the Demon War Eminent Domain Act, we could have simply annexed her entire farm at that point, but we negotiated a fair price and sent her funds.

"Main Gate tower to Gillian. One occupant visible in the vehicle. No movement."

That complicated matters. Veering into the ditch at low speed surely wouldn't cause a loss-of-consciousness injury. I debated rescinding the do-not-approach order in case the driver needed immediate treatment. "Heart attack? Stroke?"

Szerain revved the ATV to breakneck speed. "Dunno. I'm not picking up *anything.*"

"Shit," I muttered. Even from this distance, his demonic lord senses should've been able to lightly assess the driver. Either they were dead, or there was enough arcane energy on the car to shield it. Or both. The possibility of intentional arcane shielding ratcheted up the danger for my personnel. So much for the hope that a nice, benign arcane dust devil had taken out the car.

"Gillian to Compound. Level four alert. I repeat, level three is now four. Maintain twenty-yard distance from the target."

"Anything?" I asked Szerain as we approached the gate and watchtower.

"Zilch on the driver. There's definitely shielding, though."

Sharini Tandon and Jordan Kellum flanked the driveway sally port along with three other members of Bryce's Security Unit One. A sixth was in the three-story watchtower, ready to cover and spot for the sniper also stationed therein.

Szerain pulled the four-wheeler into a butt-clenching skid-stop. I leaped off and shouted, "Open!" as I ran toward the inner gate of the prison-style sally port—a twelve-foot-tall, no-nonsense chain link and steel-barred monster that was warded to hell and back. As the gate rolled, I squeezed through and entered the sally port corridor: bounded on the left by a concrete wall and the watchtower door, on the right and above by warded bars and chain link, and on the far end by a matching outer gate.

Bryce exited the watchtower. "Still no sign of movement in the vehicle, but Krawkor and Sloosh say there've been some wicked arcane flickers in the last minute."

"Make sure the holding cell is prepped and ready," I told Bryce. "I don't like how this is stacking up." The driver could be playing possum to lure us out. Or there could be threats hunkered elsewhere in the vehicle.

"Here's more for your assessment. The car approached from the east and did a U-turn right before reaching the gate. Everything looked okay, but then the car veered hard left into the ditch."

"Huh." I didn't know what to think of that right now, but maybe it would make more sense once we investigated. "Szerain's assessing before we go out. Alpha Squad's on the way for backup, but keep everyone else inside the perimeter until we give the all clear."

"Will do. What about Zenra?"

"Have her on standby until we know what we're dealing with."

The subject of our exchange emerged from the watchtower, shrugging on the bulky fluorescent orange backpack that held her medic supplies. Like most everyone else, she sported a maroon down jacket and knit cap. But instead of fatigue pants, she wore a utility kilt, and beneath that she had a cat's hind legs and tail—proportional to the rest of her—and all covered in calico fur. "I'll be ready when you need me, AC."

Rania Zeno, who now went by her demon name Zenra, had come to us almost two months ago, along with another pod person: Kinsavi nee David Hawkins and former owner-operator of the Grounds For Arrest coffee shop. Zenra had spent the last fifteen years as an Emergency Room NP and, like Cory/Krawkor and David/Kinsavi, had been exposed to the ground zero mutagen. I'd first seen her months ago in the Fed Central medical center shortly after she mutated. But with everything else in turmoil, I hadn't given much thought to what would happen to either her or David.

Turns out, it sucked being a mutant hatched from a demonic goo pod when a government agency decided to lock you away "for your own protection," which was actually "so we can experiment on you in the name of research." Using hidden aspects of his own mutant skills, David managed to get a two-word message to me: *help us.* It took calling in favors and a buttload of arm twisting, but I finally got Zenra and Kinsavi released from a lab hellhole and placed under my supervision. Where, of course, "my supervision" was their own damn supervision because they were both intelligent sentient beings and not pets, projects, or slaves. Both now thrived in their compound roles: Kinsavi as head of the commissary and mess hall, and Zenra as the primary medic for Alpha Squad and the compound in general.

I gave her a thumbs up. "Hopefully we won't need your skills this time, but you know our motto."

"If shit can happen, it will!"

"And it'll find the nearest fan!"

She grinned and retreated into the watchtower. As soon as she was safe inside, Szerain called for the outer gate to be opened. I mentally traced a *pygah* sigil for calm, clarity, and focus before joining him. "You heard what Bryce said about the arcane flickers?"

"Yup. The day just keeps getting better." As the gate slid aside, we crossed over the culvert spanning the ditch and stepped onto the asphalt of the two-lane highway.

About thirty yards to our left, a blue sedan angled nose down in the three-foot-deep ditch. The same distance to our right, a trio of riders on mules approached single-file along the verge of the highway, mounts and men kitted out in arcane-enhanced, matte-black Kevlar armor. In the lead was Marcel Boudreaux, ex-pain-in-my-ass Beaulac PD detective and current head of the DIRT First Cavalry Unit. Behind him was new recruit Delphine Reddappachar a.k.a Redd, along with an older Black man: veterinarian, barn manager, and long-time mentor to Boudreaux, Lenny Brewster.

"Gillian to Cav 1," I said into my comms. "We don't know what we have. For now, hold at the driveway."

"10-4," Boudreaux drawled. *"Be advised there's a drone overhead."*

When *wasn't* there a damn drone in the area? Aggravated, I swept a glance up and spied the compact grey drone across the highway and a hundred feet up. Could be military. News. Lookie-loo. Didn't matter. It wasn't ours. Most of the time, we didn't bother with countermeasures since the compound's warding distorted imagery, so no harm done. But our current activities were outside the warding, and I preferred to not have unknown observers.

Yet before I could tell Bryce to shoot it down, a sleek emerald green shape launched from the roof of the watchtower toward the drone. I reassured myself that the compound warding would keep the flying cat from crossing the perimeter, then jerked in shock when she disappeared and reappeared a dozen feet above the drone—most definitely *outside* the property boundaries.

"Squig, NO!" I screamed, as if the mutated cat—who had just *teleported*—would pay the slightest attention. Cursing under my breath, I added *check compound security* to my lengthy mental to-do list. Was there a weak spot in the perimeter warding? Or had Squig used this new-to-me teleportation ability to get past it? But for now, I could only watch in stunned helplessness as she dove on the drone. If the cat got hurt, Ashava would absolutely *freak*.

Claws extended, the flying feline struck the drone like a falcon on a pigeon, both hurtling downward in a tumble of wings and rotors that would land them some fifty yards beyond the trees that lined the other side of the highway.

"Shit! Cav 1, track her and bring in the damn drone." I fully trusted Boudreaux's judgment and ability, something I'd have scoffed at myself for thinking a year ago. But then again, neither of us were the same people we used to be.

"Kara," Szerain called, shifting my attention back to him and the matter at hand. "Check it out."

He eased toward the car, hands raised in readiness to counter any arcane shenanigans. A red mist like atomized blood swirled around his feet as he summoned rakkuhr, increasing in volume with every heartbeat.

I tapped the nexus in my back yard to boost my senses, then assessed the situation.

Over the car's entire surface, a barely detectable web of blue and green potency strands writhed and shimmered. The web was both meticulous and deliberate, but from this distance, I couldn't discern its purpose. To contain the occupant? Protection, like an arcane airbag? A trap? Or something else entirely?

I took one cautious step at a time, not a bit averse to using rakkuhr myself if the situation warranted. I'd first wielded it nearly four months ago during the battle with Xharbek at Ground Zero, and since then had grown a bit more accustomed to using the unsettling potency.

We stopped about ten yards from the car, a late-model Audi A3. Szerain crouched and placed his palms on the asphalt. Rakkuhr wreathed him as he lowered his head in concentration. My arcane senses tingled with a maddeningly familiar resonance that awakened visceral dread, but I couldn't place it for the life of me.

A couple hundred yards past the car, two DIRT Military All-Terrain Vehicles roared through the east gate and onto the highway. In addition to being armored against mines, ambush, and the arcane, each M-ATV held four members of Alpha Squad, including a turret gunner for the belt-fed M2 machine gun up top. Overkill for the win.

"Alpha Roller one to Gillian. We have eyes on the vehicle and you." Sergeant Debbie Roma's voice rasped over the comms.

"Gillian to Alpha Rollers one and two. Set up twenty and fifty yards from the target. Eyes and ears three-sixty and on the sky. We don't know what we're dealing with."

"Ten-four."

I placed my hand on Szerain's shoulder. Squeezed. "Movement."

The driver shifted, seemed to fumble with the door, then slumped. Szerain gathered the swirling rakkuhr into a dense ball the size of a grapefruit as he stood. "This is high-level arcane work. By a lord. Or demahnk. Or both. I can't fully assess until we move in."

"I can't do shit from here, either." I met his eyes. "Trap?"

"Could just be a bomb."

"Oh, gee. I feel better now." Following a fist bump of commitment, we advanced, Szerain on the asphalt as he headed toward the car's rear, while I jumped down into the ditch to approach the side. Frozen mud crunched under my boots as I moved forward, Glock at the ready.

A dozen feet from the car, my assessment of the arcane resonance finally kicked in with a known signature. "Jesral!" I called out, lip curling at the *feeeeel* of Demonic Lord Asshole, even as Szerain growled, "Ssahr." Jesral's demahnk ptarl.

The arcane webbing flared, and before I could react, a third resonance slithered into my consciousness. Insidious. Familiar. *Vile.* Red-tinged darkness enveloped me. I fought to draw breath, but merciless pressure constricted me, held me fast.

The voice of torment snaked through my essence, whispered promises of anguish. Promises it always kept. *You are mine.* The eleven sigil scars on my torso ignited with impossible heat.

Existence is pain. Pain is existence.

"Kara!" Szerain's voice and mental touch, yanking me back to myself.

I staggered and nearly went to my knees in the ditch . . . not Rhyzkahl's summoning chamber. Not the torture ritual that had sought to make me into a thrall, into Rowan, a tool for the Mraztur. But still, my mind yammered at me to run, far and fast. To be anywhere but here.

No. A quick pygah brought me a semblance of rational thought and slowed the frantic slamming of my heart. *I am Kara!*

I refocused on the threat before me. The arcane webbing covering the car pulsed a dull grey now, as if the web of exceptionally sophisticated wards—created to trigger specific-to-me memories—had spent their power.

I didn't buy it for a minute.

Potency from the nexus and grove tree answered my call, swirled before me like a mini tornado of glass shards. "Go to hell, motherfuckers," I hissed through gritted teeth as I pelted the car with power, smashing the web trap and leaving the car looking sand blasted. Yet for all my will and bravado, I still trembled, my logical brain understanding I was safe while my body refused to forget so easily.

"Kara! Driver!"

Though it seemed as if an age had passed since I'd entered the torture chamber memory, Szerain had moved only a single step. The driver shoved the door open and tumbled into the ditch.

Trusting that Szerain had arcane threats covered, I raised my weapon—mentally cursing the unsteadiness of my hands. "Stay where you are! Keep your hands where I can see them!"

The woman floundered onto her back, blood oozing from her ears, eyes, nose, and mouth. Her breath plumed in the cold air, alive with arcane sparks that danced like bloated fireflies—a phenomenon I'd never seen before.

I stared, lowered my weapon, then jerked it right back up again. "Tessa?!"

Chapter 4

Szerain cursed in demon. "She's been disrupted."

"What the hell does that mean?"

"She's dead without intervention."

My feelings toward Tessa were complicated, but I sure as hell didn't want her dead. "Well, intervene!" I shouted.

Szerain slid an arch look my way, and I stomped down the impulse to rush to her. He was right. Charge in without a thorough assessment, and we could end up in the same condition as Tessa—or worse.

Tessa coughed a gout of blood and stretched one hand toward me like a claw, then went limp, eyes glazed.

"Tessa!" I eased closer and dropped to my knees, stopping a foot short of contact. If not for her faint breath still pluming the air with sparks, I'd have been sure she was dead. "Are we clear?" I called to Szerain.

"There's still interference, but I'm cleaning it up."

Good enough. I touched my fingers to her throat and found a thready pulse. "Gillian to Medic 1. Prep the holding cell for an incoming casualty. Female. Forty-nine years old. Possible internal bleeding. Potential arcane complications."

"Ten-four," Zenra replied.

Tessa sucked in a wet breath. Her eyes flickered open and focused on mine, widened. "Kara," she gasped. "RUN!"

The left sleeve of her sweater vaporized in a flash of violet flame to reveal a glowing arcane construct on her forearm—much like the mark Rhyzkahl had once placed on me. But this one was interwoven with Jesral's sigil and exuded his devious energy signature.

"Shit shit shit! Szerain!"

Szerain lifted his hand, and the essence blade Vsuhl appeared in his grasp, green gem sparkling in its pommel. He strode toward us, expression grim and determined.

Tessa scrabbled at my ankle. "Run . . . run."

Bryce's voice crackled through the comms, arcane interference making it damn near unintelligible. "Security to . . . above . . . stand by . . . can't . . ." The radio squealed and went silent.

A twisted-gut feeling of wrongness flowed through me, even as Szerain pivoted away, face tilted toward the sky. "Kara! Get Alpha Squad behind warding!"

My gaze snapped up, stomach dropping at the sight of the inky circle rimmed with chartreuse arcing electricity in the otherwise blue sky. I stared in horror for barely an instant, then leaped over Tessa and slammed my palm against the car horn in the triple-blast pattern used to signal retreat when comms were out.

"You go, too," Szerain commanded, gaze still on the expanding widening aberration.

"Fuck that! Help me get Tessa through the gate then we'll—"

Brilliant light streamed from the circle, bathing Szerain in a compact circle of illumination, like a UFO encounter scene from a cheesy B-movie.

"Listen to me for fucking once and go. NOW!" He shifted his grip on the blade and traced a flickering crimson circle of rakkuhr around himself as he began dancing the first ring of the shikvihr, the versatile power-augmentation ritual that was the foundation of an arcane user's arsenal.

Shit. Guess I was going to continue my streak of not heeding him, because no way could I abandon Tessa even if we hadn't cleared her yet. Our warded holding cell would contain her and any nasty arcane surprises. I quickly wrapped her in a web of potency to protect myself from any such surprises, then wrestled her into a fireman's carry and staggered up the embankment.

The circle of light expanded, washing over me in a disorienting wave that vibrated my bones and carried the scent of burned hair. Dammit. Too late to get clear. I settled Tessa on the shoulder beside the ditch. She was still breathing but limp and pale.

"Kara!" Szerain called.

I prepped a biting comeback for whatever reprimand he had in store, but instead, he tossed a multicolored sigil my way. It flowed around my fingers when I caught it, like a watery snake.

"Put it on her sternum and bind it in. To stabilize her."

Unspeakably grateful, I wove the sigil to her chest then threw a more robust web of warding over her for extra protection.

The light now formed a circle about ten yards in diameter, with Szerain at its center. Colors beyond the perimeter dulled to monochrome greys, and sound grew muffled and faded.

Searing heat flared and subsided over Jesral's sigil scar on my lower abdomen, followed by a wave of vertigo. In the next heartbeat, the aberration above snapped closed in a flash of chartreuse accompanied by a ground-shaking *boom*. The UFO light winked out, leaving us in eerie and unnatural twilight even as the colorless world beyond deepened to the blackness of the void, blotting out the view of the compound and everything else. The darkness converged above, rapidly enclosing us in a unpleasantly familiar bubble. "Shit." I breathed. "Dimensional pocket."

Szerain continued to dance rings of sigils, now on the penultimate tenth. "Shikvihr! Hurry."

My sense of the nexus and its super shikvihr—my megaconnection to the arcane on Earth—began to fade, and unexpected panic squeezed my chest. Fighting it down, I envisioned a stark-white tree trunk, called to Rho just as the void-blackness sealed the dome—then breathed a shaky sigh of relief. The tiniest chink in the darkness told me they heard, and together we forged a spider silk thread of connection. I was hamstrung but not completely out of the game.

After a final check on Tessa, I hurried to stand at Szerain's left. "Can't shikvihr," I told him, "but I should have enough mojo to support."

"Whatever you can do. I'm trying to rouse Zakaar for aid, but for now we're trapped."

Though the demahnk Zakaar a.k.a. Zack Garner was currently sequestered within Szerain, even his noncorporeal presence provided a smidge of reassurance.

Eleven concentric circles of sigils floated around Szerain, sparkling ruby but still quiescent. With the tip of Vsuhl, he ignited the first sigil of the innermost ring. The rest of the shikvihr flared incandescent, the activated rings orbiting him now as a cohesive whole.

My turn. I pressed my palm over the grove leaf that hung on a slim cord around my neck. Over Mzatal's sigil scar. Over my own heart. I drew on the thread of connection with Rho and traced anchoring sigils of support.

That done, I took a moment to assess our situation. As weird and hazardous as the run-of-the-mill rifts between the demon realm and Earth were, they still somehow felt natural. Yet this aberration, with its crazy UFO light and dimensional pocket, all had a distinct vibe of wrongness, as if the universe itself rebelled.

"What the hell is this?" I asked. "A trap? Or is someone coming through?"

Szerain stood at the center of his shikvihr, looking dangerous in the shifting glow of the one hundred and twenty-one sigils as he scanned the pocket's dome about fifteen feet overhead. "The aberration was a void breach, though not like anything I've seen before—and I've seen many. But as far as who? Jesral." He snarled the name through clenched teeth.

The answer didn't surprise me, considering the mark on Tessa.

But there was also a chartreuse elephant in the room, namely the flash I'd seen when the dimensional pocket slammed closed on us. I'd only ever seen arcane energy that color associated with a certain strange and unsettling Lord. "Why did Kadir's color show up?"

"No clue, but I don't sense anything of him. Only Jesral."

I nodded, obscurely relieved. Kadir hadn't been associated with Jesral—or the Mraztur—for some time, as far as I knew. Both Paul Ortiz and Vincent Pellini were with Kadir—and those two were definitely our allies. Though I hadn't had direct communication with them in months, Paul often gave us indirect and useful info.

My completed grid of support sigils hovered before me like a dozen bejeweled hummingbirds. "What's Jesral waiting on?" I asked as I channeled potency into Szerain's shikvihr. "I know Lord Smarmy Butt hasn't decided to play fair and give us time to get ready."

"Your guess is as good as mine. We can hope it's because things aren't going as planned, and he's not busy charging a death ray, but somehow I don't—"

My knees buckled from impossibly oppressive gravity, but before I crashed to the asphalt, it reversed, and I felt as if I could fly with just a gentle push off. With effort, I kept my focus on managing the potency flow.

Jesral appeared, framed against the inky backdrop, sharp features fixed in a smirk. He twitched the sleeves of his ostentatious blue velvet jacket into place with refined elegance as if teleportation was an annoying necessity. While I was fairly certain Kadir had recently awakened the ability to teleport, I seriously hoped the skill continued to elude Jesral and that he'd instead utilized a demahnk for transport. Not that a demahnk with a mind to meddle was a brighter prospect.

At least I didn't have to worry about Jesral—or any lord *or* demahnk—being able to read my thoughts without my consent, thanks to shielding Zakaar had placed last year.

I was so focused on Jesral I almost missed the ilius winding around his legs like a friendly housecat—if said cat was made of smoke and teeth. The same kind of demon that merged with the pod people. My stomach gave an unpleasant flop as I realized it was Dakdak, longtime associate of Mzatal. The implications were deeply unsettling, and I stomped down my musings on the demon and focused on the matters at hand.

Good thing, because in the next breath a powerfully built man with red hair fading to grey appeared behind Jesral: Angus McDunn, ruthless bodyguard to the now-deceased J.M. Farouche, and . . . Boudreaux's stepdad. That confirmed my meddling-demahnk theory, since there was zero way Angus could have teleported himself. Not only was Angus physically dangerous, he also had the ability to augment or degrade aptitudes—whether arcane or innate talents—and who knew what else. He'd once stripped my arcane abilities, yet covertly left a seed that allowed me to eventually recover.

Jesral glanced over his shoulder, and mercurial annoyance passed over his face. Though he managed to keep his smug mask from slipping too far, I had a feeling something hadn't gone quite to plan. Good. We needed every possible advantage.

Szerain subtly gathered potency in his palm for a strike, which told me he, too, suspected events hadn't unfolded quite as Jesral expected.

"Hey, Jasshole," I said in my perkiest voice. "What's your game?"

Angus started toward Tessa as if following pre-arranged instructions, but Jesral stopped him with a slight wave of his hand.

"No *game*," he purred. "Simply reclaiming that which is mine."

Tessa, who bore his mark like a brand of ownership. Except he'd stopped Angus from retrieving her. He was stalling. Whatever he was waiting for, no way would it be good for us.

It was time to pull the ace out of my sleeve: my secret one-time-use weapon against lords who were too big for their britches.

"Think hard on this, motherfucker." I paused for effect,

relishing the debilitating effect this question would have on him. "Who's your *daddy*?"

Jesral took a staggering step back, eyes wide as agony twisted his sharp features. Feral delight wound through me as he dropped into a crouch, head gripped between his hands. Apart from Szerain and Rhyzkahl, the lords didn't know about their true parentage—and even thinking about it triggered intense head pain. With any luck, Jesral would remain incapacitated until Szerain and I could find a way out of this mess.

Angus went to one knee beside Jesral and, after a second of hesitation, tentatively put a hand on his shoulder.

Vsuhl in hand, Szerain wound potency through the gathered mass of rakkuhr, expression tight and grim. "Stay on your toes. Even with Jesral incapacitated, we're not out of the woods."

I gave a sharp nod and fed power into his shikvihr, then jerked in dismay as Jesral let out a mocking laugh. My stomach dropped as he stood smoothly, zero trace of pain on his face.

Angus scrambled back as if he'd grabbed a viper. Jesral sent him a scathing look, then made a show of dusting off his jacket where Angus had touched him, while potency built in his other hand. "Kara Gillian, you are as amusing as ever. I, *of course*, know I am Ssahr's progeny. In fact, you'll even have the honor of meeting him quite soon."

Szerain hurled the mass of rakkuhr at him with shikvihr-backed might. Jesral's mask of confidence flickered as he raised his prepped potency to shield.

Even as the rakkuhr left Szerain's hand, gravity abruptly increased—only for the blink of an eye—but the shift was enough to adulterate both the strike and Jesral's shield. My support grid imploded, sending me staggering back.

Szerain's shikvihr disintegrated into chaotic sparks—except for the first ring which constricted around him, sigils distorting as if melting together. "Demahnk incoming."

My heart hammered as I hurried to rebuild my grid. Szerain worked Vsuhl furiously through the weirdly distorted sigil ring as Jesral watched our frenzied efforts with amusement and casually examined the state of his fingernails.

But the incoming demahnk wasn't Ssahr.

Ilana appeared in elder syraza form next to Jesral, her teeth bared, and clawed hand clamped on Mzatal's shoulder.

A storm of emotion roiled through me. Mzatal stood utterly still, dark expression inscrutable. Close-fitting leather as black as the void clothed him throat to toe, and his thigh-length, ink-black hair was bound in a thick braid, tight and intricate. Two sheathed essence blades hung from his belt: his own blade, Khatur, and Xhan, which had been held by Rhyzkahl until Zakaar broke their ptarl bond during the battle at the Farouche plantation.

His gaze swept over me as if I didn't exist. Yet the covert, silk-thin thread of connection we held open between us whispered acknowledgment.

The ilius DakDak growled low at Mzatal and pressed back against Jesral's legs.

The air shimmered, and a wiry man with golden skin and bright white hair bound in a man-bun appeared, breathing hard. Jesral's ptarl Ssahr. He slapped his hand onto Mzatal's other shoulder and gripped so tightly his knuckles paled. I clung to the belief that Mzatal's resistance to the demahnk control had something to do with Ssahr's delayed arrival.

Smug arrogance returned to Jesral's demeanor, and he gave a head nudge toward Tessa. Angus met my eyes for the barest of instants before hurrying to where she lay on the highway shoulder.

"Don't you fucking hurt her," I shouted. A waste of words considering how grossly outgunned we were. I could only hope the warding I'd thrown over her would at least slow him down.

Jesral laughed, and I swung my focus back to him. "Oh, I get it now," I said with a patronizing smile, then gestured to Mzatal. "You were waiting for the alpha lord to arrive so you could proceed with your plan."

Jesral's smirk twisted into an ugly scowl. "How can he be alpha when he is vanquished thus? *I* control Mzatal—and the situation."

I scoffed. "Oh, please. You're nothing but a middle of the pack poser wannabe—and you know it."

Fury swept over his face. "Foolish child," he hissed, then snapped his fingers in Mzatal's direction and pointed to the pavement. "Witness your ignorance."

Mzatal shrugged from the demahnk's grasp and dropped to one knee, head lowered. I clenched my hands, knowing—hoping—Mzatal's acquiescence was merely a ploy.

Jesral held his hand out, palm up, in front of Mzatal. To my horror, Mzatal unsheathed Xhan. Its nightmare voice wormed into my skull, whispering and seething, even as phantom pain burned in the sigil scars it had carved on my torso.

Listen. Mzatal's voice? A murmured imperative near lost among Xhan's vile whispers.

Eyes locked on mine, Mzatal lifted the tip of the knife ever-so-slightly. He wanted me to listen to Xhan? Then he ripped his gaze away, reversed his grip on the blade, and offered it to Jesral.

"No!" Szerain thundered, an echo of my own alarm. Even Ssahr looked aghast. He spoke urgently in his ptarl's ear, but Jesral dismissed it with an impatient wave of his hand, full focus on Mzatal and Xhan. Jesral wanted that blade. *Needed* to bear it, not only because he hungered for the power it offered, but to prove to me and everyone else that he was a force to be reckoned with. Respected and feared. Not a poser. Not middle of the pack.

"Mzatal is *mine*, Kara Gillian." Jesral slid a look my way. "And soon Szerain shall be as well . . . after I resubmerge him to live out his existence as Ryan Kristoff."

Szerain continued to work Vsuhl through the melted sigils, but his sharp intake of breath told me Jesral's barb had struck home.

I gave an exaggerated yawn. "Sure you will, big guy. And I'm going to take a summer vacation on Mars."

Jesral sneered and returned his attention to the blade but hesitated as he reached for it. I was damn near positive he'd never actually wielded Xhan. At the Farouche plantation, he'd picked it up with a cloth to keep from touching it—and not long after that, Xhan was in Mzatal's possession.

Xhan's tone shifted from nightmarish to inviting, as if luring Jesral to take it.

"Yeah, grab that blade and show it who's the boss, Jesral," I taunted. "What are you afraid of? I mean, you're a super powerful lord, right? Oh, wait, didn't it burn the fuck out of you the last time you grabbed it? I'm sure you're sooo much more powerful now."

Jesral shot me a look of pure venom, then seized the hilt. His expression melted into near orgasmic bliss for an instant before turning to teeth-clenched effort as he fought the will and dominance of the essence blade. Ssahr gripped his elbow, eyes darting from person to person, as he assessed the shifting scenario.

I clucked my tongue, even as I worked the last sigils into my repaired support grid. "Oh, Jesral, sweetie, be careful now! Just remember, Mzatal can take Xhan back if you can't handle wielding an essence blade. No shame in giving up!"

I flicked a glance back at Tessa while Jesral battled the blade. Angus spoke to her, low and urgent, but with every attempt to touch her, he yanked his hand back as if shocked. Good. My warding was doing its job.

Expression haunted, Szerain thrust Vsuhl through the last melted threads of the ring to dispel it, then straightened, hand white-knuckled on his knife. Vsuhl's voice mingled with Xhan's, sharp and dangerous.

Yet instead of taking any kind of action against Jesral, Szerain stood stock still, features set in a rigor of concentration. Trying to bring Zakaar to the surface to save our asses, I realized, though he seemed to be meeting resistance?

I had no idea why Zakaar would refuse to help, but I couldn't spare the focus to figure it out. Jesral let out a howl of anguish and staggered back, Xhan gripped between both hands and pointed straight at his heart. The blade's ethereal whispers rose to an obscene shriek, but I willed myself to *listen* anyway.

Ilana and Ssahr retreated a step, leaving Jesral to wrestle the blade on his own. Both demahnk appeared willing enough to aid and abet, but dire punishment awaited them from the Ekiri collective if they took direct action against us—or interfered with the blades. Though it sure seemed as if the lines in the sand had blurred in the last few months.

Mzatal rose to his feet, and I had the distinct impression his captors' distraction had loosened their control of him—even if by only a razor-thin amount. Now was our chance to strike back.

"Szerain, rakkuhr," I said softly. Rakkuhr was toxic to demahnk.

He ignored me and continued to struggle with Zakaar. I could almost *almost* sense his presence within Szerain, as if it thrashed at the periphery of my awareness. Zakaar definitely wasn't on board with surfacing, but instead of taking no for an answer, Szerain remained distracted, prepared to . . . what, *force* Zakaar out?

Mzatal summoned Khatur directly into his hand from its sheath as his gaze locked onto Szerain. Xhan's shriek eased to a litany of almost-words before the voices of all three blades entwined in a cryptic whispered chant. Jesral took a stumble-step forward as Xhan apparently abandoned its quest to taste lord blood and acquiesced to his control.

Fuck.

Mzatal's aura rolled over me, fiery and smothering. Lightning flickered impossibly in the darkness of the void, and Ilana's startled gaze tracked upward before her lip curled in a smile.

Fuck this shit. Fuck Ilana. Fuck Xhan.

And fuck Szerain for stubbornly persisting against Zakaar instead of using rakkuhr to press our brief advantage against the demahnk.

"Mzatal!" I shouted, seeking to send my true support and love through our thread of connection while my words wove lies. "Never figured you'd end up as Jesral's lap dog."

"Hubristic fool," he said, voice potent and flint hard. "Far out of your depth."

He spoke *to* me but *of* Jesral, the only hubristic fool present. "Oh yeah?" I yelled, putting on a show of incredulous shock and fury. "You're the one who made me what I am now. My faults and flaws lie with you!" *Beloved, I am with you always, body and essence.*

"Submit," he commanded, "and the fight will be over."

Zharkat, if you submit, the fight is over, and all is lost.

His gaze flicked over me—only for an instant—but the intensity nearly sent me to my knees. He resisted Ilana and the others with his entire essence. He waged an unending battle, and the instant he wavered or weakened, the walls would fall.

If I submit, the fight is over, and all is lost.

He needed me, drew on our bond, relied on our tenuous link. A distant whisper of sensation passed through his sigil on my chest, echoed in his ring on my left hand. I'd forged that ring as a token of connection, of our union. And now, perhaps, it could add a thread to that connection.

I allowed anger to suffuse my face. "You think you're the *boss* of me?" With a swift movement, I yanked his ring off and hurled it at him with force backed by potency.

Without even looking, he snatched the ring with his free hand, expression remaining dark and hard. But I had only an instant to feel a flare of hope before he clenched his fist and disintegrated it with a savage burst of potency.

I recoiled, as shocked and hurt as if he'd kicked me in the chest. Why did he have to destroy it? To keep it from Ilana? Surely there was another way.

Or, worse, what if I'd been letting my hope mislead me. Was he that far gone?

Mzatal raised Khatur high, and dazzling incandescence streaked the void beyond the bubble. Szerain thrust Vsuhl skyward in a mirror of Mzatal's action, rakkuhr snaking from his hand to wrap Vsuhl—yet Szerain appeared to be resisting the movement, as if something or someone else forced his arm up. Zakaar? The blade itself? Mzatal?

Khatur and Vsuhl's voices shifted from whispers to harmonic tones. Mzatal thrust Khatur higher, and a thin streak of lightning struck the blade, then arced to Vsuhl.

Szerain let out a guttural cry and crumpled to the pavement, unconscious. Vsuhl skittered across the highway and came to rest midway between Jesral and me, electricity crackling over it and spiderwebbing the asphalt.

Jesral sucked in a sharp breath, eyes locked on the loose blade. Mzatal had used Vsuhl to take out Szerain—and could do the same to me—but I had no time to overthink this. Two bounding strides, and I dove on the electrified blade, gripped its hilt, and rolled—even as an arcane strike from Jesral zinged overhead. My palm burned, but I kept my fist closed tightly on the hilt.

I scrambled to my feet and backpedaled, nearly stumbling over the prone form of Szerain before standing my ground, breathing hard. The lightning was gone from Vsuhl but still arced and danced in the darkness of the void. Yet now I struggled to maintain focus as the harmonic blade song of the trinity vibrated between every cell.

Jesral gave me an ugly, oily smile. He knew I had no chance of holding out against him with Xhan, Mzatal with Khatur, and two demahnk—even though the latter were deeply focused on constraining Mzatal and supporting Jesral.

His eyes lit with predatory intensity as he stalked closer, like a jaguar considering the most satisfying way to dispatch his prey.

The blade song's intensity increased. I angled the tip of Vsuhl toward Jesral and didn't waste my breath with taunts. My grim silence would get under his skin far more.

I took a half step back. Mzatal made no move to aid me—not that I expected him to. I was truly standing on my own, and Jesral was going to—

Listen, chorused the blade song.

I ceased my resistance of the song. Welcomed the vibration, the harmonies. Immersed in the song. Called what little grove support I could muster, and . . . ethereal tones burst forth from the depth of my essence, filled my mind, melded with the blade song I *knew* Jesral couldn't hear.

He snarled and lunged at me.

One with the song, I danced aside and parried, the clash of blade on blade sending notes of pure malice into the ether as lightning flashed and flickered. We broke off, eyeing each other and circling as we sought an opening, a weakness.

Jesral smirked and shifted his grip on Xhan. I breathed deeply and steeled myself for another round.

But before we could engage again, a sharp tremor sent us all staggering. Kadir shimmered into the dimensional pocket, androgynous features intense and as pissed as I'd ever seen him. He traced chartreuse sigils, one after another, and sent each off into apparent nothingness. "Meddlesome *fool*," he growled at Jesral. "You bring ruin to all."

"*I* am the fool?" Jesral scoffed. "It seems I have outplayed you, considering I now have access to your precious interdimension."

"The Between is not *mine*, and your graceless means of access is cancerous." Kadir continued tracing and dispersing sigils with shockingly dexterous speed. I suspected he was stabilizing interdimensional damage caused by Jesral.

DakDak slunk away from Jesral to coil and uncoil beside Mzatal's boot. Ilana and Ssahr eased away from Jesral again.

Still immersed in the blade song, I called rakkuhr to me, then sent it washing toward both demahnk like a bucket of water dumped on the road. I didn't have Szerain's skill with rakkuhr, but with the blade in hand I could keep sending toxic ripples toward the already reluctant demahnk. Semitransparent now, the two shrank back to the boundary of the pocket, though Jesral didn't notice.

Lightning flashed and zig-zagged in the void, this time followed by a deep rumble of otherworldly thunder.

"No more games." Jesral snapped his fingers at Mzatal and lifted Xhan. "Take Vsuhl from her and bring the blade home."

Mzatal didn't move except to lower his head, eyes on me and expression intense. I knew that look. With the demahnk cowering from my rakkuhr, I'd bought him a little wiggle room, and now a smackdown was coming. But for who? Me? Jesral? The demahnk? Szerain, just for good measure?

Jesral laughed. "*Now*, Mzatal."

I started to send Vsuhl away to its pocket dimension storage, but the trinity's song shifted to an intricate discordance that urged me to lift the blade. Mzatal's aura ramped up to hurricane-of-lava intensity, and the barest touch of contact came through our thread of connection—a wisp of reassurance.

Mzatal was the creator of the blades, the trinity. Master and maker. That feather-light touch was enough for me to trust him.

Jesral's satisfied smirk melted into uncertainty. He felt Mzatal's mojo, too, and it wasn't at all what he'd expected.

I thrust Vsuhl skyward, ready for Mzatal to do something spectacular, fierce and overpowering, to finish the bullshit once and for all. *Come on, beloved. We have them on the ropes, right where—*

DakDak darted forward and bit the shit out of my calf.

I barely processed the pain before blinding light and concussion sent me flailing. Searing heat ripped through every cell, then just as abruptly receded to a nagging ache in silent darkness.

Calm. Blissful, even, despite the ache.

Okay, this wasn't so bad. This was a good place.

To rest.

To drift.

Kara. Mzatal's voice. Distant. Commanding. Shredding my peace. Dispelling the darkness.

Blue skies. No more dimensional pocket. A basketball-sized crater smoked and flamed in the asphalt where Jesral had been, and there was no sign of Angus, the demahnk, DakDak, or Mzatal.

Szerain still lay in the middle of the highway. Tessa moaned on the shoulder. Within the sally port, Bryce shouted garbled orders I couldn't make out.

Kadir straddled someone in DIRT fatigues lying motionless on the asphalt. Curious, I wandered their way.

"*Wykgak,*" Kadir snarled, the demon equivalent of either fuck-this-is-bad or fuck-this-is-awesome. "Nexus! Now!"

Bryce shouted another series of unintelligible orders, and Zenra grabbed her orange backpack and sprinted toward us.

I struggled for context, but memories slipped and slid through fog. The world transformed into flowing pastel light while distant voices whispered themselves into silence.

Only Kadir remained, still standing over the DIRT person, his entire form now a bazillion transparent prisms apart from the vivid violet intensity of his eyes—which were fixed on me.

Full-on Mr. Sparkly mode. *That means something. But—*

"Worlds are breaking, Kara Gillian."

His words knifed through me, propelled by icy wrath—a message of absolute truth I felt in the core of my being. Discord and disharmony. New fractures threatening to implode all. Essence-twisting *wrongness*. So very wrong.

Kadir's perception. Kadir's existence.

Kadir.

I sensed his monumental struggle even in this moment to stabilize the interdimensional space between the worlds.

He called chartreuse potency to writhe between his palms like a tangle of scintillating worms, alien yet hauntingly familiar. In an inhumanly quick move, he slammed the construct onto the sternum of the downed person.

Searing pain flashed through me, then faded to an all-over miserable ache. I dragged in a breath as I stared up at Kadir framed by the sky, my bitten leg feeling as if it was being eaten from the inside by fire ants.

Kadir cursed again in demon. And then he was gone, a final word drawing its finger through my mind. *Nexus.*

Nexus. Yes. That's exactly what I need.

Memories tumbled. Tessa needed the nexus, too.

People bustled around me. Kellum and Tandon jogged toward Tessa with a field stretcher. Turek crouched like a huge crocodilian guardian beside Szerain, clawed hands tracing unseen sigils on his stricken lord's chest. Zenra knelt beside me. I tried to say I was okay, but I couldn't speak, couldn't move. I felt as if I should be panicked about that, but I wasn't. Then wondered if I should be panicked about not being panicked. Okay, I wasn't panicked, but definitely scared shitless.

Zenra wrapped a quick compression bandage around my calf, then she and Krawkor loaded me onto a stretcher and hurried toward the gate. Bryce dropped the tailgate on a pickup in the sally port as we approached. Sonny followed us into the truck bed. He put his hand on my arm, and the fear and pain and confusion eased a bit. "You're going to be okay, Kara. Promise."

Krawkor bailed off the tailgate, using his tails for balance, leaving Sonny, Zenra, and me on board. "I'll see if I can get the comms back online."

Bryce gave him a sober thumbs up. "Anything you can do. We're crippled."

Krawkor's fingers danced over his sound deck as he dashed into the watchtower. Turek bounded by, cradling the unconscious Szerain.

Bryce slammed the tailgate shut. "Tandon, Kellum, take Tessa to the security cell. Keep an eye on her until I send instructions."

"Will do," Kellum said and angled toward the watchtower door.

No no no!

Zenra wrapped a blood pressure cuff around my arm, and I felt the faint prick of her claws as she used her unique talents to check my blood stats. Bryce leaned over the side of the pickup and gave Sonny a rare worried look. "You got this?"

"Yeah," Sonny said, his hand firmly on my shoulder. "Just drive."

Tessa needs to go to the nexus!

"Wait," Sonny said. "We really should take Tessa, too."

Bryce slammed his palm against the side of the truck in an uncharacteristic display. "Goddammit. I can't make that call without Kara's—"

Sonny grabbed Bryce's wrist while keeping his other hand firmly against my arm. "Hey, bud," he said, voice soft and compelling. "I think Kara'd want her aunt on the nexus. It feels right. It *really* feels right."

Bryce cursed under his breath, but it didn't carry much heat. "Kellum! Tandon! Load her up. We're rolling."

A moment later, Tessa's stretcher lay beside mine. Lenny clambered in and clapped Zenra on the shoulder before settling beside Tessa. "I'm a vet not a medic, but I got two able hands and I aim to use 'em."

"They're damn good hands, and we're all animals, right?" Zenra said as she prepped an IV. The engine revved, and the pickup pulled through the inner gate.

Lenny cupped Tessa's hand between his. "You don't know me, ma'am, but that's okay. There'll be time for proper introductions when you're up and about."

"Her name's Tessa," Sonny said.

Tessa. My aunt. Wild, curly blond hair now cropped short. Eccentric. My guardian after my parents died. I was her sweetling.

The ache squeezed.

Until I wasn't, and she betrayed me.

Manipulation and misguided actions, whispered something deep within me.

Tessa's head lolled as the truck sped up the driveway, and Lenny steadied her. "Won't be long now, Miss Tessa. We'll get you to the nexus, and you'll be right as rain. You just wait and see."

Get to the nexus and then . . . *what*?

Szerain? Incapacitated. Zenra? Aces with medical stuff, but arcane shit wasn't in her wheelhouse. Me? Out of my depth even if I wasn't paralyzed. What the fuck was I going to do?

Lenny's voice wove a soothing tapestry of sound as he talked nonstop to Tessa.

The truck pulled to a stop, and the tailgate slammed down. Bryce and Zenra lugged my stretcher to the center of the nexus, with Sonny still maintaining contact, then shifted me to lie directly on the stone slab. It felt warm and tingly against my back. Comforting. Overhead, the gleaming arcane circle of the super shikvihr—created by Mzatal and me—drifted around us, and the branches of the grove tree shimmered with emerald and amethyst leaves.

"Now what?" Bryce said, voice strained.

"Here, like this," Sonny said as he arranged my limbs Vitruvian Man fashion, matching the pattern of silver sigils embedded in the inky stone. My sigils, imbued by Mzatal. My silhouette.

Soothing heat drove away the all-body ache as if some critical missing element had been replenished, though the fire ants remained relentless. I called on the nexus, the shikvihr, Rho. Called on my coworkers, my teammates, my friends, my aunt. Called on Mzatal. Called myself home.

I sucked in a gasping breath.

"I'm . . . okay," I croaked. "I'm here."

Chapter 5

My calf still felt like fire ants were eating it from the inside out, and I jerked involuntarily as Zenra cleaned the wound.

Sonny gripped my shoulder. "Hey hey hey. Breathe. *Breathe.* You're okay." I was certain he said it as much to reassure himself as to calm me, but I focused on his voice, his mega-chill vibe, and breathed through the pain.

Weirdly, the fire-ant sensation traveled up my leg and through my torso, diffusing and diminishing as it went. By the time it reached my head, it was little more than a vague tingle, and the pain in my calf had receded to a normal and tolerable bitten-by-a-toothy-demon ouch.

I pushed up to my elbows as Zenra finished securing the bandage. Turek crouched at the base of the grove tree, Szerain limp in his arms. Lenny sat cross-legged near the edge of the nexus, cradling the blanket-swaddled Tessa in his lap. Tandon and Kellum stood beside him, and while they didn't have their weapons trained on Tessa, their postures made it clear they were on high alert and could react in a fraction of an instant.

Bryce scrutinized me. "You back with us? We don't know what happened out there. Y'all vanished into some sort of distortion."

"Dimensional pocket. Jesral and—" A spasm of worry tightened my gut. "Where's Vsuhl? Was it out on the road?"

"Didn't see Vsuhl."

Shit. But no time to fret about the blade's whereabouts now. "Tessa. Bring her over here." I clambered to my feet with Sonny's help. "She's been disrupted. Jesral's mark is on her. Szerain stabilized her with a sigil but—" Shit! "Turek! Is Szerain all right?"

Turek rumbled, "Unconscious. Time is needed."

At least the answer wasn't "dying." Fortunately for Tessa, I still had the nexus and the grove tree as resources. "Rho?" I murmured. The leaves whispered above, supportive, but I had the impression Rho's attention was focused elsewhere, distant.

Bryce and Lenny placed Tessa in the center of the nexus. Her breath rasped in shallow, irregular puffs, still carrying a hint of the unnerving arcane sparks. Congealed blood clogged her nostrils and matted her hair, and her skin and lips had a bluish tinge. Szerain's arcane construct on her sternum flickered in time with her heartbeat.

Expression grim with focus, Zenra unzipped the oxygen tank from her bag. Lenny held Tessa's right hand and talked to her nonstop about the weather, horses, mules, puppies, and Jontari antics, his voice calm yet carrying a pure intensity. I drew on the combined energy of the nexus and super shikvihr, summoning all of the lordy sense I could muster.

Zenra passed the tank, tubing, and mask to Lenny. He settled the mask on Tessa's face, adjusting the flow while Zenra prepped an IV, her expression focused and determined.

I dropped to my knees beside Tessa. The vortex of potency generated by the nexus rose around us, and I connected with it, let it flow through me. Jesral's mark lay suspiciously inert on her forearm, while three glimmering arcane implants coiled in her chest like dormant parasites. Flickers of potency covered her, so fleeting and pale I'd have missed them if we weren't on the nexus. They exuded a sense of wrongness, as if every flicker disrupted Tessa's life force in a miniscule way. Szerain's stabilizing sigil on her chest was likely all that kept them from ravaging her.

I placed both hands over the mark, gritting my teeth against the overwhelming feel of Jesral, like rancid oil seeping into my pores. The mark seemed inactive, at least. Probably. I was sooooo out of my depth.

I wrapped potency around Tessa's forearm like a bandage. "I could *really* use Ashava's help."

"I'll tag Jill," Bryce said.

"Tessa, can you hear me?" No response. I began a careful assessment of the implants. Lords sometimes placed them so they could recall a person at will. However, Jesral *hadn't* recalled her, so either these implants had some other purpose, or the compound's protections and the nexus shielded her from being yanked back to him.

The first implant seemed dormant, but the second shimmered at the edge of my perception, its feel of wrongness matching the flickers of the arcane disruption. It needed to be neutralized, but that wasn't something I dared tackle on my own. I shifted my focus to the first implant, but the instant I engaged in full assessment, it flared bright orange and began to exude a distinct pull as if trying to suck me in.

Leaves rustled, and "recall" whispered through my awareness.

Fuck! Rhyzkahl had once ripped a recall implant from me, but I had no idea how to attempt it—or if it was possible for a non-lord. I drew potency to contain it, but to my dismay the pulling sensation doubled.

Leaves rustled. I let myself listen.

No one was trying to call Tessa away. Someone was being pulled *to* her. A reverse recall.

My heart hammered. "Bryce! Potential unknown incoming."

But not if I could help it. I had no idea how to remove the implant, but maybe I could fuck up its outgoing signal. Working as quickly as I dared, I cocooned the thing in layer upon layer of potency, adding a veil of rakkuhr for good measure. The pull diminished, but I kept on cocooning.

Bryce barked out orders, calling more security teams to the nexus, while Zenra snapped crisp instructions to Lenny to prep meds as she pricked Tessa with her claws to do her health assessments.

"Where the heck is Ashava?" I snarled.

"Jill's looking," Bryce said. "She wasn't in the basement— where she was *supposed* to stay until the all-clear."

I gritted my teeth. This was a lousy time for her to be in rebellious-teen mode. Not that there was ever a good time for a demonic lord to be in rebellious-teen mode.

Without warning, Tessa writhed and let out a near airless shriek before going limp again. My potency cocoon burned away in a flash of phosphorescence, and the implant's pull redoubled. And now the *feel* of Jesral flowed through me. My heart slammed. I had to stop this. Reverse the pull. Reverse—

"Turek! On my honor, I ask a boon. I need you to bleed on the nexus. Please." When the Jontari Imperator Dekkak bled on the nexus during the ritual sealing of our pact, the potency flow reversed. I had no idea if blood from a different demon would have the same effect—or if it would even help—but I was out of options.

"Upon my honor, Kara Gillian, I will comply. Upon your honor, you will be in my debt."

"Understood."

Turek settled Szerain at the base of the tree while I tried again to wrap the implant in potency, heart sinking as it immediately burned away.

"C'mon Tessa. Fight back against that piece of shit."

Zenra muttered a curse. "Pressure bottomed. Prep a ten mill syringe with point one per mill epi and saline. Zero point zero one per mill. One mill bolus doses."

Lenny maintained his calm focus as he efficiently followed her directions.

Turek bounded onto the nexus and drew a claw across his forearm. Blood spattered the stone. Within three heartbeats, the vortex reversed into an arcane downdraft that made me feel as if I weighed a ton. The pull of the implant was lost in the shift, and the feel of Jesral's aura dissipated.

"Not today, you worthless prick," I growled.

The implant dimmed from brilliant orange to a burnt umber. "Almost there, I think." I felt more than heard a sound like a rock falling into an empty oil drum, and the implant contracted into a dull grey lump.

I sagged in relief. "Turek, you can—"

Ashava appeared beside Turek and gave him a mighty arcane shove off the nexus—an impressive feat considering she was a slim teen a foot and a half shorter than he was and a quarter his weight. "Stop it! You're making me nauseated." She turned to me as the vortex resumed its normal upward flow. "I took care of it, Kara."

I bit down hard on the scathing admonishment that wanted to leap out, then threw an apologetic look to Turek, even as he returned to Szerain's side beneath the tree. I'd deal with Ashava's rudeness later. Somehow. "Glad you're here. I really need help. I think we shut down the reverse recall implant, but she's been disrupted."

Ashava crouched beside me and peered at Tessa as I quickly

recounted what happened. "This is new to you, so just take your time and—"

With a quick twist of her hand she yanked the flickering disruption implant from Tessa, strands of dull purple potency stringing from it like tentacles. It thrashed in her palm like a dying jellyfish before she fisted her hand, dissipating the implant into a cloud of sparks.

I blinked. "Or you can do that."

Tessa moaned. To my relief, all signs of the arcane disruption flickers were gone, though Zenra and Lenny still worked diligently to stabilize her.

"Ashava, any danger from Jesral's mark?"

She closed her eyes, silent for a moment. "It's burned out. No use to him anymore."

Leaves rustled as Rho offered confirmation.

I took Tessa's hand and gave Ashava a smile. "You saved her life. I couldn't deal with the disruption. Thank you."

Ashava beamed. Though she looked like a teen in her sweatshirt, jeans, and auburn ponytail, she was actually only six months old. As the half-human, half-demahnk daughter of Jill and Zakaar, she'd matured quickly. Probably too quickly. "See? That's why you should call me when there's trouble. It's dumb sending me to the basement."

My smile tightened. "It's our most secure spot, and best for you until—"

"Until what?" she snapped in a mercurial twist of mood. "I'm old and wrinkly? Not going to happen. I can help *now*."

She placed both hands on Tessa's chest and closed her eyes.

"Hold on. Check in with Zenra before you do anything."

She scoffed. "I have healing ability, remember? I've got this."

For a moment, I thought she did, indeed, have it. Tessa's breathing eased into long, even breaths and the tension in her face softened.

Zenra grabbed Ashava's wrist. "Stop. Now."

Ashava jerked her hands back, face pale.

Zenra barked instructions to Lenny. "Pressure dropped again. Fast." She turned a hard eye on Ashava. "Did you take the drugs already in her system into account? No. If someone's already working a scene you don't just waltz in and do your own thing—even if you have superpowers. Get a report. Get on the same damn page."

Ashava stood, her humiliation at the rebuke morphing into defensive anger. "Maybe I was about to fix the drug balance. You don't know! I can still do it."

I looked up at her. "Ashava, I think you've done enough here, for now. We can talk more later, okay?"

"Talk talk talk," she snapped, a tremble in her voice. "That's what you'll do. No one *ever* listens to me. EVER." An arcane glow suffused her skin and fine tendrils of light snaked around her—a clear sign her control was wavering. And as an unfettered demonic lord, a loss of control could have catastrophic consequences.

"Ashava," I said, keeping my voice even and calm, "this isn't the time. We're still in crisis. You did a great job, but—"

She jerked her chin up. "But I'm not needed anymore. Fine." She vanished.

Zenra grimaced. "Sorry, Commander. I was out of line."

"No, you absolutely weren't. It's your scene and you said what needed to be said. I'll deal with it. How's Tessa?"

"Stable. Ashava did some good work apart from the drug error."

"You and Lenny did a great job. I'm incredibly grateful." I told Bryce to have security stand down, then caught Lenny's eye. "Could you help move Tessa under the tree? I think it will be good for her, and I need to make amends with Turek."

Zenra removed Tessa's oxygen mask and disconnected the saline drip. Together, Lenny and I carried Tessa the short distance to Rho.

Szerain sat slumped against Rho's white trunk, head pitched forward, chin on chest. Vines with leaves of jewel-tone purple and green draped his shoulders. "Here," he murmured, eyes barely open. "Bring Tessa Pazhel. Here."

Turek shifted to make room for us. I started to apologize for Ashava's behavior, but a quick flick of his claw told me now wasn't the time.

Tandon spread a thick and soft blanket beside the tree, and we settled Tessa on it, curled on her side, with her head close to Szerain.

Szerain stared at his hands, opening and closing them, then lifted his head, eyes closed, and ran his fingertips over his forehead and down his jawline.

I peered at him. "Hey, Szerain, you okay?"

"Flesh," he said in a voice deeper and more melodious than Szerain's. "It has been long."

"*Rho?*"

"I am here." They placed a hand on Tessa's head, and she shifted and sighed. "Sit with us."

A bazillion questions tumbled, but I pushed all aside except the matter that drove Rho to turn Szerain into, well, a meat puppet. "You came for Tessa?"

"For Szerain. For Tessa Pazhel. For the unfettered Ashava. For the End."

"We are honored. What can I—" My breath caught. Grove energy, wild and unique, flowed over and through me, carrying the scent of earth and rain, and the feel of spring sunshine. The lingering pain in my wounded leg dwindled to nothing. Cares melted away, and tension left my shoulders as if I'd had a long massage. "What of Szerain?"

"Burdened by that which only he can unlade. His physical form recovers now."

"And Tessa? I can't trust her." Even as I said it, my heart ached for it all to be a bad dream I'd wake from at any minute.

Rho remained silent.

I took a moment and reframed my thinking. "How can I trust her? Help me understand. Please."

"Tessa Pazhel has been an unwitting instrument since she conceived a child with Rhyzkahl."

The demahnk hid children from the lords by returning women to Earth and manipulating them to forget their time with the lord. Zakaar had done so with Tessa. But Xharbek then took it a step beyond and manipulated her to believe her baby—Idris—had been stillborn. "Xharbek's pawn," I said. "Then he groomed her through Katashi?"

"Not groomed. Manipulated. Heavily and ruthlessly for two decades. Anathema. Xharbek lost his way."

I swallowed, mind reeling as I struggled to reframe *everything*. Nearly half her life hadn't been her own. Twenty years meant she'd been manipulated even before she became my guardian. My entire relationship with her had been shaped by Xharbek. "But why Tessa?"

"She is but two generations descended of Jesral, has grove affinity, and carried the issue of Rhyzkahl. Add to that her quick mind and sharp summoning skills, and Xharbek had an ideal victim."

Jesral was Tessa's grandfather and my great-grandfather. I had grove affinity, and so, of course, Tessa did, too. It came to us through our distant ancestor Aphra, once Szerain's companion and lover. Aphra had adored the groves, spent countless hours in them, and that connection to Rho remained through her bloodline over the past several hundred years.

My eyes narrowed. "Xharbek went for her pedigree and hoped for a purebred pup in Idris—who he failed to collar, though not for lack of trying." Anger bubbled up on her behalf, but mellowed in Rho's aura of calm. "Can the manipulations be undone?"

"Not long past, Rhyzkahl removed all he was able and placed protections Jesral could not and Ssahr would not breach."

Holy shit. My lingering doubts about Rhyzkahl's loyalties continued to be steadily eroded away. "What about the manipulations Rhyzkahl couldn't find or strip?"

Rho stroked Tessa's hair, no longer matted with blood. "The deepest and most insidious are gone now."

Words couldn't convey the depth of my emotions, and I could only hope Rho sensed the true measure of my gratitude. "Does she . . . I mean, will she remember everything?"

"After Rhyzkahl's intervention, Jesral was only able to manipulate her lightly, nothing more. She became a liability, and he fogged some of her recent memory. That cannot be undone."

"What about past memories? Our relationship? Where do we stand?" I desperately wanted to know, yet at the same time an odd terror gripped me. What if her care and affection had all been a lie as well? What if she carried deep resentment? What if she'd despised being saddled with me? What if—

Rho brushed their fingers against my cheek. "Ask her."

With a start, I realized Tessa was conscious and watching me. She groped for my hand, and I let her take it.

"Sweetling," she said in a voice thin and weary. "I remember all of it. I'm so sorry. I should have been stronger. It seemed so right, but it was so very wrong."

In Rho's presence, I felt the truth of her words. The dam that held back my anger and hurt and grief broke, and I gathered her into my arms, succumbed to some deeply cathartic ugly-crying. Between sobs, I babbled that everything was going to be all right and that she was safe here and could rest and recuperate for as long as she needed, and that I loved her.

Eventually I calmed, and by a Rho-assisted miracle, my total snotfest cleared up to little more than a delicate sniffle. I settled Tessa back on the blanket and tucked a second one close around her. "Do you remember what happened today with the car?"

Her eyes widened. "Jesral wanted me here. In the compound. He was going to bypass the protections using a reverse recall implant. I fought it! I turned around, tried to drive away." Her breath came in short, shallow puffs as panic filled her face. "I *tried*."

Rho touched her lightly on the forehead, and she slipped back into sleep. "Too much. Too soon. Rest and time are needed."

"Thank you." The words seemed so inadequate for the situation, but I doubted Rho needed words to know the depth of my gratitude. With my worry for Szerain and Tessa settled for the moment, my mind turned to the next glaring problem on my infinite To Stress About list. "What about Ashava? I'm concerned." For so *so* many different reasons.

"She comes now." They dropped their head and looked very much like Szerain dozing.

Sure enough, Ashava appeared a heartbeat later, face flushed and frantic. "Why isn't anyone looking for Squig? She's *gone*!"

I did my utmost to maintain a calm tone. "She teleported out of the compound and attacked a drone. I didn't see what happened after—"

"Bryce did! He said she took the drone down and disappeared behind the trees. A team recovered the drone but no Squig! We have to *do* something."

Calm tone, Kara. Calm fucking tone. "You said yourself the other day how fierce and independent Squig is. She'll be okay. But after we get some things settled, I bet your mom will let you go out with the Riders to look."

"What needs settling? No time to waste!"

"Tessa needs settling. How about taking care of warding on the guest room. We'll be moving her in there, and it needs to be private and secure. And you do kickass warding."

"On it." And she was gone.

I let out a slow breath. "I'm worried about her. She's testing boundaries and chafing against restrictions. Typical teen stuff, except she's exceedingly more dangerous and unpredictable than any human teen."

Rho lifted their head and regarded me for a moment. "Your doubts about her maturity and stability are not unfounded. Out of necessity, she has gone through years of maturation in a span of months. Apart from Kadir, other Ekiri offspring were nurtured to mature at the human pace, but even then, management was challenging."

Kadir was the exception because he was literally stolen from his mother's womb. I couldn't hold back a shudder at the thought. "And y'all developed the mental governors to keep the young lords in check. Like what Zakaar implanted in Ashava. I wasn't on board with the whole thing at first, but I've come to see the need." Ashava's governor took the edge off the intense and chaotic mood swings that came from such rapid maturation and also kept her from casually reading thoughts, as mature lords were able to do. She still had the ability, but the governor meant she had to touch the person and focus on reading them.

"The offspring are hybrids. Each unique. Without the implanted focus-control in early life, they would self-destruct."

"But it got out of hand with the lords," I said. "Too much control, for too long."

Rho offered no denial.

"That said, maybe Ashava's governor needs a boost? Shouldn't it have prevented a tantrum flare like what almost happened earlier?"

"It is the crux of why I am here, embodied. Zakaar is unavailable, and there was no other to make the adjustment. It is done." The vines on their shoulders shifted, and I sensed Rho's departure from Szerain was imminent.

"Will I speak with you again?"

"Not in flesh."

On impulse, I took their face between my hands and touched my forehead to theirs. "Thank you. For everything. For sacrificing yourself to save the demon realm. For supporting the lords. For being there over and over for me."

A sense of comfort and understanding washed over and through me, like a hug from an umpteenth-great-grandparent who just happened to be an immortal and unfathomable being.

The vines withdrew into the branches above, and Szerain slumped, his head lolling. In a heartbeat, Turek scooped him up.

"Hey," I said. "I owe you a boon for the blood, and an apology. Ashava was—" I grimaced, trying to think of something other than "being a little shit."

"I will treat with the qaztehl directly," he growled, then bounded off toward the house with Szerain.

Lenny and Zenra had retreated to a polite distance while I spoke with Rho. I waved them over and explained that Tessa's physical issues were resolved but she'd be emotionally fragile for a while. "Could y'all take care of getting her to the guest room while I do some potency clean up?"

Zenra summoned Kellum over, who lifted Tessa as if she weighed no more than one of the cats and gently carried her to the house.

I watched them go, then settled in for a bit of arcane house-keeping.

Chapter 6

I stepped off the nexus as compound personnel resumed their usual duties with none of the frenetic energy of a half hour ago. Barely an hour had elapsed since we'd mobilized to deal with the car in the ditch. And now everything was back to . . . well, not normal. Nothing was ever *normal* here. But back to the usual routine. People working toward a common goal. Blah blah, save the world. The usual.

A distant growl of a diesel engine was joined by the sound of a winch and the screech of metal on asphalt—the car being removed from the ditch to be relocated someplace well away from here. Even though I was fairly certain it held no more traps or unwelcome surprises, why take a chance?

David Nguyen continued to clean up detritus from the downed tree while Tandon and Bryce conferred about security rotations. Two women on mules chatted as they passed by on their way to the horse farm. The Horsemen of the Apocalypse had been renamed the Riders of the Apocalypse—not only because of the shift to using mules, but also because a good third of the team were women.

Near the side of the house, Michael sat in the grass and animated little golem mice that two cats, Bumper and Dire, eagerly pounced on. Michael was a seriously gifted pianist and also had the ability to make golems from dirt. He'd suffered a traumatic brain injury when he was twelve but had thrived during his time with lords Seretis and Rayst in the demon realm. In fact he could sometimes "see" the lords and what they were doing, though lately that had been hit or miss due to the various arcane instabilities.

"Jill told me to bring this to you."

I blinked out of my reverie to see Giovanni Racchelli holding out a napkin-wrapped bundle. Giovanni was a highly skilled artist and the lovemate of Elinor Bayliss, a summoner whose essence had been attached to mine for most of my life. Both had been born in the seventeenth century yet had adapted quite well to modern life with a little help from an arcane crash course in necessary knowledge.

"She said to tell it is not cookies"—he grinned as my shoulders slumped—"but that you may have brownies if you first eat something resembling a proper meal."

I peeled back the napkin to reveal an egg and bacon biscuit sandwich. "She's so bossy," I said, though it came out as "shush-obsshy" since my mouth was already full of egg, bacon, and biscuit.

Giovanni laughed. "She reminds me of a housekeeper long ago employed by a patron of mine. Terrifying woman if you defied her, but she ensured all needs were met. She carried a long switch on her belt and did not hesitate to use it on any who crossed her. Rumor had it she once smacked the lord of the manor, but he dared not dismiss her over it for fear he would never find anyone to run his house as well as she."

I swallowed my bite of biscuit. "If you love your life—and your hide—don't you dare tell Jill that story."

Giovanni's eyes went wide. "Oh. Yes. I see."

I almost laughed at the consternation on his face, not to mention the image that leaped into my head of Jill walking around with a riding crop in one hand. "I'm kidding. Jill is more than able to keep us all in line without beatings."

He let out a sheepish chuckle. "And now that you are eating, I am allowed to tell you there is a tin of brownies in the bottom drawer of the filing cabinet in your office."

"That sneaky bitch," I breathed.

"She is the best kind, yes?" With a jaunty wave, he jogged off toward the pond trail, satchel with his drawing supplies looped over one shoulder. No doubt he was continuing his quest to get one of the Jontari warlords to sit still long enough to be sketched. I'd told him he could simply take a picture and use that as a reference, but Giovanni didn't feel he'd be able to capture the warlord's true spirit from a mere photo.

Since my artistic skills were limited to stick figures, I had no standing to argue the point.

Warmed by the food and the thoughtfulness, I made a bee-line toward the house.

Bryce had moved to sit on the porch steps, where he scrolled through messages on his phone. The distinctive *bloop-beep-dings* of Pro Krasta Nation kept sounding in the background, signaling there were Cornyacs ready to be farmed, but he kept thumbing through messages without even seeming to read them.

Brownies could wait. I plopped down on the steps beside him. "You sick of the game?"

"Huh? Oh." He focused on the screen, apparently only now realizing it was bleeping at him. He sighed and set his phone aside. "No, I'm just . . . Got a lot of things on my mind, y'know?"

"You're worried about Seretis, and you miss him." He and Bryce had an essence bond, but Seretis was currently Dekkak's prisoner. He'd gone to the imperator and struck a deal, essentially giving himself to her, and in exchange Dekkak hadn't slaughtered me outright when I summoned her. None of us would still be here if not for his actions.

"Yeah. He seems to be doing a lot better and isn't being mistreated." His brow creased.

"But?"

He grimaced. "I don't know what to make of some of the images I've gotten from him. There've been several of Gurgaz. Y'know, Slugthing."

"Right." I nodded as if I totally wouldn't forget and go right back to calling him Slugthing in my head. Dammit, he looked like a giant tentacle-y slug!

"Anyway, remember how when you summoned Dekkak, Gurgaz had skulls and guns from the Dirty Thirty on some of his tentacles? Well, in these latest images I've been getting from Seretis, Gurgaz is wearing more military stuff—guns and gear and the like, and I can't be sure, but it didn't look like DIRT equipment."

"Well, shit."

He gave me a pained smile. "That was my reaction, too."

The Dirty Thirty were an elite strike team who'd been sent through a rift to take the fight to the demon realm. As anyone with half a brain could have predicted, every last one of them were slaughtered. Part of the deal with Dekkak stipulated the return of the remains and equipment of the Dirty Thirty, and she'd kept up her end of the deal. Therefore, these adornments were new. I'd assumed the colossal failure of that mission would have convinced everyone that those kind of attacks were a criminal waste of lives. But someone somewhere was taking invasive action, and no one saw fit to inform me.

"I'll see what I can find out," I said, "but ever since the incursions dropped to a trickle after the Dekkak truce, I'm not in the loop on half as much as I used to be. Maybe some mutual distrust. Who knows."

"When incursions were hot and heavy, the bigwigs couldn't get enough of you. 'Why's this happening? What the fuck was that? How do we kill whatever?' Blah blah blah. Gotta be frustrating getting shut out now that they *think* they don't need you as much."

"We're all much better off if I have complete intel, but it is what it is."

He thrust a hand through his hair. "I also saw a glimpse of Kadir."

I blinked. "Wait. With the Jontari? I thought they hated all the lords."

"Yeah. It was just a quick image, but definitely Kadir. I tried to ask Seretis for more detail about why he was there, but no luck."

Weird. Very weird. Yet Kadir marched to his own beat, and I'd need way more information before I could begin to draw any conclusions. Still, I mentally filed that tidbit of info away.

"Have you heard from Paul lately?" I asked. I had a feeling seeing Kadir had reminded Bryce of his friend, compounding his pensive mood. Paul Ortiz was a gifted computer expert and hacker who'd been kidnapped by J.M. Farouche. Bryce had been his bodyguard, best friend, and most of all, he'd helped Paul escape Farouche's clutches. But then Paul suffered life-threatening injuries after getting caught in Mzatal's arcane flare during the battle at the Farouche Plantation. Kadir was the only one capable of saving his life, and so Paul went to live in his unsettling realm. To everyone's shock, Paul thrived and soon formed an essence bond with Kadir, like the one I had with Mzatal and the bond Bryce shared with Seretis.

Bryce managed a smile. "We message back and forth several times a week. He sends me the most ridiculous videos. Like this one." He scrolled to a page then held the phone so I could see the video—from one of our own security cameras—of Bryce falling on his ass in muddy slush. It then cut to a view from another camera, with a super slow-motion close up as Bryce landed in the muck, then the same thing sped up and looped back and forth, backed by ludicrous Benny Hill music.

It was impossible not to laugh at the utter absurdity. "That little fucker has eyes everywhere." That wasn't hyperbole, either. Paul could tap into damn near any audio or video feed. I glanced at Bryce. "But messaging and sharing videos isn't the same as seeing him in person."

He blew out his breath. "Not the same at all. Especially after so many months. I miss the guy. Worry about him."

"Pretty sure he feels the same way about you. Paul sends you dumb shit like that to make you laugh, Mr. So Fucking Serious."

"He knows me pretty damn well." He swiped to another video—this one of me getting a snowball right in the face.

"Ah, yes, I'm so glad that one of my finer moments has been immortalized."

Bryce grinned. "At least he hasn't put it online."

"Yet."

"Yet," he agreed.

"Still nothing from Paul about Kadir's plans, right?"

"Not a word. And I've learned not to ask."

Movement across the yard drew my attention to the Jontari kehza Weyix as he bounded over the rift, then flew up to land atop Jill's trailer. A heartbeat later Sloosh streaked across the yard and melted into the shadows at the base of the equipment shed.

I knew what was coming next, and barely a heartbeat later the two warlords began a no-holds barred spar, with both physical and arcane attacks. Weyix dove on the zhurn then leaped into the air to avoid strikes. The kehza was fast and nimble, able to turn and change direction in physics-defying moves. Yet Sloosh moved with a speedy, sinuous grace, peppering Weyix with balls of stinging potency, even as he evaded his opponent's claws. Out in the open, the two demons appeared to be evenly matched, but once their battle progressed amongst the trees, my money was on Sloosh. The zhurn easily vanished into shadows, defying even Weyix's ability to detect him.

Or so I thought. Weyix went still, teeth bared, sensing. His nostrils flared as he scented the air, and a ball of sparkling potency formed in his right hand.

An instant later Weyix lobbed the potency into the woods,

bathing a ten-foot-wide area—and the zhurn—in what was essentially arcane glitter. Sloosh snarled and leaped from the shadows, but Weyix already had his follow-up attack ready for the now-highly-visible-and-glittery warlord and, with a roar of triumph, delivered another strike, this one non-glittery. Sloosh screech-snarled, then did a complicated claw-click that indicated defeat.

Weyix let out a window-rattling bellow of triumph and flew off.

"That glitter thing was a pretty cool trick," Bryce said.

"No shit. I'd love to learn how to do that, but who the hell knows what kind of price the Jontari would ask in exchange for teaching me." And there was no way to predict what might seem a fair price to them. Never anything as simple as gold. Sometimes it was an exchange of favors. Other times it could be a physical object the warlord found interesting or appealing. Like the time Dagor took a liking to an old quilt Jill had been airing out on the porch. Though it wasn't a family heirloom or anything, she'd put on a good show about how it had great meaning to her and that she was so very reluctant to part with it. He'd ended up trading her a heavy gold ring for it, then carefully gathered the quilt up and bounded away as if he'd gotten the far better end of the deal. Meanwhile, Jill had a solid gold ring large enough to wear as a bracelet in exchange for a quilt she'd bought for ten bucks at a thrift store. Of course, for all we knew, a quilt like that could be worth a dozen gold rings in the demon realm, and Jill was a sucker who should've held out for more.

"Or you could figure out how to do it yourself." Bryce shrugged. "I mean, I don't know shit about the arcane, but you've made glowy things to light a room before. Isn't that sparkle grenade kind of the same thing?"

I blinked. His tone was utterly matter-of-fact, as if it made no sense to him that I'd need to be taught how to make such a thing. "Er, well, not exactly."

He snorted. "So figure it out. Hell, when Rhyzkahl was a prisoner here, you were a pseudo-lord. You can't tell me he didn't know how to make a fucking glitter bomb."

I started laughing. His brow creased. "What? What did I say?"

"We're sitting here thinking about arcane glitter bombs, but it just hit me: why the hell does it have to be arcane? Why not just use regular ordinary glitter? Fill some balloons with the shit. Then anyone can use them."

He chuckled. "That makes too much sense. But I wonder how DIRT will react when you put in a requisition for twenty pounds of glitter and a case of water balloons."

"Please. That's not even close to being the weirdest thing I've asked for."

"Yeah. Like the pinwheels to detect shifts in arcane flows."

I grinned. "Which didn't work at all."

A comfortable silence fell.

"So," Bryce said after a moment. "You want me to ask the recon teams to check the stores for glitter and balloons?"

"Damn straight."

Chapter 7

Bryce went off to deal with security-related stuff, and I continued inside, nearly bowling over Sonny.

"The phone has been ringing off the hook for you," he told me.

"*Quelle surprise*!" I replied, edging around him to continue toward my office. "Ooooh, I wonder, could the calls be from"—I sucked in a dramatic gasp—"Pushy Luschka?" Colonel Hanna Luschka was General Starr's aide de camp and was constantly hounding me for intel, updates, and projections.

"A few, but not all," he said, following me. He grimaced when I shot him a dubious look. "Okay, many, but not all. There was one from the Spires, two from Fed Central, four from Colonel Luschka, and one from Nandi Chola in Capetown."

I retrieved the tin of brownies from the filing cabinet, frowning as I tugged it open. Nandi was one of the eleven summoners who worked with DIRT, though Idris and I were the only ones who had ever actually summoned demons. The other nine still possessed the innate ability, but it had never been fully tapped. In fact, I was certain their "virgin" summoner status was part of the reason they hadn't pinged on Xharbek's radar, and thus hadn't been scooped up and subverted.

Fortunately, the arcane skills we needed didn't require actual summoning experience. After the initial screenings to be sure the non-summoning summoners could handle the stress of incursions, Idris and I had assessed their basic ability to shape potency, then given them a crash course in essential wards and sigils.

"Well, shit," I mumbled around the brownie in my mouth, then absently held the tin out to offer one to Sonny. "Any idea what Nandi needs?" I'd much rather talk to her than any of the others clamoring for my time and energy.

"I have a feeling all the calls are in some way related to this." Sonny took a bite of his brownie then held his phone out to show me a picture of a demon realm grove.

It took a second for comprehension to hit me. "Wait. Is that on *Earth*?!"

He swiped to another pic, this one from overhead and obviously taken by a drone.

"Holy shit," I breathed. "That's ground zero." No wonder everyone was shitting their pants. I looked out the window at the grove tree beside my nexus. "You could have warned me," I grumbled at Rho. I stuck the tin back in the filing cabinet. "When did it appear?" Though I had a feeling I already knew the answer.

"Within the last hour. From what I was able to gather, the entire thing grew right out of the ground in the span of a minute or so."

"Right when I was dealing with Lord Smarmy and the two Fuckface demahnk." I headed into the conference room, scanning the screens and news feeds for any mention of earthquakes or new volcanos or any other inexplicable natural disasters.

And there they were. A giant whirlpool in the English Channel. A sinkhole in Central Park. A lava-spouting fissure in Tiananmen Square. Smarmy and the Fuckface Duo had created stability issues for more than just the interdimensions, and Rho was responding as best they could. "I'll touch base with Nandi, but I'd be grateful if you could call back whoever else needs calling back and let them know I'm aware of the situation at ground zero and am currently making a full assessment so that I can give them a complete briefing blah blah and all that, but please make me sound more intelligent. Oh, and tell them the trees pose zero threat and to pass along the order that they are absolutely *not* to be disturbed or damaged in any way whatsoever."

"I'll work what miracles I can," Sonny said with a wry smile, then departed.

"Miracle working is in your job description," I called after him, then yanked my phone from my belt as it rang with Idris's ringtone. "Dude! I guess you heard about the grove at ground zero?"

"I . . . wait, what? No, I hadn't heard, but that ties in to why

I'm calling. A grove tree just sprang up in Yorkshire, England, a bit north of Leeds. I'm about to hop on a transport to go assess it and make sure, but from the pics I've seen and on-the-ground reports, it looks like the real deal."

"Yeah, and I think I know why it sprang up." I gave him a rundown of the events of the past hour, along with my suspicion that the emergence of the grove and tree was in response to instability caused by Jesral and the two demahnk.

He was silent for a long moment. "So, Tessa's there?"

I gave myself a mental slap for not even considering how he'd take that part of the news. "Yes. But, Idris, she was manipulated heavily. And apparently had been for *decades*. It was pretty vile."

"I see," he said.

"Look, it's been super weird trying to wrap my head around it all. I thought she'd betrayed me. You thought she'd abandoned you. I'm not asking you to change your attitude about her in the span of a minute, but I just thought you should know there were some very powerful and awful factors in play."

I heard him sigh. "Okay. It's just a lot to take in. Look, my transport's about to take off without me. I'll touch base with you as soon as I know anything."

"Please do. And stay safe, okay?"

"Right back at you."

I plopped into a chair and put it into a slow spin, then sent Sonny a text about the Yorkshire tree. After that I called Nandi, who confirmed my hunch that Capetown had a Grove tree as well. I reassured her that it posed absolutely zero danger and should be left alone, and to notify me if anything changed or if more trees appeared.

Then I went for more brownies.

I decided to work from the conference room, mostly because I still couldn't get the stupid stuck window in my office closed, and the towel I shoved into the gap did a piss poor job of keeping cold air from seeping in. For the next hour I studied old and new satellite and drone footage of ground zero—so named because last July an arcane valve exploded in the parking lot of the Beaulac Police Department, causing massive destruction along with considerable injury and death. Then four months ago, Xharbek ripped the valve open and unleashed a flood of arcane mutagen—which Squig and Fillion were inadvertently exposed to. Through a massive combined effort of summoners, arcane users, and lords, we were able to seal the valve and scatter Xharbek—the closest we could come to killing him—but not before much of downtown Beaulac had turned into a bad Sci-Fi horror movie of mutated flora and fauna. Massive hives of rat-roach things the size of chihuahuas. Carnivorous flowers. Fire-breathing birds. Horseflies the size of your face. Your basic nightmare.

Within a few hours of our victory over Xharbek, DIRT command and I agreed the area needed to be sterilized for everyone's safety. By the next morning, the heart of Beaulac was a smoking husk, buildings reduced to rubble and melted slag, and mutated infestations eradicated.

Ever since then, the area had been a grey-toned wasteland, with the exception of small clumps of weeds here and there, which—after determining they were normal ordinary weeds from normal ordinary seeds that had blown in on normal ordinary winds—had delighted me, because it proved that life had a way of prevailing. Though that didn't stop DIRT and Fed Central from overkill-fire-bombing them anyway.

And now it was a grey-toned wasteland with a brilliant splotch of white, purple, and green right smack atop the valve.

I was going to have to investigate this new grove, but the day had been long and exhausting on a number of levels, and no way did I have the energy to deal with it. It would still be there tomorrow. Or maybe it wouldn't, but in that case I wouldn't need to go investigate it, right?

I made my way to the guest room, checked to be sure the warding on the room was keyed to alert me if Tessa needed any help, then quietly stepped in.

She lay curled on her side with one hand tucked under her cheek. Even asleep, lines of stress creased her forehead, and I instinctively reached out to stroke her hair in the hopes of easing some of what troubled her. She'd done the same for me, in this very room, so many years ago, when I was still reeling from the death of my father and adjusting to having this aunt, who I barely knew, as my guardian. That part hadn't been manipulation. She'd cared about me as a person, a grieving child. In fact, she was as good a mother figure as she could have possibly been to me, considering what she was up against—not only with the manipulations and coercions of Xharbek and the Mraztur, but also suddenly being a parental figure to a traumatized tween.

Sonny cleared his throat softly from the hallway, grimacing

in deep apology. "I'm *so* sorry to interrupt you," he murmured, "but Colonel Luschka insists on speaking to you and made noises about escalating things to General Starr if you continue to duck her calls."

"It's all right." I stepped out of the room and closed the door behind me, double-checked the warding then returned to the conference room.

I didn't bother sitting down, and just hit the blinking button on the speakerphone in the middle of the table. "Colonel Luschka," I said in my warmest, friendliest tone possible, "I'm so sorry to have kept you waiting, and I appreciate your patience. I hope the updated report addressed your concerns. How can I help you?"

She cleared her throat with a *hmmf*, clearly unaffected by my overt niceness. "Arcane Commander Gillian. You can start by briefing me on what happened at your compound this afternoon."

"Could you be more specific?" I asked. "We stay pretty busy here."

"I'd appreciate it if you didn't play games with me, Commander. We have satellite imagery and drone footage of a vehicle going into the ditch near your main gate. A figure then exited the driver's side door and collapsed."

"All right."

I could practically hear her teeth grind as she realized I wasn't going to elaborate on that confirmation, such as it was.

"We believe the person in question is your aunt, Tessa Pazhel."

No point denying it. "Yup. It was, indeed."

"And?"

"And what? She's my aunt. She was popping by for a spot of tea and had a bit of a crinkle-fender in the ditch. But she's fine now and resting. It's nice of you to be so worried."

Luschka made a noise as if choking back an unkind retort. "We also have satellite imagery that shows a distinct area of distortion on the road between the vehicle and the main gate. An area where you and Szerain had stood only a moment before."

I was very tempted to repeat the *All right*, but didn't want to make the poor woman's head explode. Not yet at least. "Huh. Sounds like you might need a new camera on that satellite."

"Commander Gillian," she ground out, "I realize you're accustomed to playing your cards close to your vest, and I respect that you have your own security concerns, but you're part of a larger organization, and we're all working toward a common goal."

"Of course, Colonel Luschka," I replied, my tone all business now. "And I define that common goal to be the preservation of life and liberty throughout the world, with stalwart opposition to all entities who would seek to deprive anyone of such, whether by direct action, indirect action, criminal negligence, or merely callous disregard for the safety and well-being of those under their command."

"Well . . . yes, but I don't see what that has to do with—"

"Colonel, why wasn't I informed that strike teams are *still* being sent through rifts? I assumed that all such futile missions would be prohibited after the tragic and pointless loss of the Dirty Thirty."

She stammered for a second before finding her voice. "No DIRT units have been—"

"These weren't DIRT units," I snapped. "But I know damn well that DIRT works in cooperation and coordination with the majority of the other nations on this planet. Are you going to tell me DIRT had zero knowledge of these missions? Or worse, will you tell me they *did* know, yet made no effort to convince the commanders that they'd be engaging in willful dereliction of command by sending these soldiers into certain death?"

Luschka fell silent for several heartbeats. "Commander Gillian," she said, tone a bit more subdued, "I have no reason to doubt your intel, but I give you my word I knew nothing of this." She took a breath. "I'll see what I can find out."

"Thank you, Colonel. I appreciate that."

"No more deflection. Tell me about the highway distortion," she said in her best command voice.

"We both know I'm not going to do that."

Silence for a good ten seconds.

"Will you at least tell me if the arrival of your aunt or the cause of the distortion will impact any aspect of DIRT?"

"I truly don't have an answer for you at this time, Colonel." Which was no lie. Until we knew more of what Jesral was up to, I had no idea how DIRT and the rest of the world would be affected. "For now, we all need to keep our eyes open and stay on our toes."

She sighed, clearly accepting defeat for the moment. "I'll be in touch."

The line went dead.

I plopped into a chair, weirdly exhausted.

Sonny stepped into the conference room. "I've made the needed calls, passed along the orders re the grove trees, placated those who needed placating, and am now here to remind you—by your very own standing order, I should add—that you're scheduled for range time in half an hour, and after that you have a lesson with Tandon."

I groaned and slouched more deeply into the chair. I'd given myself a regular schedule to go to the range because I was a decent marksman but wanted to actually become a *good* marksman. And Sharini Tandon had a bazillion black belts in styles I couldn't pronounce and was slowly but surely getting me to where my hand-to-hand combat skills were approaching "might actually have a chance of winning this fight."

Sonny smiled. "Also, this evening is movie night at the rec center. They're showing *Secondhand Lions.*"

I loved that movie. "Will there be popcorn?"

"With fresh-churned butter, even."

I heaved myself out of the chair. "Butter: yet another reason to save the planet."

Chapter 8

I stared at myself in the bathroom mirror. I'd been awake for maybe three minutes, so I wasn't completely sure I was seeing what I thought I was seeing. But as more seconds ticked by, I had to accept that yes, my body had indeed undergone yet another modification—one I hadn't noticed until now because yesterday had been a bit, um, *busy*, and come nighttime I'd changed into a sleep shirt and fallen right into bed. Hell, I could have turned purple and not noticed.

But this morning I'd done the usual sensible thing and disrobed before getting into the shower, then stopped in my tracks as I caught sight of my reflection and the new scar on my chest.

Except it wasn't really a *scar*, as far as I could tell. Certainly nothing at all like the eleven sigil scars that covered my torso—one for each lord. Rhyzkahl had carved those with the essence blade, Xhan, in the torture ritual designed to turn me into Rowan. Mzatal had saved me from the ritual, but the sigils would be with me forever. Even the one that was no longer a scar. Rhyzkahl had carved a twelfth—Ashava's—but Szerain resolved it and only the arcane sigil remained.

Now, a lightning bolt wove through Mzatal's sigil, though not a cheesy or cartoonish one. Achingly beautiful, it looked more like a snapshot of a brilliant and complex lightning strike, a delicate silvery white pattern I could barely detect with my fingertips. Yet I felt it with a sense beyond touch that affected me far more deeply.

"Damn, Boss," I murmured. "You sure do send mixed signals." He'd destroyed his ring but then marked me with something so incredibly *Mzatal*. What the hell was I supposed to make of any of this?

For now, all I could do was shove it into my brain's attic, where it could join the many other things I had no idea how to deal with.

It was starting to get pretty crowded up there.

After a quick shower, I dressed in the same thing I wore every single day: fatigues and combat boots. Back in the pre-DIRT days, I'd have tugged on comfy sweats, fluffy socks, and I definitely would *not* have wrestled my way into a sports bra. After all, I'd seldom needed to worry about people popping in and out of my house. But now the house was more of a command center, and I'd been damn near living in fatigues since the demon incursions began. Couldn't complain too much, since they were fairly comfortable and easy, and I was so used to them by now it felt odd to wear anything else. Plus, I currently had the luxury of someone else doing my laundry. Almost made all the other shit worth it.

Dressed and vaguely presentable, I made my way to the kitchen, automatically side-stepping to avoid the cabinet door that would never stay closed. After fixing myself a cup of coffee, I grabbed a cinnamon roll off the tray on the stove. Still warm. *Bless you, Jill!*

I sipped my coffee and smiled at the sight of new artwork on the fridge. Giovanni had a habit of doing sketches of people and animals and demons and then leaving them on the fridge with the understanding that anyone who wanted one could have it—with priority going to the subject of the drawing. His artwork seldom remained on the fridge long, for there was no denying he was incredibly gifted. But a new piece graced the fridge this morning, and not one of Giovanni's. This was an exquisite depiction of both Giovanni and Elinor, showing Giovanni sketching Elinor as she created complex arcane sigils. It spoke to Szerain's skill that Elinor appeared strong and confident as she worked the arcane, and it also spoke to how much he cared—and worried—about the two of them. Understandable, as she was his daughter via Aphra.

Ever since Elinor had been restored, she'd gladly pitched in to help with basic arcane maintenance on the compound, including crafting the "shieldbuster" enhancements that helped ordinary ammunition penetrate the arcane protections of most demons. In fact, thanks to her zeal to pitch in and be useful, we now had a truly impressive stock of shieldbuster ammunition for every type of firearm on the compound. Yet it was clear she had little desire to do more or work toward becoming a stronger practitioner. Szerain and I both knew self-doubt plagued her, fed by the constant, nagging worry the demon realm cataclysm hundreds of years ago had been her fault. That the collapse of the ritual to raise Szerain's Earthgate happened because she'd erred or hadn't been strong enough.

And while none of us knew for sure what destabilized the ritual, Szerain and I clearly shared the belief that, not only was Elinor blameless, she was also a skilled arcane user who could rival any of us if not for her crippling insecurity.

I suspected Giovanni would waste no time in claiming the sketch.

As I finished the cinnamon roll, I moved to the window to observe the goings-on in the back yard, but my gaze went instead to a wicker love seat on the porch where a petite figure sat, blanket wrapped around hunched shoulders, and feet tucked underneath her.

I gulped the last of my coffee then grabbed a few items on the way out the door.

Tessa looked up at me, and I gave her a smile as I tugged a knit hat onto her head, gently pushing a few stray curls out of her face.

I blinked away a brief sting of tears as an old memory surfaced, from when I was about seven and I'd brought a scarf out to my mother as she sat in almost the same place as Tessa was now. Mom had been going through chemo treatments for ovarian cancer and was always cold. I'd carefully looped the scarf around her neck, then to be silly I kept wrapping it until it covered her entire face. She laughed. I laughed. And then I arranged the scarf properly and we snuggled together and watched the wildlife in the back yard.

I let the lovely memory linger as I handed Tessa a pair of fluffy slippers. "Put these on your feetsies," I said. "It's too chilly to sit out here in just a blanket."

Tessa pulled the slippers on, then simply stared at her feet. "Thank you."

"C'mon, I have a better place for you to sit."

Her brow puckered. "Am I in the way here?"

"Nooooo, that's not it at all." I took her hand and tugged her to stand, tweaked the blanket so it stayed wrapped around her shoulders, then grabbed a cushion off one of the chairs. "Just come with me, okay?"

She offered no resistance as I led her to the grove tree or when I set the cushion down at the base and guided her to sit. I settled beside her so that our shoulders touched and let the peace of the tree flow through me.

The tension in her body seemed to slowly unwind. After a few minutes, she tipped her head back and peered up at the canopy, brow slightly puckered. "Is this a *grove* tree?"

"It sure is. Just kinda popped up a while back."

She smiled, already looking a little less likely to break apart at the slightest touch. "It's so lovely." Her gaze skimmed the yard. "So much has changed since I lived here with you, and yet it's still very much *you*. Your home. No matter what else."

A thread of uncertainty I hadn't even realized I'd been holding unraveled. There'd been so many times when I rather selfishly grieved the loss of my quiet private home, despite the need and necessity for the many *many* changes the property had undergone. But now I looked at it through Tessa's eyes. Birds in the pines. Bright red berries on holly trees. Camellia bushes along the side of the house with a pink snowfall of petals on the ground beneath them. The windows of Jill's trailer with lights strung around them. A battered tinsel garland that I remembered from my childhood adorning the roof of an equipment shed.

And, leaning drunkenly against the shed's exterior, was an ancient wire and plastic Santa from my very early childhood that now looked more demonic than the demons. I'd unearthed it from the attic a couple of weeks before Christmas but hadn't fully realized how decrepit it looked until seeing it in the light of day. Yet by then, others had taken note of it and refused to let me toss it out. Even now I suspected there'd be an uproar if I tried to get rid of it, but I at least managed to get it relocated to where it wasn't right out in the open, leering at everyone with its cracked plastic smile and one good eye.

Yes, Evil Santa and all, this place would indeed always be my home, even if it was now home to so many more. And it wasn't a bad thing at all to share it with people who had absolutely become family in all the ways that mattered.

"I'm glad you're here," I said, the four words carrying far more weight and impact than I'd intended when I spoke them. I was glad she could be here, at my home. I was glad she was safe. I was glad she was becoming herself again. And so much more.

Tessa reached for my hand and laced her fingers through mine. "I'm glad I'm here with you."

We fell into a comfortable silence and watched the various activity in the back yard. It wasn't quite as hectic as it had been before we acquired the forty acres and moved the admin and barracks, but there was still plenty going on.

Two Jontari played some sort of dice-like game on the roof of the security offices. Krawkor gave us a cheery wave with his tails as he carried an armload of radio equipment across the yard. On the porch, Zenra sat in a crouch, flicking her tail for Cake and Bumper to chase. At the side of the house, Pellini's chocolate lab, Sammy, dashed to retrieve a tennis ball thrown by David Nguyen, then raced back to drop the slobber-covered ball at his feet.

"Have you heard from Idris lately?" Tessa asked, pulling me out of my reverie. Her expression remained even, but her eyes betrayed her desperate desire to know.

"He's been in Corfu this last month and was in Uruguay before that. But I heard from him just yesterday. He sounds like he's doing pretty well. He's on his way to England to do some assessments."

A variety of emotions warred on her face. "I . . . I saw him several months ago, fighting demons at the Mumbai rift. He was amazing."

Did she know he'd seen her there? Did it even matter anymore?

"He's been doing really well." I smiled. "He's insanely talented. A couple of months ago, he completed the tenth ring of the shikvihr."

Pride lit her face, but tears glimmered in her eyes. "I should have been there for him. I should have trained him." She looked at me and swallowed. "I should have trained you as well. Properly. I . . . I didn't know I was holding things back. I mean, I did, but it felt like I was supposed to."

I started to reassure her, but she shook her head. "I remember. I remember all the terrible and selfish and . . . and *evil* things I did. And yes, I know I was manipulated, but it was still my voice, my hands, my actions." She broke off with a sob.

I wrapped my arm around her shoulders and pulled her close, let her cry.

"You were *used*," I told her, drawing on the feel and essence of Rho to add emphasis to the truth of my words. "It was obscene. Your body and will were taken and perverted in order to further the goals of others."

She nodded against my chest, slowly easing. "Thank you." She sat up and wiped at her eyes with the scarf.

"I love you," I said, relieved to find I truly meant it, especially after so many months of despising her.

"I love you, too," she whispered.

We sat in silence for a time before she spoke again. "Angus."

My attention sharpened on her. "What about him?"

"Out on the road. He wanted Marcel to know that even though Catherine's a hostage, she's okay. I've spent some time with her. She puts on a good show of being docile and keeps a low profile."

"Smart lady. Boudreaux will be glad to hear his mom's okay. It's been eating at him."

"Jesral will lose Angus's compliance if he hurts her, and he can't afford that now."

"Is Jesral short on people?"

Her brow furrowed. "Everything's hazy. I think Jesral muted and muddled and muffled my memories."

"No worries. Just rest for—"

"No! I don't want to forget more."

I gave her a squeeze. "It's okay. Take your time."

"Jesral has people. But there's a project he's obsessed with. Secret. But he lost someone."

"Someone he needs for the project? Who? Tsuneo?" Tsuneo was one of Jesral's long-time summoners.

"Not Tsuneo." She paused for a long moment as if gathering her thoughts. "Tsuneo is part of it. Any summoner would do for that aspect, though, I think."

"Did Jesral lose a summoner?"

"No. An operator. Highly specialized—in what, I don't know—and with a healthy dollop of arcane talent. He'd been instrumental in the project, then about three months ago, poof! Gone."

"Gone how?"

"Vanished. Arcanely abducted from the project wing, the most secure area of the facility."

I sucked in a breath through my teeth. "Huh. I'd love to know how *that* happened." As well as who pulled it off.

"Jesral was furious. Project was at a standstill. He's tried six or seven candidates since then, but they failed one after another."

I didn't want to think what might have happened to those candidates after disappointing Jesral. "So no operator yet?"

"He found a workaround about a week ago. Two operators

with Tsuneo, but Jesral is still surly. I don't think they're anywhere near as good as the original person."

"Ugh. How does Angus fit into the picture?"

"The arrangement only works if Angus is in physical contact with both of them *and* Tsuneo while they work. Like a battery backup to make up for arcane insufficiencies. It's grueling on the lot of them, but on Angus most of all."

"Without Angus, Jesral's super-secret pet project fizzles." That was a damn good data point.

"He hasn't given up on finding the original operator." Tessa let out a long sigh as if releasing the burdens of a million lifetimes. "He did something to me."

"Who? Jesral?"

"Angus. Out on the road. Something loosened inside me. He said, 'I'm sorry. It's all I can do.'" Tears welled in her eyes, and her voice broke. "Kara, I know he's done horrible things, but he wasn't always that way, and he's been a real friend in these past months. When I needed someone."

I cuddled her close and let her cry on my shoulder. Twenty years ago, J.M. Farouche founded the Child Find League: a legitimate non-profit dedicated to locating missing children, prompted by the loss of his own daughter. Angus was his right-hand man from the beginning.

But after about a decade, the two gradually sank into the quicksand of shady dealings with demonic lords and exploitation of emerging arcane talents in humans. Murder, kidnapping, and torture became their norm, somehow twisted from the noble goals of finding lost children. Before all that, Angus had been a great dad to Boudreaux and, even up until very recently, he'd kept his ruthless henchman life well away from his family. On the road yesterday, he'd shown a little decency by passing the message to Boudreaux about his mom via Tessa, and I held out hope that "all he could do" was a covert way to resist Jesral while benefitting my aunt. Especially since he'd told me almost the exact same thing when he took the majority of my arcane abilities.

"Everybody changes," I said. "Most of us have regrets."

Sonny softly cleared his throat. I looked up to see him grimacing in apology. "Sorry to interrupt, but Fed Central needs transport approval for that new shipment of graphene netting. Won't take a minute."

"Tessa, I need to take care of this. You want to go in?"

"If it's okay, I'd like to stay for a while."

I smiled and tucked the blanket around her. "I think that's an excellent idea."

I murmured a request for Sonny to please check on her in a bit and not let her get too cold, then headed into the house to deal with administrative minutiae.

Chapter 9

As soon as I dealt with the administrative crap, and with Tessa's revelations in mind, I shot a text to Boudreaux.

<You got a few minutes to talk?>

The reply came only seconds later. <Yep. In the stables. FYI it's gonna be cold AF in about ten minutes. But no snow>

I cocked a quick glance at the sky before I climbed onto an ATV and headed toward the horse farm. Clear with some scattered clouds, and the temp was mild and pleasant. Still, over the past few months I'd grown used to bizarre changes in weather, which meant I always had a knit cap and gloves stuffed into my jacket pocket, just in case. Even if Boudreaux was right about no snow, there was still the chance we'd get sleet or freezing rain or some other miserable form of precipitation. The weather patterns had been utterly wonky for months now, so anything was possible—and the back yard rift seemed to make the local climate even more chaotic.

And we'd definitely had hella more than our share of snow, which had always been a rarity in south Louisiana. It had snowed two days before Christmas—thick fluffy flakes that didn't stop until it was over six inches deep. Though of course everyone stuck to their usual duties.

Hah. Right.

The entire compound engaged in a full-out snowball war to end all wars, and even managed to do so without ever compromising or neglecting security and safety. The whole thing was glorious, and a much needed mental break—for humans and demons alike. While it would be a stretch to say the compound

Jontari stooped to *playing*, they certainly engaged in some exuberant and violent snow-wrestling.

By the next day everything had melted, leaving a muddy mess. And on Christmas day the temps climbed into the 80s, and anyone who could wear shorts, did.

Still, it was a good—though strange—Christmas.

A five-hundred-foot border of thick woods separated my original property from the horse farm. We'd decided—at my insistence—to keep the majority of the trees and take out only what needed to go in order to make a road. I'd given up so many other trees around my house that I dug my heels in hard about cutting down anything that didn't *need* to be removed for essential expansion or security.

Once past the woods, the road connected to a gravel lane that ran along the perimeter of a generous expanse of land. Before me was a full-size racing track, along with a large pond, covered and open-air training arenas, paddocks, and several fenced pastures. Two of Boudreaux's people were exercising horses on the track, while a handful of others ran combat drills on mules in one of the arenas. With the latter group was Griz, the bear-sized demon-killing Caucasian Shepherd Dog, who was clearly enjoying both the cold weather and the training.

When Boudreaux first told me he was transitioning the Riders to mules, I'd been deeply dubious—mostly because I was clueless and thought mules were plodding beasts meant for hauling plows and the like. I quickly learned mules were sure of foot, hardier and less likely to spook than horses, and had greater strength and endurance. Moreover, they were smart and generally had more common sense than most horses. In other words, far superior for dealing with demonic incursions.

Off to my left was yet another asphalt road—laid by us so we could access the same highway my own driveway opened out onto. We'd briefly considered blocking off the horse farm's original driveway that connected to the road north of us, but finally decided it would be tactically beneficial to have an alternate access to the property. Instead, we installed a heavy duty physical gate and also created what Ashava dubbed an "arcane boulder"— akin to a giant rock rolled in front of a cave entrance, except this one was made out of loads of powerful wards and nifty traps.

Over the past year, Zakaar had crafted the perimeter protections—high-level arcane that would hold off anything but another demahnk. After we acquired the new property,

Zakaar—working through Szerain—extended the protections to include the additional acreage. Since the demahnk had *very* strict rules about non-interference, we'd always considered Zakaar's warding more than sufficient. Yet immediately after the ground zero showdown with Xharbek, Szerain went and added rakkuhr to the perimeter as a bit of added insurance and peace of mind, since it was anathema to the demahnk.

I turned right, toward the stables—an impressive structure that Boudreaux fervently approved of. Beyond it was the main residence, a.k.a "The Big House," along with a caretaker cottage and various outbuildings. Boudreaux and Redd had taken up residence in the house, but even though it was at least three times the size of mine, it couldn't comfortably house all the Riders, so a well-supplied barracks building had been erected behind the stables.

A stiff, icy breeze kicked up, just as Boudreaux had predicted. I tugged on my cap and gloves, but the temperature plunged another dozen degrees during the short drive to the stables, and I cursed myself for not having grabbed a thicker coat and a scarf.

I leaped off the ATV and dashed inside, then let out a deep sigh of relief as the warmth wrapped around me.

I didn't know anything about stables, but even I had recognized this was a pretty nice one. First off, it was *huge*, with an enormous indoor arena attached, along with more than enough climate-controlled stalls for the mules, the back-up/reserve horses, and a number of non-combat horses belonging to the Riders and other compound personnel. In addition, it had features that made Boudreaux and the other Riders damn near swoon in delight, such as a well-equipped farrier stall, water trough indicators, an enormous tack room, and a solar power array on the roof to help run it all.

A short distance from the door, Dire and Cake lounged on a neat stack of blankets while two of the resident barn cats strolled down the breezeway. The barn cats hissed and ran from me as I proceeded further in, but Dire and Cake allowed me to give them skritches. For some unknown reason, cats disliked summoners. However, Fuzzykins's spawn had been conditioned since birth to not totally hate me. Several of them had decided to explore the whole barn cat lifestyle and found it appealing, and though the barn cats were wary of the newcomers at first, they all managed to reach some sort of detente. Weirdly, they even accepted Squig and Fillion, despite the wings and spikes.

A big copper-colored horse stuck his head over his stall door, and I paused to give him a good nose rub. Copper To Gold had fractured a cannon bone in a bad spill during a race thirteen years ago and had been retired. Boudreaux went down with him and broke his femur in three places—the end of his career as a jockey.

"Boudreaux?" I called out.

"Yo, I'm down by the pups," came a shout from a side corridor.

I headed around the corner. The reyza Prikahn crouched in the center of the breezeway, a sleepy puppy held in his wicked claws.

Prikahn bared his teeth at me and stroked a clawed finger down the puppy's back.

"Hey, Prikahn," Boudreaux said from within a stall. "Can you hand that one to me real quick? Just needs his dewormer."

Prikahn growled but relinquished the puppy. As soon as the medicine was administered, he snatched the pup from Boudreaux's hands and cradled it close.

I rested my arms on the stall door and peered in. Five more puppies romped enthusiastically, while Katy, the mother, lay coiled in one corner. She was a perfectly normal-looking Irish Setter—if you ignored the furry serpentine body supported by a couple dozen normal-ish dog legs. Ground zero mutagen had changed this sweet dog into a fifteen-foot-long dog-ipede. After she mysteriously showed up on the compound, Boudreaux told me one of the Riders was a great big softy and had rescued the poor girl before ground zero could be fire-bombed. I secretly suspected the great big softy was actually Boudreaux, especially since he cared for her as diligently as any of the horses or mules.

Unfortunately, due to her elongated body, no one realized Katy was pregnant until eight weeks ago, when she gave birth to six ordinary—we hoped—puppies. Their wide variety of coloration made it evident the sire had been a "Heinz 57" mutt, but so far the puppies remained wonderfully normal. Phew.

Katy lifted her head at the sight of me then flowed up and over the stall door to wind around my legs, wagging her tail—and much of her body—as I gave her pets and told her what a very good girl she was.

As soon as she was satisfied with my offering of affection, she planted herself in front of Prikahn, eyes fixed on the puppy in his hands.

Boudreaux grinned. "Sorry, bud. Mama says it's naptime for these guys."

The reyza snarled but reluctantly returned the puppy to the confines of the stall. Satisfied, Katy climbed back over the door and proceeded to inspect and sniff all her babies.

I sighed. "They're adorable, but what the hell are we going to do with them?"

Boo shook his head. "Beats me. Lenny spayed her as soon as the pups were weaned, which means we won't run into this issue again. But as for these guys, I got nuthin'. They're old enough to be adopted out, but . . ." He gave a helpless shrug.

I rubbed the back of my neck. The shelters were closed, Beaulac was all but abandoned, and the remaining residents weren't exactly clamoring to adopt. We had plenty of animals on the compound already. And while Szerain assured us the puppies were unmutated, did he really know for sure? Regardless, none of us were keen on having a pack of dogs—mutated or not—roaming around. "Okay, well, I'm not going to stress about this right now."

"Yeah. Prioritize your stresses. Make those fuckers wait their turn."

"The puppies or the stresses?"

"They're kind of the same, aren't they?" He grinned. "'Cause all sorts of mayhem. Eat up resources. And will only get bigger."

"Well, at least puppies are cute."

Boudreaux gave Katy a good head rub, then exited the stall. Prikahn had left without my noticing. For a big demon, he sure could move silently.

"You were spot on about the change in the weather," I said.

He snorted and slapped his leg. "Ever since the accident, I got me one of those old man weather-wise aches."

"Um, yay?"

He laughed. "At least I got something out of all that, right?"

"Handy trick when the weather can't make up its mind."

"And can't rely on a weather app on your phone anymore." He chucked a manure fork into a wheelbarrow and headed down the breezeway.

I kept pace beside him. "I talked to Tessa, and she told me about your mom."

He paused. "I wondered when you were going to get around to why you came by."

"It's not—"

He cut me off with a raised hand. "Let me get started here, okay?" he said, voice tight and strained, and I suspected he needed a minute to prepare himself for whatever I was about to say. He slid open a stall door and gripped the halter of a lanky white mule. "C'mon, Betty Lou, let's get you mucked out." He drew her out into the breezeway, positioned her near the stall door, released her halter and said firmly, "Stand."

She shoved him once with her nose but didn't move when he rolled the wheelbarrow into the vacated stall. I patted Betty Lou's neck as he started shoveling. After about a minute of silence, he cleared his throat. "What did Tessa say?"

"It's not bad news. Catherine is a hostage, but she's not being mistreated or abused—part of Jesral's deal with Angus, I think. She's not manipulated, either."

He exhaled, shoulders relaxing. "That's really good to know. Thanks."

"Apparently your mom's doing a really good job of playing the part of a cowed prisoner." I snorted. "I could never pull that off."

"That's because you wear your emotions on your sleeve."

I considered that. "You're probably right."

He crooked a half-smile. "That's not a bad thing. People know what to expect from you, which means it's easier to trust you."

Holy shit. That was one hell of a compliment, especially coming from Boudreaux, who'd spent years disliking me intensely. I felt a couple of dumb tears prick at my eyes, and I focused intently on stroking Betty Lou so I could get my silly—and apparently very obvious—emotions under control.

"I heard my dad was out on the road with you," Boudreaux said casually, not looking at me as he sifted the bedding with the fork.

I had extremely mixed feelings about Angus, but no matter what other crimes he'd committed, I had zero doubt he loved Boudreaux—despite not being his biological father—and would destroy heaven and earth if necessary to keep him safe. "Angus was pretty damn stone-faced for the whole thing . . . and party to Jesral's agenda. But he helped Tessa and wanted her to pass word to you about your mom."

Boudreaux slung a forkful of bedding and manure into the wall—hard.

Unfortunately, a few months ago I'd been forced to shatter

subject. But then he added, "Too bad the online stores won't deliver here anymore."

"OH MY GOD," I shrieked, torn between horror and laughter. Laughter won, and Boudreaux grinned as if he won the round. Which, I supposed, he had. He'd certainly chased away my brief gloom.

"For your information," I finally managed, "I am indeed capable of taking care of my, ah, personal needs. Also, I never in a million years ever expected you'd someday be giving me sex toy advice." And the weirdest part was that it wasn't creepy in the slightest. Maybe because it was given out of what seemed like a genuine desire to help me out? Along with something oddly resembling friendship?

His grin widened. "I have layers."

I laughed and rolled my eyes. "You have something, that's for sure." Just then my phone buzzed with a text from Scott.

<ETA 45 mins with Walter>

"I need to head back," I said. "Scott's on the way here with Walter."

"You got it. Thanks for helping with the puppies."

"This was just what I needed. Sex toy talk and all."

"Anytime, Kara. We all have your back."

I gave him a mock scowl. "And now you've ruined it by being a fucking asshole and trying to make me cry."

He laughed and sauntered off. "Leopards don't change their spots!" he called over his shoulder.

Chapter 10

I glanced at my watch, stunned to see it was nearly midday. Time kept slipping by at light speed, which wouldn't have been so bad considering the godawful state of the world—because why would anyone want to linger in this crap timeline?—except for the pesky and gigantic looming "get the blades or become Dekkak's bitch" deadline.

But for now, the fact it was almost noon meant I'd have no trouble finding a good chunk of the command staff, since they were no doubt being sensible and attending to the needs of their corporeal forms, i.e., eating lunch. And I needed to fill them in on the various revelations from Tessa.

I drove the ATV east, past the house and on to the first chunk of land Jill had acquired for the compound expansion, unofficially dubbed "the Forty." Most of the facilities were in this eastern section, including offices and admin, infirmary, mess hall, more barracks, and a rec center. They were all important, but the rec center had been an absolute must in order to keep people from going completely batshit. Or, in some cases, *more* batshit.

Damn near everyone had contributed in some way to the rec center—occasionally through judicious acquisitions from abandoned properties—which meant it not only had a well-equipped gym, a kickass library, an impressive stock of movies and video games, but also resources for any number of hobbies, including various musical instruments, art and crafting supplies, yarn, and fabric. As the weather grew colder, the number of people who'd taken up knitting or crocheting had expanded dramatically, which meant there was no shortage of scarves and hats. Michael started giving piano lessons and turned out to be a really good teacher, patient and encouraging. Giovanni had even tentatively offered to give art lessons and was thrilled by the enthusiastic response.

These new buildings were the fast and basic kind that could be assembled cheaply and easily—pour slabs, throw up a metal warehouse type of building, frame out some sort of interior, and voila. I wasn't sure how any of them would hold up in a hurricane, but the tropical season didn't start for another five months—not that I could count on normal weather patterns—and one way or another all this mess would be dealt with long before then. Either I'd get the blades or I'd be Dekkak's slave in the demon realm, at which point keeping the compound intact during a bad storm would be someone else's problem. If the Earth itself was even still intact, of course.

With that cheery thought, I parked by the mess hall and headed in. It was set up like a basic school cafeteria but without the ever-present miasma of old green beans and cardboard pizza, or whatever the hell the smell was that seemed to pervade every cafeteria everywhere.

This one smelled like heaven, and I owed it all to the man behind the counter: Kinsavi, formerly David Hawkins. He'd owned and operated the Grounds For Arrest coffee shop that had been located across from the Beaulac Police Department—until the valve explosion wiped it out, along with most of downtown Beaulac.

Kinsavi was now a far different person than the one who'd sold me countless coffees and chocolate donuts. He'd been affected by the mutagen spread during the explosion—the same that affected the two cats and the dogi-pede—and had "podded" just like Krawkor and Zenra. Kinsavi's physical form was still human, though perhaps a bit leaner and sleeker, but his skin was now a deep iridescent indigo, and his eyes a sparkling silver. But that was nothing compared to his hair. Jet black, it was still very much normal-looking hair, with normal-looking individual strands, but it was as alive as one of his limbs, and he could control it and even change its length at will. Weird had become normal around here.

As I'd expected, the rest of my command staff were there. Jill and Bryce occupied a table in a corner, looking as if they were going over compound business stuff, but sitting juuuust a bit closer than two ordinary associates would. And they sure did smile at each other a lot. I let out a small sigh. It was clear there were feelings between them, but Jill seemed unwilling or unable to pursue them out of a sense of loyalty to Zakaar—Ashava's father. And Bryce was far too honorable to push the issue if there was even the slightest hint of doubt in Jill's mind.

Sergeant Debbie Roma sat at a long table with several members of Alpha Squad. She'd become one of my favorite people, with her gruff, no-nonsense attitude and keen sense of tactics and morale. But I also deeply appreciated how well she'd integrated Alpha Squad into the compound life, working with Bryce and the existing compound security. There was quite a bit of overlap of duties and specialties, but she and Bryce both put in considerable effort to foster a good environment of cooperation and a strong "we're all in this together" attitude.

Off to my right, Giovanni and Elinor shared a table, eating together but like an old married couple who enjoyed the other's company while they each did their own thing—Giovanni sketching, and Elinor reading a book and making notes in the margins. A couple of months ago, and to my intense relief, Jill had obtained a decent-sized camper for them to live in, which meant I no longer had to hear them having lots of very enthusiastic sex in the guest room of my house. Both had been incorporeal for several hundred years, and they'd sure been making up for lost time.

Two wrist-thick locks of hair snaked behind Kinsavi like a pair of tentacles, lengthening to scoop up a mug, pour coffee into it, and add the enormous amounts of sugar and cream I preferred. By the time I reached the counter, his hair had my coffee ready for me.

"You are giving me life, Kinsavi," I breathed with deep gratitude. I wrapped my hands around the mug and took a long sip.

"Got something even better for you," he said with a wink as his hair wound itself into a waist-length braid. He reached under the counter and retrieved a plate bearing manna from heaven.

Or, as most people would perceive it, a chocolate donut.

"You're going to make me cry," I said, and then my mouth was full of still-warm chocolate donut. "Hmrmw?"

He grinned, able to translate that into *How?* "Jill asked the squad to start checking for stashes of dry goods in abandoned areas while doing their usual recon sweeps. They found a restaurant supply place untouched by looters, probably because half the building had been consumed by a rift. Long story short, they got a lot of useful stuff."

I swallowed down the bite of donut. "That's excellent." Even though chocolate donuts were essential to my life, I felt a stab of guilt at the fact that we were doing a whole lot of—for lack of a better word—looting. On the other hand, considering how much I had to beg, plead, and whine to get the bare minimum of funding and supplies from the DIRT higher ups, if it wasn't for the general "foraging" we did, we'd never be able to keep doing the work to, quite literally, save the world.

But it definitely helped that the looting was enhanced by Kinsavi's unique new talent. Along with his changed appearance and magic hair, he now had the ability to keep food and staples fresh a lot longer. In addition, he seemed to have a knack for making plants grow a bit faster and better than usual, and had three small greenhouses behind the mess hall, built from kits that had been "borrowed" from a big box home improvement chain. They were nowhere near large enough to provide all the compound's food needs, but they were useful for supplying some fresh fruits and veggies, spices, and herbs—including a variety of obscure medicinal plants Zenra had requested.

I again thanked Kinsavi profusely and obtained some actual lunch-type food as well—fried catfish, hush puppies, and cole slaw—then I gathered Jill, Bryce, and Roma for a quick, informal meeting in a quiet-ish corner of the cafeteria and filled them in on the revelations from Tessa, including the info about how she'd been heavily manipulated.

Jill touched the back of my hand. "That had to have been very hard to hear. Are you doing all right?"

I took a quick gulp of coffee to cover my sudden attack of watery eyes. "Yeah," I said once I was fairly sure my voice wouldn't crack. "At least I will be. Before, I couldn't help but wonder if all the shit she did to me had been easy 'cause she'd never wanted to be saddled with a kid anyway. And, turns out it wasn't like that at all."

Roma smiled. "I'm looking forward to getting to know her better. She sounds tough as nails to have resisted Jesral as much as she did."

Bryce gave a firm nod. "If Jesral had gained access to the nexus . . . well, no more chocolate donuts for Kara."

"I'm glad someone recognizes what was truly at stake!" I said with a laugh.

After a change of topic and a conversation about what to name the new chickens—during which my suggestions of Alfredo,

Tetrazzini, Parmesan, and Stew were shot down—the others headed off to resume their various duties.

My phone buzzed with a text from Scott as I was disposing of my trash. <Arriving in 5 minutes, east gate>

I sent up a silent plea to whatever gods had yet to give up on me that this Walter thing wouldn't blow up in my face. I didn't even ask for a good outcome. I wasn't foolish enough to ask for the moon. I just needed a lack-of-disaster.

Next, I texted Ashava to ask if she was available to do an assessment on Walter. A few seconds later I got "KK" in reply which I assumed was an "Okay," but for all I knew it might have meant "Kkill yourself," considering her meltdown yesterday.

I could have easily walked from the mess hall to the east gate, but I told myself I'd then have to walk back to get the ATV which would surely be a waste of valuable time, and besides I was pleasantly full of all sorts of very excellent food. Plus, I was feeling lazy, and there were few enough times I was allowed to feel lazy without also feeling guilty about it. Therefore, I cajoled one more donut from David, then drove the ATV the not-even-quarter-mile to the gate, parking just as Scott pulled into the sally port.

Ashava teleported to just within the security gates, gave me a bright smile, then waited patiently as the passenger door swung open and an older man, who I assumed was Walter, climbed out. Average height, maybe five foot eight or so. Lean, wiry build. Silver hair, lined face—about what I'd expected for someone in their eighties. But he stood straight and seemed hale, an advantage over the alternative in this unpredictable environment.

I hung back as Ashava introduced herself. He shook her hand, then the two conversed for a moment or two. They were too far away for me to hear what was being said, but whatever the topic, she would occasionally touch his arm, which told me she was doing her assessment at the same time.

Finally Ashava gave him a radiant smile, then headed my way.

"He's all clear and good to go," she told me. "I like him," she added with a tilt of her head. "He didn't talk down to me."

High praise indeed. Though I wasn't sure if that last bit was a dig at me and/or some of the other adults in the compound. Did we talk down to her? I held back a sigh. Like I needed something else to worry about right now.

"Excellent," I said. "Thanks for doing the assessment for me. Any sign of Squig this morning?"

"No, but Fillion isn't worried, so I'm trying not to be."

"Fillion is a smart demon kitty. Oh, and Kinsavi has chocolate donuts in the mess hall."

Ashava grinned and vanished.

Walter twitched in shock at her departure, but he recovered his composure quickly enough. I grudgingly awarded him a mental point for not freaking out.

Scott lifted his chin in greeting as I approached. "Kara, this is Walter Harrison. Walt, Kara Gillian."

"Arcane Commander," he said with a nod, shaking my hand with a firm yet friendly grip. "I appreciate your generosity in taking me in," he added, though I didn't miss the slightly disgruntled glance he flicked in Scott's direction. Yeah, he'd given in to Scott, but he wasn't thrilled about it.

"Just Kara is fine. Glad to have you here," I replied, carefully masking my own disgruntlement. A whisper of it must've slipped out though, because a wry smile twitched at his mouth. Well, we had that much in common at least. "Scott will fill you in on the security rules and procedures. Did you bring much with you?" I glanced through the window of the horse trailer, somewhat dismayed to see the interior nearly filled with large heavy-duty plastic containers.

"A suitcase with clothes and a few personal items. The rest is my tools."

"Oh, we have plenty of tools here," I said. "Probably could've saved yourself the effort."

His eyes crinkled. "I appreciate that, but the ones you have here aren't *my* tools."

"Understood," I said, even though I didn't.

Scott cleared his throat. "Anyway. Just let me know where you want him, Kara."

"Caretaker cottage on the horse farm. Walt, it's not fancy, but it has a bedroom, bathroom, small living area, and even smaller kitchenette. Plus, there's an attached workshop you're free to commandeer if you want."

His eyes brightened at that. With any luck that would keep him out from underfoot.

"Once you're settled, Scott will give you a tour so you know where you can and can't go, introduce you to our resident demons and personnel, and let you know who to contact if you have issues. Hint: it's usually not me."

He chuckled. "I get that. Don't worry. I'll stay out of everyone's hair—including yours. Thanks again."

"No problem." I gave him a parting nod then made my way back to the ATV, praying he'd keep his word. Last thing we needed was a vulnerable civilian octogenarian underfoot.

I sighed. Perhaps if the gods smiled upon me, I'd have a few easy days before this Walter situation—or anything else—managed to go pear-shaped. A girl could dream, right?

I'd just made it back to the house when my phone dinged with a text from Sonny, proving beyond a doubt that the gods had been ready and waiting to slap down my dreams.

<Rhyzkahl wants you to call him re Squig>

I let out an incoherent shriek and dialed the number Sonny had provided.

"Rhyzkahl!" I snapped, the instant he picked up. "What the hell did you do?"

"Ah, Kara. Lovely to hear your voice as well."

"Yeah yeah yeah. Great weather we're having. How are the wife and kids? I swear, if you hurt Squig, I'll—"

Rhyzkahl muttered an oath in demon. "I'm not a monster, Kara."

"Riiiiight."

He made a noise that sounded suspiciously like a chuckle. "Very well. I'm not a monster in this scenario. I give you my oath I will not harm Squig."

"We'll stick a pin in that argument. How the hell do you have my cat?"

"She sought out my company."

I choked back yet another shriek and took a deep breath instead. Perhaps I could not sound like a complete lunatic? "I guess that means you're still lurking in the immediate area."

"Not as immediate as you might expect, which made her arrival all the more surprising. As was her appearance. I take it she came into contact with the mutagen at ground zero?"

"She and Fillion were hiding in Jill's truck. Now, when are you going to bring her back?"

He was silent for only a heartbeat or two, but it was enough.

"Ooooooohhhhh," I breathed, unable to keep from grinning. "You wike da widdle kitty and want to keep her and pet her and wuv her—"

"Are you quite finished?" he growled. "The creature has obviously grown attached to me, and even were I to return her to you, I have little doubt she would seek me out yet again."

He was probably right. Squig had snuggled with Rhyzkahl on multiple occasions during his imprisonment in my back yard. Still, I wasn't about to lose this chance to give him shit. "Whatever lets you sleep at night, big guy. Anyway, she's had all her shots, so you're good to go there until this summer. Plus she's been spayed, so no need to worry about more mutant kittens running amok. We usually feed her two-thirds of a cup of grain-free cat food once a day, but for occasional treats you can't go wrong with small cubes of Spam. Seriously, she loves that stuff. She also likes pieces of cooked egg whites, but turns her nose up at turkey and acts like you're a monster for even offering it."

Another beat of silence. "I will tend to her needs," he finally said, with the gravitas of an oath.

The rest of my snarky comments fled. "I know you will, Rhyzkahl," I said with a smile. "Thank you for letting me know Squig is with you, safe and sound. Ashava has been very worried about her."

"You are welcome, Kara."

"One more thing," I said, then took a settling breath to keep my voice from quavering with emotion. "Thank you for what you did for Tessa. Removing her manipulations, and whatever else you did to help her."

He exhaled very softly. "It was my honor."

The line went dead.

It wasn't the first time he'd mentioned his honor. A few months ago, during the battle at ground zero, Rhyzkahl helped me achieve the eighth ring of the shikvihr and had responded to my thanks with "*Tahnk si-ah kahlzeb.*" It was my honor.

Not long before that, I'd forgiven him for the torment he'd put me through. That forgiveness had next to nothing to do with absolving him of responsibility and everything to do with my own path to healing and peace. He had yet to apologize to me, and perhaps he never would speak those words, but part of my forgiveness was realizing I didn't need the words. Or at least I wouldn't get butthurt if I never heard them. Besides, there were plenty of ways to make amends that had nothing to do with the power of speech.

But now I needed to let Ashava know Squig was safe with Rhyzkahl and would apparently be staying there. However, I honestly wasn't sure if I was up to dealing with whatever reaction she might have to the news. Would she be relieved or furious? Teen hormones already made her reactions all the more uncertain, but combine that with the power of a demigod? Yikes.

Therefore, I did the only sensible thing that a badass demon-summoning arcane commanding ex-cop bitch like me would do in a difficult situation.

I texted Jill, asked *her* to tell Ashava, and dodged that bullet like a Matrix-level boss.

Chapter 11

After returning to the house, I made my way to the conference room to see if any new disasters had sprung up around the world. I flopped into one of the chairs by the table, resisting the urge to spin around in it.

Oh, what the hell. A couple of spins wouldn't hurt. Not like anyone would see me.

The volume was muted on all the wall screens, but the closed captioning was on. DNN—Demon News Network—had a round-table going on about some of the stranger cults that had sprung up since the demon incursions first began. I was used to ultra-conservative religious types decrying the demons as a sign of the end times and so on, but apparently the topic of the hour was about groups who'd begun *worshipping* the demons or insisting the demons were actually angels.

I grabbed a remote and raised the volume.

A pinch-faced woman jerked her chin up. "People insist on calling them demons, but how do we know that's what they are? It seems more likely they're avenging angels, preparing the world for Armageddon."

I snorted. In a way the lady was almost on the right track. They definitely weren't hell-spawn demons. Merely sentient and powerful creatures from the sister-world to our Earth, connected by interdimensional pathways. And, more recently, rifts.

The moderator leaned forward. "Agatha brings up an inter-esting point. Are there any actual descriptions of angels in the Bible?" He looked around the table. "Or demons?"

An earnest young man in a red bow tie brightened. "Well, in

A Swiftly Tilting Planet, Madeleine L'Engle described an angel as being made of wings and eyes and wind and flame."

The third panelist, an older man with ruddy cheeks and wispy hair, scoffed. "L'Engle did not write the Bible!" He slapped his hand onto the table in emphasis.

Earnest Young Man narrowed his eyes. "Did I say she did? Don't put words in my mouth. I was merely trying to explain that mankind has been exploring the nature of—"

"If you knew anything about your Bible, you'd know angels are spirit beings who can take human form with burning eyes if God wills it. And as far as demons are concerned, since their purpose is to draw people into sin, they can take any form that will facilitate—"

Yeah, this roundtable was totally going to devolve into a throwdown. Damn, people sure could get worked up about their personal views of supernatural creatures, mythical or not. I was sorely tempted to keep watching to see if it really would turn into a brawl. My money was absolutely on the pinch-faced lady. She looked like she'd fight dirty.

Instead, I muted the volume and checked the other screens for actual news or useful updates. The grove tree in Leeds earned a mention, but since it wasn't doing anything destructive or exciting, they didn't linger on it for long—more interested in the miraculous appearance of four new grove trees in Baghdad, Wuhan, Adelaide, and Reykjavik, which of course generated all sorts of buzz and speculation as to their nature and origin. However, the whirlpool in the English Channel was gone, and the fissure in Tiananmen Square had ceased spouting lava. In other words, Rho was indeed getting things somewhat more stabilized. Nice to have some good news for a change.

Unfortunately, I now had no choice but to turn my attention to the not-so-good news. Currently at the top of the list were the three essence blades which I'd sworn to turn over to Dekkak. But the unknown whereabouts of Vsuhl left a knot in my stomach. Szerain couldn't have picked it up. He'd been unconscious when everything went tits up. I always knew it would be insanely hard to get Szerain to turn it over to me, but if Jesral or Mzatal now had Vsuhl—especially when they already had the other two blades? Yikes. But at this point, becoming Dekkak's slave or sacrifice or whatever wasn't even at the top of my You're-Fucked list. We absolutely had to figure out what Jesral and the demahnk were plotting, because if we didn't stop them, nothing else would matter.

First things first. Not only did I need to find out what Szerain knew about Vsuhl, but it was also time to tell him about the deal I struck with Dekkak—info I'd kept hidden from him for months.

"Shit," I breathed. This was going to suck.

I headed outside, oddly unsurprised to find him resting, alone, against Rho's trunk. I dropped to sit cross-legged in front of him, plucked a blade of grass and threaded it between my fingers. "Just got off the phone with Rhyzkahl." Best to test his mental state with a relatively neutral topic. "He has Squig. As in, she went to him after attacking the drone. And he doesn't seem inclined to bring her back."

Szerain's eyes flashed with amusement—an encouraging sign. "They do seem well-matched."

"How are you doing?"

"Shaken, but okay. Mind's clear now. What'd I miss?"

I gave him a quick rundown of events, including the Tessa trap, the new Rho-grove at ground zero and the grove trees scattered around the globe, the earlier bullshit with Colonel Luschka, and my general unease with the current state of affairs.

He cursed softly in demon. "I don't like when our supposed allies feel more like enemies."

"I intend to have a little chat with whoever put in the requisition for Economy Size Complications."

Szerain snorted a laugh then sobered. "Luschka doesn't know what happened on the road, but then neither do I, after Mzatal struck me down. He's insanely dangerous."

"Dangerous is an understatement. But I still have to believe he's doing everything he can to resist his captors and help us." Szerain looked dubious, and I filled him in on the dimensional pocket happenings after he went down. "I had Vsuhl when he made the final kaboom," I said, frowning, "but it was gone afterward."

"Vsuhl is in its storage pocket."

Relief and confusion swept through me. "You were able to store it after you collapsed?"

"No clue. But it's there."

Relief swept through me. Perhaps Mzatal had a hand in stowing the blade away from Jesral's grasp? However it happened, that was one less thing to worry about.

Now for the hard part. "Speaking of Vsuhl, it's time you knew about the deal I made with Dekkak." There was no way words would be sufficient. Sighing a curse, I grasped his hand and slapped it onto the side of my head, making sure to keep everything mentally shielded except the exchange and bargain with Dekkak. "Go ahead and read it."

He went still. If I hadn't been watching him closely, I might have missed the terror that flashed oh-so-briefly across his features. I remained quiescent and waited for him to finish.

When he pulled his hand away and spoke, his voice was rough. "You have to understand—"

"I know," I said quietly. "If the demahnk chose to submerge you again, it would destroy you."

He gave a single jerky nod. "They can't do it while Zakaar is—" He broke off as if he'd said more than he intended. "They can't do it while I possess the blade. Before I was exiled to Earth, I sent it away to hide it from everyone but lost its protection in the process. I didn't understand . . . could not comprehend that submersion would be so vile."

"I know," I repeated. "I swear to you I do. And I promise I won't take Vsuhl away from you." I took a deep breath. "You were submerged beneath the Ryan Kristoff overlay for a decade and a half. But, the essence within that blade has been trapped—*submerged*—for millennia. The very existence of the blades is vile."

"I am aware of the depth of the anathema," he said, voice hollow. "But I . . . I *can't* give up Vsuhl. I don't have the will."

"You're not weak," I said, voice firm, even as my heart broke for him. "You've been damaged, but you have significant allies now." I put a hand on his. "I'm not going to ask you to give me the blade now, not only because you're not ready, but also because it's safest with you for the moment."

He closed his eyes and nodded once.

"And even should the time come that's no longer true," I continued, "I won't try to force you. Because I won't need to."

He snorted softly and met my gaze. "I wonder if perhaps you have too much faith in me."

"Not possible." I squeezed his hand. But now I had another concern apart from his possession of Vsuhl. He believed Zakaar's presence helped protect him against submersion. But after seeing Zakaar resisting Szerain during the Jesral confrontation, I had to wonder if that protection was given willingly. I needed to talk to Zakaar. *Without* Szerain. I also needed to reconnoiter just the place where I might be able to achieve that. "And now that I've bared my nefarious blade plans to you, I need you to come with me to assess ground zero and the new grove."

The destruction from the ground zero event formed an eleven-pointed star a half mile in diameter with the ruins of the Beaulac PD at its center. Ever since the valve explosion, the entire area had been cordoned off by DIRT and Fed Central and was heavily patrolled and restricted.

Fortunately, my rank and status meant I had no trouble gaining access. With Ahmed in shotgun position, Scott drove the Humvee carefully through the rubble, char, and ash, then eased it to a stop a couple hundred feet from the ruins of the PD. "Holy fucking shit."

"Ditto," I murmured. Towering near the valve location was a circle of a dozen trees with stark white trunks, stately and surreal, each an arm's length in diameter and at least eighty feet tall. Leaves of shimmering emerald and amethyst crowned the grove, giving off a light that seemed more arcane than physical, but subtle enough that I couldn't be absolutely certain. Though this simple circle didn't have multiple rings of trees or tunnel-like pathways to the center, it carried no less presence than its demon realm counterparts.

Szerain and I clambered out of the Humvee and took a moment to assess the area. Apart from the grove, there wasn't another living thing in sight. I reached out to Rho, and though I felt a welcoming response, I had the distinct impression their attention was elsewhere.

We started toward the grove, but before we'd taken even a dozen steps, a distinct and familiar diesel-engine growl cut the air. Seconds later, a heavily armored tactical vehicle came around a collapsed building and rumbled to a stop just ahead of us, not thirty feet from the grove. An MRAP—Mine-Resistant Ambush Protected—like the one Alpha Squad had at the compound.

A squad of four bailed out and began unloading equipment I recognized just enough to know it was for blowing things up, confirmed when I saw the last item was a case of C-4.

"Fucking shit," I growled. I'd clearly and specifically given orders to leave the trees and grove alone. Obviously, someone either hadn't taken me seriously or was overenthusiastic about purging. Or both.

I double-timed toward the crew. "Hey! Hold on! Stop whatever the hell it is you're doing."

A chipper young man wearing corporal stripes broke away from the others and headed toward us. "Afternoon, ma'am," he said with a crisp salute.

I returned the salute. "Good afternoon, Corporal"—I peered at his name patch—"Grayson. What's going on here?"

"Level 3 eradication protocol, ma'am. Had no luck last night with the standard heat-based sterilization procedures. This demon-blight resisted everything. We're going at it with C4 now."

"Like hell you are," I snarled. "It's NOT demon blight, and these trees are one hundred percent *not* a threat. Who authorized the extermination?"

"Er, Major Rennek, ma'am," Corporal Grayson said.

"Well, I'm here now. Report back to Major Rennek and tell him the trees are not to be damaged in any way, by my previous *very clear* order which he should be aware of."

Grayson swallowed. "But, ma'am—"

"Is there an immediate safety issue I should be aware of?"

"No, ma'am, but Major Rennek said—"

"Did you miss the part where I outrank him?"

"No. No, ma'am."

"Is there some other extenuating reason why these trees require eradication despite my explicit direction otherwise?"

"I, um, don't believe so, ma'am."

I smiled, sharp and unwavering. "Then I would be most grateful if you would please be so kind as to convey my orders to Major Rennek. Now."

He saluted again then jogged back to his squad, no longer chipper.

I dropped the smile and muttered a curse under my breath as Szerain caught up to me. "You know that thing you said about not liking it when allies feel more like enemies?"

Szerain continued toward the trees. "Best get this done before anyone else is sent to ruin our day."

Corporal Grayson was already on his phone and not looking very happy. Szerain and I walked briskly past the MRAP and on to the shelter of Rho's trees. The instant we passed between the trunks of the ring and onto lush grass, the rumble of the engine faded to nothing, replaced by the clear song of a single bird.

I exhaled in relief as the tranquility of the setting wrapped around us. Rho's single tree by the nexus offered a measure of peace, but this ring of a dozen rivaled the serenity of a full demon realm grove. "Hey, I'm going to take a few minutes to, uh, recharge."

Szerain waved his hand in absent acknowledgment as he slowly paced the perimeter, assessing. I settled cross-legged on the grass. Now what? I'd hoped for Rho's assistance in contacting Zakaar, but they still felt distant and occupied. Though maybe not completely out of touch? I laid my hand over the grove leaf on its cord and visualized communicating privately with Zakaar. Like a ripple of wind through leaves, I received the unexpected impression of Zakaar desperate to speak to me.

A heartbeat later, I found myself in a snug dimensional pocket about eight feet in diameter, its sparkling transparent perimeter bounded by tangles of stark white roots. Zakaar shimmered in, translucent and barely corporeal.

"Kara," he said, voice thin and vulnerable. He took a step toward me, then drifted to sit on the floor as if he had no more substance than a ghost.

Alarmed, I shifted to kneel in front of him. I'd thought he was recovering while sequestered with Szerain, but he seemed more fragile than ever. "Are you all right? What's going on?"

He met my eyes and steadied a bit. "You first. Please."

"It's about Szerain and, well, *you*. There was some weirdness during the encounter with Jesral yesterday, like you were resisting him. That had me baffled on its own, but then when I was talking to him about Vsuhl, he didn't say it outright, but I got the idea he considers you to be his ultimate protection against re-submersion, with Vsuhl as his backup."

He took my hand between his. It felt like being held between layers of cool, tingly linen. "You're right. Not long ago, he realized that as long as I reside within him, he cannot be re-submerged."

"That seems like a good thing, but I'm getting the feeling it's not?"

"It's great—when mutually beneficial."

"Wait. It's still beneficial to him, but not to you?"

"He's terrified of submersion and has convinced himself that keeping me is in my best interest."

"*Keeping* you? Like trapped?"

"For all intents and purposes. I was already suffering every time he used rakkuhr." That made perfect sense since rakkuhr was toxic to the demahnk. "Unpleasant, but I could shield and recover. But then"—his voice broke—"but then he veiled me in rakkuhr, and I can't . . . please help me."

Fury and aching disappointment swirled in my gut. "That stupid, selfish jerk! As soon as I get out of here, I'm going to wring his—"

"Gently, Kara, gently," Zakaar murmured. "PTSD has led him down a dark path that's not his nature—some of it conscious, other subconscious self-preservation."

I took a deep settling breath. "Okay. Fine. I won't instantly kill him."

Zakaar's hands tingled around mine, and a faint smile curved his lips. "I am relieved to hear it."

"So, what happened on the road yesterday? He was trying to bring you up to help, but you resisted?"

"A twisted mess. Yes, I could have helped during the encounter, but not without revealing my presence. The demahnk assume me scattered, and I'm still vulnerable and not ready to re-emerge—especially with the rakkuhr veil continuously sapping my strength. Szerain knew this but was driven both to defeat Jesral and to show that he couldn't ever be submerged."

I grimaced. "I guess you're lucky Mzatal zapped Szerain before Ilana and Ssahr got wind of you."

"No luck involved. I took a huge risk and reached out to Mzatal. He made a swift decision and acted on it."

My brow furrowed. "And you trust him to keep your secret despite Ilana and company?"

"He's formidable, even as a captive. Even as controlled as he is. And if he cannot keep it from them, it was better they find out about me later from him than there on the road."

"I guess that makes sense." I tilted my head. "Rho implied you were desperate to talk to me. Was it about this situation with Szerain?"

"In part. There are two other topics even more vital. The first is that Rho is weakening."

Alarm shot through me. "I thought they were thriving since they were able to bring this grove through."

"They were strong in the demon realm but are now stretched thin with both worlds unstable and the interdimensions threatened. They are doing all they can to stabilize everything but can't continue like this. We're coming to a crisis point, and I don't know the solution."

I shoved a hand through my hair, frustrated and unsettled. "The only one that comes to mind is to neutralize Jesral and the bad demahnk as soon as we can. But that's a whole lot easier said than done. In the meantime, is there anything we can do to directly support Rho? I'm always looking to them for help and guidance, and I've never really thought of how to give back."

"Communion. Sitting under any of their trees with no agenda. Not just you. Can be anyone. It's intangible but beneficial support."

"I'm sure that won't be a problem. Plus, it's a good way to unwind." I fought down a snicker at the thought of including "tree time" on the compound duty roster. "What's the second topic?"

He withdrew his hands from mine and seemed to shrink in on himself. "They are coming."

"Who?"

He gripped my head between trembling ghostly hands and pressed his forehead to mine.

We were in the cosmos, stars everywhere, but that was as nothing compared to the expanse of billions upon billions of what I could only describe as prismatic light crystals.

The Ekiri collective. Innumerable timeless non-corporeal immortals who basically role-played embodied beings on various planets, as they had in the demon realm and then on Earth, inadvertently damaging both worlds in the process. Zakaar, Ilana, Helori—all of the demahnk—were Ekiri who'd been left behind in corporeal form to right the wrongs or be forever scattered into non-corporeal fragments.

Potency beyond anything I'd ever imagined speared through my entire being, and I had the distinct sense they were keenly aware of me. Awe, dread, and a strange longing squeezed my chest. They were coming. For me. For us. For the worlds.

The return of the Ekiri meant judgment of the progress the demahnk—the Ekiri in exile—had made over the past few thousand years to stabilize the demon realm and manage the lords. Never mind that it was the presence of the Ekiri themselves that had caused unbalancing potency shifts between Earth and the demon realm.

From what I understood, if the assessment was favorable, the demahnk could abandon their corporeal forms and return "home" to the Ekiri collective, leaving the worlds to fend for themselves. If not, the demahnk were stuck, and the Ekiri would take whatever action they saw fit to rectify the situation. Xharbek, Ilana,

Ssahr, and possibly others seemed willing to do *anything* to go home. And they were out of time to rebalance the worlds gently.

I swayed as Zakaar released me, then had to work moisture back into my mouth before I could speak. "When?"

"Soon. A heartbeat? A year?" He shrugged.

"Can we stop them?"

He went even more ghostly. I reached for him, but my hand passed right through. "It's okay," I said. "Don't think about it." When the demahnk Lannist shared taboo info with me, the Ekiri collective scattered him on the spot. I had no doubt they could sense Zakaar, even if the demahnk could not.

"Even with this news, neutralizing Jesral is still a priority. We'll press on with that. And I should go have a chat with Szerain about this torment he's putting you through. What else do you need?"

His voice was barely a whisper. "To re-embody. Within a pavilion. Soon."

"Not long after you withdrew into Szerain, Ashava said that you'd be able to separate from him when the demahnk reached out to you to rejoin them."

"We . . . *they* . . . are fragmented. No longer unified. Rho and Helori are unwavering and will not forsake me." The final word faded away with what remained of his form.

I took a few minutes to collect my thoughts, then sent an impression to Rho of leaving the dimensional pocket—and found myself back on the grass. Szerain was only a step beyond where he'd been walking when I left. "Szerain. Come have a seat."

"Hang on. I'm—"

"Nope. *Now.*"

He muttered something dark under his breath but complied. "What's up?"

"Look, this isn't going to be easy." I met his gaze steadily. "I know about Zakaar and the rakkuhr veil."

Szerain recoiled as if I'd slapped him. Fear and desperation lit his eyes and he scrambled to his feet—or rather, he tried to. Before he could get halfway up, roots snaked around him and drew him down again. He thrashed against their hold at first, then a calm came over him, no doubt induced by Rho.

"We have to talk about this," I said. "You can't imprison Zakaar."

"I'm not!" he said, voice cracking. "It's not like that. You don't understand."

I kept my tone calm and measured. "I understand more than you might think. Plus, I just talked to him."

A measure of fear returned to his eyes along with a hint of chagrin. "He . . . he's—"

"Just stop. I know you're terrified of being re-submerged, and I don't blame you. But this isn't the way. You're *torturing* Zakaar for something he would freely give you."

Szerain squeezed his eyes closed, body sagging in defeat. The roots unwound and slithered into the ground.

"This isn't who you are," I said gently but firmly. "Let him go. We'll find other ways."

He lowered his head and took a shuddering breath. A whisper of leaves told me the rakkuhr veil was no more. Szerain's body shook in silent sobs, and I wrapped my arms around him. I held him until I felt his tension ease as the calm of the grove seeped through his body and essence.

He took a deep breath as I gently released him. "I'm so sorry."

"You did the wrong thing, but you've made it right. Zakaar understands. I understand. We'll get through this together."

He gave me a shaky smile and stood, offering me a hand up. "We should probably check on the demolition team since we can't hear them in here."

"Rho doesn't seem worried about them, but I *hate* having orders ignored. I don't know what I can count on."

It was twilight beyond the ring of trees, yet the headlights of half a dozen vehicles had me squinting. "Well, this is just lovely," I grumbled.

"Commander Gillian!" a gruff voice called out. "We thought you'd been et."

"By the trees?" I shielded my eyes from the glare and spotted a stocky DIRT captain heading my way. "As you can see, we're fine."

"No one else has been able to enter, ma'am. These days we assume the worst, I'm afraid."

"Did none of you receive the orders I issued yesterday with regards to these trees?"

"Yes, ma'am, but—"

"But? But what? But you thought you could ignore my expertise and make your own call?"

"No, ma'am, but—"

"But nothing. Despite the blatant disregard of my orders earlier,

I expect these trees to be cordoned off and left undisturbed. Is that understood, Captain?"

He nodded, jaw tight as if holding back yet another "but."

"Thank you, Captain. I appreciate your cooperation." I swept a gaze over the grove. "Besides, defying my orders would simply be a waste of C-4." With that I strode off toward our Humvee. Rho could certainly protect themself but deserved a reprieve from these numbnuts.

Didn't we all.

I blinked in surprise when I saw the intricate hedge of vines around the Humvee. And I couldn't hold down a laugh when I noted the bright yellow flowers in Ahmed's beard and the ivy crown on Scott's head. "Dare I ask?"

Ahmed grinned. "The captain kept asking us what you were doing in there and threatened to arrest us if we didn't come clean. All of a sudden those vines came up and pushed him back. I mean, they were nice and gentle, but he got the message and slunk back to his vehicle, growling about insubordination and crazy wizards."

"Crazy wizards." I snickered. "It's actually a pretty apt description."

Szerain settled in the back of the Humvee, quiet and contemplative. I climbed in beside him, smiling as a net of tiny silver flowers grew over his hair and shoulders like a mantle.

I looked down to see delicate crimson leaves wrap gently around my wrists like bracers. "All right, let's take this garden party back to the house."

The drive back to the compound was quiet—in the back seat at least. Up front, Scott and Ahmed kept up a steady chatter about anything and everything: the non-existent football season, best methods for making sourdough starter, how to sew a French seam, the fact that Roma used to make kickass pottery in her spare time, and opinions about various motorcycles.

We were nearly at the main gate when Szerain touched the back of my hand. "Thank you," he murmured. "It's a good and rare friend who'll tell you when you're being a complete ass."

I tweaked a flower on his shoulder. "I'll always be here for you. Especially when given the chance to tell you you're full of shit."

He cracked a grin for the first time in, well, a very long time.

"You are remarkably good at it." He took a deep breath. "When we return, I'll need to commune with Zakaar for a while."

"I'll do my best to stay out of trouble."

He snorted, smiled. "Don't make promises you can't keep."

I snickered. "Low blow."

When we arrived at the house, Szerain gave my hand a light squeeze, then climbed out of the Humvee and headed inside. As he crossed the threshold, the mantle of flowers swirled away in a cloud of rainbow sparkles.

Scott glanced back at me, grinning. "Hope you enjoyed the ride! Don't forget to give me five stars!"

I scoffed. "Five? With no snacks or bottled water?"

"There's plenty of snacks," Ahmed said. "Abercrombie dropped some M&Ms back there the other day."

Laughing, I hopped out and waved as they drove off. The bracers of leaves on my arms glowed bright crimson, then drifted away on a windless breeze.

Mood light, I started toward the house but froze at the sight of arcane shimmering on the asphalt and front steps.

I frowned then crouched. No, not arcane. Glitter.

A laugh bubbled up. "Oh dear."

I continued up the stairs and inside. Szerain had already gone down into his basement, no doubt already settling into communion with Zakaar. More interesting to me at the moment was the glitter that led down the hall. Not a lot, but it was definitely present and doing what glitter does best—getting on everything.

I followed it through the kitchen and out onto the porch. In the back yard, Bryce, Hurley, Roma, and half a dozen other members of Alpha Squad clustered around a box that contained a measly seven water balloons.

And glitter was *everywhere*.

"Y'all have been busy," I said, struggling oh-so-very-hard to keep a straight face.

Bryce stood, grimacing as he tried without success to brush glitter off his hands. "Let's just say this 'glitter grenade' thing sounded a whole lot easier in theory."

Roma snorted. A sparkly streak ran down one side of her face, making her look as if she'd spent the night at a rave. "Bryce told us what you were trying to do, and I was all for it. We've always had a hell of a time with zhurn, and this sounded like a great idea. But putting it into practice was another story."

Wohlreich blew out a sigh. "Mixing the glitter with water made it easier to fill balloons, but then the glitter doesn't really stick to the target."

"Sticks just fine to us, though," Landon grunted.

My eyes went to the equipment shed where half a dozen slightly sparkly splotches stained one side. Damn. "Well, I guess it's still better than nothing," I said with forced cheer. "Sorry it turned out to be more of a chore than I expected."

"We haven't quite given up yet," Hurley said.

"I appreciate that, but it might be time to step back and re-group, or just cut our losses on this concept. Maybe tomorrow we can come up with a better system." I grinned. "Plus, y'all need to shower before you track glitter everywhere."

Bryce groaned. "Shiiiiiit. I went inside to look for funnels. There's glitter in the house, isn't there."

"Maybe just a wee bit," I said, trying not to snicker.

"Jill is gonna kill me."

"Nah, she'll just give you that narrow-eyed *look*."

He shuddered. "That's worse."

"Tell her it was all my idea. Then she'll do that thing where she purses her mouth, shakes her head, and walks off muttering."

Bryce barked out a laugh. "I've been on the receiving end of that before."

"We all have," Hurley said, grinning.

"Oh, one more thing. Rho—the grove tree—is working hard to keep everything stabilized and could use our support. I know this is a really big ask, but whenever y'all or anyone else in the compound has a bit of free time, if you could just sit and chill at the base of the tree, that would be great. Believe it or not, that kind of thing really helps them."

"Talk about rough duty," Wohlreich said.

"Right? I might have to put everyone in for hazard pay."

With that settled, I helped the squad clean up the failed glitter bomb project and somehow even managed to stay mostly glitter free. Alpha Squad headed to their barracks, but Bryce lingered.

"Everything okay with Szerain?" he asked.

"Yeah. I think he's going to be all right. We got some stuff straightened out when we went to the grove at ground zero."

Bryce gave a nod, eyes on me. "How 'bout you?"

"Oh, I'm hanging in there," I replied with a breezy smile.

He made a little *hmmph* noise. "You look wiped out."

"Gee, thanks!"

He smiled. "The last couple of days have been a lot. Changes. Stress. Questions. And when shit like this starts hitting the fan, you push yourself hard, because the stakes are so high and you feel responsible for the world."

A curl of irritation wound through me. "Are you saying I shouldn't push hard when the stakes are high?"

He tilted his head. "I'm pretty sure I didn't say that."

I scowled. "Well, what am I supposed to do then?"

"Seriously? Take your own advice. Regroup. Recover. Don't work until you drop. You just got back from ground zero, and I bet you were planning to go straight to the nexus and do whatever shit you usually do there, and spend a good hour doing it."

I hunched my shoulders. ". . . maybe."

Bryce grinned. "Instead of that, how about you go inside and do this weird thing called 'Go to bed and get a full night's sleep.'"

"Pffft. Sleep? Who needs sleep."

"You do." His eyes narrowed to slits. "And if you don't take better care of yourself, I'll tell Jill."

"Ohhhhh, you bastard. Fine, I'll go to bed. But that's really dirty pool."

He chuckled low. "It's the only way to play."

Chapter 12

I looked out at Paris from my vantage atop the Arc de Triomphe. A brilliant blue sky spread above, and a light breeze danced around me. Low white buildings crowded between tree-lined streets that radiated out like spokes on a wheel. In the distance the Eiffel Tower speared upward, straight and tall—a welcome change from when I'd last seen it: the top third slumped at a twenty-degree angle after being melted by arcane blasts.

I inhaled deeply of the crisp air then dropped my gaze. The buildings and streets were gone, replaced by gently rolling green hills. A shepherdess tended a flock of fluffy white sheep as they grazed along what should have been the Place de l'Étoile. The sheep sprouted white bat wings and flapped here and there, hunting the best grass. And somehow the Arc de Triomphe had shrunk to the size of my house, allowing me to easily see a pair of curved horns peeking from beneath the shepherdess's bonnet, and a clawed hand wrapped around a crook crafted of bones.

"Zharkat," Mzatal murmured behind me. I turned and drank in the sight of him, powerful and unfettered.

"Lover," I said with a broad smile. He pulled me close, groaning under his breath as he wrapped his arms around me. I relaxed into the embrace and released a deep sigh.

Dry heat rolled over us. I pulled back, frowning. The grassy hills had become a lake of lava, and the demon-shepherdess and her flock floated on chunks of rock, oblivious to the peril that surrounded them.

"Er, is that going to be a problem?" I asked, gesturing to the lava that churned below us.

"The worlds break," Mzatal replied. "Time grows short."

The sheep began to bleat in unison. *Baaaaa Baaaaa Baaaaa Baaaaa*.

I jerked awake, struggling to get my bearings as I continued to hear bleating sheep, finally realizing it was the alert tone of a callout.

I fumbled my phone to me and read the alert. "Fucking geckoids," I groaned. Another invasive demon species. They had a hard-to-pronounce demon name, but since they looked like fox-sized geckos on insane amounts of steroids they'd been dubbed geckoids.

They were also largely impervious to fire, so burning them out wasn't an option. Though, to be fair, firebombing was a last resort anyway. What was the point of saving the planet if everything got destroyed in the process?

The one bright spot was that geckoids could be herded fairly easily with aversion wards. Sometimes Szerain would handle the wards, but he was currently indisposed, in deep communion with Zakaar. Though I was sure he'd come out of it to help, the Zakaar connection was more important. That meant I needed to go with the squad and couldn't pass the duty off. Not that I *would*, but technically, if it was just ratos, I *could*.

I skimmed the rest of the text and noted the location of the geckoid incursion, then forwarded the alert to the command staff along with a request to Boudreaux for a couple of Riders. Sgt. Roma would have received the alert at the same time I did, and was no doubt already mobilizing personnel.

Time to mobilize my own ass. I dressed and kitted up with the speed and efficiency of a shitload of repetition, buckling on my helmet even as a distant throaty growl of diesel engines told me Alpha squad was on the way.

I grabbed my collapsible "wizard staff"—which was basically a heavy-duty cattle prod—clipped it onto my belt, and scurried to the kitchen, automatically swerving to avoid the cabinet door that refused to close. Then stopped and stared at the closed cabinet door. I opened it, then closed it again, oddly astonished when it stayed closed.

But this was no time to marvel at miracles. A go-cup of coffee sat on the counter next to a protein bar. I murmured a fervent thanks to the universe for giving me Sonny, shoved the bar into a pocket, grabbed the coffee, and stepped out the front door as an MRAP pulled up with Scott in the driver's seat and Hurley manning the M2 .50 cal turret gun. The two smaller M-ATVs stopped behind it, with Kowal and Ahmed in their respective turrets. We dealt with so many airborne threats, procedure dictated we always had someone in the turret.

Behind the second M-ATV was a big-ass pickup hauling a horse trailer. Clearly Boudreaux and the other Riders had been drilling hard to get mounts ready and loaded so quickly.

"You call for a ride share, lady?" Scott shouted above the engine noise. "But I gotta warn you about the surge pricing!"

"You're a dork, Scott." I climbed into the MRAP to take the vehicle commander position in the front right seat. Wohlreich sat in the back with Blauser and Zenra—who was kitted out in combat gear like the others except for her feline lower half. As soon I was strapped in, Wohlreich passed me a mini tablet that I secured to my left forearm. He operated the drones for recon, and with this tablet paired to his, I could see everything the drones did and without having to peer over his shoulder.

"What's this?" I asked Scott, nudging a cardboard box at my feet.

"Glitter bombs." He laughed at my very dubious expression. "Trust me, these actually work. Walter suggested putting the glitter in some kind of thicker suspension, to help keep the glitter on the target. Next thing I know he'd scrounged up a bunch of glue and detergent and who knows what else, then rigged up a funnel system to fill the balloons and tie them off. Oh, and he also made us slingshots so we can glitter baddies from a distance."

"Holy shit." I laughed. "I guess the worst that can happen is we all end up covered in glitter. Forever." I tugged the protein bar out of my pocket and took a swig of my coffee. "Let's roll."

The hot zone for this callout was situated between a high end assisted-living/retirement complex and a swanky private school—both empty of residents and students now, of course. The area in question was wooded, with numerous nature walks and running trails winding through it for both kids and retirees to enjoy. Apparently the geckoids were now having their own fun and exercise there.

It was because of the woods that I'd requested a couple of Riders. Many of the trails were too narrow for ATVs, plus Riders generally had an easier time herding geckoids, since mules were able to make quick direction changes to deal with the nimble creatures.

Access to the school grounds was via a twisting, scenic, and tactically godawful driveway, and I didn't argue one bit when Roma suggested we instead deploy and set up on the far side of the woods in the retirement complex parking lot.

With the vehicles spaced out in an appropriate tactical formation, personnel dismounted with crisp efficiency, while Boudreaux and Redd unloaded two mules with practiced ease. After a quick comms test to make sure radios were in working order, the dismount squad moved out while drivers and turret gunners remained with the vehicles to cover the area.

This wasn't our first geckoid callout—or even the fifteenth—and Alpha Squad and the Riders knew what to do and how to move in coordination with intel from the drone. The geckoids' skin was bright red and yellow, which might have served them well for concealment in parts of the demon realm, but made them stand out nicely in the green and brown of Louisiana woodlands. Moreover, they were hot little beasties. Literally. While they were impervious to fire, their higher body temp made them glow bright in infrared—which the FLIR-equipped drone picked up.

Boudreaux, too, had a nifty drone-view tablet strapped to his forearm. He and Redd mounted and went down the easternmost trail to drop warded rocks which would serve as short term "fencing" to keep the geckoids from going farther afield. Meanwhile, I created an arcane holding pen at the edge of the parking lot and held the wizard staff at the ready to help nudge the little beasties in the desired direction.

The comms crackled as Wohlreich sighted geckoids on his monitor and relayed their locations. Pops of gunfire and scattered, shouted orders peppered the morning air.

Soon enough, the first geckoid came streaking out of the woods, though instead of being sensible and letting itself be funneled into the holding area, it decided to leap toward Kowal, claws and teeth bared. She calmly shredded it with a quick burst from her rifle, then gave an "oh yeah" hip shimmy.

Two more geckoids left the woods and let themselves be penned, perhaps realizing resistance was futile. Or maybe they understood that geckoids who behaved would get sent back through the rift that belched them out. Sure, it was a bit more work on our part, but the rift was only a couple hundred yards away. Besides, unlike ratos who were more akin to cockroaches, intelligencewise, geckoids seemed to have a sentience on the level of a dog, and I wasn't keen on slaughtering them all simply for taking a wrong turn back in the demon realm.

Another four entered the pen in quick succession, then two more who needed encouragement in the form of a quick zap from my staff. Soon enough we had nearly a dozen in the pen. I beefed up the wards containing them as they snarled and sniffed along the perimeter, seeking a way out.

"How many more, Wohlreich?" I asked, peering at my tablet screen. I thought I spied a few more heat signatures amidst the trees, but Wohlreich was far more adept at interpreting the drone video.

"Just three more in the woods," he said, eyes never leaving his screen, "but I thought I saw movement over by the school." The view swung over the trees, then the parking lot and vehicles, and then toward the school—a pretty campus even after being neglected for months. "I'm trying to—"

A flash of vivid purple lit the tablet screen, and the feed went dead. "Shiiit," he breathed. A bad feeling settled like a rock in my gut.

"That looked like an arcane strike," I called over to Roma. "Fall back until we know what happened."

She keyed her mic, but a sharp squeal of static had everyone wincing. "Comms are out," she growled.

The bad feeling tripled in intensity. They'd been working fine not even a minute ago, and normal arcane interference didn't usually make our shielded radios completely useless.

"Scott," I yelled. "Recall the squad!" We encountered radio issues too often to not have a backup method of giving orders.

He immediately gave three short blasts of the MRAP's horn followed by two longer blasts. A brief pause, then he repeated the sequence.

Personnel streamed back to the vehicles, all on high alert, while the gunners kept a sharp eye out for threats from above.

"Phones are out, too," Roma said, voice tight.

Yeah, this was bad.

In less than two minutes Alpha Squad was all accounted for, with the exception of Boudreaux and Redd, and I had to firmly remind myself they'd gone farther afield in order to make the arcane perimeter. Still, it wasn't until I heard the unmistakable pounding of hoofbeats that I let myself breathe.

Yet my heart dropped to my toes as the mules came into sight: Redd was in the lead, but the mule behind her had bleeding claw marks on its flank. And no rider.

"It got Boudreaux!" Redd gabbled, eyes wide in barely controlled panic. "Snatched him right out of the saddle!"

"What snatched him?" I demanded as Hurley and Ahmed rushed up to take control of the injured animal.

"Reyza," Redd gasped. "Came out of nowhere. Passed right over me like I didn't exist and grabbed Boo. Took off toward the school. Not even a minute ago."

Fuck. Fuck. "Wohlreich, you got another drone?"

"Way ahead of you, ma'am," he said, already firing up the backup drone.

"Send it toward the school. Need to see where the demon took him."

I held my breath as the drone raced over the woods and to the school. In addition to the usual playground and courtyard areas, the campus held two gymnasium-sized structures, along with a half-dozen rectangular buildings that were each about twice the size of my house. No demons or humans anywhere in plain sight, but there were numerous heat signatures scattered around the campus. Demons, no doubt. Fuck.

As Wohlreich took the drone over the smaller structures, two spots glowed in the one farthest to the east—with one of the glowing spots nearly twice the size of the other. Could be two demons, except the smaller spot didn't glow with the same intensity as the other. Demons were hotter than humans, except for zhurn which barely had any heat signature at all.

Once again the tablet screen flashed purple and went dark, but I'd been expecting it this time. "Roma, mobilize the squad for a rescue mission," I snapped out as I secured the geckoid holding pen. "Pretty sure this whole fucking thing has been a setup, and there's a one hundred percent chance some nasty surprises will be waiting for us. And I need intel on what kind of building that is." I firmly shoved down the awareness that Boudreaux could be dead and still have a heat signature. Didn't matter. We were going to operate under the assumption he was alive and kicking.

"AC Gillian!" Blauser ran up to me. "My niece used to go to that school. I've been to the campus a few times for family days and ball games."

"Oh, hell yes." I fumbled with the tablet screen and managed to scroll the feed back to the view of the building with the two heat signatures. "Tell me everything you know."

She peered at the screen. "That building holds the second-grade classrooms. Double doors on either end with a central corridor. Three classrooms on each side. Each classroom also has an outer door. And lots of windows on those outer walls."

"I don't think we're going to be sneaking up anyway. But no windows into the corridor?"

"Just small windows in the doors, ma'am. Going in via the corridor will at least give some cover."

"Excellent intel, Blauser." I met Roma's eyes. "You got a plan in mind, Sarge?"

She gave a humorless smile. "Roll up. Shoot every fucking thing that moves. Get our boy."

"Works for me. Let's do this."

We left one M-ATV in the retirement center parking lot as backup and to watch that flank, and the rest of us rolled out. The comms were still useless, but I had zero doubt it was deliberate arcane interference.

Since chances were high the source of the interference was somewhere on that campus, I told everyone to keep an eye out for a possible focal point. Most of Alpha Squad had some small measure of sensitivity to the arcane—not enough to see or manipulate the energies, but over the past months they'd learned to recognize the vague sense of unease or prickling on the back of the neck that often meant they were close to something arcane and possibly dangerous.

Stealth wasn't an option with the noisy vehicles. Not that it mattered in this scenario, since our opponents knew we were coming. Therefore, we'd developed a tactic for dealing with the noise.

We leaned into it. Hard.

"Whose turn is it to pick?" I asked Wohlreich.

He grinned. An evil grin. "Mine." He hit the play button on his tablet.

"You bastard," I breathed, trying not to laugh as Hanson's "MMMBop" blasted from the top-mounted speakers and shook the air.

"I'm betting the demons will hate this even more than Hurley's twangy country shit."

How could they not? But whatever the music, we'd found that, at high volume, it messed with the demons' ability to coordinate and communicate.

Except for opera. Ahmed once tried assaulting everyone's

ears with *The Marriage of Figaro*. The demons had fucking loved it, and we damn near got our asses handed to us.

But so far every other human musical genre had annoyed the ever-loving shit out of them. I was more than happy to put up with goddamn perky teeny-bop crap if it gave us even the slightest edge, because we sure as hell needed it. The aerial images of the campus had already convinced us the approach up the driveway would be a tactical nightmare, yet there was literally no other way to get the vehicles where we wanted and needed them.

The reality was no better. The driveway wound past gorgeous hundred-year-old live oaks, with vast canopies of branches that we had no choice but to go beneath. Canopies that offered too damn many places for demons to lurk and attack from. The infrared gave us an edge to detect most demons, but zhurn were a lot harder to spot since they not only disappeared into shadows but also gave off very little heat.

"You know it's a trap," Scott murmured, eyes scanning as he drove.

"Yeah," I said. "Got no choice though, do we?"

"None at all," he agreed.

I had zero doubt Jesral was behind all this, but what was he trying to accomplish? If he wanted to take a bunch of us out, why not simply have all the demons attack at once and overwhelm us? Maybe he was trying to keep Angus in line by threatening his son? But it seemed to me it would be easier to simply kidnap Boudreaux outright and hold him as a hostage. Why allow—and practically encourage—us to mount a rescue mission?

For giggles, I tried to key my mic again, unsurprised at the furious squeal of interference.

The MRAP rumbled up the driveway while the three Hanson boys belted out upbeat relationship advice. The turret gun spat, and Hurley shouted, "Kehza down!"

Good. The teeny bop worked.

Blauser leaned out the window and aimed a slingshot into the canopy of an oak tree, scattering glitter over branches and leaves. A section of glitter shifted, and a burst of fire from the turret gun shredded the bedazzled—and now-visible—zhurn.

"Hot fucking DAMN!" Blauser crowed.

We continued up the driveway with the turret gunners targeting the visible demons and other squad members painting the shadows with glitter. A few spider-like graa tried to rush the vehicles but were easily picked off. Alpha Squad knew from experience not to pause to watch demons discorporeate. As soon as their physical body began to crack and fracture, it was over for them and time to move on to the next target.

A quarter mile in, the M-ATV behind us veered off onto a driveway that led toward the gym and sports field—and, more importantly, would cover our approach on the classroom building and set up a pincer maneuver. As soon as we passed the Admin building, we took a hard right. Ahead and to our left was the second-grade building with the M-ATV and the sports field beyond it. In a sad display, a weather-worn and tattered American flag still flapped morosely at the top of a flagpole by the field.

Even as I took in the sight, Petrev hopped out of the M-ATV and fired three grenades at the flagpole. Dirt and concrete burst from its base as explosions reverberated through the air. The pole swayed then crashed to the ground.

"Why the—" I began, but the crackle of Roma's voice on the radio stopped me.

"Petrev realized it was the flagpole!" Some interference remained, but at least we had something resembling comms now, though I quickly discovered I still couldn't reach the compound. I needed to strip the rest of the arcane off the pole, but that would have to wait until after we found Boudreaux.

Scott brought the MRAP to a halt a hundred yards from the classroom building. Blauser's intel had been spot on about the layout, including the windows that covered the upper half of the outer wall, which allowed me to easily see the reyza crouched in the middle classroom. I grabbed a pair of field glasses in the hopes of getting any sight of Boudreaux, but no luck.

"We know it's a trap," I murmured, "so hopefully that means Boudreaux is still alive."

Scott scowled. "Yep. Now we're just waiting for the other shoe to drop."

"Then we need a shoe of our own," I said and laid out what I had in mind.

Scott and the others nodded. "Nice," he said. "Violent. I wish it could be called something other than 'a shoe of our own' but hey."

Blauser snorted. "Yeah, well, our shoe is a four-inch spike-heeled Rockstud Ankle Strap Valentino Garavani pump." At my blank look, she grinned. "About a thousand bucks a pair, but gorgeous and badass."

The vehicles moved into position by the target building. Blauser and I did a fast dismount from the MRAP and ran to the double doors at the north end, with Zenra right on our heels. I trusted that Abercrombie and Chu were doing the same to cover the south entrance and didn't waste time to check.

The double doors were ajar, and a smeared trail of blood led inside and toward the door to the middle classroom. Blauser took point since she had far more combat experience than me, but I stuck close and kept a sharp eye out for arcane surprises.

"This is way too easy," Blauser said under her breath. I followed her gaze to see the classroom door was a millimeter ajar and not latched.

Definitely a trap. But with Boudreaux's life on the line, we had no choice but to spring it.

I went through the door first, crouched and rifle at the ready. A reyza the size of Dagor crouched behind Boudreaux, who lay crumpled on his side, bleeding and unconscious.

I didn't waste time ordering him away from Boudreaux and simply squeezed off a burst of rounds.

The demon roared and staggered a step back, though he had enough arcane shielding that even shield-buster rounds didn't drop him.

Not that I'd counted on them to have much effect, hence the rest of the plan.

"PLOW THE FIELD," I screamed into my comm, then my team and I hit the deck.

Outside, the turret guns roared. Classroom windows exploded in a shower of glass. The reyza screamed as the heavy rounds tore through his arcane shielding and shredded his flesh, even as concrete, wood, and plaster burst from the far wall and rained down on us.

The guns stilled. I lifted my head to see the demon in the process of discorporeating, then pushed up and ran through the debris to Boudreaux. Zenra bounded forward, knelt, and started pulling supplies out of her bag with practiced efficiency.

"Just hang on, Boudreaux," I said, heart sinking as I took in his injuries. He gasped for each breath. One eye was swollen closed, and wicked claw marks punctured his shoulder. An evisceration-level gash traversed his abdomen, and a section of his chest the size of my hand moved in the opposite direction of the other ribs with each breath.

Zenra thrust a half liter bag of saline into my hands. "Commander, tape that over the flail chest," she snapped out. "Blauser, Ambu bag with O2. Starting a line."

I wiped blood and sweat from Boudreaux's chest and secured the full saline bag over the broken segment, which seemed to help keep it from sucking in and out quite so much. Between Blauser's O2 ventilations and the saline bag splint, we had his airway somewhat under control, but Zenra's grim expression as she worked at a fevered pace made my heart sink. And when she met my eyes and gave a slight shake of her head, I knew Boudreaux was fucked unless we could find some serious medical help fast. It would take way too long to return to the compound, and the nearest staffed hospital was at Fed Central by ground zero, which was more than twice as far away.

Boudreaux needed qaztahl healing. My mind raced through my meager options. I'd used my sigils to call on the lords once before, when we united to defeat Xharbek. Who the hell was on Earth *and* an ally *and* had a way to get here immediately?

Rhyzkahl? The only way he was able to travel instantaneously was with the help of a syraza. I didn't have time to waste on hoping he had a way to get here—if he was even still on Earth and agreed to come. Ashava was the most logical choice since she was able to teleport. I ripped off my ballistic vest and thrust my hand beneath my shirt at the small of my back, but a whisper of doubt in my gut had me hesitating. It killed me to think it, but I didn't trust her current judgment after her irrational behavior the other day on the nexus. And though she'd performed basic healing, would she be able to handle injuries this dire? Szerain could, if Ashava brought him here, but I'd still need to deal with her. I doubted she'd be content to step aside while Szerain did the healing—and another meltdown could be fatal for Boudreaux.

That left only one qualified option. An unwelcome one, but I had no choice. I shifted my hand to the twisted and chaotic sigil carved along my right side, spread my fingers to span as much of it as possible, and focused on the only other lord besides Ashava who could teleport.

<Lord Kadir. Please. I need your help. Pellini's best friend, Boudreaux, is dying>

Nothing. No tingle. No whisper of arcane or mental touch.

<Please. Help us>

Still nothing. FUCK. So much for Kadir. Which meant I had no choice but to call for Ashava. I shifted my hand toward the small of my back where her consummated sigil lay. No scars there—just smooth skin and a sigil visible only to those who could see the arcane.

Yet before I could even brush her sigil, the schoolroom vanished, replaced by flows of achingly beautifully light of the interdimensions. Kadir stood before me in all his prismatic glory, sparkly Boudreaux at his feet.

I scrambled to my feet, pulse racing.

With a complex hand motion I couldn't follow, he encased Boudreaux in chartreuse potency like an arcane stasis chamber. "There is a price."

"You'd let Boudreaux die?" I demanded, even though his desire for compensation didn't surprise me. "He's really important to Pellini."

One corner of his mouth twisted upward. "It is your choice to allow him die. Or not."

Ugh. "What do you want?"

His eyes dropped to the right side. "My sigil. Consummated."

A visceral spasm of terror robbed me of breath for an instant before I could push it down. The sigils had been the Mraztur's foundation for turning me into an arcane thrall—one that relegated my *self* to ever-diminishing awareness. Kadir had played some role in that plot, and the thought of him anywhere near the sigils sent icy claws through my essence. I covered the small of my back with my hand. Surely safer with Ashava.

Kadir's eyes tracked my movement. "As Jesral desires."

I blinked in confusion. "Huh?"

"A trap for Ashava. There. Within the heart of Marcel Boudreaux."

A cold wind rushed through me. I didn't doubt his words, because now the whole thing made sense. The geckoids. Grabbing Boudreaux. The ease with which we'd made entry into the building. Everything. And if Ashava hadn't lost her shit the other day—which Jesral would have zero knowledge of—I'd have called her to me without a second thought.

"I have conditions," I said, jerking my chin up as I struggled for composure. "You can't use your sigil to control me, or influence me to do things against my will, or hurt people close to me. Or hurt anyone at all, for that matter."

Kadir tilted his head, regarding me with keen curiosity and interest. "Still you know not what the sigils do or are."

I scowled. "Then enlighten me!"

"That is not my role. This is." With the lift of a finger, he diminished the potency of the stasis chamber. "Make your choice. The consummated sigil for the life of Marcel Boudreaux."

I gulped. "Will you have any hold over him?"

"I have no need for such."

Small relief, even though he hadn't exactly answered the question or acknowledged my conditions. What if consummating the sigil screwed everything up? What if this was the biggest mistake of my life? What if . . .

Get a grip, Kara! After the final lightning strike on the road, Mzatal had wholly entrusted my disembodied self to Kadir. That situation wasn't tied to this one, but my gut told me it meant *something*—and I was out of time. "Agreed."

Kadir moved in close and pressed his hand over my side. Icy arcane needles prickled and jabbed where he touched, and my knees buckled. He caught me with his free arm around my waist and pulled me close as if we were in a creepily surreal slow dance. Chaos-awareness—*Kadir's* awareness—awoke within me: breaking worlds, seething energies, images and visions beyond my comprehension. The icy jabs called me to focus, and I flowed with the pain, set boundaries for the chaos, sensed the touch of order.

Kadir's voice slid through me. "And so it is done, now and for all time, Kara Gillian."

I sucked in a sharp breath as I found myself back in the classroom. A heartbeat later, Vince Pellini appeared beside me.

Blauser startled, but Zenra seemed completely unsurprised to see him appear out of thin air.

Pellini dropped into a crouch and slapped a weird tangle of chartreuse potency onto Boudreaux's forehead. Though barely visible in a corner-of-my-eye sort of perception, I could make out a sparkly Kadir-shape standing behind him, but my head hurt when I tried to focus on it.

Pellini wore an expression of total calm focus as he made seemingly random changes to the potency. I hadn't seen him for months, not since we faced down Xharbek at ground zero. We'd been in the midst of trying to keep the PD valve from rupturing when, without any warning—and with the worst possible timing—Kadir had teleported Pellini away.

Pellini muttered under his breath as he manipulated the squiggle of potency, then with a sharp motion jerked the tangle from Boo's head and squeezed it in his fist until it vanished with a pop.

"That takes care of the trap," he said, exhaling.

"You're the bomb. No pun intended. And his injuries?"

"Working on it." He pulled another squiggle of green potency from thin air and attached it to Boudreaux's chest.

Boudreaux's eyes struggled open. A calm descended over his face that had nothing to do with any of Zenra's meds. He groped to touch Pellini's knee.

"It's okay . . . dude," he slurred. "Gonna be . . . okay. Just . . . take care of my mom . . . and my horse."

"Oh, for fuck's sake," Pellini growled. "Fuck that, and fuck you if you think I'm going to let my best fucking friend die! You dumb fucking fuck." He continued to draw more potency, muttering under his breath *Stupid dramatic bullshit* and *goddamn whiny idiot* and other expressions of endearment.

"You're good at this," I said, truly impressed by his dexterity and skill under Kadir's direction.

"Tell me something I don't know." He grinned when I rolled my eyes.

After several more minutes of writhing sigils and arcane tweakings, Boudreaux finally took a deeper breath, his skin now the color of actual living flesh rather than spoiled milk. Zenra gave me a relieved nod.

The not-quite-visible Sparkly Kadir vanished.

Pellini sat back on his heels and exhaled a shuddering breath. "I told you I wouldn't let you die, you stupid fuck," he muttered to Boudreaux.

Boudreaux lifted a shaky middle finger. "Fucking . . . prick."

"Yeah yeah yeah. You and me both, brother."

Chapter 13

While Zenra and the others loaded Boudreaux onto a stretcher and into the MRAP, I stripped the rest of the comm-blocking arcane off the flagpole. My radio immediately crackled to life.

"Compound to Gillian, come in Gillian, godfuckingdammit."

That was Krawkor's voice.

"Gillian to compound, we're code four," I replied. "It was a fucking trap. Boudreaux's messed up but stable."

"Two pronged," he said, voice grim. "We got hit hard about forty minutes after you left."

Son of a bitch. That coincided with when the comms went out. "How badly?"

"Injuries, some serious, but no fatalities on our side. Fair amount of damage to the physical perimeter, but warding mostly held."

I breathed a sigh of relief. "Ten-four. ETA fifteen minutes."

As soon as I lowered the radio mic, my phone rang. Szerain.

"Kara! What the" —*crackle*— "did you do?"

Shit. He'd no doubt sensed the business with Kadir's sigil. "What? Who is this? I can't hear you. Too much interference!"

"You can hear me just fine!"

"Boudreaux got ambushed and nearly died," I snapped. "Jesral laid a trap on him for Ashava, and Pellini is with us. I'll tell you more when we get back."

I hung up without giving him a chance to respond. He must've realized I wasn't in the mood for judgy bullshit because he didn't call again.

"You handled that like a boss," Pellini said as he waited for Zenra to get settled beside Boudreaux's stretcher.

"Asshole," I said without specifying whether I meant Szerain, Pellini, or both. "Good seeing you again."

"Ditto," he said. He closed the back doors, then came around to take the seat behind mine. "And thank you for, um, whatever you did to save Boudreaux."

He didn't know what deal I struck with Kadir and wasn't going to ask. Would Kadir really have let Boudreaux die, even knowing how much he meant to Pellini? Hell, I supposed anything was possible.

We rounded the last curve before the compound. Good thing I already knew the attack had been largely unsuccessful, because *holy shit*. Gut tight, I took in the damage. The sally port by the horse farm was a twisted heap of chain link and metal poles. Craters the size of sedans broke the fence line in at least a half dozen places, and stray arcane energy crackled and flashed between trees like static on a giant blanket fresh out of the dryer. But to my relief, the arcane defenses appeared to all be intact, and I sent up a silent thanks to Zakaar for spending so much time and effort crafting, laying, reinforcing, and maintaining those protections.

At the main gate, the sally port listed drunkenly but was still functional enough for personnel to haul it open as we approached.

Once inside, Pellini and I hopped out of the MRAP to yank the back doors open. Szerain loped our way and climbed in, then splayed one hand on Boudreaux's chest, assessing.

"Well?" Pellini demanded.

"He's stable enough," Szerain said, and Pellini visibly relaxed. "Ashava and I will ease pain and do a more thorough assessment once he's settled at the infirmary." He shot a narrow-eyed glare my way, likely fueled by the issue with Kadir's sigil.

I met it with stone-faced professionalism. "Any residue from Jesral's efforts to trap Ashava?" Might as well remind him what the stakes were.

"The trap is gone, but some shadows remain." He cursed in demon under his breath. "Jesral would have captured her, for sure."

A shudder ran through me. "That would have been an unspeakable disaster on *so* many levels. She's powerful but inexperienced. Wouldn't stand a chance against Ilana, Ssahr, and whoever else is aligned with them."

"No doubt about it." He withdrew his hand. "They'd subvert, control, and use her against us. Between the attempted infiltration via Tessa and the attacks today, they came close. Too close." He paused. "During the assault on the compound, Bryce spotted Mzatal *in chains* with Ilana and Ssahr. But only for an instant. I suspect they didn't trust their hold over him and departed."

"Fuuuuck." I focused on my breathing to control the wave of fury and grief that threatened to swamp me. "If he'd joined the attack, they'd've gotten the nexus. With you and Vsuhl as lagniappe."

"Even without Mzatal, Jesral would have had me if Ashava hadn't deflected a strike sure to take me out."

I let out a sigh of relief. "Sometimes I don't know whether to hug or strangle that girl. Er . . . that unspeakably powerful but hormonally challenged being."

Szerain failed to suppress the twitch of a smile as he climbed down from the MRAP and closed the doors. Once the vehicle lumbered off with Zenra and her patient, he turned his penetrating gaze on Pellini.

Pellini gave him a nod of greeting. "You want to verify I haven't been manipulated, right?"

"It would ease everyone's mind." And there was no mistaking the unspoken *And no fucking way are you getting into the compound proper until I make sure you're not a threat.*

"Have at it. If I'm not clear, I want to know as much as you do."

Szerain set his fingers on Pellini's temple for a good minute. "You're as clear as any of us," he finally said.

"So, completely fucked up, right?" I said wryly.

Szerain let out a low snort. "Here comes your ride. I need to reassess the fence line and other compound entrances, then head over to the infirmary." He leveled his gaze at me. "We'll talk later."

"You're goddamn right we will," I muttered as he strode away.

Bryce drove up in a four-seat utility vehicle, smear of blood down one side of his face, and a long scrape on his left forearm. Nils Engen started toward him, medical kit at the ready, but Bryce waved him off with a murmured, *I'm good*, along with instructions to see to a laceration on David Nguyen's back.

Bryce shifted his attention back to me. "Roma gave me the quick and dirty debrief of what went down at the school."

I took shotgun while Pellini clambered into the back. "Knowing her," I said, "she covered pretty much everything, but I'll fill in any missing details as soon as you brief me on what happened here."

Bryce drove toward the house, expression tight. "Demons and humans using rocket and grenade launchers they'd enhanced with arcane, like nothing I've seen before." He gestured toward the energy still dancing between the trees. "When Mzatal popped in, I thought we were done. But he was here and gone in a flash, and I think that broke the attacker's morale. Gave us the advantage we needed to drive them off."

"Krawkor said there were no fatalities, right?"

"Not on our side," Bryce said. "Killed two, maybe three, of theirs. Took out a handful of demons. Watson took a shard of wood in the neck from an exploding tree. Missed major vessels and was lucky as hell to have Ashava nearby to stabilize him. Tandon caught some shrapnel in the thigh, and Kellum has a badly broken arm. Not to mention a dozen or more relatively minor injuries."

Relieved, I gave a quick recount of the ambush, including my theory that Jesral had chosen Boudreaux because he needed a target who was not only close to me but also relatively easy to abduct. Hence snatching Boudreaux from a mule out in the open as opposed to targeting Scott who typically remained in or around a vehicle. "We're so much more vulnerable when away from the compound. The protections here still good?"

"Wards held but took a beating in a couple of spots. Ashava reinforced them, but they could use more work." He hooked his thumb toward the main gate. "We're going to have to bust ass to get the perimeter repaired and secure."

"You have a backhoe to fill in all those craters?" Pellini asked.

Bryce stopped in front of the house and we piled out. "Yep. Ronda is laying out the rebuilding plan now."

"Hell," Pellini said. "Y'all could just dig a bigass trench around the whole compound. Build up a berm. You already have the ditch along the highway and the bayou to the west."

My gaze arrowed in on a tall figure rounding the corner of the house. "Good idea. And we have something better than a backhoe," I said. "Hey, Michael! Can you come here a sec?"

Michael gave a happy wave and trotted over. "Whatcha need, Miss Kara?"

"Could you get your golems to help Miss Ronda fill those holes by the fence with dirt? Plus, it'd be smart to make a ditch around the compound in all the places where we don't already have a ditch or bayou."

"Like the moat around Amkir's palace?"

"Um, sure? Not as big, though. Check with Miss Ronda about it, okay?" She'd rein him in if needed.

He beamed in utter delight. "Yessiree! I'm a big help. Mr. Walter said so when I handed him missiles during the fight!"

"Excellent!" I said and somehow managed to keep a bright smile plastered on my face. Missiles? What the actual fuck?

As soon as he ran off, I rounded on Bryce, aghast. "Am I to understand an eighty-year-old civilian was involved in—"

Bryce held up a hand. "Hang on. First off, there's no way we could've made Walter hole up while shit was going down."

"Handcuffs?" I sputtered. "Duct tape?"

"Kara. Walter was *useful*. He rigged up a goddamn ballista to lob homemade incendiaries onto the attackers. What Michael called missiles. Plus he had the idea to reinforce the main gate with some of the leftover I-beams from the barracks and rec center construction. On top of that, he *somehow* convinced Prikahn and Dagor to transport the beams and drive them into the ground by the sally port. That's a big reason it's not completely wrecked like the other ones. Walter held his own and then some."

"Okay, fine," I muttered. I had to admit his glitter bombs and slingshots had worked pretty darn well on the zhurn at the school. I just hoped he hadn't bargained away something he couldn't deliver in exchange for the Jontari labor. "But you can't blame me for—"

A high-pitched canine yelp cut me off as seventy pounds of chocolate-brown dog cannoned into Pellini. To his credit, Pellini merely staggered and went to one knee instead of being knocked on his ass. Sammy let out ecstatic barks and yips, flailing his tail at light speed as he slobbered all over his hooman's face.

"Jesus Christ, get a grip, you stupid fucking mutt," Pellini said, laughing, then delivered belly rubs and skritches until his dog whimpered with joy.

Bryce's habitually inscrutable expression softened a tad. "How's Paul?" he asked Pellini.

"Doing great! Misses you like crazy. He always fucking brags about you. Bryce did this. Bryce did that." He chuckled. "Could give a guy a complex, y'know?"

Bryce cleared his throat. "I, uh, miss him, too."

Pellini climbed to his feet and dusted off his pants. "Paul has a boyfriend now," he added with a nonchalant shrug, humor dancing in his eyes.

"Wait, what?" I said.

"How?" Bryce demanded.

"Well, when two people really like each other—" Pellini began, as if speaking to a three-year old, then danced back from Bryce's swing.

"You're such a fucking jerk," Bryce growled. "Who the fuck is this guy?"

"Dominic. Another computer nerd type Paul gamed with for years online." Pellini snorted. "And trust me, ain't nothing *innocent* about Paul anymore. Christ almighty, no room is sacred. They could at least put a sock on the door!"

"Fucking hell!" Bryce sputtered. "And Kadir's okay with this?"

Laughing, I put a hand on Bryce's arm. "Dude, Paul's in his twenties. Also, you know damn well Kadir would never allow anything or anyone to harm his essence-bond mate." Kadir was weird and unsettling and, well, *Kadir*, but I had zero doubt Paul was safe.

Bryce grumbled something under his breath but gave a reluctant nod, no stranger to essence bonds. He worried about Seretis almost as much as I did about Mzatal.

I glanced at Pellini. "Do Kadir and Paul have a relationship? I mean apart from the bond. I've seen them together a few times and they seem . . . close."

"If you mean a physical relationship, yeah. They do. But *nothing* is straightforward with Kadir. As far as I can tell, he has no interest in sex. With anyone. I'd say his relationship with Paul is complex. Intimate, physical, and platonic. It works for them, and Dominic is cool with it."

"Good to hear. Paul seemed at ease when I saw him, but it's a relief to get confirmation without Kadir around."

"No worries on that front," Pellini said. "And Paul's really good for Kadir. Keeps the chaos at bay."

Krawkor opened the screen door and stepped onto the porch. Pellini waved. "Hey, it's Rainbow Furby! How's it going, Sarge?"

"I see you're as much of a prick as ever," Krawkor said, grinning. "Never change."

"Don't intend to. This is just another layer to my charm. By the way, I like the new hardware."

Krawkor snaked a multicolored tail around to thump the side of his prosthesis. "Latest and greatest technology, or so I'm told."

"Sweet. You in contact with any of the other pod people besides Makonite, Kinsavi, and Zenra?"

"Nope. Should I be? DIRT tracks 'em, I think."

"Nah. Just wondering. Kadir keeps tabs on them." At Krawkor's scowl, Pellini hurried to add, "Not to hurt them or anything! Just to make sure they're, uh, where they need to be."

"And where is that?" I asked. Krawkor's brow remained puckered as well.

"No fucking clue," Pellini said cheerfully. "But Kadir seems satisfied with where they are for now." He shrugged. "I've learned not to ask too many questions."

"Does Kadir get angry when you do?"

"Nah. He'll just *looooook* at you with that utterly inscrutable expression, then walk away as if he hadn't heard a word you said."

"Crap. On my way," Krawkor said into his comm. "Duty calls. See y'all later." He bounded off, more agile than he'd ever been back in the day.

"For me as well," Bryce said, and headed off in a different direction.

"So, are you back with us for a while?" I asked Pellini.

"Not quite yet," he said. "I'm actually here for something unrelated to saving Boudreaux's skinny ass." He glanced around. "Maybe we could take this inside? It's going to take a bit of explanation."

"That's fine, though can we hold off for just a few? Also, is this something the rest of the command staff should be present for?"

"I got some time, and yeah, they should probably be in the room."

"Good deal. Need to do a quick debrief with everyone anyway, but Roma's going to need some time to get the squad settled. How's an hour sound?"

"Works for me. Don't suppose Jill has been baking recently?"

"Are you kidding? It's how she deals with stress."

He let out a happy sigh. "And sometimes all is right with the world."

Chapter 14

We headed into the house where Pellini swiped a Danish from a tray on the kitchen table. I stripped off body armor, then shot a quick text to the rest of the command staff regarding a debrief in one hour.

Sonny's phone pinged with said text as he entered from the conference room, but he didn't even spare a glance at the message. "Kara," he said, voice low and urgent. "The IDTF reps are on the line and want a video conference right now. They aren't fucking around. You'd better take it this time."

I groaned. "Is it the whole enchilada or just the U.S. reps?"

"Just the U.S.," he said, to my small relief. "I have everything ready to go on the conference room computer."

I thanked him, grateful I didn't have to fight with technology on top of everything else. I started toward the conference room, but Pellini caught my wrist.

"Hang on," he said, peering at my face.

I frowned. "Am I all dirty?"

"Yes, but the bloodstains can't be seen against the maroon of your uniform, and somehow you kept your face relatively clean—which is what they're going to see. You need to actually *look* like you've just been through hell. Remind these desk jockeys you're out there in the trenches." He pulled the oven open and swiped up a bit of soot from the bottom, carefully smudged my jawline and one cheek, and even did something under my eyes. "That should do it."

I checked my image on my phone. "Daaaamn, you're good at this." I looked war-weary and fierce at the same time, and the effect came across as one hundred percent authentic.

He grinned. "I used to do a lot of cosplay, remember? I have some makeup skills. Now go knock 'em dead."

True to his word, Sonny had already pulled up the video conference window, where all I had to do was hit the "join" button. I avoided the worldwide IDTF meetings whenever possible, but had semi-regular meetings with the U.S. contingent as a general "keep everyone updated" kind of thing. But getting results happened about as often as with any bureaucratic committee.

I joined the call and took note of the people in the other three video windows. Two, I knew from previous meetings. Richard Hershberg was a former congressman with a brief military background and a purple heart for an injury that left him with a scar along his jawline—described as "dashing" by a few news outlets. I suspected his PR team had a hand in that. Though he'd lost his third election by a not-insignificant margin, he'd managed to wrangle his way onto various committees and task forces related to the Demon Wars by citing his experience. I doubted the man had ever seen a demon in real life, hence I had Questions about that experience.

Carolina Soldado was a former big wig with the CIA, sharp-faced and keen-eyed and quick to point out mistakes, but generally not unfair about it. I didn't completely dislike her, which said a lot.

The third person was new to me—a fifty-something clean-cut man in DIRT dress uniform bearing a colonel's rank insignia.

"Where's Luschka, and who's the new guy?" I asked, though I had an uncomfortable feeling I already knew the answer.

New Guy gave me a pleasant enough smile. "Colonel Luschka has been reassigned. I'm Sim Jiwoo, General Starr's new aide de camp."

Shit. Had she been reassigned because of her investigation into strike teams being sent to their deaths? I tabled that worry for later and kept my expression neutral. "Nice to meet you, Colonel Sim. And now that we've dispensed with the formalities, how may I help you all?"

Sim's smile never wavered. "Well, first and foremost, we'd appreciate details about the attack on your compound."

"I wasn't here. I was on a DIRT callout." I kept my expression guileless. "Are you sure you weren't told about this? Seems like you'd be on top of that kind of thing."

Hershberg scowled. "We know you weren't present for the attack, but surely you've had ample time since your return—"

"*Ample time*?" I made a point of glancing at my watch. "I literally just got back not even fifteen minutes ago. The one debrief I've had—and the most important—was whether my people were all right. I'm relieved to report that we suffered no fatalities, however there were quite a few injuries. Some serious."

Hershberg grumbled but didn't have much of a comeback for that.

"Speaking of the callout," Soldado said, voice cool, "I have some questions." A picture came up in a new window—drone imagery of us herding geckoids into the warded pen, then a second picture that was simply a bright flash of purple. "Namely, this habit your people seem to have for destroying our monitoring drones."

"Oh, *hell* no. You don't get to blame that shit on me. Our two drones were taken out in the exact same fashion. In fact, I'll ask my operator to send you the footage." I quickly tapped out a message to Wohlreich to that effect. There was nothing in the geckoid roundup that needed to be kept confidential. "Considering the timing of the attack *and* the destruction of the drones, I have every reason to believe the geckoid callout was a diversion to get Alpha Squad and me away from the compound. Especially since we encountered arcane interference that rendered our comms useless, which meant the compound had no way of notifying us of the situation." I had zero intention of telling them the callout was also an ambush, since that was shit they wouldn't understand, plus it would invite questions about how I'd dealt with it.

A bit of the chill left Soldado's manner. "We experienced issues with the satellite imagery around the area of the callout during the time in question."

Which meant they missed everything that happened at the school. Thank the universe for small favors.

Sim steepled his fingers in front of him. "What do you know of the motives for the attack on the compound? Are you engaged in any activities we don't know about? Activities that would invite such an attack?"

"Are you absolutely one hundred percent fucking shitting me?" I blurted, abandoning all pretense at civility. "Have you missed the part where there are literal bad guys out there and we're at war with them?"

Sim frowned. "Yes, we're aware there's a war going on, but I'm interested in what might have precipitated this particular—"

"You're seriously going to waste my time with this bullshit? I'd like to refer you to my previous comment regarding the fact I've only been back for *fifteen minutes*."

Hershberg made a *hmmfing* sound. "I'll address some older business then." He shuffled some paperwork in front of him. "Namely, what is the meaning behind the scars on your body?"

A chill went through me. I'd been asked this question before—repeatedly—not long after the valve exploded at ground zero. I'd been arrested and held for six days, during which I was searched and questioned—thoroughly and not always gently—about my role in the "terrorist attack" on downtown Beaulac. They'd of course poked, prodded, sampled, and photographed the sigil scars—and the rest of my body—from every possible angle.

I kept my expression utterly placid and gave Hershberg the same answer I'd given my not-gentle questioners. "I'm into extreme body modification. Next question."

His gaze skimmed over the papers. "Why is it that one of the designs is exactly the same as the symbol on the Spires?"

My pulse quickened, but I managed to keep from reacting. I hoped. Clearly someone who could see the arcane had made a sketch of the sigil on Kadir's Earthgate for the official records.

He scanned his papers again, then lifted his gaze back to me, smug and arrogant.

No, those weren't papers he was shuffling through. He was trying to unnerve me. Humiliate me.

As if.

"I have a question, Mr. Hershberg," I said, hard, feral smile on my face. "Are you seriously sitting here in an official, re-corded, government-sanctioned meeting, looking at eight by tens of *my nude body*?"

Soldado jerked in shock.

Hershberg gulped. "They're not—"

"Really?" I said, voice sharp as a razor. "Then hold them up and show the class."

He flushed. "This is evidence—"

"No, this is *harassment*, full stop," I snarled, "and I will absolutely be filing a complaint."

"Hershberg," Soldado snapped. "Leave this call immediately. I'll deal with you later."

Hershberg's window disappeared.

Sim looked pissed, but I wondered how much of it was because Hershberg had fucked things up and the balance of power was now most assuredly on my side. And though I didn't doubt that Soldado's anger was genuine, I still wasn't going to let her or anyone else off the hook.

I kept my extremely righteous fury on full display. "THIS is why I don't trust you people. I'm out here on the front lines, and I get fucked up shit like this pulled on me. I'm going to demand a full investigation as to who has access to those images. Not to mention, why Hershberg felt it was okay to try and use them in some stupid psychological ploy against me. Pretty sure that would fall under any number of revenge porn statutes."

Sim's face was tight. "I want to personally apologize for Mr. Hershberg's inexcusable behavior."

I sneered. "You don't get to apologize for his behavior. Only he can do that. But you can apologize for your part in whatever bullshit lack of security and oversight made it possible for him to have access to what should have been highly classified information."

Sim took a deep breath. "I apologize—"

"A true apology pairs admission of fault with *action*," I snapped. "Get back to me when you've actually done something about it."

"Commander Gillian is right," Soldado said. She tapped something on her keyboard, and Sim's window disappeared. "Be that as it may," she continued as if she hadn't just kicked Sim the fuck out, "we still have questions regarding what precipitated this attack, and how it relates to the incident outside your main gate two days ago. You have not been forthcoming at all, and it's very difficult for us to coordinate and analyze intel when we have little to no intel from your end."

I looked up and tapped my chin in an exaggerated Deeply Thoughtful expression. "Gee, I can't imagine why I'm not forthcoming with every aspect of the operations here." I sucked in a breath and widened my eyes. "Oh wait! Maybe it's because of the time I was in a video conference with y'all and one of the participants was drooling over naked pictures of me."

The muscles in her jaw twitched, and I could practically hear the grinding of her teeth. "That will be dealt with. Severely."

Somehow I doubted the "severely" part. Didn't matter. I had ways of dealing with that shit, too. "Well, I'm sure you're aware the best way to keep information secure is to severely limit who knows it."

"And we need to be in that 'who knows it' group!" Anger

warred with frustration in her eyes. "Especially if you want continued funding. Not to mention, there are those who would dearly love to see you as the former Arcane Commander."

I summoned a bland smile. "Well, that's quite a threat." I didn't actually give that much of a crap about my rank, but continued funding was a little more important.

Soldado lifted her chin. "No, not really. A threat would be if I were to say that your compound and personnel will be placed under strict government control unless you start keeping us fully informed of all activities and events related to the demon realm, demons, arcane structures and the rift on your property, as well as any and all contact and communication with the entities known as the demonic lords."

I had no idea how much they knew about either the nexus or the rift, but I wasn't about to add a single speck to that knowledge.

I leaned back and laced my fingers over my stomach. "Nah, that's not a threat," I replied, tone mild. "That's blustering, and you know it. If your people had the ability to take control of this property, they'd have done so quite some time ago." I raked a hand through my hair and pretended to look tired. Okay, maybe I wasn't actually pretending. "Look, I've explained this before, but I'll do so again." I resisted the urge to say something petty like, *And I'll use small, easy-to-understand words.* "Earth has some extremely powerful enemies. Most of these enemies have the ability to read thoughts. And *change* thoughts. They can influence people to take actions they might not ordinarily take—and then make those people forget they took them. Now, I don't know about you, but the thought of someone doing that to me or someone I care about pisses me off, and yes, scares the bejeezus out of me." *Like what was done to Tessa.* "I maintain absolutely strict security on this compound because I have to, in order to protect everyone. Not just the people here. The entire damn world. Would you let just anyone saunter into the Pentagon and start poking around? Or fly a drone down its halls?"

"Be that as it may—"

"You seriously need to stop using that phrase."

Her glower turned darker. "I'm done catching flak over your secrecy."

"I file reports on a regular basis." Technically, Sonny filed them, but the point remained the same. "I'm sure your superiors have full access to those."

She pressed her fingers to her eyes and let out a noise that sounded suspiciously like a moan. "Look, I respect why you keep so much info to yourself. But I'm caught between a rock and a hard place."

Oh, sweet, now she was playing the Sympathetic Ally. Well, I could play that right back. I softened my expression. "I know. And I'm very sorry. But my people are on the front lines here, and we're dealing with literal demigods." I let my shoulders droop a bit. "We recently recovered Tessa Pazhel—my aunt, who raised me after my parents died. She's in real bad shape." I swallowed and did what I could to summon a haunted expression. I really needed to start practicing this shit in a mirror. Maybe the rec center could start offering acting lessons? "Every time I look at her, I'm reminded of the depths our enemies will sink to."

Soldado gave me a look of deep sympathy that was probably as sincere as the tremble of my lip. "I'll talk to my superiors. But"—she exhaled and shook her head—"I can't make any promises about continued funding if you don't keep me *thoroughly* informed. And, you should be aware, there are some who would gladly resort to more strenuous reprisals if they felt it suited their purposes. Earth's purposes," she hastily added.

Nice catch there. Their purposes were probably along the lines of *How can I finagle this situation to benefit my quest for power and/or wealth.* "I understand. I really do." I donned an earnest and contrite expression. "I'll do everything I can to find out who was behind the attack, and I promise to pass it along as soon as I can verify its accuracy."

A relieved smile curved her mouth. Totally sincere. No, really. "Thank you, Commander Gillian. I knew I could count on you."

"Absolutely. And likewise." I clicked off. Waited for the screen to go dark, checked that it was well and truly disconnected, then let out a guttural scream of *Fuck all of this bureaucratic bullshit.*

Sonny stepped in, grinning. "You rang, madam?"

"I need to bottle your calming mojo in a flask and carry it with me always."

"Yeah, that's called whiskey."

Chapter 15

Szerain was pacing in the hallway when I stepped out of the conference room. I caught his eye and tilted my head toward the basement door, more than ready to deal with him, now that I was fired up from the IDTF bullshit.

The instant we reached the bottom of the stairs, he laid into me.

"I'd appreciate an explanation for why you chose to call *Kadir* as opposed to me and Ashava, or even Rhyzkahl." He crossed his arms over his chest while giving me a narrow-eyed glower. "You knew nothing of the attack on the compound or the trap on Boudreaux—which I'm quite certain I would have seen and neutralized before it could be triggered on Ashava—so that can't possibly be your reasoning. After that, we can discuss your spectacularly irresponsible decision to allow Kadir to consummate his sigil."

Cold fury filled my belly. Oh, he was definitely poking the wrong bear. "First off, you can tone down this whole Mad Daddy thing you have working here." I swept my hand up and down to indicate his entire posture.

He scowled and dropped his arms. "Mad . . . Daddy?"

"Yeah, like you're a parent ready to berate his teenage daughter for being out past curfew." I crossed *my* arms and glared at him. "You weren't there for the callout or the ambush. You didn't have mere seconds to make life-or-death decisions based on scant information. Even now, you don't know squat about the extenuating circumstances. I asked you down here so I could brief you, not so you could chew me out without witnesses."

"You have no idea what the sigils can or can't—"

I cut him off with a loud buzzer noise. "Wrong answer, and you lose extra points for not listening to a fucking thing I just said. Let me know when you're ready to talk to me like a peer." I stalked up the steps, closed the door behind me—proud of myself for not slamming it—and returned to my office. There was always paperwork to be done, and maybe I could shock the hell out of Sonny by getting some of it completed before he had to beg, nag, and coerce me to do so.

Alas, for Sonny's sake, Szerain stepped into my office only a few minutes later, while I was still trying to get pertinent files opened. I looked up, prepared to kick him right back out if he was still determined to be a dick, but the scowl was gone, and he almost . . . *almost* looked chastened. Maybe he'd communed with Zakaar?

"I apologize for my earlier behavior," he said. "You're right. I have no business judging your actions when I know little of the surrounding circumstances."

"I accept your apology. If you'd care to close the door, I'll explain my thought process behind the decision to call Kadir— and tell you what I didn't share with the others."

He closed the door and took a seat. "I'd appreciate it."

"I didn't call Ashava or involve her to transport you because, frankly, I don't trust her judgment, especially after her behavior on the nexus."

A faint wince crossed his face. "Understood. But why not call Rhyzkahl?"

"Boudreaux was at death's fucking door. Knock knock, he's gone. I had no way to know if Rhyzkahl was with a syraza who might get him to us quickly."

He let out a breath. "So you went with the next best option. The one you *knew* had the ability to travel to you. Fast."

"You got it. I didn't have a clue if Kadir would answer my call or not." I leaned back in my chair. "Fortunately, he did."

Szerain went quiet for a moment. "And he had a price for the healing and trap removal."

"His sigil, consummated. So, yes, I agreed to it. No way in hell would I let a teammate die when he could be saved. I figured I'd deal with the consequences in their own time."

"Of course." He sighed and rubbed the back of his neck. "I'm sorry I was such a . . . Mad Daddy dick earlier."

"You're forgiven. We're all scraped pretty thin lately. But it's a good thing I *didn't* involve Ashava, considering the trap was laid for her."

"No shit. And with her known ability to teleport, Jesral would have naturally assumed you'd call for her."

"It would have been a bad decision all the way around."

Szerain exhaled. "You're right to have doubts about her maturity and stability. She's gone through years of maturation in the span of weeks, with inconceivable pressure to live up to sky-high expectations and potential. She is, ah . . ."

My mouth twitched. "Astronomically more dangerous and unpredictable than your average bratty teen. And, as much as I want to, I should resist the urge to strangle her."

"Precisely."

My smile faded. "What doom should I expect to rain down on us because I consummated Kadir's sigil? And what does that even *mean* other than it's not a scar anymore and is invisible except to arcane sight?"

"It's not just invisible. It's fully integrated with you now."

"What does *that* mean?" I splayed my hand over my right side. "I feel its presence, and it resonates of Kadir like the scar did, just more potent and refined."

"When I completed and consummated Ashava's sigil, it was so much more than simply creating an arcane version to replace the physical scarring. I engaged the Rowan construct in the process."

"Yeah. Hard to forget the whole stabbed-in-the-heart-with-an-essence-blade fun."

He grimaced. "It was the only way I could come up with to stop the arcane virus from overwhelming you and obliterating Kara. I used the Rowan construct as a framework to attach Ashava's sigil to you. To your essence."

I stared at him, my mind struggling to comprehend the implications.

"The framework is still there," he said, grimace deepening. "I didn't think Kadir or anyone else would ever discover it."

"You didn't even tell *me*! What the actual fuck, Szerain?"

He sighed. "After that night, I was struggling hard with the whole Ryan/Szerain identity crisis, and we never really talked about what happened. I didn't see it as an issue, so the specifics never cropped up again."

"You attached Ashava's energy signature to my essence via a psychotic arcane construct whose framework is still there, and that's not an *issue*? And Kadir somehow got wind of it, and I've fucking integrated him, too? Sounds like an issue to me!"

"I'm not arguing the point."

He sounded so deflated, I couldn't help but feel a little sorry for him. Besides, he *did* manage to save me from losing my entire Self back then, so I had to give him a few points for that. "We all make mistakes. We're cool. I've definitely dropped the ball a time or three." I massaged my temples. "Let's move on to what might come next. Can Kadir do anything to me through the integration? I mean, what's the payoff for him, and is there a penalty for me? And if you say you don't know, I might just slug you."

"I don't currently possess that particular piece of information."

"You mean you don't know."

"I *mean* I have no desire to be slugged."

Despite my best efforts, a snicker escaped me. "Just like a qaztahl to find the loophole. Fine. See what you can figure out." I stood and hiked up my shirt. Szerain stepped around the desk and splayed his fingers along my side.

After a long moment, he withdrew his hand. "It was wrong," he muttered, as if to himself.

"Huh?"

He pulled my shirt back into place. "The original sigil. It was discordant, because Kadir has always been discordant. Out of phase. But it seems he's no longer *as* discordant."

"Because of Paul." I dropped back into my chair. "I bet you anything that's what happened. Pellini said Paul is good for Kadir. Chills him out, so to speak."

"You're most likely correct. And with Kadir's sigil modified and consummated, Paul can stabilize him even more. That's fascinating and brilliant," he concluded, his expression one of not-so-grudging respect for Kadir.

"That's a payoff and potential advantage for him. Is there anything I need to worry about?"

"You have a stronger direct—and likely permanent—connection to him now. Could be two-way. Could be nothing more than a sense?"

I gave him a sour look. "Just admit you have zero clue."

"Guilty as charged." He spread his hands. "This is completely new territory. To be honest, I don't know what the sigils and the entire construct are capable of at this point."

It took me a second to regain the power of speech. "What the flipping hell? Kadir flicked the On switch for his sigil and *integrated it with my essence*, and you're just like, 'Eh, it's a mystery'?"

He shook his head. "Consummating the sigil isn't the same as activating it, so no, he didn't flick the On switch. I'm not even sure there is an On switch."

"Well. We can at least acknowledge that our ignorance is vast." I frowned. "What about *your* sigil? It was carved on me while you were still fully submerged as Ryan. Now you're unsubmerged. Talk about some huge changes."

He shook his head. "I'd know if it wasn't right."

"Would you, though? It would've been a gradual shift, and you're not hypersensitive to discordance the way Kadir is. Maybe your sigil not being quite right wouldn't bother you the same way."

He regarded me in silence for several heartbeats, then abruptly pulled me out of my chair and placed his hand over his sigil where it flowed from my upper back to coalesce between my shoulder blades. "Huh. You might . . . *miiiiiiiight* have a point."

Laughing, I shifted to punch him in the bicep. "Y'know, you could just say, 'Wow, that was a stellar insight, Kara!'"

"Okay, okay!" He grinned and made a show of rubbing his arm where I'd hit him. "That was a pretty hot shit observation, and after further review—as much as it pains me to say it—you're right. It doesn't quite resonate."

"Ha! Score!" I did a victory dance.

"And this calm, measured response is precisely why I don't tell you how brilliant you are."

I showed him the utter brilliance of my middle finger. "Okay, next question. Would it help you if you consummated your sigil?"

He pondered the question for a moment. "Another thing I don't know. But in any case, I can't even try until Zakaar is embodied."

"So it probably wouldn't be a bad thing, once Zack has been Zakaar-ified, for your sigil to be consummated."

He hesitated. "I don't think it would be bad."

I narrowed my eyes. "Seems like since you created the Rowan thing, you should know a lot more than you do."

"I created the construct, yes. But Rhyzkahl and Jesral made subtle alterations so Rowan could better serve their purposes. And, the manner in which it was placed upon you undoubtedly shaped it as well. Plus, the night I bladed you, when you were fully embodied as Rowan—you added your own nuances. It's not the same Rowan I originally created."

"But you still know it, right? I mean, even though it's changed, you're the creator."

"Oh, very much so." His gaze dropped to my right side. "Yet I am starting to suspect that Kadir has more understanding than I do regarding what the Rowan construct is truly capable of. He sees things in ways the others can't, won't, or don't, and he has always had a far better understanding of the arcane than any other, save perhaps Mzatal."

"That's exactly it," I said. "He thinks and processes information in different ways than anyone else. He figures shit out. And even though he didn't make the construct, he'd have studied and analyzed until he knew it inside out and sideways. Basically, Kadir's a nerd."

Szerain sputtered out a laugh. "That's an accurate assessment."

"Sheesh, no wonder he and Paul get along so well." I mulled over the new insights on Kadir and Szerain's Mad Daddy act. "Why'd you get so upset over Kadir and the sigil?"

He was silent for a moment. "Because I didn't know what had happened. Only that his sigil changed, and that you had to have allowed it. I feared coercion at first—which in a way it was, of course, considering he threatened to withhold healing for Boudreaux—but then a mean part of me became convinced you'd simply made a foolish decision. And, as you've pointed out, it threw into sharp focus that I don't fully understand what the sigils are capable of now."

"And Kadir does."

He shook his head. "I don't know. More than I, but does he fathom their full measure? He's brilliant and has unique insight, but I doubt even he has gleaned their entire potential."

I grinned. "But by discovering the framework and consummating his sigil, you realized he knew more than you about your own creation, and it made you jealous."

He rolled his eyes. "Yes. Fine. I experienced a moment of envy."

I rubbed my hands together in glee. "Good enough for me! I need to have a quick chat with Pellini before the staff meeting, and then we can debrief the hell out of this day."

Chapter 16

Pellini was hanging out in the kitchen, sipping coffee and finishing the last crumbs of his Danish. "I'd forgotten how good these were."

I laughed. "Kadir needs a personal chef to make some for you."

"Oh, he has one," he said, then grinned. "A human one. Not a faas."

I kept the smile on my face and fought the desire to press for more details. I won the battle, but only because I knew Pellini was waiting for me to ask about humans working for Kadir. Yes, I was wildly curious, but I didn't want to give him the satisfaction.

"Glad to hear it," I said with an overly cheerful smile, then made a rude gesture at him when he laughed. "Anyway, can we have a quick chat before the debrief?"

"Private?" he said and pushed up from the table.

"Yeah. Figure we can take a bit of a nature walk."

He gestured grandly to me. "Lead the way."

I snagged my coat and hat then headed out toward the sanctuary of the pond glade. Even as other parts of the property were cleared and developed during the compound expansion, I'd insisted the area within twenty-five yards of the water be maintained as a natural retreat. To my relief, no personnel were currently taking advantage of the peace, and no Jontari lounged in the pond.

Still, I sketched a quick privacy ward, just to be sure.

Pellini settled on the lone bench, and I plopped down on a stump.

"Sooooo," I began.

Pellini laughed. "You have questions."

"Fine. Yes. I have questions. I always have questions."

"Fire away."

"My first question is about what happened at ground zero, back when we were trying to control the mutagen. Kadir pulled you away at a really crucial moment, and I was just wondering why he'd do something so risky? It could have been pretty disastrous."

"The Between was fracturing, which would have been *more* disastrous," he said. "Xharbek's actions threatened the very foundations of the worlds." He scowled. "Fucking dumbass."

"Holy shit. Okay then. One point to Kadir."

He snorted a laugh. "You have another question?"

"Yeah. Not long after we locked down the mutagen and scattered Xharbek at ground zero, I saw a video of Kadir and you and Paul at a school auditorium with Senator Olson and a bunch of little kids."

"Yep. Hawk Butte Elementary. Olson was hosting a town hall with parents about his education platform."

"Right. I'm aware that Kadir is super protective when it comes to kids, but I can't help but wonder what he's doing? I mean, is he looking for kids like you? Er, like you were when you were young? Fuck, you know what I mean."

His grin widened, clearly enjoying my interrogational flailing. "Yeah, he searches for kids, typically under eight, who have potential to develop their arcane pathways in a Kadir-ish way. Older than that, it's risky work."

"You do know how cringy and exploitative that sounds, right?" I said, wincing. "Lord Creepy scopes out kids to find the best ones to groom."

"If it was that one-sided, I'd agree wholeheartedly." He held up his hand when I opened my mouth to protest. "Look, I'm not saying the kids are old enough to consent or that it's right to work with them without their parents' okay, but there's more to it."

"I really do want to get rid of this sick knot in my gut." I leaned forward and rested my elbows on my knees. "Help me understand. Kadir picks some kids and then makes sure their arcane pathways develop the way he wants them to?"

"No. I mean, yes, but not immediately after those initial assessments. It's a massive undertaking. From what I gather, nearly every child has arcane pathways, ranging from vestigial to vibrant. I'd say out of every fifty assessed, only one makes that first cut, but Kadir's criteria for that are a mystery to me. It's not just about the current state of the kid's pathways or their degree of development."

I took that in. The idea that most children had arcane pathways wasn't as much of a surprise as it might have once been. The rebalancing of potency and rakkuhr on Earth was awakening latent "magical" talents and senses that had been dormant for millennia—and had nothing to do with Lord ancestry the way summoning ability did. And since kids were still developing, physically and mentally, those once-dormant talents and senses were more likely to emerge, and with far more potential. "You said first cut. What comes next?"

He lifted a shoulder in a shrug. "A bunch of meticulous assessments to determine if they'd do right by the arcane, if you know what I mean."

"Like, if a kid is a little shit, Kadir's not going to hand him magic to be a better bully."

"In the broadest sense, yeah. And it knocks out about half of the candidates."

Another uncomfortable thought surfaced. "Does Kadir have to wipe the memories of the ones who don't make the cut? Messing with their minds like that would suck."

"Oh *hell* no," he said firmly. "Now that he's on Earth, he sometimes assesses in person, like in the video you saw, but he mostly works from the Between, usually near a valve. The kids are never the wiser."

Still creepy, but not *as* creepy. "Okay, he picks a bunch of kids, then he cuts the ones he feels would abuse the power or whatever. How the hell does he approach training the ones who remain?"

Pellini shook his head. "Not so fast. For those still in the running, Kadir delves much deeper. Not saying he looks into their heart for goodness and light or that kind of shit. But more like whether the arcane would actually benefit them, or be too much stress, or freak them out. He only proceeds with those he's certain would thrive and flourish with it. Once those assessments are complete, there are only a scant handful that he deems, er, satisfactory on all levels." He shrugged. "It's a long game, though."

"Are the kids still unaware at this point?"

"Yep, though this is when Mr. Sparkly finally starts to interact. First, it's through dreams from the Between then, eventually, in the Between itself. The few kids who make it to in-person assessments tend to be excited and eager. But if they aren't, he gently blurs their Kadir memories into a dream rather than wiping."

"And he hasn't done anything to coerce them?" I asked, frowning.

Pellini spread his hands. "He just unobtrusively evaluates the fuck out of them. No manipulation. No psychic suggestions. Nothing like that."

I cocked my head. "Do you trust him?"

He went quiet for a moment. "Maybe if I hadn't gone through the process myself, the whole thing would be a lot tougher to swallow. But between my own experience plus confirmation from Paul, yeah, I trust that he doesn't manipulate the kids into wanting to work with him."

"Fair enough." I exhaled. "Once he has an eager and viable student, Kadir then goes ahead and forms the pathways?"

He looked up as if seeking the right words. "It's not like digging a ditch. More like training ivy to climb a trellis. Kadir guides development but doesn't force it. He moves at the pace of the child. Allows them to determine the scope of their growth while offering support and training." He shook his head. "I'm not explaining this very well, but I think you get the gist. Just trust me that Kadir would never do anything to harm a kid."

I met his eyes. "But he harmed you."

Pellini recoiled as if I'd slapped him. "When he essentially abandoned me, it hurt like all fuck, but I was twenty-four, not a child. I *chose* the path, back when I was a kid *and* when I was nearly an adult. Even after everything that's happened, and knowing all I do now, I'd choose it again."

I toyed with a pine needle. Kadir started visiting when Pellini was four and continued for three years, until it became too difficult to reach him. A decade later, Kadir returned and trained him in the Between every three months for seven years. Then one day, he showed up and ripped an arcane implant from Pellini's chest—an implant likely meant to keep him off some enemy's radar—and told him to hide. No other explanation.

It had devastated Pellini, and for the next twenty years he felt the keen loss of his mentor, and wondered what Kadir had found lacking in him.

Still, I couldn't deny Pellini seemed to be at peace with it all after recently reuniting with Kadir. He was thriving. "I believe you," I said. "And you're right, you weren't a kid when he hurt you. Circumstances were dire, and, in his way, he was still protecting you."

I'd witnessed how protective Kadir was of children on more than one occasion, though it still bugged me that he had to start training them so young. How could they know what they were getting into? But at least he seemed to try his best to do no harm.

A chill went through me. For summoners in the last century, harm was inherent. The heartless machinations of bad actors like Xharbek, fake Katashi, and the Mraztur had wrecked families and twisted lives. It had happened to me. To Tessa. To Idris. They made *sure* we became summoners.

My talent had been cultivated, but not in a way I'd have chosen. What if I'd had a summoner version of Mr. Sparkly to help develop my skills from the time I was little, rather than being forcibly crammed into someone else's mold? An unexpected wave of longing and envy struck me. Envy of Pellini, of all people, because as insane as it sounded, Kadir had nurtured and trained him with genuine care.

I took several slow, deep breaths to get my emotions under control before I spoke again. "When you were a kid, did Kadir have any other protégés?"

"Yeah, though I've never met any of them, other than Olson, and he's older than me by at least a decade. I don't know if there are any others still around who retained skills."

I gaped at him. "Hold on. *Senator* Olson is a Kadir Kid?"

"Yep." He grinned at my reaction. "And fully aware of it."

"Holy shit." I tried to picture Senator Olson working the arcane and failed miserably. "That's, uh, unexpected."

Pellini laughed and tunneled a hand through his hair. "That's one word for it. You do remember we're talking about Kadir, right? It's only ever been me, Paul, Dominic, and the housekeeper with him, er, where we're living. But Kadir can teleport now, and spends a lot of time in the Between, so who knows?" He sobered. "That said, I asked him once if there were other older students besides Olson, and all Kadir would say was that they'd been suppressed for their own safety."

"Did you ask him what the danger was?"

"Yup. He didn't want any other lord—or demahnk—to scoop them up. Apparently he also placed implants to help shield them if they get scanned."

That made sense. The demonic lords were already ruthless enough about getting their hands on anyone having the chops and genetics to be a summoner, and they'd likely be just as eager to control someone with well-honed non-summoning skills. Kadir would hardly want his protégés at risk of going through the kind of shit I'd experienced.

"And Kadir wouldn't simply outright kill them," I said, "even if they could end up being a danger to him."

"Even after they're grown, they're still *his* students. Killing them would be a last resort, and only to protect them. He doesn't kill the innocent."

I pursed my lips. "He almost let you die after the Jontari gutted you."

"That's different."

I let out a disbelieving snort but wasn't going to push the argument. "But here you are, a Kadir Kid all grown up."

"And you're fucking stuck with me." He laughed.

"Or vice versa!" I grinned. "At any rate, there's certainly been a lot of obvious arcane activity on Earth in the past half a year, so I wonder if it's nudged any suppressed protégés still out there."

"Maybe?" He shrugged. "Kadir just might have more people like me waiting in the wings. An army of middle-aged folks ready to tackle the great interdimensional menace."

"Oh fuck me. More Pellinis."

"You're going to feel really dumb when the Pellini Patrol saves the world."

Chapter 17

Pellini and I returned to the conference room for the debrief and barely had our butts in chairs when Jill and Ashava filed in with Roma close on their heels. Jill leaned in and gave Pellini a quick hug. "It's good to see you."

He gave her a quick hug in return. "Thanks. You, too." Then he gave Ashava a smile. "I hear you've been kicking ass and taking names."

She shrugged. "I'm *trying* to," she said and flicked a telling glance in my direction.

I kept my expression even. "Where's Bryce?"

Roma hooked a thumb over one shoulder. "On the porch, arguing with Szerain about repair priorities."

I grimaced. "Do I need to intervene?"

"Nah. Ronda's out there, too. She'll set them both straight."

She would indeed. And it wasn't long before Bryce and Szerain entered, neither looking pleased.

Once everyone was settled around the table, Bryce went right into details of the attack on the compound. There was no doubt it was coordinated with the geckoid callout and ambush of Boudreaux, with the likely goals of not only capturing Ashava, but also to gain control of the nexus and capture Szerain—and by extension, his essence blade.

Regarding the callout, I shared my suspicion that the geckoids had been purposefully driven through the rift, then gave a rundown of the sequence of events, including the initial deployment at the retirement village, Boudreaux's capture, the rescue, my request for Kadir's intervention, and his revelation that a trap had been laid for Ashava. I glossed over the reason I didn't call for her, merely saying the extent of her healing ability was unknown and time had been of the utmost essence.

"I absolutely *could* have healed him!" Ashava insisted, with more than a touch of belligerence.

I gave her my most placid look. "Regardless, it's a good thing I wasn't sure, right? Or you'd be with Jesral right now, and I doubt he wanted you over for a tea party."

She slumped back in her seat.

"But I'm glad your healing skills are up to par, since Boudreaux could use more help, as do several other people."

"I *just* got back from the infirmary," Ashava muttered.

Jill gave her hand a squeeze.

Roma was up next and listed the—thankfully few and minor—injuries suffered by various Alpha Squad members, then Bryce followed with an injury report for compound personnel, as well as the newly minted plan for repairs to the perimeter defenses, both physical and arcane. The main addition to the arcane defenses would be arcane "boulders"—like the one at the north horse farm entrance—to be positioned and ready for deployment as needed at the three south gates.

"That covers the debriefs," I said. "Pellini, you have something you wanted to discuss?"

"I'll cut right to the chase," Pellini said. "We need another summoner. I can handle a lot of arcane tasks, but I don't have the genetics or whatever that a summoner does."

My wariness skyrocketed, especially with this pronouncement coming so soon after my discussion with Szerain regarding Kadir. "Who are y'all trying to summon? And what do you mean, 'another summoner'?" I sucked in a breath. "Oh shit. I forgot Kadir took Asher to the demon realm after the showdown at the Farouche Plantation." Aaron Asher was a summoner who'd worked for Jesral and the Mraztur, and had been involved in the ritual murder of Idris Palatino's sister. "Are you shitting me? You're working with that slimy—"

"Nooooo. Christ, not Asher." Pellini snorted. "Trust me, that motherfucker is *dead*. I wasn't there for it, but apparently Kadir was beyond livid at how Asher fucked with the arcane node at the Farouche Plantation. Not to mention, he was an asshole, complicit in more than one murder, and a general waste of oxygen."

I frowned. "Then what summoner do you already have?"

"Rasha Hash ummm—"

"Rasha Hassan Jalal al-Khouri," I said with relief. I'd last seen her housed in a dimensional pocket inside the column in Mzatal's realm.

"Yeah, that's her. Apparently Mzatal made arrangements a while back for Kadir to acquire and protect her in case certain events came to pass—which I guess they did. But right now she's hip deep working on a special project for Kadir."

That was interesting. Mzatal was already under Ilana's control by the time I saw Rasha in the column, so apparently he'd made those arrangements quite some time in advance. Another example of Mzatal's tendency to think and plan many moves ahead.

"Okay, but who are y'all trying to summon?"

"No one," Pellini said. "I swear. There's this machine, kind of like a virtual reality game system. The thing needs a tech operator and an arcane user for basic functions, plus a lord for full capabilities. I tried to use it with Dom, but got really sick and—"

"You need a summoner for a *video game*?" I asked, incredulous.

He shook his head. "No, it's not actually a game. More like a game console type device that integrates with, er, that taps into, kinda, the Between, where Kadir spends a lot of time . . . Damn it. The tech is beyond me. Hey, will you please explain the Between Machine?" he said to the air, a.k.a. Paul, who was surely listening in via his ability to tap into feeds of all kinds.

The room fell silent. Bryce and I exchanged a narrow-eyed look. Szerain folded his arms over his chest, expression full of suspicion. Jill jotted notes on the back of a DIRT report. Ashava did her best to look bored, while Roma remained thoughtful.

A few seconds later Pellini's phone buzzed with a text. "Paul says he needs a minute."

Video conference with Paul? That would cheer Bryce up. Thankfully the delay gave me a needed moment to gather my thoughts. Kadir wanted a summoner. Yet even if we agreed, there was one big problem: Tessa was in no shape to be of any help to them or anyone else, and the various DIRT summoners were already spread thin, which meant the only other available summoner was Elinor. And I knew—via my own shared memories with her—that she had more than a few negative feelings toward Kadir.

I startled when Paul and another man appeared by the wall of TVs. Bryce let out a surprised curse, then came out of his chair fast enough to send it rolling back several feet. Paul grinned and ran to Bryce, who caught him in a tight embrace. Paul had filled out a bit, added some muscle to his chest and shoulders.

The other man—Paul's boyfriend Dominic, I assumed—stood back and grinned, clearly at ease despite having just teleported into a room full of strangers. He was taller than Paul by half a foot, and perhaps a few years older as well. Black, clean-shaven, hair in neat, chin-length dreadlocks. Good-looking. Nice smile.

Bryce finally released Paul and gave him a sweeping assessment. "Missed you," he said, voice gruff. "You're looking good."

Paul grinned. "I missed you, too." Then he grabbed Bryce's hand and tugged him forward. "This is Dominic. Dom, this is Bryce."

Dominic smiled and shook Bryce's hand. "It's great to finally meet you," he said, voice a pleasant baritone with a distinct south London accent. "Paul talks about you all the time."

Bryce gave a curt nod, acting for all the world like an overprotective dad. "Pleasure's all mine," he said with barely disguised suspicion. "How did you two meet?"

Paul laughed. "Dude! This is CosmicRazor—my old gaming buddy! I'll give you the gist of how we're together, though, because it ties in to why we need a summoner."

I was still in the dark about the gaming connection, but realization dawned on Bryce's face, and the protective dad vibe eased. Paul and Dominic took a pair of empty seats.

"It all started when Jesral needed a computer engineer and programmer several months ago to spearhead his plot to access the Between," Paul said. "Jesral knew about my talent and expertise from my time with Farouche, and so Dom became his target, tagged through his association with me. *Years* of gaming. Turned out Dom had the skillset Jesral needed. Boom! Entrapped and enslaved."

My semi-retired Detective Brain gave me a hard poke. This had to be Jesral's secret project Tessa told me about, with Dominic being the arcane-talented operator he lost. And since Dominic clearly wasn't with Jesral anymore, I couldn't help but think that maybe he was that someone. But if so, how did Kadir manage to snatch him away?

"Jesral sucks," Dominic said matter-of-factly. "The bellend had me snatched right in front of my house. Kept me in an actual coffin for *days*. And I'm claustrophobic."

I grimaced. "I'm sorry you went through that."

He let out a deep sigh. "As you can imagine, I was compliant once they let me out. Especially since they kept the coffin in my work area."

"Jesral's way to minimize the need for manipulation," Szerain said. "Effective, but cruel."

Paul nodded. "Kadir says there was only light manipulation, mostly to keep Dom from trying to contact authorities or dark web associates. Deeper compliance manipulation might have compromised Dom's skills."

"Apart from the existential terror aspect," Dom said, "the work was all right the first couple of weeks. Surveillance, data access, bog-standard deep hacks. I dealt mostly with Tsuneo during that time. But everything changed once Jesral was ready to launch the Between Machine project. Tsuneo's a right turd but a saint compared to him. Jesral was around more, didn't abide setbacks, and was a . . ."

Paul finished for him. "A physically and emotionally abusive asshole. Despite the fact that Dom successfully created new tech and cobbled old to do the near impossible."

"That about sums it up," Dominic said. "Ten weeks of hell to finish the project—but it worked. Fast forward to about three months ago. I was operating the system with Tsuneo and Jesral, doing a really deep hack into what turned out to be Kadir and Paul's system. I kept running into obstacles, as if someone was blocking and rerouting as fast as I could get through them. But then I found a way in."

Paul grinned. "Because I let you in."

"I know that now!" He smiled and gave Paul's hand a squeeze. "Anyway, next thing I knew *something* grabbed me—"

"By the balls," Paul added helpfully.

Dominic snorted a laugh. "Yeh, me balls and I were dragged to someplace entirely different. A bloody terrifying man crouched over me"—a shudder went through him—"and I figured I was about to die."

"You were!" Paul said. "But I was there, too, stunned that the enemy hacker was my *Red Star Sploding* gamer buddy Cosmic-Razor. I asked Kadir to please delve and figure out what the hell was going on. He found and removed Jesral's recall ward and held off on delivering a gruesome, ball-crushing execution."

Dominic gave an enthusiastic thumbs up. "Lord Kadir recruited me instead of killing me, and I spilled everything I knew about Jesral's machine."

"The machine was bad news for Kadir," Pellini said, "since the Between is where he's most at home. He navigates the flows as easy as breathing, and apart from the occasional demahnk, he's had it mostly to himself for eons. Then this machine comes along and makes it possible for others to, not exactly *navigate*, but access the Between."

"The sparkly place," I said. "I was there earlier today when Kadir and I, ah, negotiated the terms for Boudreaux's healing." I sucked in a breath. "That's how he's able to teleport! He uses Sparkleville!"

"Well, duh," Ashava said. "You know *I* teleport, and you could have just *asked* me."

"Yes and yes," I said. "My brain just now connected the dots, though. It would be great to—"

Ashava rolled her eyes in an exaggerated "whatever" expression and vanished.

"—get your input on all of this."

"Or not," Jill said, wincing. "Sorry, Kara. She's been super prickly lately. Do you need me here?"

"I always need you, but she needs you more right now, mama bear."

"I'm off then. Good to meet you, Dom. See y'all later." She hurried out.

I tapped the table. "Tessa told me Jesral's hacker got kidnapped, and the various successors haven't been up to snuff. He resorted to a workaround plan but is still hunting his original operator." I gave them a quick summary of Tessa's intel.

Dominic swallowed hard. Paul took his hand, expression fierce. "He won't get you back."

"Thanks, love," Dominic said with a crooked smile. "But, here's the thing." He glanced around the table. "My skills are amazing, but there are other computer geniuses and hackers out there just as amazing or more so. Jesral still has the machine I made for him, but the hitch is that the operator also needs the ability to perceive and tweak the arcane. As Tessa reported, finding one person to fit his needs is near impossible. The dual operator workaround was passably successful day before yesterday, but I don't see that arrangement being sustainable, and he won't give up the search."

I tugged both hands through my hair. "He wants Dominic back, but he'll take whoever he can get. Can y'all put out some kind of warning on message boards or something? Like, 'Hey, don't answer this job listing.' Or 'Avoid this smarmy fucker as if your life depends on it.'"

"Job market is uncertain," Dominic said, "so people might ignore a warning." He shrugged. "But it can't hurt. Especially if it can save one person from going through what I did."

"Good enough," I said.

Szerain's expression darkened. "With our luck, he'll find someone who fully aligns with his agenda."

"And while Szerain's maintaining a cheery positive outlook," I said and flashed him a teasing grin, "I'm still wondering why Kadir needs a Between Machine if he can already access Sparkleville?"

"Kadir doesn't need it for *access*," Paul said. "But because Jesral has invasive tech, we still need counter technology to monitor and block anything he tries. We were even thinking of building one for the compound here, but we don't have the resources or another operator."

"How hard is it to make one of these machines?" I asked.

Dominic snorted and glanced at Paul. "Tell her about the phosphorescent snail resin that's a vital component of the arcane insulation."

Paul groaned. "Let's just say it involved learning far more about the inside of a giant carnivorous demon snail's asshole than any human should ever know. Not to mention how hard it is to get to said demon snail's lair in the first place."

"Gotcha," I said. "Can't exactly pop into the local Buy More and pick up the needed parts."

"The good news is that it's just as hard for Jesral," Paul said, "and we suspect his machine was damaged when Mzatal blasted the dimensional pocket. Not just anyone can build or repair one of these things. Dom has serious hardware skills as well as the ability to integrate esoteric arcane aspects."

"Okay, so Jesral has a roadblock," I said, "but so does Kadir. I gather Pellini tried to operate the machine and failed—"

"Spectacularly," Paul confirmed, then snickered when Pellini muttered something about throwing up stuff he'd eaten three weeks before. "But through no fault of his own."

I nodded. "Because he's not a summoner."

"Right." He spread his hands. "Jesral kept Dom in the dark

about that aspect. Hence Pellini's puke fest and our current need for a summoner."

"Well, the only one available is Elinor," I said. "However, I have to warn you that she has an unpleasant history with Kadir, and I can't and won't make her go with you."

"Oh, absolutely!" Paul said with a fervent nod. "Full willingness or not at all. But could we at least ask her?"

"Lemme see if she's free." I shot off a quick text to tell her Pellini and Paul wanted to talk to her about possibly helping them and Kadir with something, and that she was under zero obligation to agree to it. Though Elinor had never actually met Pellini or Paul in the flesh, she had some familiarity with them from briefings and, vicariously, from when her essence was attached to mine.

She replied with <Willing to listen. Be there in a jiffy> followed by a dizzying array of random emojis.

I relayed the message to the others even as Jill returned with a non-committal shrug that either meant *Ashava is fine now* or *The world is about to end and there's nothing we can do about it*. Or both.

Fillion jumped up onto the table in front of me, and Pellini recoiled. "Give me a freaking heart attack, why don't you?" he growled, staring at the silver-furred, bat-winged cat.

Laughing, I gave Fillion careful skritches behind the ears and wings. "Ground zero mutagen for the win! This is Fillion. Squig took up with Rhyzkahl, weirdly enough." A wisp of a thought about ground zero tried to poke its way out of my brain but evaporated before I could catch it.

Fillion gave a *brrrump* sound and trotted to Pellini.

"Petting him on the head and back is safest," I said with a grin.

He gave the cat a cautious head scratch, but then seemed a little put out when Fillion abandoned him and trotted to Paul. To my surprise and amusement, Paul *melted* over the cat, murmuring gooey babytalk and giving him enthusiastic petting and wing rubs. Fillion happily returned the affection, purring like a monster truck as he bumped his head aggressively against Paul's.

"You should see the caterpillar-dog. She's . . ." I trailed off as the previous ground zero thought finally wormed its way to the surface of my brain and triggered a cascade of other realizations.

"Kara?" Pellini frowned at me. "What's wrong?"

"Ground zero. The valve explosion last summer is what made the Spires emerge. Kadir's Earthgate." Sweat pricked the small of my back. "Dominic, when Jesral had you abducted, had the demon incursions started already?"

"Yeh, but only a couple of weeks prior."

I bit back a curse. "Which means Jesral has been operating on Earth for at least six months, probably starting right after the valve explosion."

Paul's brow furrowed. "But Kadir has only been able to use his gate for about four months—oh shit."

Szerain growled something rude under his breath.

Jill looked totally baffled. "Can someone please explain?"

"Kadir can teleport," I said, "but only from place to place on the same world. In order to travel from the demon realm to Earth or vice versa, he has to use his Earthgate—the Spires. And no way would he ever allow Jesral access to it."

Szerain's scowl deepened. "And the Jontari would *never* allow Jesral to use the rifts to travel between the worlds, which means he was either being summoned—which is pretty dicey with all the rift interference—or, more likely, he's been getting demahnk aid to do his interplanetary travel for far longer than we realized."

"Exactly," I said. "And I'm sure before we scattered his ass, Xharbek helped ferry Jesral back and forth. But Jesral didn't start his Between Machine project until after the Spires emerged, and I think it's because he'd never thought to factor the Earthgates into any of his planning. After all, they went dormant millennia ago." I took a deep breath. "But then Kadir's gate popped up, and a shiny new option presented itself. And now I think Jesral is planning to do something really extreme—and destructive—in order to activate his own gate."

Pellini muttered something foul. "That's the last thing we need."

"Son of a bitch," I said, sitting up straighter as more realizations crowded in. "Paul, you once told me that even when the Earthgates were active only humans could pass through them, right?"

"Yup. Kadir is only able to use his gate because he tweaked it via the Between. We basically did a backdoor hack on it. The other lords can't use his gate, though Kadir gave Mzatal temporary access a while ago." He let out a very un-Paul-like expletive.

"*That's* why Jesral needs the Between Machine! Kadir and I had to work in tandem to do the backdoor hack: he did the arcane adjustments, and I did the interdimensional flow recalibration. It was tricky, delicate work, and if either of us had misaligned a single aspect, the hack wouldn't have worked."

"But it's conceivable that Jesral and his new machine operator could pull that kind of hack off?" I asked.

Paul grimaced. "Well, yeah."

Jill shook her head. "But if Jesral has demahnk taxicabs, why does he even need an Earthgate? He already has a way to travel back and forth."

I blinked. "That's a good question, Jill." A low throbbing headache began at the base of my skull. "Shit. Xharbek was willing to sacrifice Earth to stabilize the demon realm, by dumping rakkuhr through the valve at ground zero—and he'd have used other valves, too, if we hadn't stopped him. But it was a bad concept because destabilizing the valve system fucks with both worlds. If he could rapid-dump *potency* via a gate instead, that would spare the demon realm, at least for now."

"Billions on Earth would die," Szerain murmured, looking stricken.

"That's Jesral's fucking plan," I said. "Raise a gate—or several, if he can swing it—and stabilize the demon realm at the expense of Earth. That kind of sudden influx would make the disasters and instability of the last half a year look like a romantic stroll along the beach. And the bad demahnk are behind it because the Ekiri are returning and they need to have the demon realm cleaned up. Ideally they'd save both worlds, but they're out of time and we're more expendable."

Roma scowled. "Well, shit."

"The other lords need to know what Jesral is up to and what's at stake," I said. "Szerain, can you call a conclave?"

A whisper of pain shimmered briefly over his face. "Since I'm kiraknikahl, I can't. And even if that weren't the case, my realm's a wasteland."

I winced. Szerain was considered an oathbreaker, kiraknikahl, for attacking his then-ptarl, Xharbek. Szerain's actions had been more than justified, but the rest of the demahnk and the other lords didn't see it that way. "Maybe Rhyzkahl—" I shook my head. "No, he doesn't have a realm either." Not since the Sky Reaper Jontari clan overran it during his imprisonment in my back yard. My gaze went to Paul, who was still petting Fillion. "Any chance Kadir might be willing to call a conclave?"

His expression grew thoughtful.

The conference room abruptly vanished, replaced by Sparkleville, a.k.a. the Between. I managed to keep my yelp of shock to a mere squeak, but I couldn't do anything about the mad pounding of my heart. Sparkly-Kadir stood before me, hands clasped behind his back in an unsettling echo of Mzatal's habitual pose.

Even in sparkle-form it was clear he was disturbed and somber. "You are correct that a conclave is needed. However, I will not host it." He held up a hand when I opened my mouth to argue. "Elofir is the far shrewder choice."

He was right. Elofir held status among the lords as a trusted mediator, though a few also regarded him with contempt for his pacifistic nature. But the thought of facing Elofir made me wince. Our last conversation had consisted of my raging at him for destroying the corpse of Bikturk, a Jontari reyza who Mzatal had killed with essence blades in Siberia. Demons slain on Earth typically discorporeated with a chance of returning to the demon realm, but the essence blades prevented that process— meaning there'd been a rare demon corpse available for research. I was all for humans figuring out how to better defend ourselves from demons, but Elofir had opted to protect the demons. We had both been right . . . and wrong. Maybe it would be good to have a chance to face him and clear the air.

And maybe cutting out chocolate donuts would be good for my overall health, but that didn't mean I was eager to do it.

"I have no way to contact him," I said, truthfully enough. "Would you?"

He inclined his head. "I will make the request."

The sparkles vanished, and I was back in my chair in the conference room. No one seemed to have noticed I'd been elsewhere, except for Szerain, who regarded me with a shrewd expression, and Paul whose gaze stayed on me.

I cleared my throat. "Kadir agrees about the need for a conclave and is going to ask Elofir if he'll call for it."

Ding-dop-ding

Bryce flushed and yanked his phone out to silence it. "Sorry."

Paul and Dominic exchanged a look and burst out laughing.

"What's so funny?" I asked.

Paul grinned. "Pro Krasta Nation. That's our game. I mean, Dom and I created it."

Bryce straightened, beaming like a proud dad. "No shit? That's amazing! I love this damn thing."

"Yeah, it's gotten pretty popular," Paul said.

"How popular?" I asked with a smile.

"Over thirty million downloads and counting."

Bryce coughed. "Holy shit. Three bucks a pop, which means you've made nearly a hundred million off this thing?"

"That's gross revenue, but yeah."

"You two created a *game* while also doing a ton of deep and intense work with Kadir?" I leaned back in my chair, eyes on them. "What aren't you telling us?"

Paul gave a wry smile. "Busted. The game is indeed a game, but . . . Okay, have you ever heard of the 'SETI at Home' project?"

"Uh, no?"

Jill spoke up. "I have. Search for Extra Terrestrial Intelligence. It used distributed computing to analyze signal data."

"Oh, yes, I understand completely now," I said. "I mean, except for almost every word in that sentence."

Pellini grinned. "Don't feel bad. I didn't have a clue either until these two chucklefucks explained it to me. Basically people would download a computer program that then ran in the background, using idle processor power. At its peak there were about a quarter million participants, which gave the SETI project an insane amount of computing oomph."

"Ah." I cocked an eyebrow at Paul and Dom. "And you have *thirty* million people participating in something similar?"

"Pretty much," Paul replied, way too cheerfully. "Integrates location data, too. And before you get scowly, I promise that no one's personal data is ever compromised. We don't access it at all."

Jill's eyes narrowed. "But what are you using all that processing power for?"

"We're monitoring and stabilizing the electronic and quasi-arcane flows, in much the same way the lords each use their plexus to monitor and stabilize the demon realm flows. With Jesral poking around in the Between, we need those extra resources to stay on top of things."

Jill's expression didn't ease. "Isn't that awfully shady to do without the user's permission?"

Dominic spoke up. "A valid concern. Technically they *have* given permission because there's a bullet point in the terms and conditions that covers network play and use of the phone or device's system." He held up a finger as she opened her mouth to protest. "And yes, I know not a single person ever reads the terms and conditions. However, we honestly don't want to screw anyone over, so we coded in a couple of safeguards. The first blocks data overage fees incurred due to our game's usage. Technically, it screws over the service providers, but it's a micro drop in the revenue bucket for them and hasn't raised a single red flag. We also included code that protects PKN users against data scraping, spyware, malware, and similar anti-privacy bull-shit used by other apps."

Jill relaxed at that. "All right. That sounds fair. It's still shady," she added with a wry smile, "but it seems you have the best of intentions and are mitigating possible harm."

Dominic's posture eased a bit, and I realized he'd been nervous about having to defend the ethical aspect to Jill. Oddly, that made me like and trust him even more. This was akin to meeting the boyfriend's parents for the first time, except there were half a dozen parents, and they were all carrying guns. And some could do magic.

Paul smiled. "Thanks for being so understanding. We went back and forth on how to best handle that stuff—hang on." His gaze went distant for several heartbeats, then he refocused on us.

"Elofir is willing to call the conclave," he said. "And, considering the gravity of the situation, he's calling it for two days from now." He paused again, head cocked. "Also, Elofir says human allies are invited and welcome, as this affects their world as much as it does the demon realm."

Relief had me sagging in my seat, both at the news of the conclave and at the open invitation for humans. The latter felt very much like an olive branch from him, as well as a thoughtful and practical consideration that might never have occurred to a different lord. Kudos to Kadir for the wisdom to tag Elofir.

"There is one more thing to consider," Szerain said. "Whoever goes to the demon realm must have their thoughts shielded against lord or demahnk prying."

Well, shit. Only a demahnk could do that level of shielding for a human. Zakaar had placed mental shielding for me several months ago to deter Xharbek, but was obviously in no condition to do so for anyone else right now.

"Maybe Helori would be willing to help," I said. Though first I needed to figure out a way to contact him. Damn it.

Elinor tapped on the door frame and stepped in, cheeks flushed from the cold. "Sorry, I came as quickly as I could."

"Your timing's perfect." I looked from face to face. "Okay, we have a lot to do in a short amount of time. If there's nothing else to discuss, let's adjourn and start prepping for a demon realm trip." I motioned Elinor in as Jill, Szerain, and Roma headed out.

Bryce pulled Paul out of his chair and into a hug. "I've got shit to take care of, but I'll see you soon."

"Yes, you will!" Paul said, grinning as he returned the fierce embrace.

Bryce released Paul, gave Dominic a short nod, then exited.

Dominic murmured something under his breath that sounded a lot like, "He's almost as scary as Kadir," which made Paul laugh.

Elinor settled into a seat and listened attentively as Paul and Dominic explained the Between Machine, how it interacted with Sparkleville, their fear that Jesral would use it to both attack Kadir and raise his Earthgate, and their hope to thwart Jesral with the machine they'd built with Kadir.

She was quiet for a moment after they finished. "I'm sorry," she finally said, deep uncertainty on her face, "but I don't think I'm the right person for this."

"Kadir isn't the same as he was when you knew him centuries ago," I put in. "With Paul as his essence-bond mate, he's not as . . ." I groped for how to say he wasn't as creepy and weird as he used to be, without actually coming right out and saying it.

"Unsettling," Paul said with a laugh. "Hair-raising. Scary."

Dominic snorted. "He's still terrifying when he wants to be, bruv."

Elinor blinked then let out a small laugh. "Oh. Well, that's quite good to hear, but you see, Kadir isn't the problem." She bit her lip. "You say this machine is like a video game. However, I've never played a video game. I'm afraid I simply don't have the skills you need."

Instead of looking disappointed, Paul's eyes lit up. "There's a VR game system in the living room."

Pellini started laughing. Elinor looked baffled. And then Paul and Dominic practically dragged her into the living room to show her how to play.

I was tempted to follow them, but I had too many other things on my mind to spare focus on killing aliens or stealing cars or whatever they decided to start her on. Instead, I headed to the kitchen and stared out the window at my back yard. And the nexus. And the rift. And the grove tree. So much at stake.

Michael stood in the center of the nexus, right in the middle of the super shikvihr, his arms pushing and pulling seemingly nothing as he directed distant dirt-moving golems. Tessa sat with her back against Rho, her cocoon of rainbow-colored blankets bright against the stark white of the trunk. Where did she even find those? Most blankets around here were either DIRT maroon or olive drab.

I felt someone come up behind me. Szerain.

"I'm going to ask Rho if they can contact Helori," I said. "He might be willing to shield the thoughts of the humans in our party. If not, it'll just be you and me going. Far too dangerous for everyone involved otherwise."

"A solid plan."

I watched Michael do his golem-dance for another moment.

"And I need to do the tenth ring. Now." I hadn't even been consciously considering it, but the instant the words left my mouth I knew I was right.

"Agreed," he said, somber.

Tessa stretched and climbed to her feet, then looked up into the tree canopy and gave a rare smile before draping the blankets over her shoulders like a bright and happy cape. She returned to the house and, without saying a word, folded me into a hug—which I returned with relief. After a few seconds she smiled up at me then continued on to the guest room.

"I think she's doing better?" I murmured to Szerain.

"She is," he said, to my relief. Another knot of worry began to loosen within me.

"I wonder if Rho warned her I was about to do stuff on the nexus?"

"If so, Rho agrees you need the tenth ring." He exhaled. "I'm sure it's difficult for Tessa to be around the arcane. And that discomfort and unease will probably remain with her for some time. She's dealing with a considerable amount of shame and guilt, not to mention struggling to figure out her own identity.

But Rho is good for her and will help her find her own way to healing."

I smiled a bit crookedly. "Weirdest therapist ever."

His eyes crinkled. "But you have to admit, Rho's a great listener!"

Chapter 18

Once upon a long time past—which actually wasn't even two years ago—I'd been absolutely certain that working the arcane took all sorts of preparation, purification, special garb, implements, and other accoutrements. I'd been taught this bogus dependence by Katashi/Xharbek via Tessa—who'd been heinously manipulated and coerced to do so. Xharbek, and later the Mraztur, had groomed me so that my arcane pathways were wide open but constrained and controllable, leaving me ready to be molded into a weaponized summoner via the Rowan construct in order to further their goals. They didn't need me to be a good summoner. They simply needed to make sure the mental pathways were properly formed. In fact, it was better for them if I was a weak and ineffectual practitioner, one who was dependent on tools and specific clothes and pointless ritual—and thus easier to subvert and use.

Assholes.

Yeah, I was still pretty salty about all that.

Of course, I knew better now, thanks to Mzatal. It was perfectly fine, even beneficial, to engage in certain practices as an aid to focus. The key was to recognize them for what they were so they wouldn't become crutches and impediments. Over the many months I spent training with him in the demon realm, along with the past half a year of battling demonic incursions, I'd confirmed that the only tools I absolutely *had* to have were my attitude and willingness to commit. And the only preparation I needed was to put one foot in front of the other and join—or start—the fight.

In this particular instance I added "check the outside temperature" to my preparation. Even though Tessa had been bundled in blankets only a few minutes earlier, given the nature of rift-influenced weather, there was an even chance temps had either warmed up to the seventies or plummeted to sub-zero.

A few degrees below freezing. Not too awful, considering. I tugged a hoodie over my thermal shirt, pulled on a cap and gloves, then headed out to the nexus, boots crunching on frost-tipped grass. A bright flare of light at the main gate drew my sharp attention, and it took me a few seconds to realize it was Walter, already hard at work with his welding equipment to repair damage from the attack.

Above, the two Jontari reyza bugled and roared in a spar, and the growl of chainsaws, power tools, and accompanying shouts made me want to go right back inside and bury my head under a pillow.

Despite the chill in the air, Michael sat cross-legged in the center of the nexus, the circle of the super shikvihr drifting lazily around him. But now, his hands rested on his knees rather than swishing through the air directing distant golems. Two of the cats, Granger and Cake, lounged on the slab not far from the rift, likely soaking up the scant heat that radiated from it, even though it would've made far more sense for them to simply go into the much warmer house. Silly cats. Then again, maybe they liked the feel of the arcane.

Michael wore only a lightweight sweater and no hat. "Hey, buddy!" I called out as I approached, "If you're done with your golems, I need to use the nexus. And you should probably go put on a—" Pleasant warmth enveloped me as I stepped onto the slab. "Whoa, what the heck?"

Michael clambered to his feet, grinning. "Hi, Miss Kara!"

"It's, uh, toasty out here," I said as I scrambled to assess *why*.

"I was pushing dirt with my golems and got *colllld*. I wished I wasn't, and then I wasn't!"

"That's pretty neat! Do you know how it happened?" I suspected the magic sentient tree towering over us had a hand—or branch—in it.

"Nope," he said as he stepped off the nexus. "Wow, it's chilly!"

"Sure is. Better go bundle up if you're going to stay out."

"Okay! Miss Ronda wants help with the big big hole on the horse fence next, but not until she says so."

"Good deal. Anything interesting with the lords recently?" For a while he'd been able to give me a near daily rundown of what he "saw" various lords doing. But in the past few weeks those glimpses had become more and more rare.

He bit his lip. "Everyone is really *really* hard to see. I can't find Jesral or Mzatal even a little bit. Those two are being sneaky, I guess."

"Probably so." I kept the disappointment off my face with effort. "Let me know if you find them later, okay?"

"You got it, Miss Kara!" he called as he trotted toward the house.

As I paced the perimeter of the slab, Granger stretched and let out a *mrow?* Meanwhile, Cake decided it was time to wash his butt.

"I know you two are comfortable, but you're in my way." I gently removed both kitties from the nexus and suffered the wounded looks they shot me before they stalked off.

I stepped through the super shikvihr to the center of the nexus. The welcoming wash of familiar energy served as an intimate reminder of Mzatal and what we could create together. "I miss you, zharkat," I murmured, then sketched a trio of pygahs that infused me with deep calm and enhanced my mental clarity and focus. As the third sigil settled, I had no trouble tuning out the Jontari and construction noise.

With practiced, sweeping gestures, I cleared the slab of stray energies, paying particular attention to the area within the boundary of the super shikvihr where I'd be dancing my new ritual.

Satisfied, I began laying the first ring of the shikvihr, aware that Szerain stood under the grove tree, arms folded and watching my progress. All flowed well until Granger returned as I finished the third ring, and I had to pause to shoo her off the nexus again.

During the fifth, both Granger and Cake sprawled on the slab, this time joined by Dire and Fillion. "You feline shits are damaging my calm," I growled as I removed the little menaces. I heard a snicker from Szerain and gave in to the powerful urge to shoot him the finger.

By the time I danced the intricate seventh ring, his snickering had turned to straight-up howls of laughter as damn near every cat on the compound decided to congregate on the nexus. Bumper eagerly stropped against my legs. Even Fuzzykins wanted a piece of the action. Apparently, chasing Kara's feet was the Best Game Ever.

I let out an inarticulate growl of frustration. "Why do you hate me, you worthless furballs?" The only ones missing were the barn cats, and for all I knew they were on their way.

Szerain wiped away tears as he did his best to level a serious look at me. "Navigating feline distractions on the safety of your home nexus is child's play compared to the full shikvihr initiation on the column. Furthermore, when you have dire need of the shikvihr, it's highly unlikely your adversary will allow you peace and quiet with no interruptions." He stepped close to the edge of the slab, rested his gaze on its inky surface, then raised it to the six completed rings and the partial seventh. "Rhyzkahl was tethered to this nexus for months. That gave you an incredible advantage—a deeper 'lordy sense,' as you put it. Tap into that, Kara. Understand it. Use it. Work around the damn cats. Or incorporate them." He fixed me with a glare. "Finish the fucking rings."

Duly chastised, I gave him a single nod and turned away. I'd engaged the lordy sense four months ago at Ground Zero when I'd completed the eighth ring. And then two months later to get the ninth. I could do it again for the tenth, cats or no cats.

I exhaled slowly and extended my awareness to include the heart of the nexus. The surrounding terrain. Rho. The super shikvihr. Szerain. My sigil scars. The cats. I called to the energy that united all.

The rest of the seventh and the eighth ring flowed smoothly from me as I danced around and over and between the cats. Midway through the ninth I was able to anticipate where the cats would be and adjust accordingly, and by the time I finished the last sigil of the tenth ring, they were an intrinsic part of the choreography.

Exhilarated, I turned in place to take in each sigil, each ring, the whole of the construct. It shimmered deep indigo, subdued, as if holding its breath in anticipation.

Szerain stepped onto the edge of the nexus. "Kara Gillian, may I enter your ritual?"

Fuzzykins headbutted his leg, and I struggled to keep my tone formal. "You are welcome, Lord Szerain."

Smiling, he stepped through the super shikvihr, paused beyond my outermost ring, then joined me in the center, hand on my shoulder. "Inhale slowly."

As I did so, he swept his free hand through each ring, priming them for ignition. "Exhale."

My breath flowed. The sigils danced and sparkled into activation, their spin a perfect harmonic counter to that of the super-shikvihr.

"Well done," Szerain said with a proud smile.

"Y'know, I don't think I could have ever completed that tenth ring if not for the lordy sense." I glanced over at Szerain. "And I don't mean that in an 'Oh Poor Me, I Suck' way, but more like how I could never be a world-class sprinter, even with years of training. I'm a skilled summoner and arcane user, but I think you just have to possess that extra Something."

Szerain lifted his hand and flicked me hard on the forehead.

"OW! What was that for?"

"You still don't get it. At least not consciously. The 'lordy sense' isn't a cheat sheet."

I rubbed my forehead. "Er, okay?" I said, certain I was missing some obvious point.

"The shikvihr is a *foundation*, in every sense of the word. Not only is it the starting point and focus for any major arcane work, but it's also a literal foundation, like one you'd lay before building a house. Or a skyscraper. Support, protection, and even grounding. And different buildings require different foundations."

"But every shikvihr is the same—"

"Are they?" He cocked an eyebrow, challenge in his eyes.

I opened my mouth to retort then closed it, instead forcing myself to carefully consider his words. There was more to laying those rings than simply sketching sigils. I'd understood that much on a subconscious level, but now Szerain was forcing me to pull it to the front of my brain and scrutinize it for myself. I'd seen various lords lay the shikvihr more times than I could count, but I'd never actually analyzed each one. If there'd been minute differences between them, I'd no doubt dismissed those variations as being part of that particular lord's style.

"Yes and no," I finally said. "In doing these last few rings of the shikvihr, it was more that I had a solid understanding of the *reason* for them—thanks to that lordy sense." And with that awareness in mind, I now looked at the ten rings with a new perspective. The basic sigils were indeed the same as in any other shikvihr, but now I understood the subtle differences, akin to the various ways a printed word could be interpreted depending on the font or color.

Szerain smiled. "Now you're getting there."

"Right. And, a foundation can also be a power enhancement. Like how jumping from a solid surface is easier than from a bog." I gave the rings a nudge to put them in a gentle spin. "And, as the foundation is refined and developed, it can be like a gymnastics floor that not only adds emphasis to your power, but provides a bit of a cushion as well."

"Very well done," Szerain murmured. "You needed to understand the shikvihr on your own as well as via the 'borrowed' lordy sense. I knew you'd get there with the right push."

I rubbed my forehead again. "You mean the right painful flick."

"Ah, but clearly my methods produced the desired results." He chuckled. "So, yes, that lordy sense has absolutely given you tremendous advantage and insight. But remember, Mzatal fully expected you to eventually complete the shikvihr initiation atop the column, and I doubt he foresaw someday tethering a demonic lord to a nexus in your back yard in order to make that possible, no matter how far he plans ahead. That said, it's true that only the most talented and intuitive ever complete the full shikvihr, column or no."

"Because you can't *learn* the sigils for the eleventh ring," I said slowly. "The ones who complete the full shikvihr have internalized the core structures, requirements, and purpose for the foundation. Learning, talent, and skills are important, but they'll only get you so far, no matter how hard you work. And internalizing the knowledge and honing the skills until you can dance the rings in your sleep isn't enough. Intuition is paramount."

He beamed and kissed me on the forehead. "I couldn't have said it better myself." His gaze swept to a man wearing a sleek, grey, demon-made coat as he rounded the corner of the house. "And for a rare, precious few, it's innate talent and unmatched drive."

"Idris!" I grinned and raced from the nexus to grab him in a hug.

"Kara!" He laughed and gave me a squeeze. "You got the tenth ring!" His smile widened as he took in my masterpiece.

"She had help," Szerain said with a wicked grin, then pulled out his phone to play a video of me dancing the shikvihr with the cats winding around my feet.

I groaned. "You fucking recorded it. Of course you did. Because you're a jerkface."

Idris laughed. "The best kind. This is epic."

"Epically insane," I said. But even I had to grin at the cats'—and my—antics while I danced around them. I flicked a glance at Szerain. "You've already sent this video to everyone on the compound, haven't you."

"Need you even ask?"

"I hate you. I really hate you."

"I expect no less." He smiled and gave Idris and me a gentle shove toward the house. "Go. Get out of the cold and catch Idris up on the semi-organized chaos that is our life."

Chapter 19

As we stepped through the back door, a wave of cheers, laughter, and shouted curses flowed over us from the living room.

I grinned, pleased that everything seemed to be going well. "Elinor is learning to play video games," I told Idris and gave a quick rundown of the reason for her sudden interest.

"This I gotta see," he said, dropping his duffle in the hallway. We hurried to the living room, arriving just as the occupants erupted in cheers. The screen was flashing a giant blue and yellow BIG BOSS SMACK DOWN!! which I assumed meant she'd beaten the level or won some battle.

Paul and Dom high-fived an ecstatic Elinor, then Giovanni grabbed her in a hug and gave her a big kiss. "I knew you would vanquish those wolf-toad bikers!" he exclaimed, grinning with pride.

"Idris!" Pellini whooped. "Hey, everyone, Idris is back!" He pushed off the couch to greet Idris in one of those back-thumping hugs guys seemed to prefer. Idris laughed and returned the back-thumping.

"Good to see you're still doing the hard work," Idris said with a teasing smile, gesturing to the game controllers.

"Livin' the life!" Pellini said. "Pathetic that Elinor can already kick my ass, though."

Elinor's face glowed with elation. "That was so much fun!"

Paul set his controller by the TV. "You were really quick to pick it up! Just remember, operating the machine isn't like a game. It's pretty grueling."

She winked. "I'm tougher than I look!"

"Does that mean you're willing to go with them?" I asked.

"Yes, but . . ." She grabbed Giovanni's hand. "Gio, do you wish to go? I won't leave you here if such is not your desire."

Giovanni lifted her hand and placed an adorably tender kiss in her palm. "Not even Lord Kadir could keep me from your side, my love."

She beamed, kissed him soundly, then leveled her gaze at Pellini. "Gio will come with me, yes?"

Paul and Pellini quickly reassured her that, yes, of course her lovemate could join them. Elinor pumped her fist in victory, then she and Giovanni dashed off to pack their bags.

As soon as they were out of earshot, I said to Pellini, "I don't know how big a place y'all are living in, but you're going to want to give them a room *far* away from yours."

"Ah, fuck," he groaned.

"Exactly. Frequently and loudly."

That sent Paul and Dom into hysterics. Pellini sighed and muttered something about investing in ear plugs. "We're heading back now," he said, then surprised me with a quick hug. "When Elinor and Gio are ready, just send them to the conference room. Kadir will take it from there. And you know how to reach us if you need anything."

"Yup. Be within earshot of any electronic device."

Paul snickered. "It's funny 'cause it's true."

A heartbeat later Paul, Dom, and Pellini were gone, leaving Idris and me alone amidst the scattered game controllers.

I gathered them up and chucked them into the box by the TV, then tilted my head toward the kitchen. "Want some coffee? Cocoa? Whiskey?"

"Cocoa sounds great," he said and followed me down the hallway. "Though I may take you up on the whiskey later."

"Excellent choice. The cocoa is Jill's recipe, and it's to die for. Figure we can fuel up while we catch up."

He dropped into a chair at the kitchen table, waited while I ladled him a mugful from the crockpot, then took a grateful sip. "Damn, this is good." He let out a pleased sigh. "How's Jill?"

"Doing one hell of a job keeping everything running smoothly here, as well as being a loving mom to Ashava. She and Bryce have been spending more time together, which I think is good for both of them."

"They seem like a solid pair."

"They do, though it's strictly platonic as far as I can tell. I suspect they both want more, whether consciously or not, but I have a feeling Jill is conflicted because of her relationship with Zack/Zakaar. She's been spending a lot of time with Szerain. Szerain-Zakaar. Szerakaar."

Idris grinned. "Zakarain."

"Ooh, that's good."

"How's Bryce holding up with Seretis as Dekkak's prisoner?"

I rubbed my eyes. "It's eating at him, as one would expect. But he's able to get images and impressions from Seretis when he's near the rift, and that helps a lot."

"Seretis is one badass motherfucker," Idris murmured.

"He's an unsung hero, for sure," I said fervently. "His resourcefulness and sacrifice kept Dekkak from turning us all into human-steak tartare, and Xharbek would have flooded Earth with rakkuhr and the arcane mutagen."

Idris was silent for a moment. "Is Tessa here?" he finally asked.

"She's in the guest bedroom, sleeping. It's warded for privacy—ours and hers. She still needs to heal, though Rho seems to be helping her quite a bit."

He wrapped his hands around the mug. "How did she end up here?"

I served myself cocoa and took a seat. "Lemme start from the beginning." And I did, from Tessa's garbled phone call, to the car in the ditch, to the reverse recall implant and mark, to Jesral's appearance with Ssahr and Ilana and Mzatal. Idris's face tightened at that bit of info, but he merely sipped his cocoa and listened without comment.

I then told him about my blade battle with Jesral and how DakDak bit me, and my subsequent out-of-body experience.

"Holy shit. And here I thought I had an exciting time last week when I had to fish my phone from the gut of a *thruggle*."

"Ew. Dude, I'd have gotten a new phone."

"It *was* a new phone!" He snorted. "I fumbled my previous one into a rift only two days before, and no way was I going to requisition another one so soon." He set his mug down, all humor in his expression slipping away. "All right. What's the full story regarding all the stuff Tessa was doing? I assume she's been cleared if she's here in the house."

"She's definitely clear now. She'd been deeply and heavily manipulated for *decades*, starting not long after I was born. When Rhyzkahl got her pregnant, she was removed to Earth and manipulated by Zakaar to think the father was just some guy she'd had a brief fling with. Which had been the MO for lord-kids forever. But, after you were born, Xharbek altered the manipulation to make her believe the baby—you—had died." I paused to get my voice under control. "She never knew about you. That's been confirmed."

Idris visibly struggled with his emotions for a few seconds before he let out a choked sob. I quickly scooted to his side and pulled him into a hug, heart breaking for him as he wrapped arms around me and sobbed like a baby on my shoulder.

I held him until the shudders eased, then gently pulled away and fetched a wet paper towel for him. "Here, put this on your eyes. It'll ease the puffiness." I smiled as he obeyed. "Voice of experience, trust me. I had a similar reaction when I learned she hadn't intentionally betrayed me." I paused. "You should know, Rhyzkahl had already removed a good portion of her manipulations by the time she got away from Jesral."

Idris let out a long breath and lowered the paper towel. His eyes were still red, but the anger and pain that had resided in their depths for so many months had faded.

"She wasn't able to shed a lot of light on what Jesral is up to," I told him, "but her bits and pieces filled in some of the puzzle. And combined with what we know from other sources, it's not pretty." I gave him a rundown of what we'd learned from Tessa, Pellini, Paul, and Dominic about the Between Machine and its operators—including our fears that Jesral wanted to raise his Earthgate and might be planning some sort of catastrophic incident in order to do so. "Long story short, Elofir has called a conclave for day after tomorrow to address all of this."

His face lit up. "A conclave. *That* should prove interesting."

I tilted my head. "You should absolutely come to the demon realm with us."

"There's so much going on here. What about—"

"You know you want to come. Two days. DIRT will survive *two* little days without you."

He gave a wry smile. "You don't know my second in command. But yeah. I don't want to miss a conclave. Especially with so much crap to be addressed."

"It's settled, then. Do you think you'll be ready to do the eleventh ring?" The final ring of the shikvihr had to be completed in the demon realm.

He sucked in a breath then slowly released it. "I don't know.

I didn't think I'd have the opportunity so soon. Or ever, to be honest. The eleventh's not gelling for me. At all."

"I get it. I really do. But maybe you're trying too hard? You have one hell of a foundation of knowledge, along with kickass instincts. You've been dealing with high pressure situations and never worried about things 'gelling' for you, right? You just did what needed doing. So do that for the eleventh."

"That's actually a pretty good way to look at it. Okay. Yeah. Why the fuck not, right?"

"That's the spirit!"

He let out a laugh that turned into a yawn. "Sorry, I'm still on other-side-of-the-world time."

"You're welcome to crash on the couch. Or, there's space in the barracks."

"I think I'll take the barracks. Feels more normal at this point."

"I get it." I gave him a smile. "I'm glad you're back."

"Glad to be back." He grabbed his duffel and headed out.

Muffled voices—Szerain and Idris—conversed a moment on the porch before Szerain stepped in and settled at the table. "How's Idris from your perspective?"

"Less angry," I said. "A lot less."

"That's the impression I got, too."

"He still has a lot to mull over concerning Tessa. Needs time on his own as well as with her." I blew out a breath. "Time's a luxury these days."

"He's strong, and so is she. They'll find a way to pull it all together. Now to get him to the conclave to culminate his shikvihr."

"Beat you to it! He's going *and* he'll do the eleventh."

Szerain laughed. "Considering I was prepared to drag him kicking and screaming, your way was probably better."

"Kara!" Giovanni and Elinor squeezed through the back door, grins a mile wide as they carried a large, flat, cardboard-wrapped parcel between them.

"We have a present for you before we go," Giovanni announced, beaming. "But it is best if you open it where there is more space."

"Um, okay?" I exchanged a quick *Huh?* look with Szerain, then obediently followed Giovanni and Elinor to the conference room.

The two carefully set the parcel down on one end and leaned it against the table. "Now you may open it!"

Fortunately there were convenient taped spots, so I didn't have to tear through the cardboard itself. The couple looked on with impatient delight as I peeled off the tape then pulled the cardboard aside.

"Oh, wow," I breathed as I took in the exquisite masterpiece underneath. "Giovanni, this is incredible!"

I meant it, too. It was an intricately detailed painting of a badass me standing back-to-back with Mzatal atop the basalt column in his realm, chaos and battle below, and a myriad of shimmering blue-gold sigils in the air around us. Painted-me gazed out of the canvas while Mzatal dealt with foes in the opposite direction, his hair flowing loose, and I found myself longing to see his face. The whole thing was so vibrant, I half-expected the entire scene to start moving.

"I love it," I breathed.

Giovanni flushed, pleased.

Elinor clapped in glee. "I'm so glad! He's been working on it for weeks and weeks and was finished with all but a few last details. I used the arcane to get it dry enough to varnish, since those brighter colors can take days, then a bit more to dry the varnish itself."

"It's utterly amazing," I said, then had to wipe my eyes. I hugged Gio then Elinor. "I'm going to put it in my office. I think it'll be perfect for that blank wall opposite the window."

Elinor gave a squeal of delight, and then nothing would do but to immediately set about hanging it up. I was all for finding a nail and some wire and being done with it, but Elinor insisted on calling Walter to come help. Probably a good thing, because he did silly things like measure and use a level and install proper mounts. As a result, by the time it was hung on the wall, it was not only perfectly placed and even, but so secure the house could collapse around it and the painting would still be there.

Then again, considering the compound did occasionally get strange tremors, that kind of structural overkill was likely a very good thing.

While Walter worked, Elinor and Giovanni gathered their packed bags in the conference room. Our goodbyes were short and heartfelt—and then they vanished.

By the time I returned to my office, Walter was gone, and the stuck window had been repaired as well.

I gazed at the painting, still mesmerized by it. Damn, I looked fucking fierce. Any time I needed a pep talk, I could just come in here and look at this glorious thing.

Smiling, I pulled out my phone and took a picture. Now it was a pep talk I could carry with me.

Szerain came in and stood beside me. "Giovanni is a very gifted artist," he said with no small amount of pride.

"Gifted *and* your student. This is awesome."

"Even though the sigils are wrong?"

I grinned at the amusement dancing in his eyes. "Yeah, I wasn't going to say anything about the accuracy, since the rest is so perfect."

"I suspect Elinor didn't see the painting until he needed help drying it, else she would have corrected them."

"And she's no doubt familiar enough with the artistic temperament to know which battles are worth fighting."

"Smart woman!"

I tilted my head. "I bet he simply went with what was artistically pleasing."

"He succeeded. It's stunning."

Ashava sauntered in, her first appearance since she rage-quit the earlier staff meeting. "I found Idris out on his own and teleported him to the barracks. It was harder than it should have been. Either of you know why?"

"Um, no?" I offered. Though I had a feeling it might be due to Rho giving the governor a slight boost. "But thanks for taking care of him."

"Sure. No problem. We talked for a while, and . . ." Her brow furrowed as she examined the impossible-to-miss new artwork. "Too bad Giovanni just made up the sigils." She must have realized how that sounded because she quickly added, "But it's still really nice." After another moment of scrutiny, she shrugged and stalked out.

Szerain and I continued to gaze at the painting.

"Charming girl," I murmured.

Szerain snorted a laugh. "May the gods take pity on us all."

Chapter 20

I spent much of the next morning dealing with stupid bullshit paperwork, which I hated, and everyone around me knew I hated it. And I felt bad for hating it because I was fully aware that Sonny and Jill did most of the heavy lifting on that end, but ugh, I hated the admin side of things so very much.

When Bryce stepped in, holding a piece of paper and looking slightly stunned, I happily seized onto the interruption.

"What's up? You need help with anything?" As long as it wasn't bullshit paperwork, I was all for it.

"You're not going to believe what I just found out about Paul's boyfriend, Dominic," he said.

"Oh, no."

"It's nothing bad! The opposite, really. Full name Dominic Gilroy. Twenty-six years old. Started university at the age of fifteen as a Computer Science major. Went on to earn Masters degrees in Computer Engineering and Software Development. And then he shifted gears and got a PhD in Physics." His gaze skimmed over the paper, expression bemused. "No wonder Jesral targeted him."

"You're telling me you did a background check on Paul's boyfriend?" I asked. "Paul's going to know."

He snorted. "Pretty sure Paul knew damn well I'd do a full run on Dom and would've called the medics on me if I hadn't."

"True enough!"

"Anyway, I guess I approve of this guy."

I tapped my computer. "And I'm sure he knows that now."

Bryce laughed and headed out.

With great reluctance, I dragged my focus back to the thrice-cursed paperwork and briefings and managed to put in another hour of tedious, mind-numbing crap.

By the time Sonny came into the office, I'd lost the will to growl about stupid fucking bureaucrats and was ready to dive into the rift and become Dekkak's bitch. Couldn't be any worse than this.

"Zenra sent word that Boudreaux's doing really well," he said. "Awake and coherent and will be fully recovered before we know it."

I let out a sigh of relief. "That's very good to hear."

"Agreed. Also, I'm kicking you out of the house."

I blinked. "It's my house. You can't kick me out."

"Try me," he said with a deceptively calm smile. "I can finish up everything else. Go work out. Or paint some flowers. Hell, milk a cow if the fancy strikes you, but you're not allowed back here for at least two hours."

"Okay!" I replied cheerfully, then dashed off to change into workout gear.

I fully intended to burn off energy with a workout, but first I wanted to see for myself how Boudreaux was doing. Half a dozen beds separated by curtains lined both sides of the infirmary. Double doors at the far end led to the surgical suite and specialty treatment rooms. A few of the beds were occupied, and I greeted patients as I passed looking for Boudreaux. It wasn't until I saw him awake and sitting up in his bed that the knot of worry finally loosened.

Zenra was taking his vitals and checking him over, while Lenny leaned back in what passed for a visitor's chair.

Boudreaux grinned. "Hey, Kara. I might get sprung from here later today, thanks to the miracle of modern *magic*!"

"I take it Szerain has been in to see you?" I said, moving to the foot of his bed. He definitely looked a shitload better than when I last saw him.

Zenra slung her stethoscope around her neck. "Actually, Ashava did most of the work, albeit under Szerain's tutelage. But she has a gentle touch and solid instinct."

"That's great to hear," I said, relieved. "I'm really glad you're okay, Boudreaux." I paused to clear my throat as a bit of pesky emotion got lodged in there.

Zenra excused herself, and I quickly took her place at the bedside. "Hey, I had an idea about the puppies, but I wanted to run it past both of you first. They're old enough to adopt, and a bunch of the lords now have human companions, and—"

Lenny started laughing. "And of course those humans would enjoy canine company, right?"

I grinned. "Exactly! I mean, why not? They'll definitely be well cared for."

Boudreaux snorted. "And if the demons there are anything like Prikahn, they'll go sloppy for them."

Lenny smiled. "He's really drawn to that one fawn pup. Pretty much ignores the others."

"I gotta say, that really cracks me up. Have any of the other warlords shown as much interest in the puppies?"

"Not that I've seen," Lenny said, "though it's possible Sloosh has come through without any of us realizing."

"Well, I'll make sure Prikahn can say goodbye to them before we relocate the litter to the demon realm."

Lenny squeezed Boo's shoulder. "On that note, I need to get going. Jill thinks one of the cows might have an infected teat, and asked me to have a look at it." He made his goodbyes to us and headed out.

I claimed his chair and looked Boudreaux over more carefully. "Ashava did all right?"

"She did. I promise. It was obvious she wanted to do a good job."

I exhaled, relieved. "Good. Sometimes her judgment is a little, shall we say, uneven."

"Yeah, but look what she's had to deal with. I mean, it's gotta be insane growing up in, what, a *year*? Hell, less than that. Kids typically learn by watching others, trying stuff, and screwing up, but the problem is she doesn't have much opportunity or time to learn like that, and the stakes are a lot higher when she screws up. Which means she overcompensates all over the place."

I grimaced. "You pretty much nailed it."

His brow creased. "It's hard on the rest of us, too, because she IS so powerful. Dangerous. It's not her fault, but there you have it." He shrugged. "I don't think she *means* to cause trouble."

"I absolutely agree," I said. "She's not malicious or evil or selfish."

"She's still trying to find her place, prove she fits in here and deserves responsibility. Sometimes that causes more problems, so she screws up in the opposite direction. Like a bigass rubber ball filled with power and magic, bouncing from one extreme to another."

I exhaled a long breath. Boudreaux was a keen observer, good with animals and kids. I trusted his instincts. I'd never consciously thought about how hard it must be for Ashava to figure so much out and maintain control. Szerain was a solid ally and dear friend, but how much did he know about raising a kid?

"For that matter," Boudreaux continued, "she's half-human, which means she has teen hormones careening all over the place. I think I already know the answer, but does she have any friends?"

I groaned and rubbed my eyes. "No. Dammit. Not peers. Definitely no human teens."

"And then she lost Squig, which hit her pretty hard. I mean, you know how much she loves animals—especially those cats. She'd turn into a dragon and go flying with Squig and Fillion all the time over at the horse farm."

I did my best to hide my guilty grimace. I had no clue she still went flying with them.

"She seems to really let her guard down with Lenny and Roma," he continued. "Can't blame her. They're solid, and I guess they both give off trustworthy vibes. Plus, they both treat her like a normal person without being patronizing."

"I'm sure that's why she likes you, too."

He shrugged. "I think she gravitates to people who don't act like she's naive *or* dangerous. And that's not a knock on anyone else, because if you know what she's capable of—which you and so many others clearly do—it's impossible to block that out."

"So what the hell can we do for her?" I asked. "It's not like I can arrange a playdate or teen hangout for her."

"Honestly? I have no idea, other than keep in mind what's she dealing with. Probably needs some time without responsibilities, but then that goes against her drive to be relevant. Does she have any hobbies? Time-wasting diversions?"

I shrugged helplessly.

He shook his head. "It's a tough situation."

"Maybe we can figure something out once we get back from the Conclave."

"Yeah. In the meantime, I think I'll teach her how to play Rummy." At my bewildered look, he grinned. "I used to play that with my grandma. Zero stakes. No pressure. Just a card game."

"Holy shit, that sounds glorious."

He laughed. "When you get back, I'll teach you, too."

"Deal!"

After I left Boudreaux, I headed to the rec center, pleased to see it was fairly empty. I considered doing a weights workout, but I had too much worry running through me about anything and everything, and no way would weights be enough to burn it off. But maybe pounding on a heavy bag would take out some of my simmering frustration and angst and fear, much of which I couldn't even articulate.

I wrapped my hands and found gloves in my size that didn't stink too badly. I started out slowly, focusing more on precision than power while I warmed my muscles up. After a few minutes, I increased my speed and worked on putting more oomph into my punches, adding in roundhouse and side kicks, and pausing every now and then to stop the bag from swinging, as well as to catch my breath. I was in the best physical condition of my entire life, but I reminded myself that mental stress sapped energy, too.

I worked on more complex combinations, trying to shut out all the brain gerbils that clamored for my attention. A door opened, and I glanced behind me to see Idris step in.

"Hey," I said, and delivered another punch to the bag, putting a bit more force into it now that I had an observer.

"Hey." He shucked his jacket and came over to hold the bag. "Been here long?"

"Nah. Ten, fifteen minutes maybe."

He kept the bag steady while I jabbed and hooked and kicked and punched.

I stepped back after a few minutes and tugged my gloves off. "Your turn."

He wrapped his hands with the speed and ease of someone who'd done it a million times, found gloves to fit, then attacked the bag while I held on grimly. Hell, keeping it steady for him was harder than actually punching it.

He went a few rounds then shucked his gloves, breathing hard. Yet he still wore an expression that I knew all too well from looking in the mirror.

"Brain gerbils won't shut up?"

He paused in unwrapping his hands. "Huh?"

"Brain gerbils. Chittering assholes that live in your brain and drag up shit you don't want to think about, or keep you too distracted to get a moment of mental rest. Bastards drown out everything else."

Idris snorted. "Yeah, I have a few generations of them living rent-free up here." He tapped the side of his head. "Any suggestions for how to evict them?"

I shrugged. "Try and find outlets that don't hurt yourself or others."

"You and I both know that's tough to do when free time is rare and fleeting."

"Sometimes you have to schedule it in. Or have someone who'll force you to take breaks, like Sonny did to me earlier. Brain gerbils will eat you if you don't slap them down every now and then." I flicked a glance at the clock. "I have forty more minutes, and if I return before then, Sonny will deliberately make terrible coffee for me."

"That would be the worst punishment ever."

"Right?" I grinned. "I'm glad you understand the severity of his threat."

"He's a brave man," he said, eyes crinkling. "Well, since we're both bored with the heavy bag, you wanna do a bit of a spar?" He angled his head toward the large wrestling mat in the center of the room. "I'll go easy on you," he added when I hesitated.

I laughed. "Oh, will you?"

We removed our shoes and stepped to the center of the mat, then began to circle each other, knees slightly flexed, hands loose. Idris made a grab for my shoulder, but I twisted away and returned with a feint of my own that he easily evaded.

He stepped in and shot a hand out to seize my wrist, but instead of twisting to escape, I stepped to his left, swinging around to break his grip, regrabbed his forearm, then continued the movement to lock my forearm against the back of his elbow and pull him off balance. A quick hook of my foot behind his calf sent him tumbling to the mat, wringing a surprised grunt from him. He rolled to try and regain control, but I rolled right with him, pulled his arm straight into a sweet arm bar, and before he knew it I had him on his back with my leg over his throat and enough pressure on his elbow to keep him immobile.

Laughing, he tapped the mat twice with his free hand. I immediately released my hold and shifted away.

"Holy shit," Idris said with a grin. "Someone's been working hard!"

I snickered. "Sensei Tandon doesn't give me a choice."

We went at it again, this time with Idris definitely *not* taking it easy on me. To my pleased surprise, we were fairly well-matched, despite the fact that he outweighed me by a good forty pounds. But I'd had a solid amount of one-on-one training lately, and Tandon had specifically worked with me on non-complex tactics, and moves that didn't rely on strength but would work on a stronger and heavier opponent.

This kind of sparring/grappling was hard, high-exertion work, and after about fifteen minutes we both lay on our backs, muscles jellified, and gasping for breath.

"That was awesome," I finally managed. "Thanks, dude. But now you have to get water for us both since I won."

He wheezed out a laugh. "*You* won?"

"Sure. I took you down way more times."

He snorted, smiled. "Not at all how I remember it, but I'll get the water." He rolled to his side and pushed up with a groan, then retrieved two water bottles from a cooler by the wall. He handed one to me then plopped back down.

I sat up and took a long, grateful glug, then pressed the cool bottle against my neck. The sound of piano music drifted from another room. Probably Michael, judging by the skill on what sounded like a complex piece.

"Did you do anything for Christmas?" Idris asked after a moment.

I snorted a laugh. "As if I had a choice! Jill went all out, scrounged up all the decorations Eilahn had acquired for the previous Christmas, made even more, and bullied everyone into compliance until I swear every fucking inch of this place was decorated to the nines for every possible religious and secular observance of the season. We had a gigantic Christmas tree in the back yard AND an enormous menorah AND a Kwanzaa display AND a nativity scene."

He grinned. "I'm surprised she didn't decorate the grove tree."

"Luckily she knows the groves are a living, sentient entity, but I half expected her to wrap the tree in an ugly Christmas sweater. But apart from Rho, I'm not sure there was a square foot of this compound that didn't have some sort of seasonal décor on it."

"She never struck me as the mega-winter celebration type."

"I don't think she usually is, but this was Ashava's first Christmas-Hannukah-Solstice-Whatever winter season."

"Ohhhhh. I guess that makes sense. Please tell me there are pictures."

"So many. But they're on my phone, which is over by the wall and might as well be a million miles away."

We fell quiet as the piano music shifted to something slow and poignant.

"We were in the demon realm with Mzatal for Christmas a year ago," I murmured, then steeled myself against the stab of pain that always came with thoughts of him.

"Yeah. That was a really nice time."

We both let out deep sighs simultaneously, then couldn't help but laugh.

Idris scrubbed a hand over his face. "Never would have thought the world—both worlds—hell, *everything*, would have changed so much in just a year."

I lay back on the mat and gazed up at the metal trusses over-head.

The music shifted to something jazzy with a complex syncopation, the kind that made you want to tap your fingers along with it. Knowing Michael, it was something he was making up as he went along.

After a moment Idris reclined beside me. "How do we get back to normal?"

"I don't think it's *possible* to get back to normal. I mean, not the normal we knew. That doesn't exist anymore. There's not a single person in this entire world who hasn't been affected in some way."

"Yeah," he said softly. "Ever since you struck the deal with Dekkak, there've been only a fraction of the incursions compared to before. Now people are struggling to regain that old, familiar feeling of living in a world that makes sense."

"The peace of mind we didn't realize was precious until it was gone."

Even people who weren't directly impacted by the rifts and incursions were still affected, still had their lives changed. No matter where you lived, there was always the knowledge, the awareness that an incursion could wipe out everything you held dear.

The entire world had lost a basic sense of security and stability, and gained the brutal awareness that no place was truly safe. Not to mention, life in general had been disrupted in a hundred different ways. Schools and businesses shut down. Supply lines disrupted.

Many of the ultra-wealthy had simply gone to live on their

yachts since ocean floor rifts had always been pretty rare and, ever since the pact with Dekkak, were damn near nonexistent. Though, in a nice bit of karma, said ultra-wealthy quickly discovered they had to either find secluded places to anchor, or constantly defend themselves from modern day pirates. Not to mention, yachts were still vulnerable to flying demons, though the risk diminished if they were far enough out to sea.

And because the world wasn't already completely batshit bonkers, there were even credible rumors of a handful of billionaires fast-tracking construction of potential space habitats.

"These last few months, I've been seeing everything through a different lens," Idris said. "The world has changed. And there are some things that can't be unchanged." He exhaled. "I feel like I've been angry forever, even though it's really only been a year or so since the Mraztur took me prisoner. When they killed my sister"—he swallowed—"I've never felt so helpless. And it was . . ."

"Evil," I murmured. Jesral, Rhyzkahl, and Amkir had planned and orchestrated the kidnapping, torture, and murder of Amber Palatino in order to ensure Idris's compliance and set an arcane trap for me. Worst of all, Idris had been forced to watch as she was violated and killed.

He let out a rough breath. "Yeah. And then Tessa rejected me, as if I was worthless and beneath her. When Mzatal chained Rhyzkahl to your nexus, I was so glad because he was finally being punished for the shit he did. I could rage at him, and indirectly at Tessa."

I didn't speak. He had more to say, and he'd been needing to get this out for a while.

"But I've accepted that she was a pawn and a tool. The Mraztur killed my sister and held my adopted mom hostage to make me serve their ends. But they took *everything* from Tessa, took her will and freedom and future, and she never even knew it."

"They stole her child," I murmured. "Not just her baby, but the whole experience of being a mother and raising you."

"They took me from her and made her forget." He exhaled. "And I realize, in some ways, Rhyzkahl was a pawn and a tool as well." He rubbed at his eyes with both hands. "Anyway, I've been thinking a lot about what you said months ago about forgiveness. How it's not excusing what they did but instead not letting it rule you. Fuck, I was so *pissed* when you set Rhyzkahl free from the nexus and told me you fucking forgave him. I didn't understand. But over these past months, I couldn't stop thinking about how you said it was easy to hold onto anger. Because, fucking hell, it really is. So goddamn easy. And sometimes anger is good, like when truly righteous anger fuels change. But that 'good' kind of anger is usually on behalf of someone else. Still, no matter what kind of anger you're carrying, it changes you, and can trap you and suck you under if you're not careful."

"That's some impressive processing," I said.

He let out a short laugh. "I've had a lot of help. One of the guys in my unit is a therapist, and he's given me a shitload of perspective and guidance. I still have brain gerbils, but at least they're not the angry kind. Anyway, it made me think hard about what Rhyzkahl did to you. With the torture and sigils to try and make you Rowan."

I pushed up to sit and began stretching muscles that threatened to go stiff. "Jesral was behind that as well."

Idris shoved up onto one elbow. "Yeah, and the fucking demahnk were pulling strings. But I finally got it through my thick head that staying angry is just playing their game. The bad guys would *love* for me to stay pissed and burn bridges and react without thinking."

"I'm so glad you talked to someone," I said fervently. "Every blessed one of us has PTSD from the events of the past year. The entire world. Even people who weren't directly affected are traumatized simply from knowing that other people *were*. Trauma, grief, survivor's guilt, you name it. And every one of us is struggling to hold it together using any number of coping mechanisms."

"Clearly one of your coping mechanisms is martial arts."

"Look, I tried knitting, or drawing, but I am seriously lacking the skills for either."

"At least the martial arts is generally healthy—for you at least."

I grinned. "For the most part!" But then I sobered. "Think about it, though: Even the demon realm is going through massive transition and upheaval. Hell, the lords definitely have PTSD, and have ever since they were stolen from Earth and their memories were suppressed. Then they were forced to maintain a planet the Ekiri had fucked up."

Idris's brows drew together. "You're not wrong."

"For that matter, the trauma is there even for Xharbek and the rest of the Ekiri who remained and became the demahnk. They were thrust into a completely unexpected situation when they realized they'd actually fathered children. Their solution sucked complete ass, but I try to remind myself they had zero clue what they were doing. And yeah, they shouldn't have been interfering in the first place, so fuck those guys—but *because* their solution sucked ass, they keep trying to tweak the same shitty fix that obviously isn't going to fucking work. And now it's like most of them are incapable of comprehending that their solution was a terrible idea from the start, and that maybe they need to stop throwing good money after bad and try something different that might actually work."

"Sunk cost fallacy," Idris said with a nod. "When you've already put a ton of time, effort, or money into something, you become reluctant to abandon it and start over, even when it's clear that chucking it all in favor of a different option will be far more beneficial."

I stabbed a finger at him. "YOU have been reading a lot of smart books."

"Gotta do something on the plane rides to the ends of the earth!"

Chapter 21

I returned to the house and took a two minute rinse-soap-rinse shower, worn out physically but nicely recharged mentally. Which was good since there was an insane amount of stuff that needed to be planned and accomplished before we left for the demon realm. This was, of course, assuming Helori would come and mentally shield people as needed.

Bryce and Jill met me in the kitchen. Rosters, supply lists, legal pads, coffee, and bacon at hand, we got down to business.

First and foremost would be deciding who needed to go to the conclave and who could or should remain behind. Protecting the compound was our number one concern, complicated by the fact that Szerain—our main source of arcane defense—was definitely in the "must attend" category. As was I, of course.

"Alpha Team will be here," Bryce said, "so the physical defenses should be solid. We can discuss the particulars with Roma at the staff meeting." He waited for Jill to catch up with notes, then glanced over at me. "And I need to go. Even though I doubt Seretis will be allowed to attend the conclave, the bond will surely be clearer. And his intel has been pretty solid so far."

"That works." I did a quick glance-around to make sure Ashava wasn't in the vicinity, but still lowered my voice before saying, "I think Ashava should remain here at the compound. I worry about, well, a lot of things. She's still a target, but mostly I don't know how the lords might react, considering everything she represents. Not to mention, how *she* might react to them in turn."

"I agree," Jill said, to my relief, but then she added, "However, *I* want to go." Bryce shot her a startled look, and she lifted her chin. "I've never seen the demon realm."

His brows drew down. "Look, you do realize—"

"Don't you *dare* say anything asinine like 'This won't be a vacation' or 'You should stay for Ashava's sake.'" Her eyes flashed. "I've been part of this fight for the future of both worlds from the very beginning, and I'd really like to experience the other world, at least once."

Frustration and annoyance swept over Bryce's face. "I get that, but . . . too bad. This isn't the time, and I really need you to stay here to hold everything together. You can do way more to help both worlds by remaining on *this* one. Then, after everything is settled, we can see if there's a way for you to do some sight-seeing." He returned his attention to the rosters before him.

I held my breath, waiting for the Jill temper to flare, expecting that any second she'd bite Bryce's head off and shove it into the now-working garbage disposal.

Instead she simply nodded, set her pen down, stood, and headed out the front door.

Bryce glanced after her, then shifted his gaze to me. "I know she's pissed, and I know she can handle herself in a fight, so it's not like I think she'd be dead weight. But this isn't the time to have anyone tagging along just because they want to see the demon realm. You agree, right?"

I winced. Outside, an ATV rumbled to life and sped off.

Bryce swore and jammed a hand through his hair as the noise faded into the distance. "I didn't mean to hurt her feelings."

"It would take a lot of worry off our plate if she stayed behind." I sighed and breathed out a soft curse. "But I don't think she walked out because of hurt feelings." No, Jill looked more sad than hurt.

"I could have handled that better." He grimaced. "Guess we're all pretty stressed. I just . . . Fuck." He pulled Jill's legal pad over to him.

"I'll be back in a few," I said, then headed out to the front porch. I spied Ronda crossing the yard with a toolbox in her hand.

"Did you happen to see which way Jill went?" I asked her.

"Sorry," she said. "I've been in the watchtower helping Walter fix the—"

We both jumped as Weyix let out a bellow from the roof. Gritting my teeth, I rounded on the kehza, anger rising at the undeniable look of amusement on his face. But I choked back a blistering takedown when he lifted a clawed hand to indicate the east road.

"Jill went that way?" I asked cautiously.

"Kri." He bared his teeth.

"Thanks." I paused. "Why are you helping me?"

"I do not help you," he sneered. "I help the *jhonktehl*. I owed her a boon, and perhaps you are not so weak that you cannot ease her. Now my debt to her is clear."

Huh. Jhonktehl was demon for respected warrior. "Nice try, but you know damn well only the one who holds the debt can expunge it. Still, I thank you for the information that you gave me freely and with nothing expected in return."

The kehza let out a hiss that *almost* sounded like laughter, then took flight toward the woods.

I hopped onto an ATV and headed toward the Forty. I didn't see her vehicle by the rec center or motor pool, nor was it by the admin building or barracks. On a vague hunch, I decided to head toward the north end of the property and the stock pond we'd dug for the cows.

There she was, sitting cross-legged on a patch of grass and staring out over the water. She gave me a wan smile, and I was gutted to see she'd obviously been crying. This was *Jill*. Tough, sensible Jill. Yeah, sure, she cried every now and then. Who didn't? Nothing weak about tears. I'd had more than my share of crying jags. But it was her expression that damn near slayed me. She looked defeated, and I'd never imagined I would ever see her like that.

I took that wan smile as an invitation to shut the ATV off and plop down on the ground next to her.

"I love you and appreciate you," I said. "But we screwed up and hurt you. And I want to understand so I can make it right."

Then I shut the hell up, leaving it up to her to talk to me or not.

After a moment she took a deep breath and released it in a sigh. "I love you, too. And I appreciate you and all you do." She paused, gathering her words. "I know my work here is recognized and respected. I *like* taking care of all the details and making sure everything is running smoothly here. I'm good at it, and it's really satisfying." She looked up at the sky then out at the water. "But when Bryce shot me down with a casual *Too Bad*, it just hit me like a hammer between the eyes that it's really not enough to be told how much everyone appreciates all I do and how well I take care of everyone and everything. It's not enough to take pride in what I've managed to accomplish with this place." She swiped at a tear. "And I started thinking about how nice it would be if *I* could be the one who was taken care of. Like, if someone would stop and think, 'Hey, Jill is a burned-out husk of her former self, and the past couple of years have been pretty hellish for her, so maybe a change of scenery and something new and interesting would be a nice change of pace.' And I know it's selfish, and the worlds are literally in peril, but—"

I gave her a little shake to shut her up. "No, it's not selfish." I pulled her into a tight hug, aghast that I'd never realized—never let myself realize—just how much she'd bottled up. "Damn it. I'm so so sorry. Shit."

Her tears turned into shuddering sobs, and I was crying right along with her. Finally, she gave me a squeeze and pulled back. "Well, it's not as if you've had anything on your mind, y'know," she said with an attempt at a laugh. She dug a pack of tissues out of a pocket, handed me one, then blew her nose with a second. Because of course Jill Faciane was always prepared for anything.

I made quick use of the tissue. "Right? My days are lazy and carefree! But it's not like you've been through anything traumatic lately. Now, if you'd gotten knocked up by a demahnk disguised as a certain FBI Agent Zack Garner and then became the target of Xharbek and then had your baby teleport out of you in the back of a truck next to an exploding arcane valve and then had Szerain and Zack steal her when she was barely minutes old and then not be allowed any chance to be with her or see her grow up or have any influence on her during her time as a child and instead you suddenly had a moody teen and were basically robbed of the chance to be her damn *mother* and all the memories and experiences that go along with that, well THEN you'd have every right to be a gibbering basket case."

She stared at me, eyes wide. My gut sank. I'd gone way *way* too far. Yeah, shove her trauma into her face. Nice going, Kara.

To my intense relief, she burst out laughing. "Well, when you put it like that." She took a deep breath and blew it out in a rush. "But I really am sorry I fell apart like that then ran the hell away."

"Jill Faciane, your emotions are valid, dammit. You are absolutely allowed to feel hurt and, well, neglected." Because that's exactly what she was. She'd been through hell, then buried herself in work as a way to slap a bandage over her trauma. Meanwhile the rest of us had accepted it without a second thought. "You're allowed to want more. You deserve more. And you shouldn't feel guilty or embarrassed about asking for more."

Some of the tension left her body. "Thanks. I *was* embarrassed, as if I'd been silly to ask to go in the first place."

"And I'm so sorry I didn't stand up for you right then and there. There's absolutely no reason why you shouldn't come along." I certainly didn't need to worry about her being able to handle herself. Jill was an excellent marksman, had a real knack for martial arts, and was in tip-top physical condition.

She squeezed my hand. "You came looking. Though I'm impressed you found me so quickly."

"Oh, Weyix told me which way you'd gone. Then he tried to say that cleared his debt to you." I grinned. "Which, of course, is bollocks, and he still owes you a debt. But I'm dying to know how that came about."

"This morning, I was carrying a container of mini pumpkin pies to the front gate. Weyix and Dagor were sparring, and Weyix happened to clip Sammy with the tip of his wing. Not enough to hurt him, but the poor dog panicked and took off running and smacked into me. I dropped the tin, and mini pies went everywhere."

"Oh nooooo." Jill *loved* baking. It was a huge stress release for her.

She grinned. "Weyix didn't expect my fury or that I'd hold him accountable for freaking out the dog. I informed him he owed Sammy for hitting him with his wing, and me for destroying my property."

"He's lucky the entire compound didn't claim an honor debt for denying them dessert."

"Don't you worry, I told him his little stunt had affected many people, and thus his debt to me wasn't minor. Also, he's now obliged to spend fifteen minutes a day for the next week playing with Sammy and throwing a ball for him."

"I should've let *you* negotiate with Dekkak!" I said, laughing. "You ready to head back? Dunno about you, but my ass is frozen."

"Yeah. Even though I know I look like I've been bawling."

"Oh, no," I deadpanned. "Bryce might realize he hurt you by being super insensitive."

A grimace warred with amusement. "And you don't think letting him see that I've been crying is a bit manipulative?"

"No, I don't," I said after considering the question. "If some-one hits you, with or without intent to harm, it's not manipula-tion if you show up later with a black eye."

She let out a whistle. "Oooh, that's a good one."

I grinned. "Besides, you're one of those awful people who still looks gorgeous when they cry. Me, I look like a depressed blobfish. With hay fever!"

She barked out a laugh and smacked me on the arm. "You are so silly. Fine, let's go finish planning this . . . mission? Cam-paign? Side quest?"

"I think we can safely call it anything we want, though might want to avoid 'Pending Clusterfuck.'"

"Roger that. I'll scratch 'Operation P.C.' off the list of possi-ble names."

We climbed onto our respective ATVs and headed toward the house, but we hadn't even reached the road when I saw a man on a horse heading our way. I was damn near positive the horse was Copper To Gold, but the rider sure as hell wasn't Boudreaux—which was concerning, because it was well known the stallion wouldn't tolerate any other rider, nor was anyone else allowed to even attempt to ride him, for everyone's safety.

Righteous fury flared on behalf of the horse and Boudreaux until I got close enough to realize the offender was Helori—riding bareback and bridle-free, no less. I stopped the ATV and cut the engine. Jill pulled up beside me and did the same, brow furrowed.

"Is that a new Rider?" she asked me. "I wasn't notified about a change in personnel."

I grinned as Helori drew close, and I took in the ridiculous cowboy getup he had on, complete with spangly shirt, bedazzled chaps, a *huge* belt buckle, bright red cowboy boots, and ten-gallon hat.

"Jill, I'd like you to meet Helori."

"It's a pleasure to finally meet you in person," she told him. "I've heard much about you."

He smiled, radiant. "All of it wonderful, I am certain."

"Absolutely!"

I gave the demahnk a mock-suspicious look. "I sure hope you got Boudreaux's permission to take his horse out."

Helori laughed. "I visited him not long after you left his side.

He is feeling much better but was fretting that this lovely creature had not been exercised. I therefore offered to do so."

"And, apart from Boudreaux, you're probably the only one who could manage it."

Helori slid fluidly off, murmured quietly to the horse, then moved to Jill and took her hand in his, expression abruptly serious. "You have borne a heavy burden with unspeakable grace and courage. We are all in your debt, my lady." Then he smiled. "And now none may read your thoughts without your permission." He gently kissed the back of her hand and released it.

She blinked, flustered, then recovered her composure. "Thank you, Helori. That's very kind of you. Oh, what about Bryce? He needs shielding, too."

"Have no fear. All who will attend have been seen to." Helori smiled and leaped onto the horse's back as gently as a feather, then murmured in his ear. Copper To Gold tossed his mane, then pranced off like a show horse.

Chapter 22

Bryce appeared appropriately contrite when Jill and I returned to the house. She maintained a professional composure and asked him to take a brief walk with her. Bryce complied readily, which was smart since it wasn't actually a request.

They returned after about half an hour, both looking far more at ease, by which time the rest of the command staff had taken their seats in the conference room.

I gave everyone a brief rundown of where we were at with regards to planning, along with our need to ensure the compound and its personnel remained protected in our absence.

"On that note, Jill will be going with us to the demon realm." I gave her a grin. "Consider yourself a part of the conclave team."

"Away team," Bryce mumbled, and Jill stifled a laugh.

"Huh?" I looked at them in confusion.

"It's a Star Trek thing," Jill explained, eyes crinkling in amusement. "The group of people who beamed down to the alien planet was called the Away Team."

"Okay."

"Just don't wear a red shirt when we go," Bryce added, which caused several people at the table to snicker.

"Uh. Sure." I knew damn well it was yet another nerdy reference, but I refused to give them the satisfaction of my asking for an explanation.

Ashava looked up from her notepad. "The security people wore red shirts and tended to be the first to die," she said in a bored tone. "So a 'redshirt' is someone expendable who'll probably meet a bad end."

"No red shirts. Got it. Thanks. Can we get back to the matter of compound security?"

"Well, the Jontari were helpful during the previous attack," Bryce pointed out. "Not out of any loyalty to us, I'm sure," he added with an eye roll. "I think they liked showing off how tough they could be."

Jill smirked. "But they do take matters of honor seriously, which means I can call in my debt from Weyix."

"Whatever works," I said. "But apart from Weyix, we can't *rely* on any of the others to lift a single clawed finger, even though they might. Fortunately, I think we're well set as far as physical defense." I glanced at Roma.

"Agreed," she said. "Last time the compound came under direct attack, the majority of Alpha Squad was deployed away from here, and the remaining personnel succeeded in repelling the attackers. Apart from, god forbid, a Weapon of Mass Destruction, we should be able to hold off a physical force."

"Right. And since they want the nexus and surroundings intact, a WMD is pretty unlikely. That leads us to the problem of an arcane attack. During their prior assault, the enemy had ample opportunity to assess our protections, and will no doubt try new and exciting ways to circumvent them. Jesral knows the Jontari aren't under obligation to help us, and he'll assume—correctly— that key members of this compound will be in the demon realm for the conclave. The bright spot is that Szerain and Ashava have repaired and fortified damaged warding, and the entirety of the arcane protections are now updated. We'll simply have to cross fingers it'll be enough."

"I'll stay," Idris offered.

I glanced over at him, brow furrowed. "I appreciate that, but I think it'll be more valuable in the long run for you to go and complete your shikvihr. Especially since we know damn well there's a world-spanning tsunami of shit headed our way. Plus, who knows when—or if—you'll have another chance."

Szerain gave a murmur of agreement.

Ashava stood up and squared her shoulders. "I can protect the compound." She lifted her chin and seemed to make a deliberate effort to rein in the attitude. "I promise, I can handle it," she said, voice soft but fervent. Her eyes met mine, and I realized she desperately wanted my approval and support.

I kept my expression as neutral as possible while inside relief ran amok. I had *not* been looking forward to telling her we didn't think she should go with us. And she was definitely a powerful arcane user.

"You're right," I said, flooding my tone with confidence, while I pushed down any worries about Ashava's judgment. "You absolutely have all the needed skills, and I think that's a good solution to the problem of arcane security. I very much appreciate your volunteering. But," I added quickly, "let's not forget Jesral tried to capture you once before, and I doubt he's changed his mind about that. So, we need to consider how to muddy the fact you're here essentially on your own."

Ashava fell silent, considering. "I have an idea." She stood and stepped back from the table, closed her eyes. A few seconds later her entire body gave an odd shudder, then abruptly flowed into a new shape—taller, stockier. Definitely male, with dark hair and a thick mustache.

I burst out laughing, and I wasn't the only one. "Holy shit! You're Pellini!" It wasn't a perfect replica by far, but she had the basic shape and size down.

Ashava-Pellini grinned, then reverted to her normal shape. "I wouldn't even have to do much in that form, just step outside the gate a few times to make it look like there was another arcane user here to anyone spying via drone or satellite."

"It's fucking brilliant," I said. "Damn good job."

Her face glowed with pleasure. "Thanks. I won't let you down."

With the decisions made of who was staying versus going, we spent the next half hour hammering out details and finalizing plans. By the time we adjourned, I thought we just might pull this off.

I stepped out onto the porch. It was a gloriously beautiful day—for the moment, at least—and I gave myself permission to pause and revel in it. Everyone who could was taking advantage of the sunny and seventies weather, even down to the animals. Bumper and Granger pounced on insects in the grass, while Sammy tried to help by snatching flies in his mouth. It was utterly adorable and enough to melt even the coldest of hearts.

An evil, devious, triumphant grin spread across my face. I had a plan that just might sway Prikahn into defending the compound. I shot a text off to Lenny and headed for an ATV, a bounce in my step.

Lenny was completely in favor of my plan, and even let me know that Prikahn was currently basking in the horse pond.

Wasting no time, I drove over and headed to Katy's stall, where Lenny helped me get the squiggling fawn puppy into a collar and leash.

I gave him a conspiratorial grin of thanks, then carried the puppy outside and set him down in an attempt to walk him. As expected, the puppy had zero idea what to make of the leash, and proceeded to be a wiggly, jumpy, yipping mess—excited and confused while trying to bite the leash, scratch at the collar, chase invisible motes of dust, and the usual chaotic things that puppies tended to do. Eventually, we made headway toward the pond, with the puppy definitely enjoying the sights and scents of the outdoors, eager to explore every inch of it Right This Second.

I didn't figure it would take long to get Prikahn's attention, what with the yapping and chasing and general romping.

We got his attention all right.

Prikahn gave a blood-curdling roar as he exploded from the pond and thundered toward me with murder in his eyes.

Oh fuck. I scooped the puppy up and cradled him close, not above using him as a puppy shield. Prikahn slid to a stop, claws gouging deep furrows in the turf as a ball of malevolent arcane formed in one hand.

"Prikahn! Wait!" I shouted to be sure I had his attention. "What's wrong?"

He pointed a wicked claw at me. "You have fettered the immature canine. Release him. NOW!"

I let out a breath of relief. We were still at odds, but at least kill-Kara-Gillian-at-all-costs wasn't the root of the problem.

"I'm just working on getting him used to a collar and leash. It's important for their safety," I said with as much confidence as I could muster, then added, "as I'm sure you know."

His breath huffed through bared teeth. To my relief the pup began licking my chin, which must have reassured Prikahn that I wasn't actively harming him.

Prikahn released the arcane, but his eyes still blazed red. "Why must he learn to suffer a collar?"

I nuzzled the puppy, being as demonstrative with affection as I could be. "Because until they're well-trained, it's too easy for them to get into trouble, or accidentally stumble into harm's way, or fall victim to wildlife predators."

Prikahn lashed his tail, probably assessing whether it would violate his oaths if he took the puppy from me by force.

I solved the dilemma by holding the puppy out for him. He snatched him from my grasp, but I didn't miss that he used care in handling him. As if perfectly content, the puppy snuggled into the crook of his arm.

"I'm trying to get them all used to wearing collars and leashes since we're taking them to the demon realm tomorrow for the humans to adopt," I said, tone casual.

Prikahn went very still, moving only to stroke a single claw down the pup's back.

Time for the kill shot. At least I hoped it was.

"I know you've really enjoyed this one's company, but it's time for him to go to his forever home," I said with a small sigh, then cocked my head as if a brilliant thought had only just occurred to me. "That is . . . unless you want to adopt him. I have to warn you, though, caring for a puppy isn't a responsibility to be taken lightly."

The demon rumbled very low and deep in his throat, gaze fixed on the puppy who was blissfully gnawing on one of Prikahn's gold arm cuffs.

"You'd not only have to make sure he has the right kind of food, water, and medical attention, but also train him, for his own protection and others. This one's very smart, though, and I'm sure would be no trouble to train. Lenny or Boudreaux could teach you more. And, of course, dogs of any age enjoy companionship and affection."

Was that too much? The Jontari were certainly a warrior class, but surely even warriors understood and embraced the concepts of loyalty and love. Right? Otherwise, what were you even fighting for?

Prikahn remained silent for what seemed like forever before he let out a low, deep rumble.

"I would be honored to be trusted with the care of this creature," he said, baring his teeth. "NONE shall harm him!" he added with a growl that shook the ground. The puppy lifted his head, then returned to gnawing on the gold cuff. "On this I give you my oath."

"I'm very glad to hear that. However, I'm not the one you give your oath to." I gestured toward the puppy. "You give your oath to him. Also, it's your right to name him."

Prikahn lifted the puppy in both hands until the pup's nose was almost touching Prikahn's snout, then spoke in demon, voice low yet shaking with force. "I, Prikahn, of the Bloodclaw clan, first of my brood, warlord of Dekkak, swear to you, Hrrk, born of Katy, that I will teach you the ways of survival and battle, will give my life blood to keep you from harm, and will deliver terrible vengeance to any who visit malicious injury upon you."

Hrrk wiggled and licked Prikahn's snout. The demon nodded as if that was a perfectly acceptable response, then returned to cradling the puppy in the crook of his arm.

"Hrrk couldn't ask for a better protector." I paused. "You should know that when we leave for the conclave tomorrow, there's a chance the compound might come under attack again. I know you and the other warlords have no obligation under the terms of our agreement to defend the compound, but I'm relieved to know this pup will be safe."

Prikahn straightened to his full height and spread his wings. "NONE SHALL HARM HRRK!" he roared, then immediately shifted to a croon as Hrrk whined.

Fighting back a grin, I gave the demon a slight bow. "Then I will leave him in your excellent care, honored warlord."

I turned and sauntered back to the ATV, resisting the urge to skip and whistle. Maybe none of the other Jontari would lift a claw to defend the compound, but Prikahn sure as shit would.

Chapter 23

Departure day dawned sunny, hot, and humid. Appropriate for August—not January.

I took a slug of coffee, then dialed the number for the Spires main security line.

"IZ-212 security," a curt female voice answered. "Corporal Barnes speaking."

"Corporal Barnes, this is Arcane Commander Kara Gillian. I'm calling to advise that I will be arriving at the Spires at 1100 hours today along with Arcane Specialist Idris Palatino and two civilians."

"I'm sorry, A.C. Gillian," she clipped out, "but access to the Spires is currently under a class Alpha restriction."

I blinked. "A what?"

"Class Alpha restriction."

"Yes, I heard you the first time," I replied, voice growing tight. And perhaps a tetch louder. "Perhaps you could explain what a class Alpha restriction is and why it would restrict the Arcane Commander."

"A class Alpha restriction bars entry to anyone who isn't on the Alpha clearance list."

"Ah. And the civilians aren't on the list."

"Without knowing their names, I can't confirm that. However, I do know *your* name is not."

My mouth worked soundlessly for a moment before I did a pygah in the hopes of finding calm. DIRT command was trying to play hardball with me because I wouldn't share sensitive info. Assholes. "I see. Let me speak to Captain Hornak. Please."

"Captain Hornak is no longer stationed at this facility, ma'am."

Crappity crap. Hornak had been a hardass and all-around pain until Kadir did *something* to make him downright friendly. Which, now that I thought about it, might be why he was no longer in charge there. "Fine. Let me speak to his replacement, whoever that is."

"That would be Major Sawyer. I'll connect you to his office."

I put the phone on speaker and paced my office while I waited for the call to transfer. Eventually a Sergeant something-or-other picked up, and after a few minutes of stonewalling, and my rising temper, grudgingly agreed to put my call through to the major.

"A. C. Gillian, this is Major Sawyer." His tone was pleasant. Conversational, even. "Your access to the Spires has been revoked."

"And *why* is that?"

"I'm afraid I'm not privy to that information."

"Who gave the order for this?"

"I'm not at liberty to say. But they certainly outrank both of us."

"I see." There weren't enough pygahs in the universe to keep the *pissed* out of my voice. "Can you at least tell me how 'temporary' this revocation is going to be?"

"'Fraid not." The fucker sounded like he was enjoying himself.

"Major Sawyer," I said, infusing my voice with sarcastic sugar. "I do so appreciate your help."

He chuckled. "It was my absolute pleasure."

Prick.

Well, I still had a few strings I could pull. I called General Starr's office—where my call went directly to voicemail.

Scowling, I tried Colonel Sim Jiwoo, the general's new aide de camp.

"Colonel Sim's office, Sergeant Cox speaking."

"Sergeant Cox, this is Arcane Commander Gillian. I need to speak to General Starr, please." See, the please meant I was being *nice*.

"I'm sorry, ma'am, but General Starr is unavailable to take your call."

"All right, then may I please speak with Colonel Sim."

"Ah, Colonel Sim is also unavailable to take your call."

I took a deep breath, plastered a smile onto my face in the hopes it would be reflected in my voice. "Sergeant Cox, perhaps you can help me. You see, there seems to be some misunderstanding—"

"Is this about IZ-212, ma'am?"

I dropped the smile. "Yes. I've been denied access."

"Yes, ma'am, that's right."

"Sergeant Cox, I need access. I would like to speak to someone who can make that happen."

"Ma'am, there's nothing I can do about it."

"Which is why I'd like to speak to someone who *can*."

"Ma'am, that's not possible at this time."

Holy fuck, I was getting tired of being called "ma'am." My hand tightened on the phone. "At what time *will* it be possible, Sergeant?"

"I'm not privy to that information, ma'am."

Yeah well, the amount of stonewalling was *information* that told me the order almost certainly originated from this office.

I hung up without bothering with any niceties. Once I made absolutely sure the call was disconnected, I grabbed a pillow off the couch, smashed my face into it, and let out a scream of pure fury. Then did it again. With the sharpest edge of my frustration blunted, I squared my shoulders and stepped out of the office, only to find Jill, Bryce, and Idris clustered around the kitchen table, all looking at me.

"Well," I began.

"You're banned from the Spires," Idris said. "We heard."

"The neighbors heard," Jill put in.

"Everyone heard," Bryce murmured.

I glowered at Jill. "We don't have any neighbors. They moved to Nebraska and California and Canada."

"I know. Trust me, they heard anyway."

"Okay, I might've been a *little* annoyed." Still was. A lot. "Stupid government bureaucratic fucknugget military clearance bullshit!"

Bryce's phone buzzed. He checked the screen then winced, smile teasing the corners of his mouth. "Oh, this isn't going to end well."

"What's so funny?" I snarled.

He turned the screen toward me so I could read the text from Paul.

My eyes narrowed to slits. "'Tell Kara to calm down.'"

Jill covered her face with both hands, shoulders shaking. Idris hissed in a breath of dismay. "Oh, dude."

"Paul, you spying little shit!" I yelled. "You did NOT just tell me to *calm down*! What the fuck! Calm down? Do you even know the YEAR I've had? You do NOT tell a woman to calm down. EVERRRRRR!"

Jill lowered her hands to reveal tears of mirth running down her face. "Oh dear god. It's a good thing he's not in this room."

Still smiling, Bryce stopped my stomp-pacing with the simple tactic of taking me by the shoulders and giving me a shake. "Breathe, Kara. For the love of all that's good and holy, take a breath. His choice of words was *unwise*, but he's telling us it'll work out. Somehow."

"But what if—"

"Stop." He emphasized the command with another small shake. "Look, I know you've *literally* been responsible for the fate of the world, but you're not alone in this. Paul is simply asking you to trust that others will find a way to do what you can't."

"Fine," I grumbled. "Can I still be pissed at stupid-ass political power plays?"

"You wouldn't be Kara if you weren't." He snorted. "Hell, you wouldn't be human if you weren't! Now, please, go turn off that brain of yours for fifteen minutes, okay?"

My gaze swept the kitchen. All I found were looks of support and encouragement, with no hint of annoyance over my temper tantrum—which quadrupled my chagrin over my loss of control. "Yeah. Sorry. I'll do that." With a parting grimace of apology at everyone, I headed outside.

Earlier, I'd been planning to do a run or maybe even go through the obstacle course, but now I just wanted to wander. I headed past the pond, then meandered down random trails and tromped through the woods. For the past half a year, I'd grown accustomed to using every spare minute to get tasks done, or check on the status of projects, or read reports detailing incursions, or write reports detailing incursions, or assess personnel and equipment needs, or fill out scads of paperwork. There were always crises to be averted or situations to be monitored. In between the admin crap and deployments, I did my best to keep my combat skills and fitness levels up, because you never knew when a lull would turn into an everything-on-fire shitshow. We mobilized for incursions and callouts at all hours of the day and night, usually with little warning.

Hell, I couldn't even remember the last time I'd taken a shower more than two minutes long. Get in, get wet, rinse the hair, then do a fast soaping of the body. If I made it that far without hearing an alert tone signaling a fresh incursion or other crisis, I'd go ahead and actually shampoo my hair. And conditioner? HA! That was a dim and distant memory.

Even after the incursions had slowed, the showers did not. There still weren't enough minutes in the day, so that hurry-hurry habit persisted. Fate of the world at stake and all that. But Bryce's kind-yet-firm words of "turn off that brain" hit home and had my mind easing toward topics I'd avoided thinking about.

I managed to hold off the deep-thinks until I found myself in a small clearing with a sunlit patch of brown winter grass. After checking for creepy crawlies, poison ivy, or other potentially nasty surprises, I flopped onto my back, closed my eyes, and let the sun beat down on me. I consciously focused on each group of muscles in turn, coaxing them to relax, and finishing with the knot at the base of my neck where it felt like the weight of my responsibility sat the heaviest.

Bryce had a valid point. I had a support network. Out of necessity, I'd gotten good about delegating. I'd assigned management roles to people who were far better suited for those specific areas. Yet the big, overriding responsibility had always stayed firmly with me. Or at least it felt that way. I'd held onto it and taken the lumps as they came.

Maybe because, in a number of ways, I felt somehow at fault for the entire world-changing mess? I'd accidentally summoned Rhyzkahl, setting off an inexorable chain of events. I'd almost broken the world when I helped Mzatal retrieve the essence blade Vsuhl and merged with potency I couldn't control. At the absolute core of it all, I was the reason the two worlds were at war. Or, at the very least, the Rowan construct that I carried was the inciting incident. All that said, Xharbek's machinations reached back at least five hundred years and had ramped up in the last hundred. I *knew* I wasn't responsible, yet the sense of guilt lingered.

I could explore those feelings until the cows came home, but now, with the quiet and grass and sun loosening knots and offering a rare moment of relaxation, my mind wandered to subjects I hadn't dared explore for a very long time. Chief among them was ME. I'd felt *odd* ever since Elinor's essence had been separated from mine and restored to her own body. I'd carried her essence for damn near my entire life. She had shaped my psyche just as I'd shaped hers. But now there were times when I struggled to define who *I* really was.

Okay, so maybe I didn't know the real me very well yet, but there were some things I could be sure of. The world was pretty fucked up—and had been even before the demons started their incursions—but it was still worth saving. And I intended to see that through, even if it killed me.

I paused, expecting a surge of fear or grief or anger that never came. Though I hadn't consciously explored the topic, I'd long ago come to terms with the fact that this conflict could indeed cost me my life at any time. Not that I was ready or eager to die, but I'd accepted there were no guarantees.

Then again, maybe I didn't let myself think about a bright future—or any future—because I was still trying to get used to being just me without Elinor along for the ride. How could I think of Future-Me when I wasn't even sure who Present-Me was?

Yet even despite—and beyond—my search for the One True Kara, when all was said and done, there was no certainty I'd get a Happily Ever After. And that was the crux of it, wasn't it? As corny and dramatic as it sounded, saving the world came first. Not everyone got a Happily Ever After. Some people did the hard work and simply got an Okay ending. And lots of people didn't even get that.

And with *that* door cracked open, I finally let my mind turn to one more subject—one I'd steadfastly resisted exploring until now: Mzatal. Even assuming we won this war and saved the worlds and freed him from the demahnk's control, the bitter reality was that he was fucking *immortal*. I, obviously, was not. How could we build a long-term relationship?

I snorted. Now I was just being silly. I was barely into my thirties and, with a lord's healing, I could conceivably see another hundred years or more. Most mortal couples had barely a fraction of that time together. Any grief I felt was more for the fact that Mzatal would have to watch me age and die. Still, I knew without a doubt he'd treasure what time we could have together.

Hand over my heart, over his sigil scar, I reached for him. I imagined the scent of the sea and evergreens, of ozone and petrichor. I felt the warmth of his body, the strength of his arms around me, his lips brushing my ear. *Tah zahr lahn, zharkat.*

"Tah zahr lahn," I murmured.

Calm, settled, and infinitely more balanced, I clambered to my feet and brushed off stray grass, prepared now to face whatever came next.

*   *   *

I returned to the house and took an honest-to-god leisurely shower: conditioned my hair, shaved various body parts, and even attacked my feet, knees, and elbows with my long-neglected loofah. And, once finished with the shower, I managed to find an ancient bottle of lotion and moisturized parched skin that I imagined sobbed in relief.

I'd just finished pulling on fresh fatigues when Jill stuck her head into my room. "Phone call. It's the Spires again."

"What now?" I grumbled. "Do they want to put me on double-super-secret probation?" But I took the phone and answered with a bright and perky lilt in my voice.

It was Major Sawyer—who did not sound bright and perky but downright miffed—calling to tell me the order banning me from the Spires had been lifted.

I thanked him for the information and managed to not sound gleeful, which was easy because mostly I was suspicious at the sudden change of heart by the higher-ups. Still, I remained professional and polite, then hung up and told the others.

"That's weird," Jill murmured.

Idris frowned. "Maybe Kadir intervened already?"

My phone buzzed, and it was with exactly zero surprise that I saw it was a text from Paul. "Paul says No."

Bryce rubbed the back of his neck. "I hate it when things get easy for no discernible reason."

"If Major Asswipe hadn't sounded so put out over rescinding the order, I'd be sure it was a trap to take me into custody or something. 'Ha! Psych!'"

"Still could be," Jill said. "Maybe he intentionally sounded put out just to throw you off track. Or maybe the higher ups didn't let him in on the plan."

"Damn your logic, Jill. Wouldn't surprise me one bit."

She nodded sagely. "Would Kadir be willing to, er, run interference and escort us through?"

My phone buzzed yet again. "Paul says 'Yes. We'll pick you up at one pm.'" I grinned, then said to the air, "Gee, I wonder if Kadir is going to swing by and pick up Rhyzkahl, too."

A pause before it finally buzzed. I burst out laughing and showed the screen to Bryce.

<We've been trying to contact you about your vehicle's extended warranty>

Bryce groaned and pinched the bridge of his nose. "I don't know where I went wrong with him. I swear to god."

"I just blame everything on Pellini," I said, still snickering. "Annnd, now Paul says yes, blame Pellini, and yes, they'll get Rhyzkahl." I shoved my phone into my pocket. "Okay, now that the transportation issues have been sorted, we have one more big, wiggly task to take care of."

"The puppies?" Jill asked.

"The puppies."

Chapter 24

Redd, Lenny, and Ashava managed to corral all five uncooperative puppies and stuff them into the sturdy pet carriers Walter had cobbled together. At ten a.m., every living creature going to the demon realm was ready and waiting on the back porch—except Szerain.

Bryce, Idris, Jill, and I each carried a small jump bag with a change of clothes and basic needs to cover the few days of the conclave. All of us were armed. Though I'd seriously considered wearing demon-crafted clothing, I defaulted to fatigues. Jill had opted for jeans and a t-shirt paired with a close-fitting and badass maroon leather jacket.

Ashava rode toward us on a tall bay mule with no bridle or saddle. She leaped lithely to the ground. "Where's Szerain?"

"Dunno," I said. "But he's about to turn into a pumpkin."

She closed her eyes for a second, then made an impatient noise. "I'll get him." With that, she whispered something to the mule—which I imagined to be "Wait here until I deal with the grownups!"—then marched into the house.

Jill gave me the side eye, and I could only offer a helpless shrug.

A minute later, the screen door swung open and Ashava emerged dragging a dazed-looking Szerain by the hand. She snapped her fingers in front of his face a few times. "C'mon. Not much longer, but you have to focus."

Szerain's features subtly morphed through hints of Ryan and Zack before resolving fully into his own again—all so quickly I wasn't totally sure I saw it. He was clearly having trouble maintaining equilibrium in light of Zakaar's impending separation.

He steadied himself on the porch rail. "I'm, uh, good. Thanks."

Ashava gave him a smile. "Stay that way, you hear me?"

"Loud and clear, squirt. Loud and clear."

The air gave a quiet little pop that I felt more than heard, and Kadir, Paul, Dominic, and Rhyzkahl appeared beside the nexus—one p.m. on the nose. To my surprise and intense amusement, Rhyzkahl had Squig cradled in one arm.

He met my eyes with a *look* that clearly said, "Don't even start." It took an enormous amount of self-control, but I managed to hold back the truly insane amount of teasing that sprang to mind. Ah well, we'd be in close company for a couple of days, and surely there'd be other opportunities to give him grief.

Kadir's gaze traveled over each member of our group, as well as the five puppy crates and their occupants, then nodded once—which I took to mean he had no objections. As we gathered our gear, a streak of silver-furred kitty dove out of the sky to land at Kadir's feet. Fillion proceeded to strop and rub against Kadir's legs, purring damn near as loud as a diesel engine.

Kadir regarded him for a long moment, eyes narrowed. I honestly didn't believe he would do anything to hurt the cat, but I was surprised nonetheless when he tapped his shoulder. Without hesitation, Fillion flew up to perch where indicated, happily bumping his head against Kadir's temple. Kadir gave a very slight nod and absently reached up to scratch the cat under the chin, as if to say the matter was settled, and he and Fillion had come to an agreement.

Paul grinned, obviously delighted. But Ashava stared in dismay as she realized what was happening.

"My lords," I said to Rhyzkahl and Kadir—earning me a raised eyebrow from Rhyzkahl, since I'd long fallen out of the habit of addressing him with anything even remotely resembling an honorific. I mentally flipped him off and continued. "May Ashava says goodbye to Squig and Fillion? She's taken excellent care of them these last few months, and though she knows they're going to good homes, she'll always have deep affection for them."

Ashava shot me a look of pure gratitude and didn't wait for any sort of acknowledgment from either lord before darting forward to lavish parting affection on the two winged cats.

"I'm so proud of you both for finding good people to adopt!" she gushed. I couldn't argue with her, since Squig and Fillion had quite obviously adopted the two lords, and not the other way around.

Of course, then my brain conjured up an image of a Demonic Lord Rescue with sappy music playing over videos of lords looking adorable and pitiful. I pressed my lips together to keep from snickering, very glad the two adopted lords couldn't easily read my thoughts.

Ashava stepped back with final skritches to both cats, shot me another look of gratitude, hugged her mother and then Szerain.

Finally, we all gathered close—three lords, six humans, five puppies, and two mutated cats.

A thought abruptly struck me. "When we arrive, nobody move, just in case they're—"

My back yard vanished, replaced by a sea of sparkles. A heartbeat later the sparkles disappeared, and the Spires towered over us.

"—trigger happy," I finished, though I wasn't sure if anyone in our party heard me over the ruckus generated by our abrupt appearance in the middle of a high-security military installation. Fortunately, either my instructions or innate survival instinct had everyone but Kadir remaining stock still. The muzzles of at least a dozen weapons zeroed in on us, and a voice over the PA blared, "Status red! Status red!"

Kadir seemed oblivious to the threat and strode to the pair of fifteen-foot, quartz-like crystalline shards that comprised his Earthgate, while Fillion spread his wings and dug in claws to keep his balance. To my relief, the furor—and weapon pointing—died down quickly after the initial shock, and a soldier snarled, "Could've fucking warned us." Since I'd seen no need to tell Major Sawyer how we'd be arriving, it might have been directed at us, but I suspected the grumbles were meant more for the soldiers' own higher-ups.

However, it was evident the security forces had indeed been told not to interfere with us. Though they double-timed into position, they assembled some distance away and took no hostile action. I suspected the sight of Kadir had them wary, considering a few months ago he'd turned all personnel in the area into temporary living statues. Not that a little distance would make any difference if Kadir decided to flex.

"A.C. Gillian," the PA system blared. "This is Major Sawyer. Your arrival has been logged. You are instructed to clear the area ASAP."

Rhyzkahl let out a low snort of amusement and shifted Squig

from the crook of one arm to the other as he followed Kadir to the space between the shards. I grimaced. DIRT and the various Powers-That-Be were getting all sorts of uninterrupted video of the two mutated cats. Nothing to be done about it now. I reminded myself that both cats were now under the protection of two powerful demonic lords, and neither Kadir nor Rhyzkahl would let any harm befall their new . . . pets? Friends? Colleagues? Mutated Feline Overlords?

While the Spires personnel watched us in hard-eyed silence, the rest of us joined Kadir and Rhyzkahl between the crystals. They hummed a quiet and comforting white noise, backed by soft chimes on some register beyond the physical. While Bryce, Jill, Paul, and Dominic stood quietly as if waiting for their turn to climb into an amusement park ride, Idris strode around each of the crystals, examining and assessing.

Kadir casually plucked a basketball-sized bundle wrapped in purple velvet from some interdimensional stash. Both Rhyzkahl and Szerain immediately tensed—which had me on alert as well.

Kadir drew the cloth back to reveal two pairs of manacles made of arcane-suppressing *makkas*, each with a foot of chain connecting them. Expression placid, he held them out to the other lords. Rhyzkahl narrowed his eyes, suspicious, but Szerain took an uneven step back, breathing hard.

I looked from Kadir to Paul and back. "What's going on?"

Kadir didn't spare me a glance. "Terms of transit."

Rhyzkahl scowled. "These *terms* were not disclosed."

"Alternate means of travel are ever your prerogative," Kadir said as he draped the velvet over the manacles again.

"Name your full terms," Rhyzkahl growled.

"Makkas during the passage. Nothing more."

"Locked?"

Kadir gave a *well-duh* lift of his chin, and Fillion spread his wings as if for emphasis.

Though Rhyzkahl kept his tone even, the twitch in his jaw told me that if he had any other means to get to the demon realm, he'd take it in a heartbeat. Knowing him, the issue wasn't the proposition of wearing makkas—not an unreasonable requirement, considering the potential for malicious shenanigans—but rather being at the complete mercy of Kadir.

Szerain, pale and shaking, took another step back. I looped my arm around his waist and murmured, "It's going to be okay," though I had no idea if that was true. He'd been brutally submerged as Ryan, and I suspected makkas played a role in it. The prospect of being *locked* into it, even for a short time, likely messed with his mind.

Rhyzkahl reached toward the velvet, then paused. "I have your oath you will unlock the cuffs upon arrival?"

"I give you my blood oath."

Without hesitation, Rhyzkahl took one set of manacles, apparently fully trusting an oath from Kadir.

Kadir turned on Szerain, lips parted slightly and eyes narrowed, like a predator waiting for its prey to bolt.

Szerain stood his ground but made no move to take the manacles. "I . . . can't."

"Then remain here." With that, Kadir sent the remaining cuffs away and stepped close to the nearest crystal.

"Kadir," Szerain said, voice tight. "I give you my oath. I will not—"

"Kiraknikahl," Kadir said so softly as to be barely audible. *Oathbreaker.*

Szerain spread his hands. "I don't deny I've given you cause to distrust me and have been a true shit more times than I care to remember. But you know—perhaps more than any—that resisting Xharbek was the right move."

Kadir remained silent for an uncomfortable moment. "Not you."

Mental facepalm time. Of course Kadir knew about the Szerain-Zakaar union. Paul had ears and eyes everywhere. And the oathbreaker was not just the demahnk Zakaar, but *all* demahnk, who had suppressed and manipulated the lords for millennia.

I glanced over my shoulder at the gathered military presence. "This isn't the time or place. Seriously."

Szerain shuddered, then squared his shoulders and took a step toward Kadir. "You now know as truth that which you always suspected." Szerain's voice, but backed with a strained resonance.

"What *truth* is that, Zakaar?"

"We—the Ekiri, the demahnk—grievously wronged you."

Fillion let out a mighty hiss. Paul edged closer to Kadir, face serious and more than a touch worried. The demahnk/lord relationships were complicated and fraught. Kadir had been estranged from his Ekiri parent, Helori, for ages, but had never broken their ptarl bond. He regarded Zakaar in silence, nostrils flaring as if he sought information via scent.

Zakaar said quietly, "What is it you want from me?"

"Your obliteration."

"If you wished to thwart me, you would have simply planned to lose Szerain during the passage."

"That's possible?" I whispered. Paul's expression said yes.

The PA crackled. "A.C. Gillian," Major Sawyer said. "Again, you are instructed to clear the area ASAP."

I switched from middle finger to thumbs up in mid-hand raise, though I had no intention of rushing Kadir into a precipitous action—like leaving without us.

"Deceiver!" Kadir said, cold anger icing his voice. "Your existence and that of your kind is no more than a masquerade that leaves shattered lives and broken worlds in its wake. Even now, you thought to deceive me. I granted you until this moment to disclose yourself, but you remained hidden within Szerain."

Paul put a hand on his arm, but Kadir shook it off.

Sweat beaded on Zakaar's forehead from the effort it took for him to speak directly through Szerain. He extended his hand toward Kadir. "Take my hand, and you will *know* my remorse and my intent."

Kadir recoiled, and Fillion took flight. "Never."

Zakaar slowly withdrew his hand. "I am so sorry," he murmured.

Rhyzkahl frowned. Fillion circled overhead, meow-growling.

Zakaar trembled with the effort of maintaining his presence. "My oath is worthless to you, I know. Still, I give you my word my intention is to preserve the worlds, preserve the interdimensions. Kadir, time is so very short." He took a deep breath and let it out slowly. "Bind me in makkas. Make the passage. I trust you to decide my fate."

Paul gripped Kadir's forearm, and this time didn't release him. "We need to go. This needs to happen." To my undying relief, a measure of tension slipped from Kadir's features. He patted his shoulder, and Fillion landed, diesel-engine purr fully engaged.

"So be it, Zakaar," Kadir said as he retrieved the makkas manacles.

"A.C. Gillian!" Major Sawyer blared. "Do you require assistance?"

"Nah, we good, fam!" I hollered, fucking fed up with Sawyer and his impatient ass.

Zakaar offered his wrists. Kadir stepped close and fastened the first cuff. As he placed the second, Zakaar gripped his hand, held tight. Kadir tried to pull away, then stilled, eyes going to Zakaar's.

It felt as if everyone in our little group held their breath.

An expression I could only describe as comprehension lit Kadir's face. Zakaar released him, and Kadir snapped the second cuff into place, then inclined his head ever so slightly.

Paul visibly relaxed and stepped back beside Dominic.

The next instant, Zakaar was gone, and Szerain crashed to his knees, shaking. I crouched beside him. "You got this, big guy."

He closed his eyes, and I imagined him doing a billion pygahs to keep from freaking out. After a moment, he staggered to his feet, and I wrapped my arm around his waist again.

The hum from the gateway increased in intensity and shifted from steady white noise to a low thrum.

Rhyzkahl snapped the manacles onto his wrists. A puppy yipped and scratched at its carrier.

"Oh, shit," I said. "Will the puppies be okay?" The first time I traveled through Kadir's gate had been unnerving and more than a little painful.

"They are under my care." Kadir's violet gaze locked on me a moment before sliding away to rest on Jill and Bryce, as if remembering there were other humans with us.

Paul smiled at them. "It's best to just sort of imagine you're already there and trust in the process."

Jill tilted her head. "Okay, but what does 'there' look and feel like?"

Kadir regarded her for a moment. "A sensible question," he murmured, then moved close and lowered his head until his forehead touched hers—a gesture I'd witnessed and experienced with other lords, but never Kadir.

Jill's breath caught, and she stiffened. A second later she relaxed. "Thank you, Lord Kadir. That helps."

Holy shit. Kadir just . . . what? Gave her a mental image? And Jill acted as if it was no big deal?

Oblivious to my surprise, Jill turned to Bryce and said, "Think of the sun rising over dunes—the kind of white sand that's on the Mississippi Gulf Coast beaches but with a warm late April breeze. There's a faint scent of char and vinegar with wisps of clove and cardamom. And it feels"—she shot a quick glance of apology to Kadir before continuing—"like the first day at a brand-new school where you don't know anyone and you're a walking bundle of uncertainty, just desperate to survive the day."

Kadir gave her the barest hint of a smile and laid his hand against the shard.

I pulled out of my surprised stupor as the world dropped away into bitter cold and absolute black nothingness. *Trust the process!* I ordered myself and clung to the sensation of warmth and sand, from my own memory as well as Jill's description. *I'm already there. I'm already there.*

And then we were through. I dragged in a breath of relief and did a quick head count to reassure myself everyone made it. Szerain sagged against me, face haunted, and Bryce looked a bit green around the gills. Squig shrank back into Rhyzkahl's hold, while Fillion washed his butt. The puppies whined, but didn't seem unduly distressed. Meanwhile the rest of the humans seemed unfazed.

Kadir dropped a key into Paul's hand, and a moment later, both Rhyzkahl and Szerain were free of the makkas.

Szerain rubbed his wrists. "Fucking hell."

A warm breeze meandered by, stirring the sand that stretched around Kadir's gate. As Jill described, the morning sun had barely cleared the horizon and cast long shadows across the dunes. A number of foot-long lizard-like creatures scuttled about, leaving shimmering trails of slime in their wake and creating a strangely beautiful sparkling-web effect. They looked like distant cousins of geckoids, smaller and more lithe, focused on sipping drops of dew that clung to grains of sand.

In the distance an oasis sparkled amid low green growth punctuated by the blackened trunks of trees destroyed by fire rain. Kadir's "palace" hunkered beside it: a whitewashed, tasteful structure of adobe and stone, no bigger than a typical middle-class home. Beyond, his grove called to me, and tears welled at the welcoming feel of it. Of Rho. It seemed an eternity since I'd been in a full grove.

Kadir's realm was as I remembered, apart from the time of day and the sparkling slime of the mini-geckoids, but I couldn't shake the sense there was something different. It was several seconds before it hit me. The entire vibe of his realm had changed. No longer as teeth-vibratingly uncomfortable as before. Kadir himself was stabilizing, so I supposed it made sense that his realm would adapt as well.

My musings sputtered as I noted a human head impaled on a spike a half dozen yards away. Kadir followed my gaze. "Consciousness remains for longer than one might think."

I had a feeling he knew exactly how long, and I managed an inarticulate noise in response. He might be more stable, but he was damn sure no less creepy.

I nudged Jill and Bryce and drew their attention to a patch of sand a short distance away. The surface rippled, as if something moved just beneath. My mind immediately went to the monsters from the movie *Tremors*, or the sandworm from *Beetlejuice*, though on a much smaller scale.

A creature abruptly popped its head up in a shower of sand. Jill and I both yelped and leaped back, then I let out a strangled laugh. Bryce muttered something under his breath.

The creature was, in a word, adorable. Large brown eyes, pink nose, and pale yellow fur on a sinuous body about a foot and a half long. It looked like the cutest cross ever between a ferret and a guinea pig.

Before I could blink, it unhinged its jaw, revealing a holy-shit number of needle-sharp teeth, practically turned itself inside out, and glommed onto a mini-geckoid, biting it neatly in half before gulping down the pieces.

"Holy shit!" Bryce shouted.

The remaining mini-geckoids scattered as the ferret-monster resumed its original shape, extended a long tongue to lick the blood off its fur, and dove beneath the sand.

"What the *hell* was that?" I demanded, struggling to get my heart rate under control.

Kadir's expression remained constant, but I could have sworn a flicker of amusement lit his eyes. "A *barg*. They are my first line of defense."

I did NOT want to find out what the second line of defense was.

Kadir met and held Szerain's eyes, no doubt somehow related to the earlier incident with Zakaar. Paul moved in close to his side. "We'll see you at the conclave," he said, the only warning I had before he, Kadir, and Dominic vanished.

We grabbed the puppy carriers and trekked toward the grove. Jill gazed around in delighted wonder, and I did my best to answer her bazillion questions. Bryce was more stoic, but seemed equally wowed. Apparently, Kadir had told the bargs we weren't snacks since we made it to the grove without losing limbs.

White trunks and overarching branches formed a tunnel leading to the heart of the grove. Jill stopped at the entrance and smiled up at the canopy. "This is *amazing*."

"It is!" I said. "Ninety-nine point nine percent of Rho is here in the demon realm. Point one percent is on Earth—by the nexus, at ground zero, and the various locations where single trees have sprung up." Leaves rustled and whispered as if in confirmation.

We lugged the carriers down the tunnel to the grassy circle ringed by white trunks that formed the heart of the grove. Sweet birdsong greeted us, and I drank in the sensation of welcome and connection.

"Rhyzkahl," I said, "Szerain and I need to make a side trip to an Ekiri pavilion before heading to the conclave. Would you mind escorting the rest of the group to Elofir's realm?"

Rhyzkahl gave me an understanding nod. "It would be my pleasure."

"I mean, you're all welcome to come with us, but I don't know how long it will take us to saw Zakarain in half."

Idris snorted a laugh.

Jill moved to Szerain and threw her arms around him. "Good luck," she murmured, and I knew she was speaking to both him and Zakaar. Szerain held her tight for a moment, then reluctantly let her go.

"Thank you."

She smiled and returned to stand by Bryce.

Rhyzkahl inclined his head to me, then gathered the others in the center of the grove. I asked Rho to please deliver them to Elofir's realm, and a breath later they were gone.

I took Szerain's hand. "Our turn." I embraced the presence of the grove. *Please bring us to a suitable pavilion.*

The light through the canopy changed from morning sun to overcast, and the trees shifted around us.

I kept Szerain's hand in mine. "Let's do this."

Chapter 25

The ambience of the destination grove blanketed me in bitter-sweet nostalgia as Szerain and I strode down the tree tunnel, and I couldn't help but smile at Rho's choice of pavilion. I'd been here twice before. The most recent was almost nine months ago, when Mzatal and I had been trying desperately to rescue Idris from the Mraztur. But the first was when Mzatal—who I thought at the time to be the villain—sought to remove Rhyzkahl's mark from me. I'd used this grove to escape to Rhyzkahl's realm, straight into his clutches and horrific plots. In response, Mzatal vented his rage and frustration by unleashing a devastating flare of potency here that reduced the rainforest in a fifty-yard radius to ash and char, the same kind of arcane-flare that nearly killed Paul during the battle at the Farouche plantation.

Beyond the tunnel, the scent of char had washed away, and the soil showed it had never been fully dead. Glorious purple and green knee-high grass rippled where the charred ground had been, like carpet unrolled from the grove. Long-stemmed crimson flowers bobbed their heads and filled the air with a spicy scent, while sparkling fairy-like creatures darted to and fro in an aerial dance I could almost understand. Across the field, where the grass met rainforest, an Ekiri pavilion stood, its milky columns and iridescent roof glistening in the sun, with a waterfall shimmering just beyond.

"Thank you, Rho," I murmured, grateful for their choice of location—and for the reminder that life was a stubborn bitch, even in the face of destruction.

Face set in determination, Szerain started toward the pavilion at a brisk jog, grass and flowers swishing in his wake.

I dogged his heels, amused when one of the fairy creatures landed in his hair, content to cling there despite the jostling. It flitted away when he stopped near the pavilion, and I had an absurd image of it returning to its buddies and getting high-fived for hitching a ride so audaciously.

"Will the enemy demahnk try to stop us?" I asked. As far as we knew, they were still unaware that Zakaar hid within Szerain, but we were about to enter one of their power centers, and that could change everything.

"Probably," he said, grim.

In other words, assume they would and prepare for the worst. A whisper of grove sense passed through me. Rho, agreeing. Rho would shield our whereabouts as much as possible, but once the demahnk sensed Zakaar and what we were doing, it wouldn't take them long to find us.

Steps of translucent white stone led up to an open-air heptagonal dais about twenty feet across flanked by seven lofty columns, all giving off a barely perceptible bluish glow. The only Ekiri pavilion I'd ever been close enough to enter had been the one in Rhyzkahl's realm. Even in its state of ruin, half-crushed by boulders during the cataclysm, it had captivated me with its grace and mysterious atmosphere. But it was nothing compared to the allure of this pristine structure that whispered at the edge of my awareness, urging me to dash, laughing, to its heart.

I resisted—reluctantly.

Szerain dropped to his knees in the grass, head lowered. I placed my hand on his shoulder. "What do you need?"

"A moment," he croaked, his whole body tremoring.

Understandable, considering his dependence on Zakaar as a protection against re-submersion. I kept contact with him and used the moment to survey our surroundings. Demahnk intervention wouldn't come in the form of conventional physical attacks, so I didn't need to know the distance to the tree line or determine lines of sight, but my arcane resources were another matter. Surface potency. The grove. Rakkuhr.

The pavilion itself thrummed with potency I was certain could be harnessed, but it would also bolster demahnk interlopers. I reached for Rho. Grass rustled around my calves, and the bobbing red flowers went impossibly still for a heartbeat. Rho likely wouldn't intervene via direct attacks, but I had the clear sense they had my back, and grove potency would answer when I called.

Rakkuhr didn't want to come out and play, though. It was kryptonite to Ekiri which, understandably, meant there wasn't a hint of it near the pavilion. I finally sensed traces a football field away, among the trees of the grove. Though Rho had once been Ekiri/demahnk—susceptible as the others to the peril of rakkuhr—they had merged with the heart of the demon realm planet, merged with rakkuhr itself, and were unique.

Szerain lurched to his feet, eyes haunted. "Let's do this."

I helped him up the steps and between the columns. A profound sense of peace and welcome wrapped me in a smile, and my steps felt light and effortless in the somewhat lower gravity. Just beyond the far side of the pavilion, the narrow waterfall cascaded over a fifteen-foot vine-covered rockface.

I led Szerain to the center of the dais. "How long will it take for Zakaar to re-embody?"

"No idea." He steadied himself on my shoulder.

"Won't Zakaar give you a hint?"

Szerain snorted. "Believe me, I tried to pry one out of him. For all I know, he'll manifest as a pile of goo covered in eye stalks and then have to go through some sort of hyper-evolution."

I snickered at the image. "While normally I'd pay good money to see Zack as goo with eye stalks, I do hope he'll be considerate enough to shift straight to normal demahnk."

A snort escaped him before he got down to business. He turned a slow circle, eyes half-closed, hands spread. Assessing. "It's on you to protect us. Zakaar and I will be quite vulnerable."

"Understood. I'll . . ." My head tipped back as if of its own volition, and I gazed upward. "Holy shit."

From outside, the roof had seemed more decorative than functional, considering the height of the columns and lack of walls. But from within, it wasn't a roof at all. Stars twinkled in limitless space framed by the columns. Beautiful. Impossible. Seductive. My stomach gave a roller-coaster-drop lurch, and I was among the stars. Galaxies, crystal clear to my unaided eye, called to me. I answered, visiting one after another in familiar timeless eternity.

Jesral was my great-grandfather. His father was Ekiri. Realization awakened, giving a deep foundation to the comparatively superficial comprehension my mind allowed.

I am of the Ekiri. Vast. Timeless. At home in the whole of the universe.

Time turned back on itself, and aching loss engulfed me. I

felt stone beneath my boots again and gasped a sob, tears well-
ing. No wonder the demahnk had lost their way, imprisoned in
bodies, cut off from their home. Able to glimpse it via the pavilions but tormented, like a starving man smelling fresh-baked
bread he could never reach.

I scrubbed away tears I didn't have time for, surprised—but
not—to see Szerain only now finishing his turn. No more than
a second, maybe two, had passed. "I'll, uh, get to work."

Work was exactly what I needed to ground myself after that
near-unfathomable experience. I started with a mental pygah,
allowing the natural peace of the structure to enhance its effect
and hone my focus. When I tapped the pavilion as I began to
dance the shikvihr, more potency than I could use leaped to my
command, and I laughed in the glory of it. With every sigil, I set
the intention for an impenetrable foundation, a robust base from
which to fend off attacks. Yet one that would augment my own
offensive strikes.

Once ten brilliant rings spun around me, I forged layers of
protection within the boundary of the pavilion's columns. Inter-
locked shields. Convoluted red herrings to trick and distract.
Anchor spikes. Potency sinks to keep everything charged.

Szerain knelt, palms upturned on his thighs. "More."

I spun out additional layers, traps, and misdirections, filling the
pavilion around us with arcane protections beyond anything I'd
ever attempted before. Finally satisfied with the construct, I summoned grove power, interwove it with the Ekiri-fueled potency
and reinforced the whole. I tested every part of it, reworking weak
points until they held firm.

I dropped my hands, as ready as I could ever be to face impossible odds. Szerain gave a single nod before shifting to sit
with his arms wrapped around his legs and forehead tucked to
his knees.

A ripple of sensation went down my spine. Not from Szerain.
Not from the grove either.

But the demahnk didn't need the grove.

I tapped into the shikvihr and pulled potency from the pavilion and grove until my body hummed. Then I waited. Tense and
hyperaware.

A willowy woman with silver-hued skin and bald head appeared a dozen feet from the steps of the pavilion: Dima. Amkir's ptarl. I could only hope Ssahr and Ilana were tied up with
their scheming.

"Hi, Dima," I called out with a bright and cheery smile. "Nice day for a picnic, eh?"

She tilted her head, gaze going beyond me to Szerain. "Zakaar has broken his vows. For the good of all, I will not allow this to continue."

I barked out a laugh. "Give me a motherfucking break. Not only have you lost all sense of what 'good' means, but you arrogant shits broke both worlds. Y'all are like the most heinous colonizers ever! Hell, you even enslaved the Jontari elders, not to mention destroying native culture and environment. I mean, seriously, did you use Christopher Columbus as a role model?"

"We do what must be done."

"That's the best excuse you can come up with?" I was happy to continue the verbal spar as long as she let me. "'They made us do it,'" I said in a nasal whine. "'No, really, the elders *wanted* to be enslaved. It was worth it because we built a new and better world for the demons. Schools! Prisons! Picturesque cataclysms!'"

Her eyes traveled over the formidable protections before returning to Szerain. I didn't dare glance back to see how things were going, but judging by Szerain's moans, I couldn't imagine the process was anywhere near complete. "You understand nothing, Kara Gillian."

"Probably a lot more than you think, honey."

"Enough! This will end *now*."

A scintillating arcane strike whipped from her hand, impacting my shields and sending me staggering back a pace. She was so not fucking around.

But neither was I. With a flick of my wrist, I spun out strands of potency to reinforce my construct and slap at her, well aware I couldn't actually do damage. I just needed to hold her off for what, a minute? An hour?

No big deal, right? Ugh. I'd have much better odds with rakkuhr, but there was none to be had here.

I funneled power from the grove and pavilion, layering barrier after barrier. Dima scoured each one away with blindingly fast strikes, expression impassive and maybe just a little bored.

Which had the benefit of pissing me off. *I'm boring you? Well, that just means I need to do something unexpected.*

Yep. Something she'd never expect. Yessirree. Clearly nothing I'd ever expect either, because I couldn't think of a damn thing. I poured more into the shielding and risked a split second glance back at Szerain. He'd stripped his shirt, and his sternum area bulged like a cantaloupe had grown under his skin. Weird shit was clearly happening, but not fast enough.

I dug in, abandoning my useless attacks on Dima and instead channeled every wisp of potency I could scrape up into the protections. She stood back, lobbing attacks without pause, faint smile touching her mouth as my defenses steadily weakened.

In a heartbeat, the pavilion energy shifted, and gravity increased to near normal. As I processed the dire implications of the pavilion now under Dima's control, the grove activated, and my gut dropped like a stone. If that was Amkir or any other unfriendly . . .

"Szerain! We're fucked. Unknown incoming. We have thirty seconds. Maybe."

And that was a generous estimate. I sure as shit couldn't maintain long against two attackers.

In confirmation, my shikvihr dimmed and whined, drained of its pavilion potency. I scrambled to reinforce from the grove, but it wasn't enough. Our outermost shielding thinned, and Dima laughed, potency coiled like a serpent in her hand. I tensed, knowing too well the chance of our protections holding out against her strike were somewhere between none and nil.

White hot potency exploded from Dima, and I instinctively threw my arms up to protect my head.

Yet the shielding held, low gravity returned, and I didn't scatter into a billion pieces. Baffled, I dropped my arms to see Dima bathed in white-blue flames, and beyond her, the utterly glorious sight of Rhyzkahl and Idris hammering her with attacks.

"Focus on the protections!" Rhyzkahl shouted. "We'll keep her occupied!"

I didn't need to be told twice. With Dima's attention diverted, I reclaimed pavilion potency and intertwined grove power throughout the shields, rebuilding and reinforcing the damaged areas. In my periphery, Rhyzkahl and Idris collaborated in an exquisite ballet of give and take. Idris snatched strands of potency from Dima and diverted them to Rhyzkahl, who in turn forged weapons from the raw material that they both used to pummel the demahnk.

Hot damn. We weren't winning, but we weren't losing either.

The air shimmered, and a second demahnk appeared, this one in elder-syraza form. Trask, Rayst's ptarl. Though I'd never had direct conflict with him, he was solidly in the enemy column, having been named by Lannist as being in league with Ilana.

Trask confirmed this by snapping a whip of potency at Idris, which Rhyzkahl barely managed to deflect in time.

FUCK

Trask pivoted and redirected his potency whips at my shielding.

DOUBLE FUCK

Despite our best efforts, the two demahnk scraped layers of shielding away faster than I could rebuild them.

<*Need a hand, beautiful lady?*> Helori's voice lilted through my mind.

I jerked in surprise at the unexpected telepathy. He stood on the steps just beyond the protections, glimmering with potency as he gathered it for a strike.

"You are definitely a sight for sore eyes!" I called out with a strained laugh.

Trask yelled something at Helori that didn't sound like a compliment. I half-hoped Helori would make a rude gesture, but he merely smiled and launched arcane barbs at Trask with blinding speed.

With Helori's aid, we were able to hold them at bay, yet I kept my elation in check. Dima and Trask were by no means beaten, and it was only a matter of time before yet another demahnk came to their aid, tipping the balance once more to their side. And meanwhile, Zakaar was *still* re-Zakaarinating.

I shifted to reset an anchor and instead found myself in a pool of dim light amid utter blackness, my face cradled between Mzatal's hands, his forehead against mine.

"Take the shikvihr to the edge," he said with intense urgency. "Foundation. Support. *More.* Look far afield. Use the outer—"

The din of arcane battle slammed into me, unwelcome and jarring after those brief seconds in Mzatal's dream-presence.

His cryptic words reverberated through my essence. Even incomplete, fragments merged and gained meaning. "Outer" had to refer to the tenth ring of the shikvihr.

With Dima focused on Rhyzkahl and Idris, and Trask engaged with Helori, I reassessed and reworked the sigils in my tenth ring. All seemed strong. Perfectly normal.

But *normal* was the problem. Mzatal said *more*, not same-old same-old.

He'd also said *look far afield.*

My gaze snapped to the grove-grass that blanketed the

once-charred ground. Goosebumps swept over me. Rakkuhr dripped from the red flowers to slither among the grass, like tendrils of sentient scarlet fog. Above the field, the fairies' dance formed and unformed a trio of mysterious sigils, each iteration nudging their meaning awake within me.

Exhilarated, I did a fist pump in honor of Mzatal and Rho's resourcefulness. They'd made magic happen. Now it was my turn.

I reinforced the shields and assessed the combat. Trask and Dima had retreated several paces from the grass and its insidious rakkuhr to the shelter of the rainforest. Unfortunately, that small distance didn't hamper them, and we continued to lose ground, even with Rhyzkahl adding threads of rakkuhr to his attacks. But with the demahnk still distracted, I just might have time to pull this off.

I lifted my hands to dispel the outer ring of my shikvihr but hesitated. This was *it*. If I was wrong, all our defenses would fail. I tipped my head back, allowed myself to brush the vastness of the multiverse. That second of connection fueled my conviction, and I dispelled the tenth ring with a sweep of my arm.

My shielding, traps, anchors, and shikvihr dimmed and flickered. The arcane battle itself faltered as all heads turned toward the pavilion. With speed unhampered by second guessing, I began to retrace the ring, allowing its pattern to flow from my essence, weaving the three fairy sigils among the standard eleven.

Helori, high on the steps to avoid the rakkuhr-laden grass, spared a quick glance at what I was doing, then grinned and darted across the field, bounding high to minimize contact with rakkuhr. Trask and Dima tracked him—which was no doubt Helori's goal—their attention off the pavilion for the moment I needed.

A shikvihr was a foundation and support. But it could be so much more. I couldn't get my mind around the new potential, so I fell back on Szerain's guidance, back when I was preparing for the impossible-to-learn summoning of Dekkak.

Be *lordy*. Be *the summoning*.

I completed the ring and set it spinning in the opposite direction of the others. "Time to *be* an Arcane Blackhole on Steroids." I imagined all the arcane around Trask and Dima flowing to my shikvihr, then let go of the imagining and *felt* it. *Was* it.

I met Rhyzkahl's eyes as I activated the unorthodox tenth ring, willing him to read the situation.

He apparently did, because he seized Idris and hauled him toward the center of the field, well away from my targets.

I breathed in. Slowwwwwwly. Blackhole-on-Steroids style. Trask and Dima crumpled to their knees while every blade of grass and tree within three paces of them flattened as if stepped on by a brontosaurus. Our protections thrummed and crackled with power, giving off coruscating light as if there was too much to hold.

Idris let out a whoop. "That's brilliant, Kara!"

My lungs full, I held my breath a moment, then exhaled, equally slowly. Ground-hugging rakkuhr flowed like flood waters from the grass and into the flattened area, then rose to engulf the two demahnk. Their telepathic screams clawed through my mind and essence, shredding my resolve—and my *be*-ingness. I blew out the rest of my breath to dissipate the rakkuhr. Enough was enough. The demahnk writhed on the ground, helpless. Still brimming with Ekiri-ness and potency, I sent them a mental message. *Go. Now.*

They vanished. And so did my protections, as if I'd held too much, too long, and they were like, "We done? Phew. We outta here."

I spun to check on Szerain. He lay sprawled on his back, breathing hard, covered in sparkly goo. Face down on his chest lay a human-looking infant.

"What the hell?" I managed as I dropped to my knees beside them. "Szerain?"

"I'm okay," he croaked without moving.

<*I am here.*> Zakaar's voice in my head, vibrant and potent.

<*Yeah, I see your cute little tush,*> I sent back, grinning in relief. <*Please tell me "infant" isn't a long-term state.*>

Rhyzkahl bounded up the steps, followed closely by Idris. The lord dropped to his knees beside Szerain and set his hand on baby Zakaar's back. Probably some sort of telepathic communication going on. Zakaar was Rhyzkahl's sire and had been his ptarl for millennia—until Zakaar broke the bond. Rhyzkahl had changed for the better since then, through both his time shackled to my nexus and Zakaar's action. Yet it was clear the more primitive bond—and perhaps the more powerful one—remained between this father and son.

I swayed, and Idris looped an arm around me. "Steady, lady. That was some show you put on."

"It all happened so fast. I'll need some time to untangle what went down."

"That's easy! Kickass awesomeness!"

I grinned. "Well, that's a given! How'd y'all know we needed help?"

He hooked a thumb at Rhyzkahl. "He had a bad feeling. We'd arrived in Elofir's realm and were on our way to the palace when Rhyzkahl stopped and did that narrow-eyed frown of his. Next thing I know, Amkir sprints past us toward the grove, and Rhyzkahl shrieks to me that we have to go."

"I did not *shriek*," Rhyzkahl said as he cradled widdle baby Zakaar to his chest, expression placid save for a faint twitch of his mouth. "I calmly commanded."

Idris grinned. "Anyway, we race after Amkir to the grove, where he's trying and failing to make an offering so he can use it to travel. Rhyzkahl flips Amkir off, calm as fuck. Next thing I know Rhyzkahl and I are at the grove here, and, well, you know the rest."

I raised an eyebrow at Rhyzkahl. "Did you really shoot Amkir the bird?"

"I did what had to be done," he said with a grave nod, but amusement danced in his eyes.

I dearly wanted to give him more grief, but he murmured something to Zakaar and headed for the far side of the pavilion and the waterfall. Szerain staggered to his feet, eyes on them. Still holding onto Idris, I threw my other arm around him, not minding the glittery goo one bit. "You did good, big guy."

With the three of us supporting one another, Idris, Szerain and I followed Rhyzkahl, who had descended a handful of steps into a shallow pool formed of the same luminescent stone as the pavilion. I flopped on the top step with a sigh of relief. Idris followed suit, but Szerain descended into the water to stand at the base of the stairs.

Rhyzkahl carried baby Zakaar under the thin stream of the waterfall, and I watched in slack-jawed amazement as Zakaar shifted smoothly from infant to adult in less than fifteen seconds. He stood facing Rhyzkahl, water glistening on skin that subtly sparkled as if from an inner glow. Rhyzkahl wasted no time gathering him into a fierce embrace, returned wholeheartedly by Zakaar.

I looked away, eyes abruptly stinging. Idris, too, seemed to have a sudden issue with "pollen" in his eyes.

Zakaar, in all his naked glory—Ekiri wang and all—finally released Rhyzkahl and approached Szerain, who hadn't moved from his place at the bottom of the stairs. He smiled gently and dissipated the glittery goo with a wave of his hand, while Szerain gazed at him with a look of pride and relief mixed with a bit of lost-child dazedness. Zakaar cradled his face between his hands and engaged in a moment of forehead-to-forehead communion. When he released him, Szerain's face held an expression of peace I'd never seen on him before.

I climbed to my feet as Zakaar ascended the steps. "You're looking good, my friend."

"Thanks to you and our allies."

"What do you need? Besides a loincloth, that is."

He laughed, a joyful sound that wound through me like fuzzy kittens and chocolate donuts. "A little time to reattune, so to speak."

"Take what you need. We'll get ourselves to the protections of the Conclave."

He leaned in, kissed my forehead, and was gone.

I made a show of dusting off my hands. "Well, now that we've checked 'Re-embodify Zakaar' off our to-do list, we should probably get to the conclave before *ruugi* root is the only thing left on the buffet."

Chapter 26

Rhyzkahl and Idris ended up traveling to Elofir's realm ahead of Szerain and me, since Szerain wanted a little time to collect himself before diving into the stress and drama of the conclave. I stayed with him in the safety of the jungle grove, and after about ten minutes of sitting and soaking in peace and tranquility, he took a deep breath and gave me an *I'm ready* nod.

Our arrival in Elofir's grove left me staring in slack-jawed wonder. As with other groves I'd visited, the tree trunks were white—but these were *huge*. Sequoia huge, though with the familiar emerald and amethyst grove leaves rather than needles. However, instead of the typical couple dozen normal grove trees surrounding the central glade, there were only five of these megatrees, and the glade itself was twice the diameter of every other grove I'd been in.

A slender brook bisected the glade, water burbling between opalescent stones. Vibrant green lizards with lilac eyes scurried upward to watch us from the lowest branches, their intricate calls an eerily beautiful play of tones reminiscent of a pipe organ. I craned my neck to peer at the patch of blue sky nearly obscured by the canopy.

Szerain muttered, "Where's the damn tree tunnel?"

That got my attention, and I turned in place. Beyond the five trees, another ring of fifteen or so white giants circled us, and beyond those was dense growth of smaller white trees that looked more impenetrable than welcoming. "Okay, this is strange."

A streak of blue dashed from the far side of the glade, leaped over the brook, and scampered up to us.

"Jekki!" I exclaimed, delighted to see the faas, though his

presence raised a number of questions, the first of which was, "Is Mzatal here?"

"Dahn dahn dahn!" He waved his two right hands. "Not here. Far far away."

Disappointment washed over me followed by an immediate wave of relief. I'd only just faced down enemy demahnk and, though it felt a bit like betrayal, I needed some time before dealing with Mzatal and his handlers again.

"How and why are you here then?" I asked the faas. I'd never known Jekki to be away from Mzatal's realm without Mzatal. Admittedly, my lens was skewed, considering my experience represented only a tiny fraction of the ages Jekki had worked with Mzatal.

"Conclave!" He vibrated in what I could only interpret as excitement, sleek peacock blue fur rippling with iridescent purple. "Jekki always at Conclave!"

"Honored Jekki," Szerain said. "What happened to the—"

Jekki *shrieked* and stood up on his rearmost pair of legs, waving all four clawed hands as if warding off mosquitoes. "KIRAKNIKAHL!!!"

The pipe organ lizards fell silent. Szerain's face froze between a grimace and a wince.

"Jekki," I said, trying to control my own grimace-wince, "surely you know the whole story, and that Szerain isn't—"

"Shh shh shh, Kara Gillian," Jekki whispered. "No mouths can say Jekki did not protest." He tilted his head back and faasbellowed, "KIRAKNIKAHL!"

Szerain pressed his lips together to hold back a laugh, then knelt before Jekki and lowered his head. "Duly noted, my old friend. You have well and truly announced—and rejected—my presence."

Jekki hopped up and down chittering happily. "Jekki did did did!"

I rolled my eyes. "If you two are finished with your weird honor ritual thing, I'd love to know where the damn tree tunnel is."

Jekki warbled. "No tunnel! Up up up, not out out out." He made a sweeping two-arm gesture toward the sky. "See?"

Szerain and I exchanged a baffled glance.

"Come come come," Jekki burbled as he scurried off across the brook and then between two of the massive grove trees. "Sky bridge is the way."

"What the actual fuck?" muttered Szerain.

I looped my arm through his and headed after Jekki. "Only one way to find out."

The brook proved easy to cross, opalescent rocks acting as stepping stones that were nice and grippy rather than slick. Tiny rainbow-colored fish darted here and there in the shallow water, and I longed to just sit on the bank and watch for a while.

Between the first ring of trees and the second, Jekki hopped onto a broad root protruding from the ground like a milky-white platter, more than large enough to accommodate the three of us twice over. "Come come come!"

Szerain and I joined Jekki on the root, but before I could frame a question, the world dipped and shimmered and shifted.

"Holy shit," I breathed. Sunlight bathed us where we stood on a platform of interwoven branches at the top of the canopy. Emerald and amethyst leaves shimmered a hundred feet in all directions, encircled by a wall of dark-trunked trees half again as tall as the grove giants.

Jekki scampered up a walkway of living vines that led to yet another platform at the top of the humongous trees. "Come come come!"

I unhooked my arm from Szerain's and set my foot cautiously on the vineway. To my great relief, it seemed both sturdy and stable despite the sharp incline. I focused on putting one foot in front of the other, relieved when I reached the second platform without incident.

And then I took a look around.

Elofir's demesne was literally a forest. The tops of immense trees spread in all directions like a sea of deep green and rich turquoise. Though I'd never tried to picture what his realm would be like, somehow it was exactly what I expected.

Far to the west, old rolling mountains worn down to comfortable peaks reminded me of the ancient Appalachians, and to our east, late morning sunlight glinted on water. From past perusal of demon realm maps, I knew that to be a massive body of fresh water that rivaled North America's Lake Superior in size.

The vineway—or sky bridge as Jekki had called it—extended northward along the treetops, over a break in the trees, then onward toward another platform a good quarter mile away. Rhyzkahl and Idris stood there, taking in the breathtaking scenery.

We followed Jekki along the bridge, though I came to an abrupt halt at the break in the trees, swaying from a sudden rush of vertigo. Szerain slipped his arm around me, narrow bridge be damned. Below, a ravine a hundred feet wide and miles long cut through the trees and so deeply into the ground its bottom was lost in darkness. Weird potency crawled along its edge and the bases of the trees. A stream, likely the one from the grove, formed a slender waterfall over the edge right below us.

I felt as if I was standing on the lip of an impossibly high cliff with sucking darkness below—and my body didn't want to continue across it.

Szerain blew out a breath. "This is new." He tightened his arm around my middle and urged me forward until the weird pull of the ravine lost its grip on me and retreated into the dark.

Now that I was past it, I realized where I'd experienced something similar, namely the dark void at the top of the column in Mzatal's realm. Yet another manifestation of the breaking worlds? No wonder Rho had closed the tree tunnel and created this sky bridge to bypass that bizarre hazard.

Szerain released me and led the way to the next platform. I stayed close behind him, and we made it without incident.

Idris waved as we joined them. "This is as far as we made it earlier before Amkir came tearing past us on the way to the grove."

The world dipped and shimmered again, and all four of us were back on the forest floor, well past the freaky ravine, and surrounded by dark trunks as thick as my house. I'd once gone on a callout to Muir National Forest, and after we secured the rift, I spent a couple of blissful hours simply wandering amongst the amazing trees. Elofir's forest made even those giant redwoods look like saplings.

Idris, Rhyzkahl, and Szerain started down a luminescent stone path, Jekki chittering happily alongside them. I kept my steps slow in order to soak in the peace and unique quiet, but then hurried to catch up when the others went out of sight around a bend. Maybe I could take a more leisurely walk at some point later on.

I fell in beside Idris, who trailed a dozen or so feet behind the lords, giving them space to talk. He elbowed me and pointed off to our right. "How is that even possible?"

Among several downed and shattered trees stood a massive hunk of stone at least fifty feet tall. I started to ask what he found so unusual, then realized it wasn't stone at all, but the remains of a huge tree that appeared to have *melted* from the top down like a giant candle. "How is that even possible?" I echoed.

We gaped for a moment, neither of us coming up with any reasonable explanation, before hurrying on. We passed other evidence of catastrophic damage: many more shattered and fallen trees, odd upthrusts of chaotic roots, and what had once been a large pond but was now a bed of cracked mud littered with bones of various aquatic life, as if the water had evaporated in mere seconds.

Soon enough, the trees gave way to a broad swath of cobalt blue grass skirting Elofir's palace, and I abruptly felt a frisson of betrayal to Mzatal.

I adored Mzatal's palace, with its incredible glass and sweeping balconies and breathtaking views. But the instant I saw Elofir's, I fell madly and deeply in love. It was, indeed, clearly a palace, yet by its very nature it blended perfectly into the surrounding trees—primarily because it *was* trees. Half a dozen trees well over a hundred feet wide at their base formed towers. Balconies flowed around the perimeter—not carved, but more as if the trees had been convinced to grow that way, asked kindly to please create rooms and hallways and exquisite connecting walkways both high and low.

Hell, for all I knew that's exactly what Elofir had done. *You are beautiful, and I would be honored to live within you. Will you accommodate me and mine?*

Elofir's palace hadn't escaped the ravages of the recent cataclysmic events. One tree tower lay on its side, gouged deeply into the earth, leaving behind a trunk with wicked shards of wood spearing fifty feet into the air. Yet another was little more than a smoldering stump, charred and broken, walkways terminating where the tower once stood. But it all still exuded welcoming peace and serenity—a perfect reflection of Elofir.

"Wow," I breathed.

"Opposite end of the spectrum from Kadir's realm, isn't it?" Idris said. "I know this sounds odd, but I think Kadir's is beautiful as well—though in a vastly different way."

I glanced over at him, oddly pleased that he, too, looked upon the mega forest with reverence. "I know exactly what you mean. They're both closely aligned with nature."

"Yes! That's it."

A huge tree trunk lay across the stone path, though this one was "only" about thirty feet in diameter. Cracks in its bark glowed from unnatural fires deep within. A tunnel had been carved through it, and wards lined the interior to protect those passing through from the heat.

The scent of smoke mingled with a far more pleasant aroma of flowers and growing things. Amidst the ruined areas, blue grasses and green shoots already poked forth. The sight lifted my spirits. Life stubbornly persisted.

No sooner had we passed through the burning tree than a syraza swooped down to land before us. Pearlescent white skin shimmered in the dappled sunlight as slanted violet eyes regarded us from an elegant, almost human face.

"Greetings and welcome, Rhyzkahl, Kara Gillian, Idris Palatino," he said, pointedly not acknowledging Szerain. "I am Nagoh. Elofir has set aside an apartment for you and your associates in the Ambrosial Tower. The other members of your party have opted to wait until your arrival before proceeding to the rooms and are currently enjoying the aquatic courtyard. Select and trusted demons are attending the juvenile canines."

I held back a snort of amusement, because I'd seen how demons were with Fuzzykins' kittens. I had zero doubt the "select and trusted demons" were getting sloppy-gooey over the puppies.

"When you reach the main entrance," Nagoh continued, "Jekki and Keku will escort you to your rooms and see to your needs and comfort. The conclave proper will not begin until the morrow." The syraza directed his attention to Rhyzkahl. "Elofir has asked that you proceed to the Fountain Arbor to swear the conclave oaths to him. Moreover, he offers reassurance that all companions—human, demon, animal, or"—his gaze swept over Szerain—"*other* will be covered by said oaths and offered full protection."

Szerain remained unperturbed by the slight, so I did my best to follow suit. Rhyzkahl looked from Nagoh to Szerain and back. "I do not agree to sponsor Szerain."

I winced, though it was probably a wise decision on Rhyzkahl's part. Szerain was a renegade, essence blade holder, and dangerous.

Nagoh extended his wings. "Understood. The kiraknikahl may plead his case with Elofir."

Hopefully Elofir would be reasonable about Szerain's presence. "Which other lords are here?" I asked.

"Vahl and Amkir, along with their respective companions.

Others will continue to arrive throughout the day and tomorrow morning."

"Do you know if Lord Elofir might spare a moment for me after he administers the oath to Rhyzkahl and, um, deals with Szerain?"

Nagoh inclined his head. "He will be closeted with other lords at various times, but if he has availability I am certain he will welcome your presence."

I thanked the syraza, though his certainty did nothing to alleviate my nerves about speaking to Elofir. Nagoh had sounded a bit too much like an efficient administrative assistant who knew just how to screen visitors. While I doubted Elofir had been cursing my name for the past few months, he still might not want to deal with me or my issues.

Nagoh leaped into the air, and we continued down the pathway with Jekki leading the way.

As promised, another faas waited for us at the main entrance: intricately carved double doors surrounded by incredible inlays depicting swirls of ivy and flowers. And once again I had the impression the effect was more grown than physically crafted.

I gave Szerain an encouraging smile as he and Rhyzkahl parted ways with us for their oath-swearing and case-pleading with Elofir.

The new faas was slightly larger than Jekki with considerably more purple than blue in its fur—a sign that it was quite ancient. I crouched before it. "Greetings, honored Keku."

Keku chittered at Idris and me. "Greetings greetings, Kara Gillllian and Idrisss Palatino! Come come. Your friends await." She trundled off at a very sedate pace for a faas but still faster than my normal walking speed, which meant she had to stop every so often to let us catch up.

We passed through a spacious foyer—walls and ceiling formed of living branches interwoven with lush vines bearing golf-ball sized crimson fruit—and into a lovely open-air courtyard bounded by trees. As in the grove, a stream flowed through it, alive with sparkling fish and unusual crustacean-like creatures. Beside the stream were benches formed from living plants and extensions of trees, along with scattered cushions in a variety of rich colors. Everything about the courtyard invited quiet contemplation.

Jill sat cross-legged on a bench watching the fish. Beside her, Bryce's posture made it seem as if he too was enjoying the aquatic life, but I knew him well enough to be certain his attention was focused far more on keeping meticulous tabs on anything and everything else. Bodyguard to the core. Especially for her.

He noted our presence before we'd taken a single step in and nudged Jill, who looked up and waved. Idris murmured something about catching up with me later and headed off toward an arched passageway between trees to our right. Jekki swiveled to look at me, then at Idris's back, chittering softly in agitation.

I gave him an apologetic smile. "We're probably not supposed to be unaccompanied yet, right? Oaths still being administered and whatnot. Go ahead and go after him. I'll be sure to hang with Keku."

Jekki threw up all four hands in comical exasperation and darted after Idris as I continued to Bryce and Jill.

"Is everything okay with Zakaar?" Jill asked. "I mean, I assume it all worked out since you seem pretty chill."

"Idris and Rhyzkahl made a showy entrance just in the nick of time and saved our asses." I gave a brief summary of what went down. "Zakaar is his own man, er, demahnk now." I paused, remembering the unfathomable light in his eyes at the waterfall. Was he actually still demahnk and partially fettered Ekiri? Or had the process somehow freed him? I wanted to believe it was the latter, though it was pure speculation. "Anyway, he's off doing Zakaar-ish things. But he did say he'd rejoin us later." Though "later" to a virtually eternal being could be tomorrow or a century hence.

"Oh, that's so good," she said, a mix of grief, acceptance, and closure passing over her face. Relief finally settled in, and she glanced at Bryce and smiled. His expression didn't betray his emotions, but he put his hand on Jill's and gave it a brief squeeze.

I tried to shift my look of delight into a casual smile, which probably came across more like a weird grimace of pain. "Nagoh said demons are looking after the puppies. I hope they know about puppy piddle."

"I'm sure they do by now," she said with a laugh.

Keku tugged my sleeve. "Time to go to your rooms, Kara Gillian."

Bryce stood and offered his hand to Jill—which she readily took despite needing absolutely zero help standing. I didn't miss that it was a good five seconds before they released each other's hands.

Keku led us out of the courtyard and up broad, winding stairs of multi-hued wood, parts of which had leaves of purple and silver growing out of them, reminding me of the grove. Creatures like potato-sized fireflies drifted above, casting soft, shifting light over our path. At numerous landings, natural corridors extended, giving us glimpses of a variety of demons, from diminutive zrila to massive reyza, as well as some types unfamiliar to me.

Jill kept a smile plastered onto her face, but I'd known her long enough to recognize she was on the verge of being overwhelmed. Though she was no stranger to demons, her exposure had been to only a few at any given time. Not to mention, there was no denying we were in a completely different world—one that was going through its own apocalypse.

Despite all that, I was certain she had zero regrets about coming along. And I was glad I'd fought for her right to do so. As much as she'd been through, she deserved to see this world—both the damaged and the delightful aspects.

I gave her a light shoulder bump. "Feels different, doesn't it."

She laughed shakily. "Yeah, it's subtle, but still, it's like everything's a few degrees off-center."

Bryce nodded. "I promise you get used to it pretty quickly." He flashed a smile. "Kind of like a bad smell."

"At least it smells pretty nice here," she said. Even with the ever-present whiff of wood smoke along with that of seen and unseen disaster, the prevailing scent was of rich earth and muted spices.

She was too polite to say that Kadir's realm had an odor and feel of destruction. A lingering miasma. An acrid tang that slithered in and settled at the back of your throat.

"Once we get to our rooms we can kick back for a bit."

She blew out a relieved breath. "Yeah. That sounds like a great plan."

The stairs opened onto an elevated walkway that traversed fifty feet across the face of the palace toward another tree tower. We were about three stories above the ground, and I tipped my head back to gaze at the tree canopy as it shifted and swayed in a gentle dance.

Keku gestured toward the tree tower. "There there. Kara Gillian stays there!"

We followed along the balcony and through an arch into the tree tower. "Ohhhhhh wow." I stopped, eyes closed as I took in the incredible scent. Gone was any trace of smoke or destruction.

Still rich and earthy, but carrying an unidentified floral undertone alongside perfect notes of spice.

"Oh my god," Jill breathed. I opened my eyes to find her as rapt as I was. Even Bryce looked amazed and blissful.

Keku burbled softly, as if pleased at our reaction. "Ambrosial Tower. Favorite of Elofeeer. Honored guests to shelter heeere." With that she trundled off down a lofty corridor of interwoven branches alive with deep turquoise leaves and up to a set of double doors. She shoved them open to reveal a gloriously appointed suite consisting of a sizable central common room with a half dozen individual bedrooms around the perimeter. A gentle sound of running water provided a soothing backdrop. Opposite the entrance was another set of double doors almost as gorgeous as the main entry below. These had thick demon-glass windows with hints of twining vines deep within. They stood ajar, allowing us to see a broad balcony, and giving us a breathtaking view of the palace and surrounding forest.

Jill all but ran to the railing, taking in everything. Smiling, Bryce followed at a more sedate pace, assessing his surroundings on the way.

Though I was dying to check out the view, I vowed to give Bryce and Jill some time alone first. Jekki scurried in—without Idris. Before I could ask, he burbled, "Elofeeeer has Idris Palatino!"

By "has" I assumed Jekki meant under his protection.

Keku and Jekki exchanged rapid-fire words in a dialect I couldn't follow, then Keku said, "Jekki chooses to remain with Kara Gillian. Welcome and farewell." With that she scrambled out the door.

I knelt by Jekki and pulled him into a hug. "I've missed you, *ghastuk*."

He burbled happily and gave me a tight four-armed squeeze. "Friend friend, friend!"

"I miss our other . . . *friend*, too."

"Kri kri kri! *Gestamar* is in trouble. Sad sad Gestamar."

I took the hint that talking directly about Mzatal, even here in the seeming privacy of the suite, wasn't a good idea—hence referring to his reyza companion instead. "I worry about him. I know he's strong and resilient, but—"

"He keeps wings folded! That is goooooood. Strong ones cannot force him to fly."

"Er, yeah. That's good," I said and took a mental step back.

Maybe Jekki wasn't using Gestamar as a stand-in for Mzatal, and was really talking about the reyza? Either way, there were too many mental gymnastics involved for my tired brain. "We'll keep hoping for the best."

"More doing than hope, Kara Gillian!"

Bryce and Jill came in from the balcony, both smiling, and settled into a cushiony sofa. I gave Jekki an uncertain smile, deciding to perhaps delve into the Gestamar-maybe-Mzatal conversation later, after I had some time to unwind.

A small and very blue faas darted in. When he spied Jill, he gave a squeal of delight. "Reft likes pretty pretty hair!"

"Er, thanks?" Jill said with a weak smile and put a hand up to touch her hair in a self-conscious gesture. She'd kept it in a pixie cut for as long as I'd known her but had let it grow over the past year or so, mostly because there'd been too much other stuff to deal with to worry about haircuts.

Reft chittered. "Bright and strong and fierce color! Reft will style for you."

Jill shot a desperate *What the hell do I do?* look my way.

"Go for it," I said. "Faas are terrific artists."

"Um, sure, thanks," she said to Reft. "It's a mess. I honestly can't remember the last time I had a trim."

Reft made a bubbly noise that was clearly a faas version of *Oh, hell nah, girl, don't slag on yourself!* then dashed off, no doubt to gather supplies.

Jill let out a weak laugh. "This is the strangest salon ever."

"Just you wait," I said as a zrila skittered into the room. The demon resembled a six-legged newt about half-again as large as Fuzzykins, with skin that shifted in hues of indigo and fuchsia. It whistled a complex tune at Jekki, who thanked the zrila and turned to us.

"Elofeeer offers zrila circle services to Kara Gillian and companions!" Jekki translated for us.

"Lord Elofir is quite gracious and kind," I replied, "and Jill would be honored to indulge." I turned to Jill, who was watching this exchange with wide-eyed confusion. "Okay, chick. You need to stand up and extend your arms and relax. This very nice zrila is going to take your measurement."

"For what?" she asked, voice a bit faint.

"Really amazing clothing."

She sucked in a breath, and astonished delight displaced the nerves. "Oh my god. Like the stuff you have in your closet?"

"Exactly."

Jill shot to her feet and stuck her arms out, wide smile on her face as the zrila scuttled all over her. Not even ten seconds later, the zrila gave another whistle, then leaped down and dashed out of the room.

Jill slowly lowered her arms. "That's it?"

"Pretty much. The zrila will have something for you by tomorrow morning at the latest. Maybe sooner."

Yet another faas darted in then, carrying a tray that it set on a side table. I grinned at the sight of the "cat turds" that had become one of my favorites, displayed beside cheesy potato skins and sliced fruit. A pot of the luscious chak steamed on one side along with a pitcher of tunjen juice—the demon realm version of a kickass sports drink, but better tasting and far more restorative.

"Jill, you have got to try these," Bryce said, offering her one of the cat turds.

"You're shitting me," she said. "Literally." She gestured toward the general turdy appearance.

Bryce laughed. "Trust me. You can't judge this by its appearance."

She gave it a verrrry dubious sniff, but gamely took a tiny bite. "Oh, damn," she breathed, eyes lighting up.

After that, Bryce was eager to have her try chak and other various delicacies. Jekki quietly informed me that oaths had been sworn on the humans' behalf by Rhyzkahl, and on Szerain's by Elofir, so we were now free to roam as we pleased—with any mischief we caused falling on the head of our sponsor. I slipped out of the common room, mostly because I had a desperate need for a bath after all the exertion from the confrontation at the pavilion, and even Elofir's fragrant palace wouldn't mask my stench when I went to see him.

The bathing chamber was like a small jungle, full of warmth and light and lovely scents. Soft reeds carpeted the floor, and flowering ivy twined up the walls in patterns of purple and gold. On one end of the room, steaming water cascaded from an intricate sculpture of hollow reeds, splashing into what I could only describe as a gigantic leaf—giving new meaning to the term "garden tub." The branches of a small tree beside the leaf-bathtub bore small orbs of crystalized sap which sparkled and winked in the light, and when I cautiously touched one with wet fingers it foamed into something akin to soap and gave off a clean refreshing fragrance that invigorated even as it calmed.

I bathed and scrubbed then lounged in the tub until some of the knots of tension in my back unwound, then reluctantly got out and dressed in some of the demon realm clothing I'd brought. And, of course, belted on my gun, because conclave oaths were fine and all, but I wasn't stupid.

I checked my appearance in a long mirror, adjusted my shirt so it covered my gun, then squared my shoulders, gave myself a pep talk, and left to speak to Elofir.

Chapter 27

Not that the pep talk was needed, since it turned out Elofir was closeted in discussion with "select lords" and not currently available to see me.

I trekked through the aquatic courtyard, tense as I wondered which lords he was conferring with and, of course, what the topics of conversation were. Closed-door meetings left me antsy, especially with so much at stake, but I reminded myself that Elofir had always been on our side and surely continued to be.

Still, that old argument between us about his destruction of Bikturk's corpse was like a rock in my shoe, and a reminder that even as allies we had very different ways of dealing with things. I wouldn't feel better until I could address it with him.

What I needed right now was something that was one hundred percent guaranteed to lift my spirits.

After getting directions from a faas, and a couple of wrong turns, I finally got close enough to my destination to follow the sounds of yips and squeals and demonic rumbles. I pushed open a door—and quickly closed it behind me as two puppies attempted escape—then sighed in delight at the spectacle before me.

It was a good thing the room was large, because there had to be damn near a dozen of the larger variety demons there. Puppies tugged on ropes or chased demon tails or attempted to chew on reyza claws. One pup was sacked out, cradled in the claws of a savik, while a kehza stroked its little floppy ears. I spied bowls of food and water against one wall with enough mess around them to confirm that the puppies had indeed eaten. And when one of the rope-chasing pups squatted to drop a puppy-sized present, a watching reyza immediately scooped up the waste and disposed of it.

I watched for another minute or so, then quietly left, satisfied that the puppies had very excellent puppysitters.

Yet since I was still too restless to go back to the rooms, I found myself heading outside to do a bit of wandering. After all, I'd promised myself that I'd take a walk and explore a bit, right? And at least there were no nagging phone calls or overdue paperwork here that needed my focus and energy.

Soon enough I found a trail that branched off from the main walkway and simply ambled, which was something I hadn't done in a long long while. I took time to enjoy the sights and sounds of the ancient forest, and also acknowledged each mark of destruction, as if that tiny bit of honoring could help everything heal.

I rounded a curve in the trail and stopped at the sight of an unfamiliar man with olive-toned skin, and grey peppered through his dark hair. He sat cross-legged with his back to me amidst a cluster of foot-high plants bearing fronds of purple and pink, while he made notes in an ordinary spiral notebook. After a moment, he gently touched the tip of a leaf with his pen. Immediately, the fronds curled inward, seizing it. Muttering to himself, he relinquished the pen, then lifted a smartphone in an oddly bulky case and took a picture. A few seconds later, the plant unfurled and dropped the pen, at which point the man retrieved it to make more notes.

He glanced back at me as soon as he finished writing and gave me a smile. "You must be one of the people coming for the conclave," he said in what I recognized as a Filipino accent. "I'm Arnel."

Now that I could see his face, I guessed his age to be mid-fifties or so. I returned the smile and approached. "I'm Kara. And yes, I'm here for the conclave."

"Ah! I apologize for not recognizing you, though of course I know who you are."

"My infamy is vast," I said with a laugh. "Are you here with one of the lords?"

"I live here with Elofir and Michelle. Have for almost three months now."

Huh. Three months meant Arnel definitely hadn't been among the humans kidnapped by Farouche's men as companions for the various lords. I wanted badly to ask him how he ended up in the demon realm and if he knew about any other new arrivals, but decided to hold off, at least for now. I'd learned several months ago that most, if not all, of the human companions had been suffering from extremely debilitating health issues. And, it really wasn't my place to pry about that sort of thing.

That said, I suspected Helori was involved in some fashion.

"What is it you're doing out here?" I asked him, gesturing toward the plant.

"Having the time of my life!" he said with a laugh. "I'm a botanist, so this opportunity to research alien plant life is an absolute dream come true. But to answer your question more specifically, I'm studying the reactions of this specimen to various stimuli. It responds in different ways depending on what touches it, and I'm trying to narrow down the various parameters."

I crouched and peered at the plant. "Just be careful not to get eaten," I said, only partly joking.

Arnel gestured toward the base of a nearby tree and a patch of darkness that I now realized was a coiled zhurn. "Koob the Shadowy," he said, eyes crinkling, "knows a great deal about the local flora and has stopped me from blundering into dangerous situations a few times. Plus, I enjoy their company."

"That's very good to hear." I straightened, relieved that Arnel had a bodyguard. "Perhaps I'll see you at the conclave at some point?"

"I'll be there. Michelle has given me no choice in the matter." He smiled indulgently. "I think she misses being around humans and is looking forward to a social gathering. Plus, I confess to being curious about the other lords."

"Some are nicer than others," I said in a massive understatement.

He nodded. "I have been well-briefed."

Whew. "Then I'll leave you to your studies. It was a pleasure to meet you, Arnel."

"Likewise, Kara."

Meeting Arnel had lifted my spirits, not only because he seemed like a genuinely nice man, but because the presence of more humans in the demon realm would hopefully help the various qaztahl see any threat to Earth as a threat to a world of actual real people with names and faces and thoughts and dreams. Though humans had been an integral part of the lords' experience for millennia, the demon realm had been mostly isolated from Earth for the past few centuries, so an in-your-face reminder couldn't hurt.

Despite the lifted spirits, fatigue began to dog my steps as I continued along the path. And no wonder, since I'd already put in a solid day and a half or so of various exertions, what with the stress of prepping to leave the compound, the hijinks at the spires, and the restoration of Zakaar and the accompanying battle. The sun was barely at its zenith here, but my energy level was diving toward its nadir.

Fortunately, my body decided to give me a second wind as I passed through the aquatic courtyard and spied Vahl. He stood near an Asian woman with short, grey-streaked hair. Looked to be in her sixties or so. Fit, with muscled shoulders, and a weathered face that held bright eyes and a strong jaw. She sat on the same bench Jill had occupied earlier and gazed down at the fishy creatures, but glanced up as I angled their way. Vahl bent and murmured something to her, and she gave me a more guarded look before nodding up at him. He smiled, rested a hand briefly on her shoulder, and strode in my direction.

It had been a year or so since I'd last seen Vahl, but little had changed about him. Tall, athletic build, perfect dark skin. He still smoldered. Still exuded sexiness.

His mouth curved into a smile as he approached. "Kara Gillian," he murmured, gaze sweeping over me.

"Vahl," I replied in an over-the-top sexy purr.

He tipped his head back and laughed. "Ah, I deserved that. How I have missed you!" Yet his expression grew more measuring as he looked into my face. "Are you still with Mzatal?"

The question surprised me, because surely by now everyone knew we weren't "together" in any traditional sense at the moment. But then I realized there was probably more to the question. "Why do you ask?" I said all innocent-like.

Caution—and perhaps uncertainty?—whispered over his features. "He has closed himself off in the past, but this time is different. More absolute."

"Indeed it is." I met his eyes. "I suppose we all react in our own ways to the influences around us." I paused for a breath, then added, "Where is your ptarl?"

Vahl's brow creased. "You came this way, I assume, for greater purpose than my delightful company."

I didn't miss how he'd skated right past my question. "Your

company is, as ever, delightful, but you're right. My purpose is more dire."

I traced a quick pair of privacy wards, then told him what we'd learned about Jesral's plans regarding his Earthgate and what we suspected his ultimate intent to be, gauging Vahl's reaction after each revelation. As I spoke, his expression grew more and more guarded.

When I finished, he remained still. "I confess it is difficult to accept Jesral would take it so far, though I cannot deny his desire for mastery runs deep." He paused a moment. "Jesral believes he has never been given the respect he is due, and thus will take it and feel justified in doing so."

"That's quite the insight," I murmured. I didn't doubt his assessment of Jesral. But I wondered if Vahl realized how much he'd revealed of his own psyche. A vague sense of self-enforced neutrality or uncertainty still lingered about him, as if he wanted to be sure he chose the path that would suit him best, give him the most relevance, whether or not it was right one.

He tilted his head toward the woman on the bench. "Suong is from your North Vietnam and has experience with dictators and tragedy. It would grieve me deeply to see your entire world in such a state."

"I imagine she has some well-honed instincts for the type of people who would crave such domination."

"The tragedy is that too often such instincts are born from bitter and painful experience." His eyes flicked to the sigil scars visible above the neckline of my shirt.

"The hope is that we can use that hard earned instinct to protect others from similar trauma." I tilted my head and put on my best innocent expression. "Has Suong met Jesral?"

Vahl chuckled low. "I assure you, I will do everything in my power to keep Suong safe and protected." He took my hands and gently kissed my knuckles. "May we be worthy soldiers in this battle."

I left Vahl with the fish and mused over the encounter. He'd put on a good show of being concerned and serious and disapproving of Jesral's actions, but my time as a cop meant I'd been around a lot of liars. Really good ones, too, who'd perfected deception and dissembling over many years with hundreds of different people. Vahl was thousands of years old, but he didn't actually have that much practice at appearing earnest while being less than truthful, considering he dealt primarily with the other lords. And even when he did have interactions with humans, I doubted he'd ever needed to lead them to believe he was being anything less than open and honest. Why would he need to when a) he could read their thoughts, and b) adjust those thoughts if they didn't suit his purposes?

But he couldn't read or adjust my thoughts, and I didn't need lordy mental powers to know he wasn't as anti-Jesral as he wanted me to believe.

I found Jekki after a brief search and crouched before him. "Honored Jekki, I have a favor to ask of you, yet I'll understand completely if it's beneath your honor."

Jekki cocked his head. "Kara Gillllian would never purposely hurt Jekki's honor."

"I certainly hope not." I smiled. "My request is a simple one. If you or any other faas see Vahl sending a message sigil within the next couple of hours or so, would you please let me know?"

"Kri kri kri," Jekki burbled, then leaned toward me and lowered his voice. "We can also see see seeeeee if any lord here *receives* a message from Vahl!"

My smile widened. "You are indeed the most clever of all faas." If none of the lords here received a sigil from Vahl, that narrowed down the possible recipients by quite a bit.

I thanked Jekki again, and he darted off, tail vibrating with excitement at the mission.

As I thought about it more, I wasn't all that surprised at how the conversation with Vahl had gone. As sexy and smoldering as Vahl could be, he sure did seem to carry a lot of insecurity. In fact, he reminded me of a girl I knew in college—always angling to be invited to whatever cool thing was going on, even if the cool thing didn't actually interest her at all. But she was so desperate to be included and part of a group that she ended up hopping from social circle to social circle and never actually did the work to get to know people and let them get to know her.

I'd told Jesral he was a middle of the pack wannabe, but Vahl was definitely at the bottom of the pecking order. Yes, even below Seretis, because never in a million years would Seretis switch allegiances just for a shot at, what, popularity?

I snorted. I couldn't imagine Vahl ever being willing to

sacrifice everything to do what was right. He wasn't a *bad* person, but he was definitely a weak one.

At the same time, I wouldn't delude myself that certain other lords would be willing to believe the worst of Jesral. Hell, Amkir was so far up Jesral's ass, I'd need scuba gear to have a conversation with him.

Lost in my musings, I damn near jumped out of my skin at a piercing whistle just ahead and above. My hand instinctively went toward my weapon until I realized the source was Janice Massi, who grinned and waved at me from a balcony that blossomed with turquoise demon-roses. I aborted my reach for my gun and shifted to an enthusiastic return wave. Janice was in her late forties, with dark hair and complexion, and was omg smart and funny. I'd "rescued" her from Rhyzkahl's clutches, back when I'd been convinced—with good reason—that the humans who'd been transported to the demon realm were there to be little more than sex slaves. Janice had quite firmly informed me that, while they had indeed been transported to the demon realm, none had been forced to remain—or do anything else—against their will. In fact, after they received healing or help, all were given the option to return to Earth. So far they'd chosen to remain as companions to the various lords.

"Hey!" she called down. "You gonna be downstairs in the Sylvan Hall later? A bunch of us pesky humans are doing a bit of meet and greet hangout thing in an hour or so."

"Count me in!" I replied, weirdly delighted to be included in a social activity that was *human*. Normal-ish. "I have a couple of extremely pesky human types of my own I can bring along too, if that's okay?"

"Hell yeah, the more the merrier!" She laughed. "Time to show these lords how to party. Maybe we'll even raid Elofir's liquor cabinet and smoke his cigars!"

"If there's raiding, I'm there!"

"And we'll get Kian to be the lookout!"

"Who's Kian?"

"You'll meet him tonight." She glanced back toward her rooms. "Hang on, Kian says we need weed."

A distant male voice shouted, "No, I said I'm trying to read!"

"Right, we need weed." She winked at me. "You got any weed?"

"Nope. Not even a weed seed!" I replied, enjoying the

ludicrous exchange. It probably helped that fatigue made me extra punchy. "Arnel's a botanist. Maybe he knows where we can score weed! Wait, does the demon realm even have weed?"

"Hell, they have giant flying sharks that eat stray magic," she said with a shrug. "Why not weed?"

I grinned, remembering the time Helori took me for a flight in the ever-gaping mouth of one of those behemoths. "I can't argue with that logic!"

The balcony doors across from Janice's flew open, putting a halt to our conversation. Amkir stepped out and sent a black glare down at me. Dark hair, strong bone structure, and built like a Russian gymnast. He'd've been damn handsome if he wasn't such an asshole.

Janice gave him an over-the-top enthusiastic wave. "Hi, Lord Amkir!" she said, tone bright and *just* shy of sarcastic. "It's so nice to see you!"

I fully expected him to snarl something nasty at her, but he merely let out a small sigh and offered up a pained expression that almost resembled a smile.

"A pleasure as always, Janice Massi," he said in a long-suffering tone. His attention returned fully to me, then he very slowly lifted one hand and extended his middle finger. He held it for a heartbeat, eyes locked on mine, then dropped his hand, returned inside, and closed the doors firmly.

Janice and I looked at each other, wide-eyed and open-mouthed in shock for an instant before we burst out laughing. *What the fuck just happened?* she stage-whispered at me.

I spread my hands in an expression of pure bafflement, then stage-whispered back, *Maybe he's been into the weed?*

Janice slapped a hand over her mouth to muffle her even more exuberant laughter, waved with the other, and hurried inside.

Spirits and energy levels lifted, I made my way to my room, reflecting on the interaction. How much did Amkir know of Jesral's plots? Amkir was one of the original Mraztur, but Jesral certainly seemed to be out for himself and no one else at this point. No way would I ever be able to have a civil conversation with Amkir, but maybe Janice could? She didn't tolerate stupid bullshit and was sharp as a tack. Here I was thinking I'd have to do all the heavy lifting when it came to convincing the other lords Jesral was up to some really bad shit, but in truth, I potentially had a cadre of astute and clever humans to do much of the legwork for me.

I entered the suite, then bit back a laugh at the sight of sleeping bodies scattered about the common room. Bryce sprawled on a couch. Jill was snuggled down in a pile of oversized cushions. And Szerain sat in an armchair with his head tipped back, eyes closed and fingers laced over his stomach. I wasn't sure if he was actually asleep, but he damn sure didn't look perky. Even the ever-active Jekki was curled on a cushion near the balcony doors.

The one fully conscious member of the lot was Idris, who sat at the table doing idle arcane exercises, the equivalent of a musician doing scales.

"When did the others pass out?" I asked him, keeping my voice pitched low.

He smiled. "About five minutes after you left."

"Good to know I'm not the only one suffering from jet lag," I said. "Or planet lag."

Idris snorted. "I've been bouncing around our own planet so much, I think my body's forgotten what a circadian rhythm actually is."

"I remember those days," I said with a wry smile. "But at least you're still young and can recover from lost sleep in no time." I tilted my head. "Tomorrow's a big day, though." The shikvihr. The whole enchilada.

"Yeah, I'm going to grab a power nap in just a few." He finished the exercise and dispelled the potency. "Eleventh ring. Feels weird that it's happening like this."

"Without Mzatal," I said, quietly.

He shoved a hand through his hair. "Yeah. But, y'know, it's cool." He jerked one shoulder up in a too-casual shrug. "He's the one who trained me. That's the important part."

I nodded, aching for him. "Have you met any of the new human companions?" I asked to change the subject. I went on to tell him about Arnel—who Idris had also bumped into—then summarized my encounter with Vahl and then the strangely hysterical one with Janice and Amkir, as well as my thoughts about getting the other humans to help sway opinions.

"Great idea." He cocked his head. "Amkir actually flipped you off?"

"Janice is my witness!"

"That is so weird."

"Speaking of Janice, she's invited all the humans to a meet and greet in the Sylvan Hall in about an hour."

"Sounds good to me," he said through a yawn. "But first, nap time."

I tried to clench my teeth against an answering yawn but lost the battle. "Damn it. Same here."

I went into my room, barely remembered to set the alarm on my watch, then flopped onto the bed and was out like a light.

Chapter 28

Szerain was gone when I emerged an hour later, but Idris and Bryce were awake and drinking chak to dispel lingering sleepies.

"I'm not much on parties," Bryce said, "but after everything we've been through, I'm making an exception." His mouth twitched in a smile. "Plus, Jill's dead set on going." He hooked a thumb toward her room. "The zrila delivered a package a little while ago. She's changing now, and that faas, Reft, is doing her hair."

As if summoned, Jill stepped out of her room, grinning a mile wide. She wore a flared forest green shirt that made her eyes look outright luminous, close-fitting pants in a dark blue that shimmered when she moved, and ankle boots made of a crimson, scale-like material. Her hair had been trimmed just a bit and now framed her face in clever waves, held back on one side with an elegant clip that sparkled and matched the rest of her clothing.

Jill laughed and gave a spin. "How do you like the make-over?"

"You look fucking amazing," I said, grinning.

"Doesn't she?" Bryce murmured, then quickly yanked his gaze away to look out the window at . . . something very important. Uh huh.

I held back a snicker with effort. "Are y'all ready to head downstairs and do that alien ritual called socializing?"

Jill smoothed her hands over the shirt, squared her shoulders as if preparing for battle, and gave a fierce nod. "Let's do this."

*   *   *

The entrance of Sylvan Hall was an impressive arch of thick,
twining vines peppered with tiny luminous white flowers like living fairy lights. Within the hall, trees and interwoven branches
and vines formed natural walls enclosing an irregularly shaped
space about the size of a basketball court. A leafy canopy arched
above as a ceiling, and a mix of opalescent flagstones and short,
dense blue-green grass served as flooring. On the far wall, a mini-
waterfall splashed onto shimmering stones, and all throughout the
room, constellations of the firefly creatures cast soft golden-hued
light reminiscent of a sunset, creating a welcoming ambience.

Clusters of cushions and low seating offered plenty of opportunities for small group conversations. Some of the people present I knew, and some I didn't. There was no sign of Paul or
Dominic, so Kadir likely hadn't arrived—or they were planning
to be fashionably late.

Even with less than a dozen of us present, we still managed
to take up a solid quarter of the room, since everyone mixed and
mingled in ever-shifting clusters. Faas circulated with food and
drink, and a pair of nine-foot reyza crouched on either side of
the arch like sentient gargoyles.

Elofir's beloved, Michelle Cleland, and a few others had
e-tablets with them, all bearing the same type of arcane shielding case as Arnel's phone. I was unsurprised to learn it was Paul
who'd provided the devices, special cases, and solar chargers to
the companions. There was no wi-fi or cell service in the demon
realm, of course, but Paul downloaded popular movies and TV
shows onto the companions' tablets on a regular basis. Could
hypothetical super-powered Wi-Fi make it through a rift? Probably not, I decided, since the arcane interference would be pretty
wicked. Still, I snickered at the mental image of humans and
demons clustered around a rift with their devices, desperately
seeking a signal.

Right now, however, apart from using the tablets and phones
to take or share the occasional picture, everyone seemed content
to simply socialize. I already knew Michelle, of course—the
lovely and vivacious human companion who'd been in the demon realm the longest. She'd come a long way from the drug-
addicted hooker I'd met what felt like a million years ago. Arnel
chatted with her, looking somewhat bemused but happy enough
to converse and mingle.

I sipped golden wine with Suong, the woman I'd seen with Vahl, and learned she was a blacksmith and had a Masters in Metallurgical Engineering. Janice also made sure I met Kian, the young man who she'd deliberately misheard earlier on the balcony. The pale and heavily freckled redhead had a perpetual grin and eyes so light blue they looked almost ethereal.

After I finished the wine I switched to tunjen juice, then met Teri, a stick-thin black woman with an amazing corona of natural hair who looked like she was barely out of her teens. Janice had told me about Teri a few months back, describing a fiercely intelligent young woman who couldn't finish high school because of extreme anxiety and panic attacks but who'd made great strides while living with Amkir. I still couldn't fathom the ever-angry Amkir having the patience—or desire—to help her, but while Teri was definitely shy and cautious around all these new people, she didn't seem as if she was about to have a breakdown either.

To my surprise, Amkir had a second human companion: Afu, a bearded and muscled Pacific Islander with an easygoing manner and infectious smile, who was developing a wave power energy system.

It had been ages since I'd attended any sort of purely social gathering—maybe a crawfish boil back with my team when I was a street cop?—but this was easily the most stress-free get-together I'd ever been to. Everyone socialized to the level of their comfort, with no pressure or expectations. Teri in particular stayed a bit apart from the others at first, and when she did cautiously join, the others kept things low-key even as they made sure she felt included. Afu especially seemed to watch out for her—which made sense considering he was also with Amkir—but he did so in a way that was considerate and not paternalistic or infantilizing.

It was, without a doubt, an exceedingly cool group of people.

"You done good, Helori," I murmured under my breath. Seems he'd made excellent choices of companions, not only with skills and personalities, but as a cohesive unit.

I plopped into a chair by Janice and Michelle and, after tracing a discreet privacy ward, gave them the quick and dirty deets regarding Jesral and his plans. I then floated my idea that the human companions could make more headway convincing certain lords—especially Amkir—to oppose Jesral's actions, or at least not support or condone them.

Michelle pursed her lips and glanced at Janice. "Teri and Afu need to be roped in on this."

"Um, is that wise?" I asked. "I mean, if they're with Amkir, aren't they more likely to just go along with what he wants?"

"Noooooooooo," Michelle said, amusement alight in her eyes. "Did you always go along with whatever Mzatal wanted?"

"Fuck no. But . . ." I groped for the right words. "I mean you've all been healed and helped by the lords. Isn't there some sense of oblig—"

"No," Janice said. Firmly. Then she smiled to take the sting out of her words. "That's not how it works. And anyway, the companions need to be informed of exactly what's going on if they're to have any hope of influencing the lords."

"You have a point," I said with a laugh.

Michelle winked and waved Teri and Afu over. "We're not subservient to the lords. There's no debt owed. While they've been generous with their healing ability, and we're grateful for it, we stay because we choose to."

Teri hesitated, then perched on the edge of a chair, hands clasped tightly in her lap. Afu settled in and leaned forward, resting his elbows on his knees. "And we have no qualms about calling them on their shit." He grinned. "It's like setting a friend straight when they're making poor choices. Besides, we all need someone who'll tell us when we're being fucking pricks. Even the lords."

I glanced over to where Jill and Bryce were in animated discussion with Suong. "Yeah, I have a few people like that."

Teri smiled. "Amkir can be stubborn."

"As cross as two sticks," Afu put in. "A giant shit."

"An ass," Teri added with a laugh.

Afu snorted. "Angry."

"Oh god, yes," Teri breathed.

Afu leaned back in his chair. "Last month, he lost his temper. Had a major meltdown—"

"—and I had an awful panic attack," Teri said, hunching her shoulders.

Afu patted her hand. "Yep. Teri ran and hid from him. Amkir tried not to show it, but I could tell he was out of his mind with worry. Couldn't find or sense her anywhere. For all his assholishness, he truly wanted to help her through the panic attack." Afu's chuckle was deep and rich. "Turned out the demons were hiding her until she felt ready to face him."

"I . . . I think . . ." Teri said quietly, "I'm sure he regretted it. When I finally got up the nerve to go back, we had a long talk, and he even apologized."

I tried—unsuccessfully—to wrap my head around Amkir apologizing for anything. "I'm sorry you went through that, and I hope it hasn't happened again."

"He still gets angry but leaves to blow up elsewhere. It's progress, I suppose."

"Amkir doesn't like me," I said, unable to keep the amusement out of my voice.

"That's not true," Afu said, then grinned. "He hates your fucking guts."

Teri barked out a laugh, then blushed. "He calls you That Fucking Bitch Kara Gillian."

I pretended to fan tears of joy from my face like a beauty pageant winner. "Oh. My. God. I have my own Amkir nickname!"

We all shared a laugh that was more about camaraderie than Amkir or my nickname. A young faas refilled our glasses—though I stuck with tunjen—and we toasted our humanity and to a bright future for both worlds.

Jekki scurried into the hall and tugged on my hand. I excused myself from the others and retreated to a quiet corner with him, where the faas eagerly shared that Vahl had indeed sent a message sigil not long after I met with him, and none of the lords already present in Elofir's realm were the recipient. Of the remaining lords, I felt safe eliminating Mzatal, Kadir, and Seretis, which left Jesral, Rayst, or Vrizaar. My money was, of course, on Jesral.

I thanked Jekki effusively, and as he scampered off, I felt the mental tingle of the grove activating. Rayst—Seretis's longtime partner—had just arrived. Rayst, who was a close second behind Jesral re who Vahl sent a message to.

I located Bryce, quietly gave him a heads up in case Rayst came through here on his way to swear conclave oaths with Elofir, and also gave him an update on the matter of the message sigil.

I returned to my socializing, and sure enough, about twenty minutes later Rayst passed under the flowery arch. Swarthy and with a stocky build, he moved with confidence and lithe grace. Three syraza flanked him, and to my delight, I recognized two of them as Eilahn and Steeev. Bryce stood with his arms folded over his chest, expression unreadable as blank stone.

Eilahn gave a soft, musical cry and darted forward to sweep me into an embrace, even as Jill leaped to her feet and ran to Steeev. She hadn't seen him since he was shot and killed on Earth, back when she was still pregnant with Ashava, though we'd received intel that he successfully recorporeated in the demon realm.

All thoughts of Jill and Steeev evaporated as Eilahn appeared determined to squeeze the life out of me.

"Ribs," I gasped dramatically. "Can't . . . breathe . . . dying."

Eilahn trilled a laugh and released her hold on me. "You are more sturdy than before!"

"Uh, thanks?" I grinned. "More muscle and less fluff than when you last saw me. I've been busy."

Rayst approached, expression filled with worry and perhaps a whisper of fear. "Kara Gillian. Greetings." His gaze flicked between me and Bryce. "Have you news of Seretis?"

The pain in his voice told me he did, indeed, care about the well-being of his life mate, yet I could hardly forget how his ptarl, Trask, had fought against us at the pavilion. Best to not overshare.

"He's doing well," I told him, keeping a neutral smile on my face and feeling no need to go into *how* I knew, i.e. via Bryce and their essence bond. "He isn't being mistreated." Rayst didn't know about the bond, and my answering rather than Bryce would muddy the waters a bit.

"You betrayed his trust but blame *him*." Bryce stepped closer to Rayst, expression and voice ice-cold. "Admit it."

Rayst lifted his chin. "I did not, and I will not. You do not know the circum—"

"I know more than you imagine," Bryce said through gritted teeth.

The months Bryce spent in Seretis and Rayst's realm last year bought him more tolerance from Rayst than would be afforded other humans. But that time, plus the bond with Seretis, meant Bryce had significant insight into their relationship.

"I worry for him," Rayst said, eyes on Bryce.

"Had you not kept ugly secrets and actually *listened* to him, he might not have had to swear away his life to Dekkak." A muscle in Bryce's jaw ticked. "Then you had the fucking gall to be angry and mock his choice."

Rayst's expression darkened. "If you cannot understand anger at a loved one who chose to so needlessly put himself into jeopardy, your emotional acumen is sorely lacking."

"Of course I can understand a kneejerk reaction of anger," Bryce said. "But that's not all it was, was it? You didn't like how his sacrifice reflected on you—or what Jesral and your other cronies thought of it—and you're still pissed as hell."

Rayst started a denial, but Bryce cut him off. "Here's where my emotional acumen shines, Lord Rayst. In the same situation, I might have a moment of anger at a loved one because I was scared shitless for them. But then rational thought would set in, and I'd trust their judgment and be proud of their strength and courage in their convictions." Though his eyes didn't flick toward Jill, I felt the direction of his words.

I touched Bryce's arm to caution him from revealing too much. "Seretis saved us all," I said to Rayst. "Not just Earth. You understand that, right?"

"I have heard a variety of assessments of the situation." He focused on me as if I might be more reasonable than Bryce. "I suppose believing the least likely does hold a measure of comfort."

Both my eyebrows winged up in disbelief. "You've partnered with him for how long? A thousand years? Two? How can you think so little of your partner and still claim to love him?"

He let out a slow breath, and a measure of the self-righteous indignation slipped away. "If you speak to Seretis again, tell him I miss him."

"I will," I said, then, grateful I had the demahnk shielding on my thoughts, added in a light, conversational tone, "Ran into your ptarl earlier today."

His brows knitted in what seemed to be genuine confusion. "Trask was on Earth?"

"Not that I know of. I saw him by one of the pavilions." I smiled. "Anyway, please give him my best the next time you see him."

Rayst glanced from me to Bryce, brow still furrowed. "I must attend to my conclave oaths. Until later, Kara Gillian, Bryce Taggart." With that, he departed in more of a hurry than warranted. Steeev and the other syraza followed in his wake, but Eilahn remained.

I exchanged a glance and shrug with Bryce. "Dunno if he's aware of what his ptarl is up to," I murmured, "but I figured it couldn't hurt to sow a bit of uncertainty."

Bryce chuckled under his breath, more relaxed now that he'd gotten some of his own righteous indignation out of his system. "A bit of a change for you. Usually you skip uncertainty and go straight to sowing pure chaos."

I grinned. "I'm trying to become a better person."

He shook his head, smiling as he returned to sit near Jill.

I turned to Eilahn. "Do you have a moment to talk?"

She trilled and rested a hand lightly on my shoulder. "Always for you, my dear friend."

Sylvan Hall vanished, and then we were standing on the shore of an enormous body of water.

Eilahn let out a musical laugh at my involuntary yelp of surprise. "I assumed you wished privacy?" she said, violet eyes crinkling with humor.

"Privacy is good, though you could've warned me." The sun seemed to be in the same afternoon position, which meant we weren't on the other side of the planet or anything. And the towering trees in the distance told me this was almost certainly the lake to the east of Elofir's realm.

"That sounds boring," she replied, twitching one wing up in a shrug.

I laughed. "Oh, I've missed you so much."

"And I, you." She tilted her head. "You are worried. About me?"

Perceptive as always. "About you and many others who are dear to me." I quickly explained about the Zakaar re-embodiment and the demahnk opposition to it, including Trask's involvement. "I know you're with Rayst now, and I can't help but—"

She stopped me with a sharp shake of her head. "Dahn. I am sworn to no lord. His demesne is a comfortable one for syraza, and thus I abide there. Rayst and Seretis have always made us welcome. Moreso recently. Despite Rayst's bravado, he truly frets much over Seretis and misses him. But it is clear you have ample reason to distrust Trask." She trilled softly. "I will be on my guard and will warn Steeev as well."

"Thanks," I said, relieved. I didn't think Trask would—or could—stoop to using Eilahn as a hostage to influence me, but at least I'd warned her where his loyalties lay. "One more thing." I pulled out my phone and scrolled to a picture of the recent holiday decorations on the compound. "This was Jill's doing last month."

Eilahn gave a delighted musical yelp and clapped her hands.

"How excellent! Has she begun to decorate for Groundhog Day? Or Mardi Gras? Or Valentine's Day? I cannot wait to hear what she has planned!"

I grinned. "If fortune favors us, you'll be able to come see for yourself."

Chapter 29

It took me a moment after waking the next morning to remember where I was, not helped by the fact that the near total lack of sunlight told me it was likely the equivalent of five a.m. Still, my nap yesterday had helped my "planet lag," and for the most part I felt fairly rested.

By the time I made indulgent use of the bathing chamber and dressed in an outfit that would conceal my sidearm, brilliant pinks and orange bathed the eastern sky.

Szerain and Idris were already breakfasting when I entered the common room. Both greeted me with an appropriately subdued level of enthusiasm, given the early hour and the late night.

I poured myself a cup of chak, took a gulp, and waited a few seconds for the warmth and spices to infuse a bit of energy into my system before speaking. "Jill and Bryce still asleep, I assume?"

"You assume wrongly," Szerain said. "They've been up for over an hour and decided to go for a walk."

"A walk?" I grinned. "What a splendid idea. I bet there are some very nice, secluded walking paths around here that they could explore. In the soft light of dawn. Alone."

Idris snickered. "They're both big fans of nature."

"Absolutely!" I widened my eyes in innocence. "It looks like a lovely morning. And a quiet walk is a very nice way to relieve stress."

"There's been just so much *stress*," Idris added with a sage nod.

"Right? Oodles and oodles of tense, aching stress."

Szerain pinched the bridge of his nose. "You're a terrible friend."

"How *dare* you," I said in feigned insult. "I'm an awesome friend! I simply want them to stop dancing around what they both clearly want and get on with it. And each other."

Idris laughed and fist-bumped me.

Szerain shook his head, smiling. "Well, you'll be shattered to know they're currently in the north preserve, looking at a giant tree burl."

I stared at him.

He took a calm sip of his chak. "Apparently it's as big as a school bus."

"Are you shitting me?" I threw my hands up in mock-disgust. "They're looking at an overachieving plant wart? That's not even remotely sexy or romantic. I don't know what I'm going to do with those two."

"I suppose leaving them in peace is out of the question?"

I made a disparaging noise. "You speak nonsense. Besides, it's not like I'm actively meddling."

"Yet," Szerain muttered.

"Says the meddler."

"How do I meddle?" he asked, looking affronted.

I scoffed. "Please. You're a qaztahl. Albeit on kiraknikahl probation, but a lord nonetheless."

Szerain opened his mouth to protest, then shut it. "Damn it."

I grabbed a pastry and plopped into a chair. "So, what's the deal with all the super-secret closed-door meetings you qaztahl-types are having?"

"They're super-secret closed-door meetings," he replied with an annoyingly bland smile.

"Seriously? You can't cough up more info than that?"

"I truly cannot," he said, spreading his hands. "Conclave oaths."

I regarded him sourly for several seconds. "Fine. Be that way. Do you happen to know when the next round of Kara-can't-know meetings is scheduled for? I've been trying to get in to talk to Elofir, but he's always occupied."

"No more meetings until at least noon. The morning has been set aside for *socializing*."

"Really?"

"Yes. This time the humans have invited the lords and any interested demons as well."

I met Idris's eyes, and a grin spread across my face that was beyond my ability to control.

Szerain gave me a penetrating glare. "What have you done?"

I took my sweet time chewing and swallowing a big bite of pastry before answering. "I've merely been my usual brilliant self, my dear Lord Szerain. With a bit of encouragement on my end, and with the help of Idris, Jill, and Bryce, the companions are doing their part to remind the lords of Earth's value. Thus more emphasis on *socializing*."

He regarded me with an oddly wistful smile. "You're also reminding them of what conclaves used to be like before the cataclysm." Before Szerain's ritual with Elinor spiraled out of control, wreaking untold havoc and destruction on the demon realm, and causing the ways between Earth and the demon realm to slam closed.

"That's a good thing!" I said. "Y'all are aching for a real party after hundreds of years of staring at each other."

Idris grinned. "Just wait until the companions get puppies. They'll be unstoppable."

"May the gods have mercy on their souls," Szerain muttered.

"The humans? Or the puppies?"

"The lords!"

I gave my best evil cackle. "This is going to be great. Maybe Michelle has some techno beats on her tablet."

"On that note, I'm outta here." Szerain pushed up from the chair. "I'll see your oh-so-brilliant selves soon enough during the very first conclave morning social soiree in over three hundred years."

"With bonus puppies! And maybe a rave!"

He stuck his fingers in his ears. "I know nothing!"

After Szerain departed, Idris went for a run since today was shi-kvihr day, and he wanted to work off some excess energy. By the time I finished my breakfast, Jill and Bryce had returned, still behaving like two people who were just really good friends. Dammit. I filled them in on the Conclave social gathering and the continuing campaign to sway lords who preferred to remain neutral, then agreed I'd meet them in Sylvan Hall later.

I made my way to the puppy room and, for the millionth time in the past twenty-four hours, wished I had one of Paul's super-shielded cameras or devices. All the puppies but one were sound asleep, each being cradled oh-so-gently by a different demon. The one conscious pup was playing a growl-tug game with Steeev and a piece of rope, but she already seemed to be losing the battle to stay awake. Good. If they all napped now, they'd have plenty of adorable energy for later.

After asking the dog-sitting demons if they could please bring the puppies to the main hall at the mid-morning tone, I left the room with a cuteness-overload grin on my face. But my humor fled at a woman's sharp cry from an open door farther down the hall, and the unmistakable sounds of struggle.

Oh hell no. I broke into a run, about to charge through the door with my gun drawn when the woman let out a laughing curse, followed by a male voice encouraging her to try again. I pygahed to slow my heart rate, reholstered my gun and tugged the shirt back over it, then eased forward enough to see into the room.

It was a dojo type place with a padded floor, which explained the thumping sounds. I hung back in the shadow of the hall and watched as Vrizaar—who must have arrived during the night—playfully and patiently taught a human woman how to do a ju-jitsu hip throw, one I knew all too well from my training with Sharini Tandon. It wasn't a difficult move, but if you didn't get the initial grab and balance shift right, you'd have trouble with the rest. The woman tried it several times, face set in determination, while Vrizaar patiently coached her through the steps, pausing and adjusting her grip or stance as needed. She looked maddeningly familiar—blonde, with a lush, curvy figure—and it was with a jolt of recognition that I finally realized this woman was Amaryllis Castlebrook. Overwhelming relief flowed through me on the heels of the realization. Last year, she'd been targeted for abduction to the demon realm, and I'd taken her place, impersonating her in order to infiltrate the Farouche Plantation. When I eventually learned that most of the abductees had been in the midst of health crises, I'd felt spasms of guilt, wondering if by taking her place I'd condemned her to a life of pain or even death. Even worse, one of Farouche's men later tracked Amaryllis down and assaulted her, and despite my best efforts I was never able to locate her afterward.

Seeing her now with Vrizaar was like having a weight lift from my shoulders. Not only was she clearly healthy, but Vrizaar was teaching her self-defense—empowering skills for anyone, but especially an attack survivor.

Finally, Amaryllis managed to put all the steps together into one smooth movement and sent Vrizaar flying over her shoulder to land with a hard thump on the mat.

"Perfect!" he exclaimed. "Now finish me off!"

She grinned, let out a war cry, and delivered a top-notch Mortal Kombat style Pro Wrestling "Finish Him!" move.

I fought down a laugh as Vrizaar gave a dramatic dying gasp. Amaryllis did a little victory dance, then gave him a hand up. He smiled and gave her a kiss on the cheek—more friendly than sexual—and murmured something I couldn't hear. She glanced toward me, nodded, then jogged off through a door on the other side of the room, clearly pleased with herself.

"Kara Gillian," he said, voice deep and resonant, and his tone more serious now. "I wondered when you would be coming to see me."

I stepped into the dojo. "Lord Vrizaar. I see word has gotten around already." I'd never met him in person, but I'd observed him from a distance and also seen portraits of him painted by Szerain. Dark-skinned and bald, he had bright amber eyes, a neatly trimmed goatee, and sported gold hoops in both earlobes. My first time seeing him, he'd been wearing flowing robes in rich, vibrant colors, but today he had on loose copper-colored pants and a simple deep blue tunic. A wiser choice than robes for grappling, to be sure.

"Vrizaar is sufficient," he said. "And yes. The lords and demons gossip like no other." A smile flashed across his face. Damn, I already liked him. I really hoped he wouldn't turn out to be a dick.

We sat on one of the benches against the wall. I wasted no time with niceties and laid out what we suspected—and knew—of Jesral's plans. By the time I finished, the joy in his expression had been supplanted by grim acknowledgment.

"I have heard the rumblings of division," he said after a moment. "And seen the stark changes in Mzatal."

"Ilana has . . . tightened their relationship," I said carefully.

Vrizaar exhaled. "I have ever sought to remain apart from the machinations that many of the other lords thrive on."

"This goes beyond the typical maneuvering, Vrizaar," I said, allowing a chiding note to creep into my voice. He lifted an eyebrow, but I went on. "There's a saying on Earth: The darkest places in Hell are reserved for those who maintain their neutrality in times of moral crisis."

His expression deepened. "Dante Alighieri. And so, if I am not with you, I am against you?"

I shook my head. "More like, if you're not against Jesral and his schemes, you support every action he takes to further his agenda."

Vrizaar went quiet for several seconds, then gave a sharp nod as he stood.

It was a dismissal but not a harsh one. More like he needed time to process it all. I couldn't ask for much more at this point. I headed for the door.

"Kara Gillian."

I glanced back at him.

"I remember another of Dante's sayings: 'The secret of getting things done is to act.' I think perhaps I have failed to act too often."

"He also said that from a little spark may burst a flame." I smiled. "It's never too late to act, my lord."

With that I strode out before he could throw another Dante quote back at me. I was fairly certain he wouldn't support Jesral. At worst, he'd remain neutral. At best, he'd take an open stand against him. But more importantly, I didn't want Vrizaar to realize I'd never actually read any of Dante's works, other than the CliffsNotes I'd used to scrape out a passing grade in my senior year of high school English.

Chapter 30

The conclave social soiree was already in full swing by the time I stepped through the arch. The vibe was different from last night's meet-and-greet gathering, especially since today was an official conclave day, with additional lords due to arrive over the next few hours.

I scanned the hall, noting the presence of Elofir, Szerain, Rhyzkahl, Vahl, Rayst, and Amkir, the various human companions, along with well over a dozen demons of various types. Not a bad crowd at all for the first official conclave soiree in centuries.

Szerain stood slightly apart from the others, head held high and shoulders back, stance and attitude one of total composure, face bearing the secretive lordy smile that I suspected the qaztahl had all perfected through millions of hours of practicing in the mirror. That is, until Jill walked up to him and poked him in the side, causing him to grin and lose the whole lordy bearing thing.

Vahl and Rayst stood near the mini waterfall, chatting comfortably with Suong, while Amkir sat not far away with Teri and Afu, his arm draped around Teri's shoulders, and in deep conversation with both. For once he didn't have his usual black scowl twisting his features. In fact, was that a smile? And not a nasty one either. Weird. I didn't know his face could do that. No sooner had the thought crossed my mind than he glanced my way and gave me the glower I was so accustomed to. I turned away quickly to hide my amusement.

Rhyzkahl lounged on a divan, and I had to roll my lips between my teeth to keep from laughing at the sight of Squig tromping over his lap, aggressively bumping his chin with her head, and occasionally smacking him in the face with a wing. Not that Rhyzkahl seemed to mind. He merely gave her skritches while he chatted with Janice and Arnel.

In marked contrast, Elofir stood off to one side, expression somber, which wasn't his usual mien at all. Not far from him, Michelle sat with Kian and Bryce, all chatting and generally looking happy and comfortable.

Michelle's group abruptly burst into laughter. Elofir's gaze tracked over to them, face softening into a fond smile as he watched her. I couldn't help but let out a sappy little sigh. It was clear he truly loved her and was pleased she was getting some other human contact.

Janice spied me from the far side of the hall and waved me over, but I held up a finger in a "hang on a sec" gesture as I approached Elofir.

His expression shifted to "pleasant" but included a whisper of caution. A pang went through me that this tension existed between us, whether or not there was a reason for it. Certainly didn't seem justified anymore.

"Thank you for hosting the conclave," I began awkwardly.

"It is my pleasure to do so." He smiled but it was guarded. Careful.

Fuck it. I seized his hand and opened my thoughts so he could read the full meaning and intent behind my words related to our grievance. "I want to clear the air about what happened in Russia," I said. "I understand why you destroyed Bikturk's corpse. You didn't want us using it to learn how to better kill demons. Not because you wanted humans to be defenseless, but because the demons are of your world, and you despise violence."

Despite the considerable number of demons killed on Earth in the Demon Wars, a demon corpse for research was the holy grail for the military. Demons killed on Earth discorporeated, with a chance to return to the demon realm—unless slain by an essence blade. There were only two known instances of this: when I unintentionally killed the reyza Pyrenth with Vsuhl, and when Mzatal bladed Bikturk.

Elofir let out a slow breath. "We both strove to protect our worlds and their denizens, Kara Gillian, but in that moment, we were at cross purposes on the best means. Your anger was understandable."

"I'm sorry for yelling at you over it. You've always been

nothing but kind to me and have done much to help protect and preserve my world."

I drew breath to say more eloquent and heartfelt stuff, but Elofir shocked any further words out of me by pulling me into an embrace.

"And I, too, regret taking hasty action without consultation and consideration of how it might affect you and others." He released me and held me at arm's length. "As Michelle would say, 'We good, fam.'"

Of course that made me snort out a laugh, especially considering the precise and measured tone he'd used. His smile widened, and true tranquility returned to his expression.

Though I hated to mar the moment, I had to ask. "Do you know if Mzatal is coming?"

Grief shimmered in his eyes. "I have heard nothing from him. He is . . . not himself."

I didn't have to say anything. He knew, and could read the rest from me, how Mzatal was locked down by Ilana and the other demahnk.

Elofir's voice dropped. "You were ever good for him. *Are* good for him. May you find one another again soon."

My throat tightened, and I blinked furiously to hold back tears. He touched my shoulder, and a wave of calming peace flowed through me like an ethereal pygah, giving me the support I needed to maintain my composure in front of the lords and everyone else.

I lifted my chin, grateful, and headed back to the others, noting with amusement that the various groupings had shifted in just the minute or so I'd been speaking to Elofir. Vrizaar and Amaryllis had arrived and were making their way over to Vahl. Suong and Arnel were in intense conversation with the reyza Kehlirik, while Jill and Bryce had joined Rhyzkahl's circle. Or rather, Jill sat, while Bryce stood slightly behind her in an unmistakably protective pose, his gaze tracking over everyone in the spacious hall.

A low chiming tone sounded, ignored by most since it merely indicated that it was mid-morning. But Bryce and Jill glanced my way, then fixed their attention on the archway.

With exquisite timing, five demons entered the hall only a few seconds later, each bearing a squiggling puppy.

Gasps of delight arose from the humans as the demons and

I moved to the center of the hall. Szerain formed a circle of potency to act as a pen, and the very excited and adorable pups were placed within. Then we all backed away to give space to any who wanted to see them.

Which was, of course, the majority of the humans in the room. And damn near every demon.

"Oh my god, they're so CUTE!"

"Awww . . . look at the widdle nose on that one!"

I scooped up a sweet brown male with white chest and paws and placed him in Teri Abraham's hands. She looked at me in surprise and delight, then hurried back to Amkir. I watched surreptitiously as he stared at it, brows drawn together, expression inscrutable. Teri laughed and plopped the puppy in his lap. He grumbled something but hesitantly stroked the puppy's back. Emboldened, I snagged a blue-eyed, black and white speckled girl and handed her to Afu, then very subtly tilted my head toward Amkir. He grinned wide and returned to Amkir with the second puppy.

A whisper of something like longing passed over Amkir's face as he reached to pet the blue-eyed puppy, never ceasing his stroking of the first.

I watched surreptitiously, because I knew this had the potential to be a pivotal moment. A few months ago, the Ekiri had scattered Seretis's ptarl, Lannist, but in his last seconds, Lannist had been able to impart to me brief flashes of the lords as they'd been before the Ekiri had stolen them from Earth. One of those flashes had been of a young Amkir leaping into an icy river to save a dog.

Amkir didn't remember any of that. Those memories had all been taken or suppressed. But somewhere deep inside him, maybe a spark of that person still existed. Hell, simply the fact that Teri had blossomed with him surely meant something, right? I was starting to think that Amkir had been angry for so long, he'd forgotten why he was angry.

He was the key. My instincts screamed this. If we could put a wide enough crack in Amkir's anger-armor, then Jesral would essentially be the last of the Mraztur. Jesral would still be dangerous and vicious and unpredictable, and still supported by an as-yet-unknown number of the demahnk, but any weapon of his we could blunt was a victory.

I dragged my attention back to the little adoption fair, and in no time at all the puppy problem was no longer ours. Michelle got a rambunctious "boss bitch"—a white fuzzball with black ears, paws, and tail. Amaryllis nuzzled a red and white male with long hair like Katy-dog, and already Vrizaar was making silly noises at the pup. Kian lovingly cradled a puppy with red curly hair that damn near matched his own. Meanwhile, Janice watched the goings-on with amusement while she cuddled Squig. Yeah, she was definitely more of a cat person.

"My god, I'm brilliant," I murmured as Szerain dispelled the arcane puppy pen.

His gaze tracked over the room, where humans, lords, and demons alike had abandoned all pretense of decorum to lavish affection on the puppies. "I hate to stoke your ego any further, but yes, this was a very clever idea." He deftly avoided the elbow I aimed for his ribs.

A distinctive aura pulled my attention to the arched entrance. A murmur went through the room as Kadir stepped beneath the interwoven vines, their tiny fairy-light flowers dimming during the moment of his passage. Paul and Dominic flanked him in an echo of how the syraza had flanked Rayst.

Kadir swept an assessing, narrow-eyed regard over the assemblage, yet I couldn't help but smile at the sight of Fillion perched on his shoulder, claws digging into flesh, one paw on his head, and wings spread for stability. Spoiling any possible chance at looking fierce, he happily rubbed his head against Kadir's temple.

Without the slightest shift in his expression, Kadir scratched Fillion under the chin, even as spots of blood stained his shirt from the cat's claws.

It was, to put it bluntly, absolutely fucking adorable. And very weird and unsettling, because, after all, this was Kadir.

Paul and Dominic moved up to either side of him, both with satchels looped across their chests that no doubt carried all sorts of tablets and computer equipment. Paul bore a wide grin, but Dominic was clearly struggling to appear unaffected and not goggle at everything around him. I knew he'd been to the demon realm before with Kadir and Paul, but I doubted he'd ever faced a group like the one before him.

I was suddenly struck by the difference between this Kadir and the one I'd met for the first time just over a year ago—during the conclave that had ended with the torture ritual intended to make me Rowan.

I'd been in Rhyzkahl's demesne, and Kadir had approached me. Though I hadn't known who he was, I would never forget the overwhelming sense of terror and dread evoked by his presence. His aura oozed like viscous, dark slime, his voice promising pain, terror, and torment. He'd leaned close and breathed, "I know your scent, *baztakh*." And then goaded me, trying to get me to, in his words, "Rise fully."

It made zero sense at the time, but now it felt like a forehead-smacking *Duh!* moment. He'd sensed the Elinor essence attached to my own. In one of my Elinor memories, he'd said the exact same thing to her about knowing her scent.

And "rise fully" was him wanting me to show what power I was capable of. Power unknown to me, considering I'd been purposefully kept in the dark about the Elinor essence and my potential.

I knew more about Kadir now, and while he'd always been—and still was—creepy and threatening and weird, I now had a glimmer of realization about that first encounter. Kadir was indeed the Nerd Lord, the one who understood deep technicalities and ethereal truths. He'd been fascinated by that hitchhiking bit of Elinor essence and wanted to assess it.

That realization fueled yet more questions. I'd been terrified after the encounter and tried to leave Rhyzkahl's realm via the grove. Rhyzkahl's demons stopped me—supposedly for my own protection—but what if Kadir had been so threatening because he *wanted* me to escape Rhyzkahl before the torture ritual? What if he'd actually been against the entire "Make Kara Rowan" plan from the start? Maybe it had threatened his anti-chaos nature in ways I and others couldn't comprehend. Which was fine with me since, if that drastic plan had succeeded, it would mean that I, Kara, would no longer exist.

Kadir had been tacitly one of the Mraztur back then, along with Rhyzkahl, Jesral, and Amkir, yet he was ever driven by an uncompromising adherence to order in the midst of his personal chaos. In fact, even when Mzatal and I recovered Szerain's essence blade, Kadir hadn't joined the other Mraztur when they sought to gain control of it.

And yeah, Kadir being Kadir, he'd definitely wanted me to be scared of him, too, which he more than accomplished.

Lost in my musings, I almost missed the infinitesimal nod Kadir gave Szerain before sliding his gaze elsewhere. My curiosity flared. What was that about? Zakaar? The conclave? Something else entirely?

And then the Kadir entourage tableau broke when Paul grinned and waved at Michelle, and Janice seized Dominic's hand to introduce him around. Kadir proceeded to Elofir, who greeted him with a surprising amount of warmth—unreciprocated, of course—before leading him off down a corridor, I assumed to administer the conclave oaths.

I accepted a deliciously tart fruit drink from a faas, then joined Rhyzkahl's group. Yet my focus sharpened on Paul as he brought Dominic over by Amkir and his two companions. What if Amkir recognized Dom from when he was working for Jesral?

I watched, tense and poised to intervene in the event Amkir decided to do something unpleasant—especially since Kadir had left the room. Sure, Dom was theoretically protected by the conclave oaths, but that hadn't stopped Amkir from attacking me at the last conclave I'd attended.

But to my relief—and no small surprise—there was absolutely zero flicker of recognition on Amkir's face as Paul greeted him, Teri, and Afu. Amkir remained aloof but not hostile during the introduction to Dominic, and continued to absently stroke the fawn pup who'd fallen asleep beside him.

My every encounter with Amkir had told me he wasn't one to hide his thoughts or emotions, and his demeanor now revealed something very important: even though Amkir was supposedly Jesral's ally, the Between Machine project was almost certainly Jesral's alone. That slimy asshole had no intention of sharing the glory—such as it was—with anyone else. Perhaps that could somehow work to our advantage?

Still, I didn't relax until Kadir and Elofir returned, and Paul moved on to Vrizaar and Amaryllis.

"I just realized something pretty darn funny," I said to Rhyzkahl and the others in our little group. "Right now, humans outnumber the lords. And not just here. In the whole demon realm."

Janice snickered. I saw Bryce do a quick mental tally. Rhyzkahl merely smiled.

"As it should be," he murmured. "As it always was, before." Squig chose that instant to smack him in the face with a wing, spoiling the gravitas of the moment.

Eventually Paul finished showing off his boyfriend—which the easy-going Dominic didn't seem to mind at all—and joined us.

"Pellini didn't come with you?" Jill asked him.

"Nah, he's getting Elinor and Giovanni settled in and is keeping tabs on stuff Earthside."

"You're not able to tap into Earth feeds while here, right?" I asked.

He grimaced. "Nope. It's one set of flows or the other, depending on which world I'm in. We're working on a way to bridge that gap, but we still have a ways to go."

"Gotcha," I said, keeping a calm smile on my face. We'd only been gone one day, I reminded myself. Ashava and Turek could handle an arcane attack. Alpha Squad and compound security could counter a physical one. Not to mention, we'd made good progress with talking to the lords while here, which meant we could likely return to Earth with our informational mission essentially accomplished by this evening at the latest. What they did with that information was another matter.

That said, the continued absence of Jesral at the conclave made me deeply uneasy. Maybe we could skedaddle home as soon as Idris achieved the full shikvihr.

Chapter 31

As if my thoughts had summoned him, Idris strode in, cool and collected. I'd expected him to wear a zrila-constructed outfit—and he was, though not in the usual demon style. Instead, it was if he'd asked for fatigues and combat boots, but made with zrila skill and ingenuity to emphasize ease of movement, protection, and durability. However it came about, the result was stunning. Fabric and leather of midnight blue a whisper shy of black. Understated antique gold stitching. Close-fitting, without being at all restrictive. And I was fairly sure the clothing included a subtle degree of armoring on the various important parts.

I wanted an outfit just like it right fucking yesterday.

Idris radiated mature confidence, as if ready to conquer any challenge the universe threw at him. It felt like eons ago that he'd been the slightly awkward and uncertain nineteen-year-old with a brief crush on me. Enough had happened in the past year to lay the weight of maturity on anyone, and he'd been forced to deal with far more than most.

Kadir and Elofir chose that moment to return from the oath giving. Idris greeted both lords, then gave Rhyzkahl a slight chin lift and smile before joining Vrizaar's group.

Paul sat bolt upright, gaze darting every which way as if trying to pinpoint a barely audible noise.

Dominic touched his hand. "You good, bruv?"

"I think so," he said, rubbing the back of his neck. "It's probably just some random interference." Brow furrowed, he pulled out his tablet and swiped through a number of screens, then locked eyes with Kadir, who frowned slightly, hesitated, then murmured something to Elofir.

Whatever he said caused Elofir to give Kadir an are-you-shitting-me look. In the next instant, a petite woman with purple eyes and short black hair appeared beside Elofir and crouched, her gaze riveted on a space a dozen feet in front of the arch. Greeyer—Elofir's demahnk ptarl.

"Paul?" I frowned at him. "Is everything okay?"

He shot to his feet. "Um, we should all back away from the arch."

"What's going on?" I asked, even as we scrambled to comply with his suggestion.

Any reply he had was lost in a screech like tearing metal. The floor before the arch shivered, and the air a few feet above it glowed like a tiny sun of bright gold and magenta.

Fillion yowled and flew up into the branches of the ceiling while Rhyzkahl and Szerain retreated from the sun-thing with the rest of our group. Amkir shouted to Afu to grab his dog and follow him, herding Teri and her pup to the far side of the room, where he immediately placed himself between his companions and the whatever-it-was and spun out a quick shield of potency. Vahl and Vrizaar hurried to usher companions and puppies well away from the arch, then stood shoulder to shoulder with Rayst, each calling arcane into their grasp.

"Qaztahl, stand down," Elofir said, voice cutting through the noise and hubbub. "You are under oath. Stand down."

I tamped down my own urge to gather potency and fought the instinct that shrieked to at least put my hand on my gun. I glanced at Bryce to see if he'd drawn his weapon, but instead of the intense expression I expected, a broad smile spread across his face.

Comprehension hit me like a punch. Only one reason Bryce would look this fucking pleased.

The mini-sun elongated into an eight-foot-tall, brightly glowing line that hovered a couple of inches off the floor. A heartbeat later the line split to form a three-foot-wide mid-air rift.

Holy shit. I'd seen this type of rift once before. Right after I retrieved the master gimkrah from the column in Mzatal's realm, the Jontari had attacked, arriving and departing through rifts like this. We'd never had mid-air rifts on Earth—thank every possible god in existence for that small favor—so I suspected they weren't possible between the two worlds.

Greeyer remained motionless, watching. Vahl, Rayst, and

Vrizaar ramped up their prepped arcane strikes. Amkir left his companions behind the shielding and called potency. Rhyzkahl and Szerain seemed wary but didn't join the strike brigade. Kadir stepped closer to the rift, lips parted and head tilted slightly as if burning with curiosity.

"Control yourselves," Elofir shouted, his voice backed by potency as he eased toward the rift. "Measures will be taken against any qaztahl who attacks another *guest*."

Elofir's emphasis on "guest" quieted the clamor to a simmering murmur, though confusion and suspicion now reigned. Though the lords relinquished their hold on potency, they didn't look one bit more relaxed.

I couldn't really blame them, since this was a power play of the highest order on the part of the Jontari. *Fuck you, we can go wherever the fuck we want.* Yet at the same time, my primary reaction was sheer amusement coupled with mad respect because of the insane balls of it all.

The rift flared, and Seretis stepped through, eyes sharp and head high, his expression one of quiet confidence. Dark hair hung in shining waves past strong cheekbones that belonged in a *telenovela*. His clothing wasn't fancy—deep red pants, a dusky blue tunic, and soft indigo boots—but even if he'd been wearing dungeon rags, they wouldn't have diminished his air of absolute competence. I beamed in utter delight, as I suspected the other lords had never seen *this* Seretis, at least not in recent millennia.

He smiled as a wave of whispers and mutters swept through the room, then he stepped aside to give Slugthing—*Gurgaz*, I corrected myself—room to emerge and . . . stand? sit? ooze? beside him, hide midnight blue with vague hints of pink shifting over it, and tentacles mostly quiescent.

The muttering immediately shifted tone and volume. Elofir didn't shout this time, but swept a scathing glare over the assembly. I couldn't help but note that, except for Elofir, Rhyzkahl, Szerain, and Kadir, the lords looked way more freaked about Gurgaz's presence than the humans—probably because humans had gotten pretty used to taking weird shit in stride. Suong and Arnel both looked intrigued, while Kian barely glanced at the new arrivals and focused on keeping his puppy calm. Teri watched with wide eyes, but there was curiosity in them as well as caution. Even so, Amkir stood between her and Gurgaz. Vahl and Vrizaar also shielded their human companions, while Rayst simply looked shocked and horrified and deeply uncertain.

Meanwhile, Kadir appeared entirely uninterested in the new arrivals, and had instead crafted a tiny arcane "laser pointer" to coax Fillion down from the branches of the ceiling.

The rift closed behind Gurgaz, contracting down to a pinpoint of light that disappeared with a soundless pop of air pressure.

Elofir stepped toward them. "Welcome to the conclave, Seretis, and welcome, Gurgaz, honored emissary of Imperator Dekkak."

Elofir knew the Jontari demon's name? My already high opinion of him climbed several more notches.

Neon pink rippled along Gurgaz's tentacles, and eerie blue light spilled from a mouth lost somewhere among those tentacles as it spoke. "Elo-feeeeer. Spawn of hu-beast and the oathless Greeyer, we greet you."

Greeyer could have been mistaken for a statue, but Elofir gave them a calm smile of welcome. "Seretis, meet me in the Fountain Arbor for the conclave oaths. Gurgaz may join you, if it is their desire."

"*Dak lahn*, Elofir," Seretis replied. "We will comply momentarily."

I tried without success to rein in my grin. Seretis had more composure than half the lords in the room combined, as if he'd found his true strength. And even though he was still constrained by his oaths to Dekkak, it was clear he knew himself and his path.

Elofir's smile widened just a bit before he strode away, as if he'd picked up the same vibe.

Bryce approached the pair, surprising me by giving Gurgaz a deep bow before seizing Seretis in an embrace. Seretis laughed, hugged him fiercely, and a few heartbeats later they separated, grinning at each other—a short, swift exchange that managed to convey more than a three-hour movie.

Bryce bowed to Gurgaz once more and stepped back.

The instant Bryce moved away, Rayst approached, hesitantly at first, then he threw his arms around Seretis.

Seretis held him close, murmuring reassurances as Rayst shuddered with emotion. Finally, Rayst cupped Seretis's cheek with one hand.

"I have you back, zharkat," Rayst said, voice cracking.

Seretis kissed him gently. "I was away but never gone from you, beloved."

Rayst gave a slight shake of his head. "Yes. You were. You *chose* to leave me. And now it is time to come home."

Seretis's expression remained unwaveringly confident, and it suddenly hit me why the change in him seemed so profound. He'd always had an aura of uncertainty, as if waiting for the approval of the other lords—approval that was never going to come. Now it was as if he realized he'd never needed it.

"Beloved," he said, voice serene and rich, "I have obligations, and there is still much to be done."

Rayst turned to Gurgaz, who he'd so far managed to avoid looking at directly. Disgust crawled over his face. "Jontari, release Seretis from his oaths, so that he may return to his rightful position and duties as qaztahl, for the sake of the entire demon realm—including your clan holdings."

All traces of neon pink vanished from Gurgaz's tentacles, and it opened its maw wide, bathing Rayst in ghostly blue light. Its voice crashed over us like surf on boulders. "No oath binds Seretis from qaztahl duties."

A buzz swept through the room.

Rayst regarded Seretis in bafflement, clearly struggling to understand. "Then why do you remain with—" He gestured at Gurgaz.

Seretis glanced at Gurgaz, then back to Rayst. "For reasons of my own. And for the benefit of all."

"Nonsense!" Rayst raked fingers through his hair. "You have lost all reason. I need you by my side. You will flounder apart from me."

"You are ever strong enough for both of us, my love." Seretis took Rayst's hand in both of his. "But I must stand on my own for this."

Rayst shook his head, a quick, sharp motion. "No. This is insanity. How can you do this to me?"

Seretis exhaled softly, regret and something very like disappointment in his eyes. "I do not seek to harm you. But I cannot go home. Not now."

Rayst yanked his hand away from Seretis and retreated a step. "You choose these brutish creatures over your kind? Over the qaztahl?" he demanded, outrage and hurt twisting his features. "Over *me*?"

Seretis straightened, quiet strength seeming to infuse his entire body. "We are an abomination, Rayst. Enslavers and defilers. Spawn of kiraknikahl."

Rayst took another step back, breath coming faster. "No. The Jontari have filled your head with lies. We protect this world! Come back to me. We can make this right."

Grief shimmered over Seretis's face. "Rayst. I *am* making this right, as best I can. You will always be precious to me, but—"

"Prove it!" Rayst's voice cracked with pain. "Abandon this hideous spectacle!"

Silence fell for several agonizing heartbeats. "*Yaghir tahn*," Seretis finally murmured in apology, expression sad and weary. "But I can no longer be with you."

"Fool!" Rayst snapped, voice shaking and agonized. "Willing to grovel to this . . . this filth." He waved a hand at the unruffled Gurgaz, while Seretis stood composed and still. "You were my life-mate—always weak—but I defended you. Supported you. No longer. Without me, your self-slaying would have succeeded! I saved your pathetic life. *This* is how you repay me? Now all will know you for the spineless coward you have always—"

A crack split the air as Bryce drove his fist into Rayst's jaw, quite effectively stopping the ugly tirade. Rayst staggered then sprawled to his back as Bryce stepped between him and Seretis, face like stone but cold fury in his eyes. Gaze on Rayst, Seretis laid a hand on Bryce's shoulder, expression alive with sadness and a touch of pity.

Rayst let out an incoherent cry of rage and scrambled to his feet, a dark purple ball of potency forming in his right hand.

Before I could react, the air shuddered, and a spinning circle of wards surrounded him. "ABIDE BY YOUR OATHS, RAYST," Elofir thundered.

Daaaaaamn. Even-tempered, pacifist Elofir was *so* not putting up with this shit.

Rayst released the arcane but not his anger. "Then I demand Rhyzkahl punish his human for attacking me."

Turning his back on Rayst, Bryce met Seretis's eyes. Neither spoke aloud, but I knew much was being communicated via their essence bond. After a few seconds Bryce gave an almost imperceptible nod and faced Rhyzkahl.

Rhyzkahl stood and made a show of tweaking his shirt into place and flicking nonexistent dust off his shoulder. "Yes, Bryce is here as my *guest* and under the aegis of my conclave oaths. And yes, the onus is on me to discipline him for . . . helping you find your center after such an unseemly loss of control."

Rayst flushed with anger but also a measure of shame. Bryce had literally beaten me to the punch but, in a way, I couldn't help but feel a weensy smidge of sympathy for Rayst—though wielding Seretis's attempted suicide as a weapon kept it a mere smidge and nothing more. Yet he'd been partnered with Seretis for centuries. This abrupt breakup couldn't be easy to process. Plus, who knew what sort of shit Trask had been whispering in Rayst's ear?

Rhyzkahl stepped to Bryce, then lightly batted him on the nose. "Bad human."

Several people snickered. Rayst clenched and unclenched his hands, expression agonized.

Elofir strode up. "Come, Rayst. We will speak." Serene, gentle Elofir was still serene and gentle, but it was very clearly not a request.

Rayst took an unsteady breath, then nodded and left the hall with Elofir.

Fillion flew down to land on Kadir's shoulder, posing with wings open and one paw atop the lord's head as if the cat took on the role of conclave guardian while Elofir was otherwise occupied.

Hell, there were certainly worse choices for a substitute Elofir.

Chapter 32

After that bit of excitement, the mood returned to something akin to normal—or as normal as a conclave could be with the motley assortment of beings assembled. Seretis took a seat near Bryce and Szerain, while Gurgaz settled nearby, tentacles restless. Idris remained standing slightly apart from everyone, loose and relaxed, but in a way that made it clear he was expending effort to stay loose and relaxed.

I startled as a message sigil appeared in front of me, shimmering black and gold. I glanced over at Szerain, assuming it was for him, but he shook his head, expression stony.

"He sent it to you."

He. My brain finally caught up. Black and gold was the color pattern for Mzatal's sigils. Mouth dry, I touched it.

Failure is imminent, short of the ultimate triumph. The heart of darkness devours all.

Even here, hope withers, baztakh.

It sucked that Idris couldn't attempt the final shikvihr atop the column—the supreme challenge. The ultimate triumph. But completing it *here* on Elofir's nexus wouldn't diminish Idris's accomplishment one bit. It was the baztakh insult that hit me like a sucker punch.

Szerain couldn't read my thoughts, but my emotions must have been clear on my face, judging by the anger and sympathy on his.

"I know," I said, summoning a more neutral expression. "He's controlled."

Rayst and Elofir returned, the former looking not so much

chastened as resigned. And sad. I almost felt sorry for him. Almost.

Szerain stood, smoothed his shirt and lifted his chin. "My lords, it is my great honor to sponsor Idris Palatino for the eleventh and final ring of the—"

"I object," Rhyzkahl said, voice clear and commanding. He rose, gaze going to Szerain and then Idris, even as my heart sank. Szerain was kiraknikahl, so of course he wouldn't be able to sponsor Idris. But to my bafflement, Szerain flashed a grin and sat. Rhyzkal gave him a slight nod, then swept an authoritative gaze over the assembled lords.

"It is *my* great honor to sponsor, for the eleventh and final ring of the shikvihr, Idris Palatino. My son."

It was everything I could do to keep from bursting out laughing. Not at Rhyzkahl's pronouncement, but at the wide range of reactions. The humans were universally in the *Awwww, that's so cool!* territory, while Amkir and Rayst looked shocked and disturbed. Vahl seemed utterly perplexed, as if only now realizing such a thing was possible. Vrizaar appeared briefly surprised, then gave a small, satisfied nod, while Elofir and Seretis seemed pleased the subject of the lords' progeny was finally out in the open.

Kadir remained utterly expressionless. But I had zero doubt he already knew the lords could procreate. Probably had for centuries. Millenia.

Idris clearly wanted to bust out a wide grin at the various reactions, but held himself to a small, pleased smile.

Elofir inclined his head to Rhyzkahl. "Has the summoner completed the ten rings required to attempt the full shikvihr?"

"He has."

"Do you believe the summoner is prepared for the challenges of the eleventh ring?"

"I do."

"Will you assume the honor debt owed should the summoner violate the integrity and principles of the apotheosis?"

Rhyzkahl's gaze tracked to Idris, then back to Elofir. "I will."

Elofir gave a nod. "Then I invite all assembled to reconvene at my nexus."

Elofir's nexus was a lovely open air courtyard paved with clear quartz that radiated prismatic colors just on the verge of sight.

As with every other nexus I'd seen, eleven columns were spaced evenly along the perimeter. These were the same quartz as the floor but carved as tree trunks—making me imagine they'd been grown from little quartz seeds.

Idris paced on the far side, managing to look both anxious and confident at the same time. I tensed as a black and gold sigil appeared before him. Idris took a deep breath and touched the sigil. Potency shimmered around him as the message was conveyed, and his face went to stone. He dispelled the sigil with a sharp wave of his hand and resumed pacing.

Infuriated and helpless, I realized the timing of Mzatal's message to Idris was perfect. I had no time to remind him that Mzatal was under the influence of two—and possibly three—demahnk.

He knows all that, I reminded myself, but it didn't help dissolve the rock in my gut. The last thing any of the opposition wanted was for Idris to have the full shikvihr.

Vahl straightened as a simple silver and black message sigil appeared before him. He read the message and dispelled it, then folded his arms as if whatever it contained was no big deal.

I leaned toward Szerain. "Whose message sigils are silver and black?" I murmured.

"Anonymous," he replied under his breath, then snorted. "As if we can't figure out who sent it."

Jesral. Duh.

Another silver and black sigil appeared, this time in front of Amkir. He read it then dispelled the message with a savage wave of his hand, face tight with anger.

"You'll want to stay back about ten feet or so," Szerain told me as Idris stepped to the center of the nexus.

I retreated, mystified when the lords moved closer to the nexus and Elofir raised a barely shimmering veil of potency just in front of the various non-lord observers. Did he think we would interfere?

Expression hard and grim, Idris took a deep breath and sketched the first sigil of the first ring. A palpable tension filled the courtyard, growing as Idris completed the first half of the ring.

I startled as Rhyzkahl set off what I could only describe as a mini-flashbang. Idris jerked but finished his sigil, even as I bit down on a *What the fuck are you doing?* None of the lords seemed bothered or surprised.

Idris flicked a quick scowl around the courtyard, eyes narrowed, then continued.

And so did the distractions. Vrizaar and Seretis unleashed screeching sigils that whizzed past him with inches to spare. Amkir delivered smoke bombs of sickly colors, and Kadir sent a cloud of tiny gnat-things to buzz around his head. Even Elofir took part, casting tiny balls of fizzing arcane on the floor, forcing Idris to alter his steps or set off a micro concussion grenade.

I grinned, amused despite everything. Of *course* the full shik-vihr wouldn't be some sanitized display of eleven perfect rings. At the Ekiri pavilion, I'd made the shikvihr a foundation of strength, stability, and defense. Now Idris had to prove he could do the same: *understanding* the shikvihr, not just knowing it.

The distractions stepped up in intensity and frequency as he progressed through the second and third rings. Jaw tight, he sketched sigils like a man possessed, even as I saw the signs of rising temper.

On the fifth ring, outright attacks began. Idris hissed out a curse and recoiled, then adjusted the sigils to defend against the stinging needles Rayst peppered him with. Kadir sent barbed coils of chartreuse to bind and tear, and Idris pinned them to the floor with a focused increase in gravity. Still, it was clear the lords were abiding by rules and boundaries as far as how much force could be used at any given time. I kept half an eye on Vahl and Amkir, but Vahl only made lackadaisical attacks, while Amkir seemed to be participating with the same intensity and effort as any of the others.

Idris finished the fifth then abruptly paused, hand in mid-air. He grinned and met my eyes. "I figured it out!" he shouted in unmistakable delight, then began the sixth ring with none of the scowly anger of before.

I had no idea what the hell he'd figured out, but whatever it was lit a fire under his ass. Good thing, because the attacks started coming harder and faster and from every direction. Newly refocused, Idris countered and blocked and redirected, sketching and adjusting his shikvihr to be an intrinsic part of his defense.

He was halfway through the ninth ring when Elofir fired a spear of arcane toward him—a split-second before Vahl unleashed a wave of arcane wind. Heart in my throat, I watched the disaster unfold as Vahl's wind accelerated Elofir's spear to near double its intended speed and force. Idris clearly sensed the attack, but I couldn't see any way for him to neutralize it or—

Moving damn near too fast for my eyes to follow, Idris

snapped out a whip of arcane to snare the spear, using the force of the strike and his own speed as he performed what I could only describe as an absolutely perfect *seio nage* judo move to slam the spear into the quartz floor.

The attacks came to an abrupt halt. Someone let out a whistle of awe. Vahl raised his hands in a "Whoops, didn't mean to do that" gesture. But he wasn't fooling anyone. It was clear he'd tried to sneak in a potentially lethal attack by piggybacking off Elofir's.

Elofir didn't say a word—merely regarded Vahl with a quiet disappointment that was somehow far more terrifying than any of Mzatal's black furies. To my surprise, Amkir gave Vahl a withering look that I had zero trouble interpreting as, *Vahl, you're a weak fucking jackass.*

Idris dispelled the arcane whip, squared his shoulders, and resumed his shikvihr.

Vahl drew back, expression bordering on sullen. Elofir shifted position around the perimeter, and I had the distinct sense he was subtly making sure everyone played by the fucking rules. Amkir didn't hold back with any of his attacks, but seemed to be working within the allowed limits just fine.

The instant Idris finished the very last sigil, the distractions and attacks ceased. Vahl had an oh-so-casual smile on his face as if he was proud of Idris. Amkir didn't seem to be either annoyed or glad that Idris successfully completed the shikvihr. His attitude seemed to be more "Okay, whatever," which made Vahl's casual mien look all the more artificial. It was almost as if Amkir was far more annoyed by the bullshit and was just glad to be done.

Rhyzkahl moved up to culminate—though he first gave his son a hug that coincided with a sudden attack of allergies that made me a bit sniffly. Damn demon dust.

Elofir shifted position again, and there was no mistaking he was on high alert for this last bit. His expression remained calm, yet at the same time focused and intense.

For a fleeting instant, he met my eyes, and I had the barest millisecond glimpse of just how fucking potent and dangerous he could be if sufficiently provoked.

The other lords remained *very* well-behaved while Rhyzkahl culminated Idris's shikvihr. And then, of course, cheers erupted.

I lingered as the nexus courtyard began to empty, wanting to give Idris my own congratulations. As Rayst and Vrizaar headed out, I heard the latter murmur, "Vahl was a fool to anger Elofir."

Rayst snorted. "Vahl's foolishness surprises you?"

I turned away to hide my amusement, just in time to see Amkir give Vahl a deliberate shoulder bump as he walked past, hard enough to make Vahl stagger. Vahl scowled, body taut with frustration. It was as if he'd wanted to be one of the cool guys, except now one of the cool guys thought he was a jackass.

As soon as the crowd around Idris thinned, I gave him a hug of congratulations. "Now, tell me what you meant when you said you figured it out?"

He glanced around, then lowered his voice. "Mzatal's message was simply, 'You are a fool to attempt this. You are not ready.' It pissed me off, then I realized *that* was his distraction, his way to participate. His final lesson as my teacher. I mean, I know the demahnk had him send it to throw me off, but Mzatal knew that if it *did* throw me off, then I wasn't ready."

"Yes! Of course he'd figure out a way to satisfy his captors *and* support you!"

"What about your message?"

I shrugged. "Just bullshit about you not completing the shikvihr on the column."

He narrowed his eyes at me. "Kara, what *exactly* did he say?"

Was I that transparent? I scowled. "Failure is imminent, short of the ultimate triumph. The heart of the column devours all. Even here, hope withers . . . baztakh."

Idris winced. "Ouch. The first part seems like a pretty straightforward dig. But you know Mzatal."

"Yeah, I do, and he's all about dual messaging."

Idris pondered. "What if 'here' doesn't mean Elofir's realm?"

I smacked my forehead. "He meant where *he* is. And I'd like to think he means the demahnk's hope withers but could be *his* hope. Or both."

"And 'baztakh' can sometimes translate to bitch, depending on context." He grinned. "Admit it, there are times when you like being a bitch—and are damn good at it."

"Hey now!" But I couldn't help but laugh.

"I'll bet you anything 'baztakh' is a substitute for 'zharkat'—in its own unique, Karafied, badass bitch way—and he trusts you enough to know it."

The coil of not-so-secret hurt unwound. "You're right," I breathed. "I let myself be distracted by the surface meaning."

"He tested my focus. Yours, too, maybe."

I wrapped him in a bearhug. "Thanks for setting me straight."

He lifted me off my feet with a fierce squeeze, then set me down and hurried back to Sylvan Hall and what was now a celebration of his achievement.

No doubt about it, I was a very fortunate woman to have people like him in my life to help me see things through a different lens.

And speaking of seeing things—or people—through a different lens . . .

I sidled up to Szerain. "Question: Is Elofir, like, the biggest badass to ever walk the demon realm?"

Szerain gave me a slow smile. "Even Mzatal would think thrice before provoking him."

Chapter 33

The mood in Sylvan Hall was jubilant, not only because Idris was the first summoner to attain the full eleven rings of the shik-vihr in many decades, but also because he'd absolutely kicked all the ass—especially with the way he dealt with the accelerated arcane spear.

Faas circulated with wine, and toasts were made. The humans started a chorus of "Speech! Speech!" which elicited a groan from Idris, but then he seemed to reconsider and climbed atop a low stump. The room quieted.

And then he launched into Roy Batty's "Tears in Rain" mono-logue from *Blade Runner*. Szerain and several humans burst out laughing as they recognized it. Hey, they wanted a speech, so he was giving them one. Even Kadir wore a very faint smile, clearly having watched the pivotal scene at some point—no doubt due to Paul's influence. I only knew what it was because Idris and Pellini made me sit through the movie many months ago.

Idris spoke with great drama of attack ships and glittering C-beams. Meanwhile the majority of the other lords looked ab-solutely perplexed, which made the whole thing all the more entertaining, especially when they clapped politely after Idris finished. Fortunately, he stopped just short of the final "Time to die" line, which would have really confused them.

Szerain clapped him on the back, then Afu and Janice grinned and congratulated him on his dramatic prowess. More wine was passed and further toasts made. Several of the human compan-ions tried to explain the movie to the lords, with varying degrees of success.

I nearly jumped out of my skin at a cry of inarticulate rage from behind me. I whirled, shocked to see Kadir standing rigid, hands clenched, and face suffused with naked fury.

Behind him, Paul went sheet-white. "Oh fuck . . . fuck . . . oh fuck . . ." He yanked his tablet from his satchel and began typing and swiping with furious speed. Dominic took one look at Paul's screen and blanched.

"Tell me what to do," he snapped, unslinging his laptop and flipping it open.

Paul gabbled out a series of instructions that made zero sense to me but Dominic seemed to understand perfectly.

"What the—" I began, then jerked in shock as Ashava appeared a few feet away, breathing hard, frantic and excited.

"Mom! Kara! Oh thank the spheres, I'm not too late—"

"WHAT HAVE YOU DONE?" Kadir roared, not at all in his usual icy cold way. This was Kadir livid with rage—aghast and . . . afraid?

Ashava recoiled. "It was the only way I could get here to warn you all! DIRT is going to—"

"You callow crucible of naïveté!" Kadir snarled.

A tremor rocked the palace. Ashava paled. "No," she breathed. "I don't understand!"

"Understand *this*." Kadir took a step toward her, expression dangerous. "Your rash and barbarous arrogation of my gate triggered rampant instability that *will* fracture the foundations of the interdimensions unless it is forestalled." Though his gaze was riveted on Ashava, his potency-backed voice penetrated throughout the hall. "If it is not forestalled, the ruination from the cataclysm will be as nothing."

Pale, Ashava stammered out, "I was just trying to help and—"

"*Silence!*" Kadir hissed. He turned his back on her to face Paul, who still worked frantically on his tablet. Around us, lords, humans, and demons appeared equally stunned into silence. Jill stood with her hands pressed to her mouth, then pulled Ashava close.

Ashava clung to her, whispering over and over, "I didn't know. I was trying to help. I swear I didn't know."

All eyes were on her, some more hostile than others.

Jill tightened her arms around Ashava in reassurance. Szerain muttered a dark expletive and moved close to them.

Kadir dropped to one knee and took the tablet from Paul, holding it for him like a lordy living desk. Paul didn't miss a beat and continued to type and swipe at an incredible speed.

Arcane energy crackled around Kadir, even as a chartreuse glow formed and expanded around Paul. I took a healthy two steps back, plus a third for good measure.

"He's acting as a foundation for Paul," I breathed. "Idris, quick! Help me lay support for Kadir."

Idris leaped to my side, and together we sketched sigil after sigil into compact grids. "What are they doing?"

"I think Paul is trying to stabilize the Between space." I began interlacing the grids as quickly as I could, surprised when Rhyzkahl joined us. The support structure dimmed as Kadir drew on it, then brightened again as Elofir, Vahl, Vrizaar, Rayst, and even Amkir added their efforts. Despite their differences in other arenas, the lords historically unified when it came to stabilizing the planet.

Ashava sat, dazed, beside Jill on the divan Rhyzkahl had occupied moments earlier. Szerain stepped away from them, but paused, eyes narrowed as if undecided about joining in the support effort. Kadir siphoned potency from our grid, and it dimmed yet again.

"Any day now," I growled at Szerain.

He moved, but toward Kadir, not the support team. Without hesitating, he reached through the crackling potency and gripped Kadir's shoulder. Kadir flinched, and the aura around Paul flickered. Another tremor rocked the trees, and the eerie sound of countless faas keening added a surreal dimension.

Szerain kept his hold even as chartreuse potency writhed around his arm and slithered toward his shoulder. "Maintain focus," he commanded. "You need my interdimensional experience."

Now I understood. The cataclysm had been blamed on Szerain, since it was his ritual with Elinor that went wrong and broke the world. He'd spent centuries in the fringes between worlds, working under the tutelage of Helori to stabilize the realm and repair damage, like a lordly version of community service. He had unique experience and perspective.

Kadir went utterly still, and the chartreuse potency wound around Szerain's neck like an arcane python.

"*Kadir*," Paul gritted out. "He's right."

The potency constrictor withdrew, and Szerain let out a breath of relief even as he dropped to one knee beside Kadir and lowered his head in concentration.

We redoubled our support, and a strange, droning potency

joined the mix—Gurgaz along with Seretis. Not even a minute later, someone growled, "Anomalies at the poles." Vrizaar perhaps. Another huge tremor rocked the palace. Paul glowed so brightly it was hard to look at him, and Dominic had to turn away just to see his screen.

The support structure shrieked incessantly, drained as quickly as we could feed it power. Another tremor rumbled but gentler. Then another, a mere vibration.

The glow around Paul faded. "Collapse of the Between . . . averted," he mumbled. Then his eyes rolled back, and he went limp.

Kadir caught him as he crumpled, and Dominic lunged to grab the falling tablet.

Idris and I dispelled the support structure. My hands shook in post-exertion stress. Idris looked furious and pale.

Kadir gently set Paul on the couch, touched two fingers to his temple. Paul's eyes slowly opened, and a wordless conversation passed between them. After a moment, Kadir stood, expression smooth and way more terrifying than when he'd been obviously furious.

In the next instant he vanished, wringing shocked exclamations from the lords who had yet to see him use his teleportation ability. A clamor of voices rose but cut off immediately when Kadir reappeared with four human soldiers in tow, each wearing a DIRT uniform and a leash of potency around their neck. He dragged them to the center of the room, and sent them sprawling with a vicious tug on the leashes.

"Helori," he murmured, tone pure ice. "A device of destruction has been set near my gate. It needs to be skillfully relocated."

Idris and I exchanged a baffled look. Helori wasn't here as far as I knew and, despite being Kadir's ptarl and demon daddy, the two had been estranged for millennia. For Kadir to call upon him—hell, to even speak his name . . .

I managed not to startle when Helori appeared in front of Kadir. He was in human form, dressed in sedate bronze robes, his expression utterly neutral. He gave Kadir a single nod, then vanished again without waiting for—or, no doubt, expecting—a response.

Holy shit. This was *huge*. Eons of enmity, set aside. Had Zakaar's earlier acknowledgment and apology for the actions of the demahnk contributed in some way?

Furtive conversation passed between knots of lords. Ashava continued to lean into the support of her mother, but she followed the hubbub and mutters with wide-eyed attention.

Barely half a minute later, Helori reappeared. "It has been neutralized," he murmured. Kadir dipped his head in the tiniest of nods. Helori mirrored the action, then vanished.

Though I wished I had time to marvel on how so much could be said with a couple of tiny chin dips, there were more pressing matters to deal with.

Kadir advanced on the soldiers, but I stepped in front of him. "You have righteous anger, Lord Kadir—but if I could have a moment before you dispense justice, it would be greatly appreciated."

"Until I lose patience, Kara Gillian."

Not wanting to waste a single second, I turned to the soldiers. Three men and a woman with varying degrees of injury—mostly slashes and bites—doubtless from the barg, the "first line of defense" creatures we'd encountered in Kadir's realm. Blood from a nasty, potentially fatal thigh wound soaked the pants of one of the men.

The woman, a lieutenant, struggled to her feet and managed a shaky salute in my direction that I returned out of pure habit. Misery clouded her eyes, but she maintained her bearing. "Commander Gillian."

"Lieutenant," I murmured, then looked back at Kadir. "My lord, will you allow healing for the man with the injured leg?"

His eyes narrowed, but then he flicked a brief glance at Paul—which told me Paul had thoughts on the matter. "Seretis may give aid," Kadir said, "if he is willing."

Several of the other lords exchanged dark glances, clearly wondering why Kadir had chosen Seretis rather than one of them. I gave a quiet snort. If they couldn't figure it out by now, then there was no point trying to explain it to them. Seretis had shown true grace, bravery, and conviction—and Kadir respected that.

Seretis tapped a rhythmic pattern on the nearest tentacle in some form of communication. With the same tentacle, Gurgaz nudged him toward the soldiers.

He crouched by the man with the leg wound, quietly asked for permission to tend his injuries, and got a jerky nod in response.

Seretis set a hand on either side of the ugly gash and went still. The man sucked in his breath and clenched his jaw, hands tightening into fists. Seretis didn't move for nearly a full minute, then withdrew, absently burning away the blood on his hands with potency.

"Nicked femoral," he said as he stood. "You won't die now, Corporal. Not from this, at least."

The corporal focused on Seretis with effort. "Th-thank you, sir."

"Dak'nikahl lahn," I said to Kadir, then gave my full attention to the woman. "Report."

She hesitated then apparently realized that she could spill her guts to me, or literally spill her guts to Kadir.

"I'm Lieutenant Bethany Cortez, assigned to IZ-212, more commonly known as The Spires. At thirteen hundred hours, my unit was mustered for an emergency callout after an unknown adolescent female appeared and transported herself through the gate." Her eyes strayed toward Ashava before snapping back to me. "Major Sawyer stated he'd received intel that the gate was now open and usable. At this time, my unit received orders to . . . to take a device through, activate it, and then return to Earth."

"Did you know the nature of this device?"

Her misery deepened. "I wasn't briefed on the specs, but I can conjecture that it was a WMD of a nuclear nature."

"And only four of you were sent?"

"No, ma'am. There were ten of us." Her throat worked. "Four never came out on this side. Two others did but were dead upon arrival."

"And then the barg . . . the ferret-like things attacked you."

She could only nod.

"I'm guessing you activated the device, and only then discovered there was no way to return through the gate."

Anger and betrayal flared in her eyes before she could control it. "That is correct, ma'am."

I shared her anger and didn't bother controlling it. "I'm sorry you and your team were treated so despicably." I pivoted to face Kadir, maintaining the formal bearing. "Lord Kadir, I accept and acknowledge that you have legitimate conflict with these soldiers, however I hope you will recognize they were betrayed most foully by their superiors, and allow them to return to Earth."

His icy gaze slid to rest on the Lieutenant. I had to give her points for maintaining her bearing as well as she did, though I didn't miss the tremble in her legs.

"They are not responsible for the conception of the plot," he snarled, "and I will not take the blood debt from them. With my gate damaged, there is no way to Earth for them at present."

Elofir strode up, exuding calm. "Lord Kadir, I can house the humans until such time as their return can be facilitated."

Kadir dispelled the potency leashes from their necks and returned to Paul, steps sharp and full of fury. That was as much of an answer as anyone was going to get, but I'd take it.

Cortez gave me an uncertain look. "Ma'am . . . ?"

"It's all right," I told her. "This is Lord Elofir. You're in his realm now and will be safe and cared for here until we can get you home."

With swift efficiency, a reyza scooped up the man with the thigh wound, and a pair of faas arrived to escort the other soldiers.

On her way out, Cortez glanced toward the archway, and her eyes widened in recognition.

I turned. Jesral. Rage burned through me. How long had he been standing there with that smug smile on his stupid smarmy face? The fact that Cortez clearly recognized him was ample evidence of his role in this entire disaster.

Ashava pulled away from Jill and stood, fists clenched at her sides. Jesral's mocking gaze swept the assemblage, and I didn't miss the flash of fury as he noted Dominic's presence.

"JESRAL!" Vrizaar snarled. "You would destroy the worlds for . . . what?"

"Don't be absurd, Vrizzy," Jesral sneered. "Why suspect I am culpable? You are ever one to believe the worst of others." He turned to the pale Ashava and offered her a sympathetic smile. "My dear qaztehl," he said, voice soft. Silky. "I apologize for the atrocious behavior of my fellow lords. So quick to blame you for existing instabilities when you simply sought to warn your family and friends." He sighed and shook his head. "This is not your fault. The governor placed on you by Zakaar and endorsed by Szerain makes it nigh impossible for you to divine truth from deception."

Ashava jerked as if struck. "The . . . what?" She went very still, eyes unfocused. "It's true," she murmured. "Jesral speaks the truth."

He smiled and took a step toward her, held out his hands. "Come with me. I will help you explore your true power *without* cruel fetters."

She ignored Jesral as her gaze swept over the rest of us, then fixed on Szerain. "This . . . this *disaster* is all your fault. You and Zakaar diminished me, put restraints on me."

Szerain's expression went stone cold. "The governor did not interfere in that way. Yes, you have limitations in place until such time that you gain the maturity of judgment to wield the unfettered power at your disposal. A child is not allowed to drive a car until they can show control *and* good judgment. Not simply when their feet can reach the pedals!"

"You fucking *prick*!" She squeezed her eyes shut, and I felt more than heard a faint pop. A shudder passed through her. She bared her teeth in feral triumph and swept a vicious gaze over the room. "It is a moot point now."

Fuck. She'd figured out how to remove the governor. And now we were faced with a not-at-all typical teen with the powers of a demi-god.

Jesral sniggered. Of course he was delighted. He'd failed to trap her via Boudreaux, so now he planned to fucking woo her to his side by being the Nice One.

Jill took a step toward her. "Ashava, sweetheart, can we please calm down and discuss this rationally?"

Ashava rounded on Jill. "Discuss?! It's too late for that, Mother!"

Jill backpedaled, grief and true fear on her face. "I didn't know, darling, but—"

"But what?" Ashava yelled. The air shimmered dark around her, like a cloak of shadows. "You've all been hiding the truth from me! And even if you didn't know, you'd've all been on board with keeping me locked down. Little baby Ashava." Potency crackled around her, lifting her hair.

Jesral's distinctive laugh cut through the wind and voices raised in alarm. He leaned against a tree column, arms folded over his chest, clearly enjoying this entire scene tremendously. "Indeed, my dear! You deserve to discover the true extent of your powers."

"Enough, Ashava!" Szerain shouted over the wind. "This tantrum is doing nothing to convince anyone that limits were unwarranted."

Fuuuuck. That was the wrong thing to say.

"You want a tantrum?" she screamed. The wind rose and expanded, dark and cutting. An angry purple glow formed around her, violent and vicious—familiar in a way I couldn't pinpoint.

She stabbed a finger at Szerain, "You're pathetic!"

Then at Jill. "You're weak!"

Then at me. "You're oblivious!"

And finally at Jesral. "You're a slimy creep!"

With a sweep of her arms, a wave of power sent everyone staggering back several feet.

"Ashava, we can talk about this!" I shouted, not even sure she could hear me over the din.

"Enough of this nonsense!" Amkir gathered potency into a malevolent ball and flung it at her.

She adroitly caught it in one hand and held it aloft for a heartbeat, infusing it with vicious purple before savagely casting it back on Amkir. Despite his effort to deflect, it struck him square in the chest, sending him flying across the room to slam into a tree and crumple at its base.

The air seethed around her. I looked around desperately for someone or some way to stop her, contain her. Kadir was nowhere to be seen, yet that didn't surprise me. He'd want to keep Paul and Dominic safe, and he obviously didn't have a way to stop Ashava's tantrum. Mzatal could possibly stop her, but of course he wasn't here—

Mzatal. Ice clutched at my chest. Now I knew why it all felt familiar. I grabbed Szerain's sleeve. "She's going to flare!" I screamed over the wind. "We have to get out of here before she kills us all!"

Bryce's gaze snapped to me. He'd experienced one of Mzatal's flares at the Farouche plantation. Paul had almost died in that one.

The wind rose to a scream as the power built within Ashava, and dark purple lightning arced between the branches of the ceiling. Szerain struggled through the arcane storm to reach her, while I turned to Jill, prepared to pick her up and carry her out if necessary.

A gunshot cracked.

The potency dispersed in a fraction of a heartbeat. Ears ringing in the sudden deafening silence, I swung around in an effort to figure out what the hell happened, feeling as if everything moved in slow motion. Szerain stood stock still. Jesral's expression of amused arrogance shifted to black fury.

Ashava stood motionless, arms limp by her sides and hair in lank tendrils, her eyes staring at nothing.

The insane silence reigned for an infinite instant while my brain refused to process the sight of a neat bullet wound in the center of her forehead.

The instant passed, and she crumpled, scattering into a billion points of light.

Jill screamed, yanking me out of my shock.

Jesral let out a howl of rage and roared a curse in demon. Blue-black potency leaped into his control, an ugly and untamed strike. But before he could unleash it, Ssahr appeared at his side, slapped a hand across his forehead, then vanished with him.

Bryce lowered his gun, looking utterly shattered.

And all hell broke loose.

Chapter 34

Lords shouted over one another while humans screamed and demons roared.

Jill stood shaking, staring at the empty bit of floor where Ashava had been but a moment before. "No . . . no no no—"

I grabbed her by the shoulders. "Call to her!" I shouted over the din. "I think she's scattered, noncorporeal. That doesn't mean dead!" I gave her a small shake. "I died in the demon realm and came back, remember? I swear, mentally calling to her will help."

It felt like a century ago that a reyza eviscerated me, and Rhyzkahl brought me to the demon realm to have a chance of recorporeating on Earth. I knew the situation with Ashava was far different, but Jill needed a life preserver to cling to. When Ekiri scattered—their equivalent of dying—they eventually re-coalesced, though it could take centuries. The lords, including Ashava, were only half-Ekiri, and as far as I knew, none of them had ever been killed. But Ashava's billion-points-of-light shattering was enough like an Ekiri scattering to give me hope. I *had* to have hope.

Rayst snaked out a rope of potency to bind Bryce, but Seretis smacked it away with enough force to send Rayst stumbling back a step. "Leave. Him. Be."

Vahl clenched his hands. "Bryce Taggart must be held accountable for a terminal attack on one of our own!"

"*Now* you acknowledge Ashava as one of us?" Rhyzkahl snarled with naked vehemence. Vahl jerked as if stung.

"And what of Jesral's illicit attack on Kadir's realm?" Vrizaar growled. "That cannot go unanswered!"

Amkir started toward Bryce with murder in his eyes, but

Afu seized his arm, shouting something lost in the tumult. Amkir whirled on him, face twisted with rage until his gaze swept over Teri huddled against the tree wall, arms clamped tightly about her head, and eyes wide in terror.

The fury dropped from his face. He darted to her and scooped her up into his arms, then jerked his head toward the arch. Afu grabbed both puppies and followed as Amkir strode out.

"We need to get Bryce out of here," Szerain said, raising his voice to be heard. "Now."

I had a moment of manic hilarity as I pictured everyone in the conclave running along the vineway to the grove, only to be forced to wait patiently in line for their turn to leave.

"Come," Seretis said as Gurgaz opened a vertical rift. "This is the fastest way out."

Across the hall, Elofir met my eyes and inclined his head as if to say, *I understand you have to get the hell away from this madness.* I gave him an apologetic grimace, then wrapped my arm around Jill's shoulders and force-walked her through the rift the instant Gurgaz opened it wide enough to pass.

Cool, dry darkness enveloped me like the depths of a desert cave, but I had no sense of movement or sound or light or the ground. And, somehow I'd lost contact with Jill—with everything. I pygahed ruthlessly in the face of rising panic, then let out a gasp of relief as light and sensation returned.

We staggered out of the rift into a stone corridor some fifty feet wide and at least that high. About ten feet to our left was a broad, claw-scored cliff ledge at least eight hundred feet above a verdant valley floor, and to our right the corridor continued into what I assumed was a mountain. The rift we'd just exited seemed to be a permanent feature, a doorway of ruby light set in a stone wall intricately carved with bas relief geometric patterns. A matching rift-door was directly across from us, on the far side of the corridor.

I pulled Jill several steps farther into the corridor to make room for the others. Bryce and Szerain came through, followed by Idris. Seretis and Gurgaz emerged, but to my surprise, Paul and Dom stumbled out next with Kadir striding behind.

Paul caught my confused look. "Kadir doesn't dare teleport since the Between is still unstable," he told me quietly. "And since his Earthgate is non-functional now, traveling via the Jontari rift to your nexus might be the only way to return to Earth."

"Gotcha," I said with a mental "duh" headsmack.

The ledge and corridor seemed to be part of a huge complex carved directly into the stone of the cliffs. Countless more corridors opened to the air, each framed by colorful abstract designs that shimmered with the arcane. Demons—some massive—landed on or departed from ledges, carrying out their daily lives. Flightless demons scurried and crawled and lumbered up and down ramps either cut into cliff faces or built from some sort of pale wood. In the green valley far below, a literal lake of rakkuhr glimmered, though the surrounding arcane residue told me it had once been deeper.

The biggest luhrek I'd ever seen crouched on this particular ledge. While the lord-aligned luhreks tended to be about the size of a large dog, this one was nearly as tall as me. Their curved horns gleamed like ivory in the early morning sunlight, and though their sleek, lion-like body seemed relaxed, one tufted ear twitched repeatedly.

Kadir stood on the very lip of the ledge beside the luhrek, toes of his boots a good two inches beyond the edge. I got dizzy just thinking about it, even more so when he casually dropped to sit, legs dangling. To add to the surreal feel of the entire situation, Kadir apparently already knew the luhrek's name—Idan—and conversed in demon with them, his tone respectful yet also . . . friendly? Not at all creepy-weird—which was, in itself, creepy weird.

Jill edged away to stand apart from everyone, hugging her arms around herself, expression stricken. Bryce watched her, looking utterly helpless and bereft.

Szerain wrapped his arms around her, pulling her close. "I feel Ashava, yet. I swear this to you," he murmured. "We will not give up hope. I'll help you call to her."

Jill clung to him. "I want to go home," she croaked. "I just want to go home."

"I'll get you there as soon as possible." He stroked her back and met Bryce's eyes as if to say, *I'll take care of her for now.*

Bryce swallowed hard and gave a short, sharp nod.

"Gurgaz," I said, using my very best respectful tone, "I can't thank you enough for giving us an escape from that nightmare." Grimacing, I tugged both hands through my hair. "But we need to get back to Earth before Jesral causes more mayhem. Would you allow us to return via the rift by my nexus?"

Seretis held up a hand. "Jesral will be incapacitated for a time. Ssahr was locking him down even as they left."

"I don't understand," I said in a massive understatement. "Why did Jesral need to be locked down? I mean, yes, he was pretty livid, but . . . ohhhhh, he was pinning his hopes and dreams and nefarious plans on having Ashava at his disposal."

"Precisely. And when Bryce took action"—he shot an apologetic glance toward him—"those plans vaporized, and Jesral's reaction was extreme."

Idris scowled. "In other words, he had a toddler-worthy meltdown, and Ssahr put him in time out before he could do something dangerously stupid."

Seretis nodded. "I estimate it will be close to a week before Ssahr and Ilana stabilize Jesral and regroup. The failed nuclear attack on Kadir's Earthgate, coupled with the loss of Ashava, have set them back."

"That's a relief," I said. "Maybe we can get ahead of them for once."

Pinks and purples rippled over Gurgaz's hide. "Permission is granted to travel through the rift. We shall provide a guide, as there are more branchings than an uninitiated hu-beast could track."

I abruptly realized I'd seen only two rifts since our arrival, and both seemed permanent. And though there were probably more elsewhere, the landscape and other ledges weren't pocked with as many as I'd expect if each rift on Earth had a counterpart in the demon realm. Duh. It was probably like the valve system, with a main trunk that branched off.

"Imperator Dekkak awaits you, Kara Gillian. Your own passage is delayed until she gives you leave." Gurgaz waved a tentacle in the direction of the others. "These may go."

"Of course," I said, keeping a bland smile on my face through sheer force of will. What the hell did she want from me now?

Bryce bowed to the demon. "Honored Gurgaz, forgive me if this is an impertinent request, but could I remain here with Seretis for now?" He glanced at Jill just in time to see naked relief skim across her face. He quickly jerked his gaze away, looking gutted.

"It is acceptable until such time it is not."

Gurgaz moved to Idan and spoke to them in demon. They trilled an affirmative and went to wait by the rift across the corridor.

Szerain looked down at Jill. "Can you manage one more journey through a rift?"

"We'll come out in the back yard?"

"I'll be with you the entire way. And then we'll call for Ashava."

"I won't give up." She gripped his hand tightly, then raked a glance around her. She gave me a shaky nod and avoided Bryce's eyes entirely.

"Let's go," she whispered and walked toward the rift-door with Szerain on one side and Idris on the other. Idan chirruped and bounded in, disappearing into the ruby light. Jill and Szerain followed without a break in stride, Idris right behind them. Paul and Dom went next, hands clasped tightly. Kadir regarded me for a moment, then stepped sedately through. The rift-doorway belched a gout of orange-red arcane and went quiescent.

Bryce scrubbed a hand over his face. "Fuck."

"You did the right thing," I told him. "I know that doesn't help right now, but it had to be done. I'm so sorry you had to be the one to do it."

"Yeah," he murmured, a funny catch in his voice. "I heard you say she was about to flare, and I can never forget how Paul almost died when Mzatal lost control. And then Seretis . . ."

Seretis exhaled. "I told him Ashava had to be stopped or we were lost."

"So you acted," I said. "And you saved us all."

His gaze went to the rift. "Yeah," he said, voice hollow. "All but one."

Seretis pulled him into an embrace, murmuring softly as Bryce began to weep.

Aching for both of them, I headed off with Gurgaz.

The demon led me down a winding corridor lit by baseball-sized orbs of arcane, each casting a soft glow that closely matched the hue and intensity of morning sun.

"Can all Jontari make rifts?" I asked after a moment.

"Few. Only Dekkak between worlds."

That explained why the ones to Earth were literal rifts in the earth, while the ones from point to point in the demon realm were more like openings in the fabric of reality. "Demons from other clans still come through the rifts on Earth, though."

Gurgaz made a noise that sounded like a prolonged wet fart. "Depredators." They smacked two tentacles together—hard—leaving no doubt what would happen if Gurgaz caught one. Probably best to drop the subject.

The corridor soon opened out into a large open air space the size of a couple of football fields. Intricate warding shimmered above—I assumed as protection from both attacks and the elements. More corridors were spaced around the perimeter, and an octagonal structure of blood-red stone and ebony wood dominated the center, its open sides allowing passage of even the largest of demons. Within, a lively marketplace bustled with activity. Off to my right was a cluster of a dozen or so smaller dome structures, made of what looked like thick, frosted demon glass. Faas scurried among them, darting in and out of round doorways. Adjacent to the domes stood a cute little cottage right out of a fairy tale, style and craftsmanship leading me to suspect it had been built by Bubba. Faas youngsters scampered over the rooftop in a rousing game of chase. Beyond it was a simple, single-story wooden structure, likely also a Bubba creation.

"Is Bubba doing okay?" I asked Gurgaz as we made our way to the right, avoiding the more crowded market area and bringing us closer to the faas domes and cottage. Now it was clear the outbuilding was a workshop, with a pile of logs and a rack of wood planks beside it.

"Hu-beast Bub-Bah Swa-Resss." Gurgaz extended a tentacle toward the cottage and outbuilding. It wasn't exactly an answer, but judging by the state of both structures, I had to assume he was settling in well enough.

Gurgaz continued on past the workshop and into another corridor. We soon entered a lofty chamber of a slightly irregular though not crude shape, about a hundred feet long and fifty feet wide. Carvings of battle scenes covered the walls, interspersed with depictions of daily life. Stone ledges along the walls held a variety of items—mostly weapons, but also unique stones and other natural artifacts, as well as a foot-long articulated wooden crawfish that was, without a doubt, Bubba's doing.

Against the wall to my right, a low stone table held the three gimkrah—basketball-sized crystal orbs with deep pulsing maroon within their depths, shot through with flickers of red-gold lightning. Each was bound in eleven bands of arcane-dampening makkas inscribed with dark sigils born of the void. Xhan. Vsuhl. Khatur.

Dekkak crouched at the far end of the chamber on a dais covered in richly patterned rugs of shifting hues. Her intimidating size and undeniable Presence still left me in awe. Blood-red hide and wings gleamed as if freshly oiled, and the craggy scales covering her head and shoulders bore the scars and signs of battles old and new. Gold bands bound her horns, and rings with esoteric symbols adorned each joint of her fingers. Though the chamber was far from small, she dominated the space, both in size and general aura of command.

I approached and gave a deep bow of respect. "Greetings, honored Dekkak. I am so very grateful you allowed us to retreat to your demesne." I flicked a glance toward the gimkrahs at a whisper of noise, then yanked my attention back to Dekkak. Probably just the demon realm equivalent of a mouse.

She rumbled and leaned toward me. "You have yet to obtain the blades, Kara Gillian."

"You're not wrong," I said, "yet I assure you, plans are in motion to achieve that end."

Kara Gillian

I shot another quick look at the gimkrahs. That was no mouse. Nor had there been any sound.

Dekkak bared her teeth. "Your time grows short to retrieve them. The elders await their freedom."

Her voice faded away beneath the call of the gimkrah on the far right. Xhan's. I extended my hand to touch that crystal—

The room tumbled and roared around me. No, *I* was tumbling, and it was Dekkak roaring after knocking me away from the gimkrah. I hadn't even been aware of walking toward it.

She leaped at me, claws ready to separate my guts from my belly. "YOU SHALL NOT DEFILE—"

"Shit! Xhan wants to talk to me!" I scrabbled back. "They need to talk to me!"

A snarl curved her mouth, and her breath hissed through her teeth. "Do not attempt to deceive me, callow human. They have never spoken. It is yet another cruelty of their prison."

Fuck. Heart pounding, I yanked my shirt up to show the scars on my belly. "Maybe these have something to do with my being able to hear Xhan."

A growl throbbed in her throat, but since she no longer seemed poised to kill me right this instant, I scrambled to my feet, tore my shirt off, and even removed my bra. Best to let her see every line, loop, and swirl.

Dekkak's eyes narrowed to slits as she bent close. I used every mental trick in the book to remain perfectly still as she examined the sigils.

"They were carved into me with the blade Xhan," I told her.

"Kri," she rumbled, somehow also conveying *No shit, Sherlock*. She moved around me, breath hot against my skin. "What of the sigil of Kadir."

I hesitated for a bare instant, then remembered how comfortable he seemed to be with the Jontari. "He consummated his a few days past."

She dipped her head in a slight nod, then straightened. "You are able to speak with Xhan?"

"I think so. I mean, I can hear them now. It's worth a try, right?"

She rumbled, and I could only assume it was assent.

I quickly pulled on my bra and shirt, wiped sweaty palms on my pants, then moved to the gimkrah, mentally bracing myself before I placed my hands on either side of it. Xhan and I had met before—during the ritual that carved the sigils—which meant this would likely be a pretty fucking intense experience.

Yet to my shock, Xhan felt nothing at all like our previous encounter. No rage, no fury, no burning desire for torment. Instead there was only a calm and gentle presence. An electric tingle passed up my arms to settle in my head like a swarm of tiny buzzing bees. *Enter.*

The invitation was simple but carried so much more meaning than a single word.

I acknowledged and did my best to convey *Hang on juuust a sec, please.*

"Xhan invited me to enter," I told Dekkak. "I'm not sure what all that entails, but I get the sense it might take a while. I need to let Bryce know I'm going to be out of pocket for some time. Also, would it be possible for me to have a letter or message delivered to my compound on Earth? No one expects me to remain behind longer than perhaps an hour or so. And, of course, I'm worried about my people and would like to get a status update."

Dekkak regarded me for a long moment before returning to the dais. "The burden of command is heavy, and one I understand well. Gurgaz will inform Bryce Taggart, and I will have materials brought for you to scribe a message. Idan will deliver it to your demesne, and any reply may simply be dropped into the rift." She sketched a violet and amber message sigil and sent it off.

I expected to be provided some sort of vellum or parchment

and perhaps a quill and ink. Instead a faas bounded in carrying a Disney Princess school backpack.

I stared at it, mouth going dry. At what age did kids stop being interested in Disney characters? Second grade? Third? "What, um, happened to the owner of that backpack?" I kept my tone as light and casual as humanly possible, even as any number of horrific mental images clashed in my brain.

Dekkak snorted out a breath. "The *nehl* fell into a rift in Ahr-eh-zonah and suffered minor injury to her knees and hands when she emerged here. We tended her wounds and fed her chak and treats, then Idan led her back through."

I tried to keep the relief off my face, but Dekkak was no dummy. She bared her teeth in amusement. "The youngling was no threat to us, and there was no gain to be had in harming her. Far more honor to be lost by committing violence on an innocent. Yulz was intrigued by this satchel and traded her a dagger for it."

"Oh. Well, that's nice." One hell of a souvenir for a little kid. Then again, her parents could probably sell it to a collector for a sizable sum. "And you aren't worried about her telling people back on Earth about the, um, nice demons?"

Dekkak made a noise that almost might have possibly been perhaps interpreted as a laugh. "Kadir blurs the memories of those who come here with no ill intent. The youngling was left with the belief she'd fallen into a ditch some distance from her abode and found the dagger there."

I'd never been literally speechless before, but here we were. Yet now I remembered how downright friendly Kadir was with the luhrek Idan, and how *relaxed* he seemed once we arrived here. Not to mention, Dekkak noticed the visible absence of his sigil on my torso. Weirdly, it made perfect sense for the Jontari and Kadir to be, well, friendly. Both were rule followers. Both believed in the power and sanctity of oaths and promises and honor. And Kadir was absolutely one-hundred-percent super protective of kids and innocents in general.

I managed to make some appropriate reply, then turned my attention to my letter-writing task. The backpack had already been rifled through, but I found a *Reading Skills for the Second Grade* workbook, and also a spiral notebook. No pens or pencils—probably already taken by Yulz or others—but I discovered a handful of broken crayons at the bottom. Eh, could be worse. I carefully tore a sheet out of the notebook and, with a purple crayon, I wrote in neat, block letters:

I'm going to be with Dekkak and the Jontari for a few days. Everything is five by five and copacetic. Please let me know how things stand at the compound. Just drop a reply into the rift. —KARA

I folded it in quarters and handed it to the faas. "Dak'nikahl lahn." It chittered a reply and dashed off. I returned to sit before the Xhan gimkrah, took a deep breath, then placed my hands upon it.

Chapter 35

My palms tingled against the surprisingly warm bands of makkas. "I'm here," I murmured. "Now what?"

Wait

Okay. I could do that. About half a minute later, my head began to feel weird, as if the bones of my skull vibrated against each other. I breathed through it and kept my hands firmly against the gimkrah.

Then fire ants came to devour my brain, and I fought the overwhelming urge to scream and pull away. But to my relief the pain subsided as quickly as it had come on, leaving only a residual tingle—almost exactly the same sensation I'd felt after the ilius Dakdak bit my calf.

Enter

Before I could frame a question as to *how*, my being shattered into countless fragments, and I sank into the oblivion of the void.

Darkness gave way to light flickering over my eyelids. Running water spoke in soothing whispers, like a brook over stones, and the delicate scent of wildflowers wafted on pleasantly warm air. I felt comfortable turf beneath me, and found myself reluctant to break the peace by opening my eyes.

Then I remembered the gimkrah and my purpose and sat bolt upright. I was on a swath of bright green grass dotted with butter-colored flowers that swept down to a sparkling stream. Around me was a wide expanse of meadow bounded by woods, and mountains rose in the distance against an achingly blue sky.

Sunlight played between leaves of emerald and amethyst

above and the white trunk of a single grove sapling stood beside me. What the hell?

A rich, bass voice thrummed. "This is not what you expected, Kara Gillian?"

The speaker—a luhrek the size of a mini-van—lounged like a burnished copper cat on a flat, sun-drenched rock, his lion's tail lazily swishing back and forth. Curved horns arced back and around, framing a face that was both dog and goat-like, with the rectangular pupils of the latter.

"*Xhan*?" I said after I recovered from my shock. I'd always assumed the elders were reyza, since my less-than-complete early summoner training had led me to believe they were the biggest baddest demon type.

The luhrek inclined his head.

"None of this is what I expected." I gestured broadly around me. "The place. You."

He laughed, a sound between a purr and growl. "It is a pleasant prison, is it not?"

"But a prison nonetheless." I let out a breath. "I don't understand. The blade Xhan is horrific, but you're, um—"

"Serene and peaceful?" he offered.

I shifted to sit cross-legged. "I have so many questions."

"There is time, Kara Gillian. So much time."

"No, I actually don't have all that long. A day or so at most. I have to get back—"

"Do you?"

Leaves whispered above me, and Rho brushed my consciousness. A specialized dimensional pocket where time flowed by their design. Now far more quickly than outside. Weeks passing in mere hours.

"Huh. I guess not," I said with a shaky laugh as I flexed my hands. "Every other time I've been in a dimensional pocket, it formed around me or I had the sense of *going*. This time, it was like I broke into pieces then woke up." I had the absurd image of being sprawled, drooling, on Dekkak's floor while I had a nice long dream of Xhan.

"Different, yes, because of the nature of this prison. Rho has taken your physical form into their safekeeping, and your full essence is here. The bite from the ilius facilitated the separation of flesh from essence."

Huh. So Dakdak had primed me for this? Even knowing Mzatal

made plans for a zillion possible outcomes, this was still pretty hard to wrap my head around.

I decided to not even bother trying to fathom the twists and turns and just accept that I'd somehow made it into the gimkrah, and my meat-based form was safe. Somewhere.

Xhan rose and shook himself, sparks of rakkuhr flying from his coat. "Come with me."

We walked in silence through the meadow and pristine woods. Along a river into a valley set between rocky hills. Plants abounded, but I saw no signs of animal life. Not even an insect.

I started to speak a number of times, but Xhan's flicked glance convinced me to bite back the words. As time and miles wore on, I found myself less inclined to question and more inclined to simply enjoy the scenery and rhythm of the journey.

We followed the river until it opened into a broad lake, surface rippling in a gentle breeze, reflecting the setting sun and a sky streaked with orange and purple. Near the water's edge, a campfire flickered beside another grove sapling, and the delicious aroma of simmering stew had my mouth watering.

Not only stew, but a pitcher of tunjen and an inviting pallet and pillow awaited me.

Xhan stretched out on the grass nearby. I ate and drank in comfortable silence before settling onto the pallet beneath a glorious blanket of stars in an inky sky.

In the morning, a breakfast of warm bread and tender meat awaited me, along with a steaming mug of chak. After I filled my belly, we resumed our silent, meditative walk.

Days passed in similar fashion as we drew closer to the mountain range. I awoke from each sleep a little more refreshed, my mind that much clearer. As we set out again on the tenth—or perhaps the eleventh?—day, Xhan finally spoke again, an alien sound after so long without hearing speech.

"What question do you have now, Kara Gillian?"

The billion questions that cluttered my mind upon arrival had stilled. Now they waited patiently, to be brought forth one at a time. "What happened?"

I didn't need to elaborate. He told the tale as we walked, the early parts he'd learned from Rho, and the rest experienced by him. I listened and absorbed the story over several days, surprising myself with my new-found patience.

He laid out the full history of the Ekiri collective's relationship with the demon realm and Earth in glorious and ignominious detail. From their arrival nearly twelve thousand years ago, to their mentorship of adept and eager demons in the use of potency, to their exodus shortly after the lords—their unexpected offspring—were born, and beyond.

The Ekiri presence had caused a critical potency imbalance, nearly draining Earth, and overloading the demon realm to the point of destabilization. They imprudently cut the conduit between the worlds, believing it would solve the problem, but it only trapped the potency in the demon realm, giving it no means of escape. Rakkuhr—toxic to the Ekiri—erupted from the demon planet's core as arcane volcanoes, prompting the abrupt departure of the collective, save for the parental "demahnk" Ekiri, along with Xharbek who would remain as a steward.

Of the Jontari—the sentient natives of the demon realm—Xhan, Vsuhl, and Khatur were the first students of the Ekiri. When the rakkuhr was forced to the planet's surface, these three were intrigued and fascinated by this new-to-them resource and its unique potential, and so they experimented with it, using their vast experience with potency to shape and tame it. They channeled it into reservoirs and became its gatekeepers and masters.

During this time, the demahnk created the Earthgates to bleed off excess potency as well as to allow human contact for their offspring. For several hundred years all remained stable, and the demons reveled in their newfound rakkuhr-fueled power and potential. While the demahnk made efforts to limit the Jontari's rampant progress, they knew the problem would eventually solve itself as the potency balanced and the rakkuhr retreated into the planet's core.

Yet the Jontari were not fools and had no desire to lose access to this most-desirable resource. Thus they targeted the Earthgates that were slowly depleting their stores of rakkuhr and forced their collapse, triggering a near catastrophic destabilization of the planet.

Rho relinquished all ties to the Ekiri collective and merged with the planet's core to prevent irrevocable destruction.

Zakaar initiated the valve system as a new way to vent potency to Earth. The Jontari viewed it as yet another attempt to strip their way of life with the rakkuhr and entered into full revolt, attacking and disrupting valve development by any means possible.

Demons less inclined to violence, and often unattuned to

rakkuhr, sought out the lords, from curiosity or a desire to gain a different perspective, or for reasons unknown. Warlords looked upon them with scorn, viewed them as weak, and named them *Jontardahnk*—"Not Jontari." But some of these demons spied upon the lords for the Jontari and earned honor among their clans.

That brought us to the evening of the third day of the telling. We made camp in a mountain meadow bounded by slim trees with bark the color of honey and leaves of the palest green. After a hearty meal, I lay back on my pallet and allowed the new knowledge and insight to settle within me as I watched the star-laden sky wheel above.

The next day, we hiked mountain trails in a light drizzle, finally stopping on a ledge that overlooked a deep valley framed by high craggy cliffs. It took me a moment to realize it was Dekkak's realm, long before excavation or construction.

"When are we?" I breathed.

"In the early days of Ekiri mentorship. Many millennia past." He crouched, sphinx-like.

I sat with my back against his side, closer to the edge than I'd have dared not so long ago. "The revolt. Is that what prompted the creation of the gimkrah and blades?"

"In part," he said, deep voice resonating comfortably against me. "As our power expanded, we grew greedy, seeking ever more. We waged brutal war among rival clans, even to the point of extermination. Khatur, ever the wisest of us, counseled temperance, both with the demahnk and our rivals, but we would have none of it. Dekkak ruled the Jontari world and was determined to remain Prime Imperator."

I took a long moment to consider his words. "Okay, so the valve attacks plus increasing violence prompted Mzatal to imprison you and the other elders. But *how*? I mean, y'all were pretty insanely powerful."

"Betrayal."

I pondered that. "You were betrayed. But not by Mzatal, since he wasn't an ally. He'd have been a means to an end." The answer was before me, but I allowed it to steep before speaking. "Khatur." Because of course Mzatal would hold the blade of the one at the core of it all.

Xhan rumbled assent. "Khatur conspired with Mzatal and Rho to lure Vsuhl and me into an inescapable trap."

"Wait. Mzatal knew Rho was once Ekiri?" I glanced at the sapling that had appeared unnoticed sometime after our arrival.

"Mzatal knew much. Knows much. He was firstborn of the offspring. Potent and deeply committed. He would repeatedly break through the demahnk controls, remembering, knowing, only to have it all stripped from him. Over and over."

I blinked away tears as grief squeezed my chest. "That's vile." But no wonder he had the fortitude to resist them even now.

"As was much in those times, and still is today."

"Why gimkrah *and* blade? How are they both you?"

"Khatur advised a splitting of essence lest the whole of us rally to escape."

"That's also horrific," I said with a deep grimace.

"But oh-so-wise," he said. "Mzatal had long worked with ilius, learned much about their ability to dissociate and reassociate their essence when podding. Between ilius knowledge and the aid of Rho, our essences were sundered. Violence and vehemence and vitriol went into the blades, fitting repositories for such. What remained"—he lifted a claw—"was channeled into the gimkrahs."

We sat in silence while the cloud cover darkened into blackest night.

As the moon peeked through a gap in the clouds, I spoke. "You were betrayed but don't seem disturbed by it. Is that because it's your placid self here in the gimkrah?"

"Even this aspect railed against the injustice and dishonor of the act. But Rho kept us connected, not only with our blade aspect, but with each other and the events of the outside world. We have had millennia to come to terms with what was done—and to understand and accept its necessity. The Jontari were bound for self-destruction."

"Everybody needed a time out." I pondered my bargain with the Imperator. "Dekkak wants you three restored. What if she goes right back to being a domineering mega-warlord?"

"She, too, has had long to reflect and evolve." At my dubious expression, Xhan added, "But even should she revert, we will not support obliterative violence."

That night I slept with my back warm against his and dreamed of Mzatal.

Morning sun revealed a very different valley, one marked with a myriad of tunnels and carvings in its cliffs, and a lake of rak-kuhr below. Eerie, without a single demon, save Xhan.

We descended steep trails toward the valley floor, talked about the taming of rakkuhr, the cataclysm, my torture at the hands of Rhyzkahl and the Xhan blade, anomalies, the demahnk, and the lords.

"Do you know why all the lords except Ashava are male?" I asked.

Xhan rumbled a laugh. "I asked a similar question of Rho long ago. They told me it related to the levels of potency on Earth at the time, much like how zrila-brood sex is determined by the ambient temperature of the egg mound."

"Gotcha. Ashava is female because the potency levels now are a lot different than they were three-thousand-plus years ago." But with the answer to my question came a reminder of how much was still in flux. I blew out a sigh. "Ashava is gone. Scattered. Sort of, I think. She was killed in the demon realm." I met his eyes. "Has a lord ever died and come back?"

"None have ever suffered death."

"I'm clinging to the hope that her Ekiri side is enough to bring her home."

He made a low sound, like a cross between a croon and a purr. Odd, yet comforting. "She is the only *unadulterated* human-Ekiri hybrid. The others have been suppressed and controlled and hobbled for near their entire lives. Of them all, she has the best chance of return."

I winced. "But she has—had—a governor to help keep her under control."

"It is not the same, Kara Gillian. Hers was subtle and to her benefit. The controls placed on the other lords are brutally cruel and contemptible."

I took comfort in his words, mood easing. As evening crept upon us, we came to rest beside a sapling of Rho's that overlooked the rakkuhr reservoir. The sheer *power* of the place took my breath away.

Xhan gazed out over the shifting potency that seemed more like dense ruby red fog than water. "You have learned the rudiments of rakkuhr manipulation. My other aspect parted your skin by Rhyzkahl's hand. You have the ability to master more."

My immediate reaction was *Oh, fuck yes!* But I made myself pause and breathe and consider the statement and the potential ramifications from all angles.

Okay, still definitely *Oh, fuck yes!* The worlds were in dire straits, and we needed every possible advantage. But apart from that, I wanted to know more, to truly understand. "You'd teach me?"

"I would, Kara Gillian."

"I accept your offer, honored Xhan. But first, I'd like to check in with my people on the outside. Is that possible?"

"With assistance from Rho, yes."

I stood and placed my hand on the sapling's trunk. "I'll be back soon."

Chapter 36

Dekkak wasn't in the chamber when I recoalesced, and I found myself grateful for the solitude, since I needed a moment to adjust to the real world instead of the gimkrah's tranquility. The peaceful prison.

"Wow," I murmured once I felt a bit more like I belonged in my body. Then said it again. "*Wow.*"

I didn't get a chance to say it a third time—which probably would have been overkill anyway—because the same faas who'd brought the backpack earlier scampered toward me from the corridor.

"Missive for Kara Gillian!" it chirruped and handed me an envelope. I had the sense he'd been waiting in the very near vicinity for my return.

"How long was I gone?"

"A day and half a day!"

I thanked the faas—whose name was Vlip, I learned upon asking—and pulled the letter from the envelope. Then I let out a laugh when I saw it had been written in green and purple marker.

Apologies for not responding in kind, but we couldn't find a single crayon.

But my amusement waned as I continued reading.

Alpha Squad was recalled while we were at the conclave. No reason given. Their order came immediately after Ashava left to crash Kadir's gate. DIRT has been completely silent, with none of the usual pestering for information. This is unsettling in its own way, of course.

Michael says Jesral is fuzzy, like he has been since the con-clave, so not back to sowing mayhem as yet. Otherwise, matters are stable for the moment and repairs and maintenance con-tinue. We are caring for Jill to the best of our ability and con-tinue to call to Ashava. Be careful, and good luck. —Szerain

Well, that was some shit news, but there wasn't anything I could do about it. I was confident the time spent with Xhan was well worth my short-term absence.

I tucked the letter into a pocket. "Will Dekkak be back soon?"

"Dekkak busy busy. Back in not long."

"Gotcha," I said, and hoped that "not long" would be enough time for me to check in on my people. "Can you tell me where to find Seretis and Bryce Taggart?"

"Kri! Follow!"

After trekking corridors, ramps, and more ramps, I stepped out onto a plateau dotted with a number of the frosted demon-glass domes—though these were considerably larger than the ones the faas were using in the common central arena. The sun blazed through low clouds to paint them in brilliant pink and gold, turning the domes into a sea of sparkling gems.

Bryce and Seretis sat atop one, enjoying the gorgeous colors of the morning skies. Seretis gave me a wave, and Bryce offered a weak smile.

"Everything okay?" Bryce asked. "The message Dekkak sent was terse, at best." He definitely looked better than when I'd seen him last, though he still carried a heavy aura of sadness. Understandable, considering everything.

"So far so good—for the most part." I clambered up to sit beside them and shared the news from the compound.

"I should probably get back to Earth," Bryce said, frowning.

I shook my head. "Jesral's still out of commission. Nothing's going to happen in the next couple of days, and I think you need this downtime."

"He does indeed," Seretis said and gave Bryce's hand a squeeze.

"Oh, I haven't even told you the absolutely bonkers reason I needed to stay." I proceeded to give a rundown of my experi-ence with Xhan in the gimkrah. By the time I finished, Bryce appeared intrigued, while Seretis looked absolutely poleaxed.

"Do Szerain and Rhyzkahl know any of this?" Seretis asked after he found his voice.

"Nope. And neither does Dekkak, but she'll be back soon, and I'll fill her in. In the meantime, I want to check in on Bubba. I spotted his house when we got here, but he wasn't around."

Seretis nodded. "That was around the time he usually plays *kessa* in the grotto. At this hour, he's likely in his workshop."

"Good deal. Is he settling in all right?" I asked.

"He is indeed. He built the house and workshop the first two weeks he was here, with the assistance of quite a few demons."

"And they don't give him too much grief?"

Seretis laughed. "Not in the slightest. Bubba charmed the Jontari from the very beginning by respecting their way of life, their attitudes and outlook. They in turn appreciate his courage and skills." He grinned. "His second day here, one of the younger reyza challenged him to a wrestling match—with sufficient rules that Bubba was unlikely to suffer any serious injury that would invalidate his pact to be a hostage. He agreed, got his ass handed to him, laughed uproariously, and asked the demon to give him lessons in the fighting style. Then he gave the reyza a gift of a puzzle box as thanks for taking the time to teach him." Seretis paused. "But what truly solidified their high opinion of him was when he fought alongside them during an attack by a rival clan. He's a fine warrior on Earth *and* here, and a fine man as well. They see that." Seretis smiled. "It has been deeply satisfying watching him win them over. Even Dekkak seems to respect him."

I exhaled. "You have no idea how relieved I am to hear that."

"He's been calling to Ashava as well," he said, expression growing more serious. "We all have. Even the demons." Seretis exchanged a long look with Bryce as they communicated without words, and a tiny bit more of the torment and guilt faded from his eyes.

I swallowed down a sudden knot in my throat. "I'd best be heading back, and I'll see if Bubba's around."

Vlip escorted me through a somewhat different maze of ramps and corridors, eventually leading me to the large open-air plaza. There were about half the number of demons as before, moving more sedately, as if relishing the moment and easing into their day.

Bubba was indeed in his workshop, sitting behind a long table, sanding tiny triangles of wood.

He glanced up as I approached, then let out a whoop of delight and ran to greet me. He was shirtless, with only a long leather apron—and an insane amount of body hair—covering him.

He grabbed me up in a big hug that I returned with gusto. "You sure are a sight for sore eyes, Miss Kara!"

"I could say the same!" I said, relieved. He looked good. Happy.

He released me, grinning. "I heard tell you was here but all anyone would say was you was busy."

"Yeah, and I have a bit more to take care of before I head back to Earth. But it's good to see you settled in."

"Sure have. The demons are hard-working folk who also know when to stop and kick back. We get along like peas and carrots!"

I smiled, the last of my knots of worry about him unwinding. "I have to go speak to Dekkak, but I'll stop in again before I leave."

"I'll count on it!" He turned and trotted back to his work table, giving me a full view of his bare—and quite hairy—ass.

I choked down a laugh and let the faas escort me back to Dekkak's chamber. One thing was certain—Bubba was very comfortable in his skin.

Dekkak was on the dais when I returned, but didn't seem perturbed that I'd left.

I bowed, then sat cross-legged in front of her.

"I have much to tell you," I said, and launched right into it—the history, the betrayals, and the stakes.

Dekkak listened, motionless as a statue. When I finished she remained silent for several moments more, then let out a low growl that seemed to have nothing to do with menace or anger.

"I do not wish to believe one elder would betray the others," she said, words slow and measured. "And yet, you speak that which no hu-man could know and bring the answer to a deep question."

"You mean, how one qaztahl could entrap the three elders?"

"Kri." Her gaze hardened. "This changes nothing about our agreement."

"I didn't expect it to. I'm just as invested in seeing the elders freed as you are. It's time. Events are coming to a head, and the Ekiri MUST be dealt with."

Dekkak rumbled deep in her chest, "Then we are of accord, Kara Gillian."

Holy shit. Dekkak actually said something nice to me? I kept my expression even and merely nodded in acknowledgment, then settled in front of the gimkrah and entered it once again.

I opened my eyes to a bleak landscape of a seemingly endless plain of fine grey dirt roofed by equally grey clouds. A grove sapling swayed in a light breeze nearby, and Xhan crouched beside a puddle of rakkuhr about the diameter of a car tire, his eyes keen on me.

"Welcome back, Kara Gillian." His gaze dropped to the rakkuhr. "Show me all you know."

And I did. I called rakkuhr. Spun it into strands. Formed sigils from it that glimmered like rubies. Exploited every trick and nuance I'd learned.

When I finally released the rakkuhr, Xhan regarded me with an unreadable expression. "What is it you just did?"

"I, um, worked the rakkuhr. Molded and shaped it to do what I wanted it to do. In that last bit, I smacked stray tendrils back in place. Rakkuhr tends to flow away more than surface potency."

He made a deep huffing noise. "What did the rakkuhr tell you?"

"Er." I shifted, grimaced. "Tell me? I didn't get anything."

He raised one paw-like hand. Rakkuhr snaked from the puddle to coalesce in his palm, then rose and expanded into a six-foot-wide fan shape of delicate red filigree. It rotated slowly for a moment before dissipating. "Rakkuhr may be bent to your will and forced into constructs, as you demonstrated. But the results are coarse and crude."

I took a moment to process his words along with what we'd each done. "Forcing and manipulating isn't the way. The rakkuhr should speak to me by some rakkuhr-y means." I looked for the logical next step. "I need to try to listen better? Somehow?"

Xhan remained silent.

Yeah, I was definitely on the wrong track. "No. Wait, I think I get it. Trying is forcing *myself.*" My experience with the tenth ring of the shikvihr had taught me to be one with the energy and construct. To flow with it. "I need to let go and follow my intuition."

He inclined his head. "Rakkuhr is far more secretive, shy, than other potencies. You have the time you need to become well acquainted."

We spent the day and most of the next in meditative sessions beside the rakkuhr puddle. Our weeks-long trek during my first visit had taught me that I could, indeed, quiet the pesky brain gerbils, but I felt nothing from the rakkuhr on that first day. Mid-afternoon of the second, I sensed a feather-light touch for a bare instant. Playful, like a child tagging and running away. Unexpected, and I couldn't help but smile.

Over the rest of the week, I built my relationship with the rakkuhr, guided with ultimate patience by Xhan. It seemed to have a degree of sentience—not like a person but still beyond an inanimate substance. By the second week, it would come to my hand when I invited it, eager and willing, unlike the stiff harshness before when *commanded*. Every day, the relationship grew stronger, mischievous at times, but serious and potent when asked.

On day eighteen, Rho shifted us to a spot beside the rakkuhr lake. Xhan continued to help me fine tune my experience as I worked with the larger body as I had with the puddle—until it invited *me* in.

My mind recoiled at the thought of wading into such a dense mass of rakkuhr—but only for a moment. Intuition, clear and vibrant, coaxed me to let go and simply *beeeee* with the rak-kuhr. I glanced at Xhan, who regarded me without expression. I approached the edge intending to wade in slowly, especially since I didn't know the depth or the consequences.

So much for thinking. The rakkuhr called, and I dove in, delighted as it buoyed me somewhere between the surface and the bottom. Soft ruby light completely surrounded me, the po-tency pressing against me like fluffy clouds. My lungs began to ache—because I'd been holding my breath. I listened to intu-ition rather than the mind and body reflex and inhaled deeply.

The sensation was heady and staggering. I sensed the heart of the planet, the whole of rakkuhr. I didn't know how long I remained in deep communion, but a full moon shone down when the rakkuhr finally lifted me to the surface and deposited me on the bank—at my request.

Xhan rumbled approval.

I couldn't stop grinning. "That was pretty fucking awe-some!"

"Indeed, Kara Gillian. Well done," he said. "You have but to practice now. For as long as you need and desire."

And I did. For nearly another month. When I felt complete, I wrapped my arms around Xhan's sleek neck and gave him a huge hug. "Thank you, honored one. I feel changed. In a good way. More connected to *everything*, not just the rakkuhr."

"You are fresh and new, Kara Gillian. Nurture that feeling."

"It's time for me to go," I said with a hint of wistful sadness, "but I will see you again soon. On the outside."

"May it be so. Go in peace and wholeness."

Chapter 37

I recoalesced and took a deep breath. Dekkak was on the dais, watching me intently but without aggression.

I shifted to face her, remaining seated while I once again readjusted to the real world.

"I'm very glad I had this opportunity," I said. "Thank you for allowing it."

"The truth was revealed after all this time. There is honor in that. What will you do next, Kara Gillian?"

"The Earthgates are key. The demahnk Ekiri originally created the gates in order to balance the potency between the worlds. Jesral—and the demahnk who are influencing him—would also use them to balance potency but in a catastrophic flood."

She nodded her massive head. "Jesral craves mastery over your world. And this world would not remain stable for long, for with your Earth so damaged, the balance would soon fall asunder once again."

"The Mraztur demahnk don't care. They just want to go home to the collective."

Dekkak rumbled her opinion of that, then stretched her wings wide before refolding them. "Regarding our agreement, I am confident you will not shirk in your oath to complete the restoration of the elders. Therefore, Bubbah is no longer my hostage."

"I appreciate that, and thank you for treating him with honor and dignity."

"Bubbah has great honor and courage. He is valued here and is ever welcome."

I smiled, pleased and proud. "He's a very good person. I'm fortunate to count him as an ally."

*   *   *

I arranged to have a message sent to Bryce telling him it was time to go home—not "Do you want to go home?" because no way was I going to allow him any wiggle room—then took my leave of Dekkak and allowed Vlip to escort me back to the plaza.

Bubba was in his workshop and gave me a broad smile as I approached. "I was wondering if I'd be seeing you again before you headed back to Earth."

"Well, speaking of heading back, I have some great news. Dekkak says you're free to go. Hostage no longer!"

"Yeah?" He smiled, but it seemed like an afterthought. "That's awesome. Really great."

I studied him for a few seconds. Oh, he was trying to act non-chalant, but he was too much of an open book to pull it off. "Do you want to stay here?"

He shrugged then shook his head. "Nah, it's okay, Miss Kara. I don't wanna leave y'all in the lurch any longer than necessary. I already hate to think how much work is waiting for me." He laughed, but it had a wistful tone, and I didn't miss how his eyes flicked to some of his unfinished projects.

I hadn't expected this, but maybe I should have. Especially since I wasn't at all surprised by his reaction. Bubba didn't have any family back on Earth, and it was clear he'd forged real connections here and was comfortable with the demon society.

"Would you be upset if I told you there's someone at the compound who's been taking care of various repairs and upkeep?"

His eyes narrowed. "That depends on who it is and if they're doing the kind of competent job y'all need and deserve."

"Well, he's an older guy, but he's been doing all right as far as I can tell. Scott Glassman recommended him. Name's Walter Harrison—"

Bubba's whoop of delight cut me off. "I know Mr. Walt! Oh man, y'all are in really good hands. He's the best. Taught me all sorts of tricks. Hell, we used to work out at the same gym before it got eaten by a rift."

I held back a laugh with effort. Of course he knew Walter. *Everyone* knew Walter. "Then, assuming Dekkak approves, you'll be the first official human ambassador to the Jontari."

He let out another whoop. "Fuckin' A! Hot diggity damn!"

Grinning, I asked Vlip if they could run to Dekkak and see if she was okay with Bubba remaining with the Jontari for the foreseeable future.

Vlip chirruped. "Dekkak say yes for Bubba stay already!"

I gave the faas a puzzled look. "Er, she did?"

Vlip spun in an excited circle. "Dekkak say value and honor in Bubba!"

I mentally replayed my conversation with Dekkak, then smiled. She'd said Bubba would always have a place there. Said he had great honor and courage. *And* didn't qualify it with "for a human."

The imperator had known all along Bubba would want to remain.

"Well, Bubba, looks like you got the gig. I truly can't think of anyone better suited. You've done us all so very proud."

"Thank you so much, Miss Kara," he said, beaming. "I'll be the best damn ambassador you ever done seen." He looked past me, and I turned to see Bryce making his unsmiling way toward us. "You gonna straighten him and Jill out, right?"

I exhaled. "I sure hope so."

Bubba nodded. "Sounds like he had a real hard choice to make. I don't envy him that. Just want you to know I been calling for Miss Ashava, too. Got some of my buddies here to call, as well. I never knew her 'cept as a bump in Miss Jill's belly, but Seretis told me lots, and I seen pictures. But mostly I know she's real special, and I'm happy to do my part."

"Thanks, Bubba," I said fervently. I had a hard time wrapping my head around the idea of a Jontari doing anything to bring one of the lords back, but I suspected if anyone could pull that off, it would be Bubba. "Every little bit helps."

He glanced over to where Vlip had begun hopping from rock to rock. "Vlip is looking antsy, so I guess y'all should be going."

"With any luck, we'll be back to visit under far more pleasant circumstances."

"Vay-cay with the Jontar-ay!" He smiled. "Is it okay if I give you a proper hug goodbye, Miss Kara?"

My mouth twitched. "As long as you're wearing that apron, yes."

He barked out a laugh, then wrapped his meaty arms around me and gave me a hug. Holy shit, what a hug. Full of gratitude and respect and appreciation and the love shared by comrades in arms. It was the kind of hug that made you feel special and treasured, where sins were forgiven and achievements celebrated. I hugged him back, hoping I could convey how truly proud I was to know him, and how I admired his heart and essence, and that he was truly a brilliant shining light in the universe. It only lasted a handful of seconds, but when we pulled apart we both had tears streaming down our faces, which made us both laugh.

"Aren't we a couple of sappy fuckers," Bubba said, wiping his eyes without shame.

I sniffled, managed a watery smile. "I wouldn't have it any other way."

"Damn straight."

I turned away before I could start bawling and walked to Bryce. "You ready?"

Doubt flickered across his face, edged with a trace of fear and worry. He opened his mouth to speak—probably something stupid like how it would be better for Jill if he stayed away—but I speared him with a hard look before he could get the first sound out.

He exhaled and squared his shoulders. Though sadness still lingered in his eyes, acceptance had joined it.

I gave him a nod. "Okay then. Glad you're seeing things my way."

He snorted. "Guess I'm not a complete idiot."

"Not at the moment, at least."

Chapter 38

I clambered out of the rift in my back yard, blinking to adjust my eyes, then moved aside to give Bryce room to emerge. It was a gorgeous day, with a brilliant blue and cloudless sky. A flare of light down by the gate signaled that Walter and crew were still welding away on the sally port, and the mouth-watering scent of roasting meat told me Kinsavi would be serving barbecue later. A single cat graced the center of the nexus. Fuzzykins, who welcomed me by walking up as if to show me some affection . . . and then continuing right on past.

An alarm blared, and it took me a hot second to realize it was because we'd just cruised out of the rift unannounced. Tandon and Watson came pelting toward us, weapons at the ready, but Bryce and I had the presence of mind to stay very still with our hands in plain sight.

Even though they stopped close enough to recognize us, they didn't lower their weapons one teensy bit.

"Welcome back, Commander," Tandon said. "What's the first throw I taught you?"

Couldn't be too careful when shape-changing entities existed. "Osoto Gari. And don't ask me how many tries it took for me to successfully throw you, because I don't think either of us can count that high." For good measure, I threw in, "And then you made me do fifty burpees. FIFTY!"

Tandon smiled and spoke into her radio. "Code four. Gillian and Taggart have returned. Verified. Code four." She holstered her weapon. "Glad to have you back, ma'am."

"Glad to be back," I said. "But I'd forgotten it's still winter here." I rubbed my bare arms and headed toward the house.

Tandon scoffed. "Like hell. I don't think seasons are a thing anymore. It was in the nineties yesterday."

Bryce trailed behind, in quiet conversation with Watson, likely getting updates on security.

Szerain stepped out onto the porch as we approached.

I gave him a mock scowl. "You could have at least brought me a jacket!"

Even as the words left my mouth, the back door opened and Zakaar exited, a coat in each hand. He looked great—bright-eyed and rested—like the old "Surfer Boy" Zack I knew way back when. He descended the stairs, giving me a broad smile and my coat before moving right on past me to pull Bryce into an embrace.

I tugged my coat on while Zakaar murmured quietly to Bryce.

Szerain eyed me. "I take it things went as well as could be expected with Dekkak?"

"I'm still alive, so I'd call that a win." Before I could elaborate, Bryce exhaled a shuddering breath and gave Zakaar a *Thanks, man* nod. I could only assume that had been a man-to-eternal-being exchange about Jill. Good.

Bryce pulled on his jacket. "Kara, I'm going to check in with the rest of the security team, unless you need me for anything."

"Do what you gotta do."

He strode off toward the security office, but he didn't look *quite* as dejected.

I grinned at Zakaar. "Good to see you, surfer dude! How long have you been back?"

"Since midnight," he said. "I'm still adjusting to this new embodiment, but I wanted to be here when you returned."

"Much appreciated," I said. "How's Jill?"

He exhaled. "She's been working in the basement library in an effort to focus on something other than Ashava and what happened. Szerain has been trying to help her cope as much as possible, but she's barely holding it together."

"Has she said anything about Bryce?"

"Not a word," Szerain said. "Helori's block is still in place, so I can't read her, but it isn't hard to figure out she's wrestling with her feelings about the incident and about Bryce."

"Everyone here has been calling for Ashava," Zakaar said quietly.

"So's Bubba," I said. "The Jontari, too."

"Boudreaux . . ." Szerain's mouth twitched in amusement. "He has this little song he sings to himself when he thinks no one can hear him."

I gave him a baffled look. "A song?"

Szerain looked around to make sure no one was nearby, cleared his throat, then sang very softly, *"Ashava come home now, you need to pet the cow. Ashava you're so sweet, you make the birdies tweet. Ashava soon you'll see, this is the place to be. Ashava we love you, it's time to come on through."*

It took me a second to speak. "Holy shit. That's fucking adorable." But Boudreaux always did seem to have a unique insight into Ashava's personality and everything she'd been going through. Somehow it made perfect sense that he'd come up with a sweet little song to call to her.

"He's a man with surprising depth."

"Is Tessa doing okay?"

Szerain nodded. "She's come a long way in the past few days. Staying busy—assisting in the library, and helping Kinsavi at the dining hall. And she and Idris have been spending time together working on the never-ending task of repairing and reinforcing warding. They're talking. Getting to know each other. Idris even"—he paused for dramatic effect—"laughed!"

I gasped. "No!"

"Yes! It's like they're bonding or something."

I put the back of my hand to my forehead in mock-despair. "Oh my god, we really are in the end times."

Idris strode from the house. "I can hear you pricks talking about me," he called out, then ran and caught me up in a hug.

I laughed and hugged him back. "Okay, show me. You know you want to."

Needing no clarification, he sketched a sigil that hung in the air, just like in the demon realm. Now that Idris had the complete shikvihr, he could make floaters on Earth, in addition to having increased power, focus, and control.

"Oooh, purty! Next Christmas, you can decorate the tree with sigils!"

"Finally, all that training will be put to good use!"

Though I could trace floaters on Earth due to my connection with the nexus, I was still limited if that connection got dampened, like it had during the encounter with Jesral in the dimensional pocket. And even with the nexus boost, it still wasn't the same as having the intrinsic ability. I needed to complete my shikvihr. But with everything else going on, who knew when I'd be able to finish my training and get it done.

"I'm going to talk to Jill real quick, then I'll fill y'all in on what I learned from Dekkak and where everything stands." Or at least the parts I was willing and able to share.

"Honey, I'm home!" I called out as I descended the basement steps.

Jill looked up from where she'd been hunched over some old book. "You're back?" She stood up. "Of course you're back. Did everything go okay?"

"Yeah, it did. Dealt with Dekkak, and Bubba's doing really great. In fact he'll be staying in the demon realm for a while—by his own choice," I quickly added. "He likes it there, and the demons seem to genuinely appreciate his skill and spirit."

"That's wonderful," she said. "He's a really good guy." She struggled for a smile, but her face crumpled. "I'm sorry. I-I'm not doing all that great."

I pulled her into a hug. "Jill, it's okay to not be okay. You've experienced an enormous trauma, and it's only been a few days. No one would be 'okay' so soon."

She nodded, a small jerky movement. "I've been calling her, but I don't know if I'm doing it right."

I took her by the shoulders. "You love her. She's your daughter. You're worried for her, and you want her back home with you. I have zero doubt you're putting all that into your call. It's instinctive for you. You're a loving mother."

Bitterness flashed over her face. "Her mother, who had no idea how . . . how dangerous she could be."

"None of us did, Jill. Not fully."

"Apparently Zakaar and Rho did! Why else lock her down?"

"Ashava is a one-of-a-kind because she was never suppressed by the demahnk like the other lords. She's unfettered. Szerain and Zakaar could only speculate about her ultimate potential, but they accurately predicted that the road to maturity would be rocky." I softened my tone. "Look, I know how hideously traumatic that was for you, but—"

"She would have destroyed us all," she finished in a low, dull voice.

"Quite possibly. Y'know, there's a good reason we don't let

kids fly fighter jets when they're five. Because that's a lot of dangerous power for someone who simply doesn't have the basic self-control or knowledge and experience to handle it."

She dropped heavily onto the couch and buried her face in her hands. "Kara, I was so terrified. Then when Bryce shot her, for a hideous, terrible instant, I felt a surge of relief. And now I have so much guilt for ever feeling that relief."

"Oh, sweetie." I sat and pulled her to me. "Jill, we humans can be very primal creatures when survival is on the line. But what never changed is that you love your daughter." I rubbed her back and let her cry, held her close while she sobbed on my shoulder. I suspected this was the first time she'd really unloaded since the conclave.

Eventually she quieted but made no move to pull away.

"I was so awful to Bryce," she whispered.

"He understands. I promise."

"I can't imagine how hard that was for him." She sat up and looked into my face. "I really love him, you know. I tried to stay just friends, because of Zack, but—"

"Jill, everyone knows you're crazy about Bryce. And he's been nuts about you for a very long time."

"I wouldn't even look at him. After."

"Oh my fucking god, you should have seen that man mooning over you while we were in the demon realm. Now, go wash your face, change your shirt, and go talk to him."

"My shirt?" She glanced down at what she was wearing. "What's wrong with this one?"

"For starters, it's not the dark bronze demon silk shirt you were wearing the second day of the conclave. I can say with absolute confidence that Bryce really liked how it looked on you."

She blushed, which I'd never seen her do. Then she rolled her eyes, gave me a hug, and hurried up the stairs. A few seconds later, I heard the back door slam.

I headed up after her, pausing when I saw my crayon letter had been posted on the refrigerator. A sticky note was affixed to one corner. *We're so proud of our little Kara for learning her letters!*

"You fucking pricks," I murmured with a chuckle. My gaze drifted over the various other notes and sketches by Szerain that also adorned the fridge, then I detoured to my office and gazed up at Giovanni's painting.

I drank in the glorious depiction. Mzatal, his entire posture oozing with fierce power and confidence, but also with joy and *freedom*. Even though we stood facing away from each other, no one could ever deny that we were together, two unique individuals in perfect harmony.

"I'm coming for you, boss," I murmured, then went out to the porch and made myself comfortable on the swing. Szerain soon joined me, and together we rocked in companionable silence. Zack came and sat in a wicker chair, then Idris sauntered up and settled on the porch rail.

A few minutes later, Bryce stepped out of the security office, frowning down at the clipboard in his hands. He started toward the front gate but stuttered to a stop as Jill emerged from her trailer. To my delight, she was indeed wearing the bronze demon silk blouse that clung to her in all the right ways.

Bryce stood motionless, expression growing uncertain as she walked toward him. I could damn near see the thoughts flitting through his head. *She's so fucking beautiful. But is she coming here to kick me in the balls? No, she's super flexible. She'll kick me right in the head . . .*

I gave a happy sigh as she reached him and pulled his head down for a kiss. He dropped the clipboard, wrapped his arms around her and returned it. Enthusiastically.

"Well, they're making up for lost time," Szerain murmured.

I snickered and was about to ask him to throw an arcane privacy shield over them when they finally broke apart, smiling.

Bryce murmured something to Jill that made her grin. Then she took his hand and practically hauled him to her trailer.

The door slammed behind them. Quiet reigned for about three seconds before everyone in the yard broke into a whooping, hollering cheer.

The trailer door opened a few inches. Bryce stuck his hand out and shot everyone the finger, then slammed the door again.

Chapter 39

Szerain smiled. "Nicely done."

"It didn't take much with those two," I said. "They'll help each other through this." I blew out a breath heavy with relief. "Let's head inside, and I'll catch y'all up."

I didn't feel like using the conference room, so instead continued to the living room and plopped into the comfy armchair before anyone else could snag it. I waited for the others to get settled, then began. "First off, Bubba is now the Earth ambassador to the Jontari," I said, and explained his easy adaptation to life there and how much the demons appreciated him and vice versa.

"I can't think of anyone more suited," Szerain said with a grin.

"Right? He's absolutely perfect! Anyway, I had an enlightening conversation with Dekkak. The most pressing problem for all of us is, of course, Jesral. Dekkak agrees that he wants a working Earthgate so he can dominate Earth without destabilizing the Demon Realm. Ideally more than one gate, if he can swing it."

Zakaar exhaled. "With the help of the demahnk—and enough brute force—it's very likely he could succeed."

"He's okay with brute force, because for phase one of his Jesral-is-a-vile-piece-of-shit plan, he only needs a gate to work well enough to allow him to flood Earth with potency—which aligns with the bad demahnk's last-ditch desperation play. Once there's a more manageable human population, he'll move on to phase two, which is where he becomes Earth's Smarmy Prick Lord Emperor."

"More manageable, because a potency influx of that magnitude would be unspeakably catastrophic," Szerain put in, voice tight.

"Yup. But he doesn't want everyone to die. Just half the world's population or so. After that, he'll have time to raise and activate several more Earthgates properly, allowing him to commute back and forth in style and ease without having to rely on demahnk help—which is vital because they want to rejoin the Ekiri, hence the whole 'dump potency on Earth plan.'"

Idris snorted. "Like realizing the parents are coming home and tossing all the liquor bottles into the neighbor's yard so you don't get in trouble."

"You're not wrong," I said. "The problem we face right now is that once Jesral raises an Earthgate, especially with Ilana and Ssahr and possibly others helping, it'll take minutes at most for him to set himself as the owner, and then it'll be next to impossible for us to do a damn thing to stop him."

Zakaar nodded slowly. "Like setting a system password when you start a new computer. That first person then has control."

Idris said, "Kadir must have secured his gate as soon as it emerged."

"Exactly right. And since the gates are usually humans-only, Kadir and Paul hacked his so he could actually use it. When Jesral realized what Kadir did, he made a Between Machine so that he, too, could backdoor hack a gate—not only to allow him to use it, but also so he can vent potency through it."

"This is a very cheerful conversation," Idris muttered.

"Ain't it though?" I grinned. "But, as Bubba would say, 'we ain't been beat yet.' Because Jesral can't do shit until and unless he raises an Earthgate. Therefore, we need to be the first to raise all ten remaining gates and immediately set ourselves as the owners—basically cockblocking him. Which leads me to my next point: Szerain, you tried to raise your Earthgate in the ritual with Elinor."

He gave me a sour look. "I seem to remember something about that."

"Okay, but with a *working* ritual, and with the proper skills and understanding, an experienced summoner could raise and lock a gate, yes?"

Szerain looked troubled. "Skill or not, experience or not, the ritual carries significant risk, as we learned when Elinor attempted it. Which is why no other attempt has been made to raise an Earthgate since the cataclysm. Though I assume Jesral feels it's worth that risk. One of the main reasons the Mraztur wanted to make you into Rowan was because you'd then be powerful enough to pull it off."

I leaned forward. "Fun fact: it's not all about power. That ritual with Elinor would have worked if not for the interference that destabilized it."

He scowled. "Fuck Xharbek to the darkest reaches of existence."

"Oh, I agree with you there." I paused for dramatic effect. "Except it was *Vsuhl* who interfered."

Szerain stared at me, gobsmacked. "What?"

It took every ounce of control I had to keep my expression annoyingly placid. "Yeah, turns out it wasn't Xharbek at all." I shrugged nice and casual-like. "Of course, in hindsight it never made sense that Xharbek would sabotage the ritual, since having a working Earthgate would've absolutely been in line with his goals and those of the demahnk. Plus, Xharbek knew how disastrous it would be to disrupt such a ritual. Cataclysmic, even. Throwing everything out of balance. And the demahnk looooove their balance." I leaned back, put my feet up on the coffee table and crossed my ankles. "But the aspect of Vsuhl that's trapped within the blade is rage and pain and a living thirst for vengeance. What better way to express it than to rebel at such a critical moment." I snorted. "And speaking of critical moments, the same thing almost happened when I recovered Vsuhl after you hid it away. We all thought it was a bad combo of the arcane, rakkuhr, and grove power—too much for me to control, and putting us on the brink of yet another cataclysm—"

"But it was Vsuhl's interference, yet again." Szerain looked at Zakaar. "Did you know this?"

Zakaar sat very still. "I could never quite accept Xharbek as the instrument of such destruction and chaos," he said quietly. "Not at that time, anyway. Yet I couldn't fathom an alternative source of interference given who was present that day. And Vsuhl was, indeed, present, but the blades are closed to me. To the demahnk."

Szerain gave his head a sharp shake as if trying to settle the pieces into place. "How can you be sure it was Vsuhl?"

"I had a chat with the Xhan aspect in the gimkrah."

"Holy shit." He straightened. "What else did the blade tell you?"

"Not the blade," I corrected. "The gimkrah. And I can't share that with you just yet. Except, I did learn one pretty cool thing."

I pulled rakkuhr to me and formed it into a complex sigil.

A broad smile split his face. "You've mastered the use of rakkuhr."

"Xhan is a very good teacher."

Zakaar shifted in obvious discomfort, and I quickly dispelled the rakkuhr. He exhaled softly, relaxing.

Szerain sobered. "Does Elinor know she wasn't responsible for the cataclysm?"

"Not yet, but I intend to tell her."

"The ritual would have worked," he murmured.

Idris leaped up, too energized to remain sitting. "We can do it. We can raise the Earthgates. Kara and I certainly have the arcane skill to pull it off."

"But doing *ten* of that ritual," Szerain said, "and even splitting the effort between you two . . . That's not something that can be accomplished in a day. Not even sure it could be done in a month."

I winced. "I know. But I can't think of any other way to stop Jesral. Which means we have no time to lose."

Idris cocked his head. "Is there a way to lock a gate on the Earth end before it's even raised? Seems like that would take a lot less effort than doing the whole ritual shit to raise one. Kind of like how putting a brick over a snake hole is easier than fighting a snake that's already out."

I sucked in a breath. "Holy shit, that's brilliant!" I looked to Szerain and Zakaar. "It's doable, right? Surely there's a way to keep it from being raised in the first place? Please say yes. Please."

"I'm . . . not sure," Szerain said, brows drawn together. "This brick has to completely block the gate's conduit between here and the demon realm, such that a ritual performed there wouldn't be able to connect to the Earth end."

Both he and Zakaar fell silent for several agonizing heartbeats, and I had zero doubt they were discussing it via their own ptarl bond. But my blooming hope crashed as Zakaar finally exhaled and shook his head. "It may indeed be possible, but no ritual or arcane construct exists that could accomplish what we need. And we don't have the luxury of time to develop one."

"And even if we could create a workable construct," Szerain

said, "you'd still have to know where all the Earthside locations are."

"Wait, what?"

His mouth curved into a pained grimace. "You forget—the lords couldn't use the gates. Only humans were able to pass through them."

"Hang on. If you didn't know where your gate was on Earth, how the heck did you do that ritual with Elinor?"

"Because, when performed in the demon realm, a considerable portion of the ritual involves finding the correct conduit that leads to the corresponding Earthside location. Like driving to a friend's house. It's one thing to get to their town, but you need to know the exact address if you want to reach the right destination."

"But if we did the rituals from the Earthside locations," I said, "that would make the whole thing a lot easier, right? We already know the gates come out in each lord's demesne on the demon realm side."

"It would reduce the amount of work considerably, yes."

"Zakaar, you know the Earth locations, right?"

"No."

I stared at him, gut sinking. "Are you shitting me? You don't remember where you parked your gates?"

"No, I know where they *were*."

"You just said . . . Ohhhhh. So, they won't be in the same place as before?" Shiiiiit.

He spread his hands. "We created the Earthgates nearly three thousand years ago. Not only has the physical world changed quite dramatically over the past twenty-five-hundred years, the drastic potency shifts, coupled with the cataclysmic events in the demon realm, have scrambled the inter-world pathways."

I sighed. "And I assume you can't sense where they might be lurking now."

"The only Earthgate I sense is Kadir's."

"And that was only after it emerged."

He nodded.

Frustration clawed at my gut. "Can you tell me where they used to be? That would at least be a start."

"I know the general locations: Egypt, North Korea, Great Britain, Somalia, the west coast of Mexico, Chile, the Lower Mississippi Valley, Ohio, in the northern part of Japan, a few hundred miles south of Moscow, and Papua New Guinea."

I perked up. "Was Kadir's gate the one in the lower Mississippi Valley?"

"No," he said, dashing my hopes for some sort of consistency. "That was Amkir's, and it was nearly two hundred miles north of here. Kadir's was in Chile."

Idris straightened. "Shit! That's what the nuke was for! Jesral was trying to pin down the Earthside gate locations. Detonating it at Kadir's gate would have sent reverberations through all the gates."

"You're right," I breathed. "That would have saved him a great deal of time and effort, because he wouldn't have to do the part of the ritual that located the right conduit. And, placing the nuke would have appeared to be the humans' idea to attack, leaving Jesral looking like an innocent observer."

"Jesral counted on Kadir killing the human soldiers outright," Szerain said.

"Instead they were able to tell him about the nuke in time for it to be dealt with," I said. "Also, Jesral didn't factor in the barg-creatures that attacked the soldiers and delayed the activation of the device."

Zakaar shook his head. "It still baffles me that Jesral chose to use such a destructive means to find the gates. Especially since there's no guarantee it would have even worked. It doesn't fit his usual—for lack of a better word—style."

"He's way more sly and conniving," Idris said.

"Honestly, it actually makes a lot of sense," I said. "I mean, Jesral's a complete sociopath with no regard for others, so why would he care how destructive it is if he gets results?" I paused as more details lined up. "And now I get why he kept trying to get his hands on Ashava. Yeah, he has summoners who might be able to raise an Earthgate, but we've already established it's complicated and long and difficult and prone to cataclysmic failure. But according to Xhan, Ashava is an unadulterated Ekiri-human hybrid. Never fettered by the demahnk beyond the mild governor to help her cope with her hybrid-enhanced development. Jesral wanted her because she'd be even better than having a Rowan, and he believes she could raise the Earthgates. Easy peasy. But then the trap on Boudreaux failed, so he couldn't capture her. And everything went downhill from there. His nuke plan flopped, so he has no clue where the gates are. And, instead of running to Jesral, who was oh-so-understanding and nice enough to tell her about the governor, Ashava had a level-ten meltdown. *Then* Bryce shot her. Now everything's a shitload more complicated for him, so he had a great big meltdown of his own."

"Gee," Szerain said with a smile. "Poor Jesral."

I exhaled in relief. "So, for the moment, we're all at the same find-and-raise-the-gates-first stage of things, but with a bit of a head start while Ssahr has Jesral locked down."

"Also," Szerain added, "any gate-raising ritual will be very risky for another day or two at least, while everything is still unstable."

"Ugh. True. But maybe we could get a start on actually finding the locations." I considered for a moment. "Dekkak referred to Rho as a Gatekeeper. Maybe Rho can help us?"

Zakaar's brows drew together in thought. "That's not a bad idea at all."

"Only one way to find out." I pushed out of the armchair and started for the back door but paused as the leaf warmed against my chest. I placed my palm over it, then slid my gaze to Szerain. "You should come with me. And bring your sketchbook."

"Any particular reason?" he asked, forehead creased.

"Because Rho's still working to get shit stabilized, and even when they aren't otherwise occupied, I usually just get impressions and images from them. I figure you could read me and sketch as we go."

"I'll gather my supplies."

"In fact . . ." I looked at Idris and Zakaar. "You should all come with me to commune with Rho. Zakaar, being the Ekiri-in-demahnk clothing that he is, might get even clearer impressions than I do."

Zakaar smiled. "Excellent idea."

"I'm game," Idris said, then lifted his chin toward the window. "But we'll need to dress warm."

I muttered a few choice words at the sudden blizzard outside. "Let's hope Rho has the heat cranked up."

Chapter 40

It was insanely tempting to wait for the freak storm to abate before trekking out to the nexus, but that pesky issue of how the survival of Earth was at stake and there was no time to waste had everyone but Zakaar piling on the cold weather gear. To my relief we found the ground around Rho to be clear of snow and relatively warm, and by unspoken agreement we each sat with our backs to the trunk, like points on a compass.

Immediately, I sensed Rho was deeply involved in stabilizing the overall damage caused by Ashava's gate-crashing fiasco, yet I also felt their welcoming touch and knew they would offer what help they could.

Communing with Rho didn't require words, and I made no attempt to start doing so now. Instead I did my best to give the sense of what I wanted to accomplish.

Find the Earthgates. Secure them. Protect both worlds.

An answering touch of acknowledgment, followed by what communion Rho could manage.

I closed my eyes and let myself sink into their presence.

Two hours later we thanked Rho and stomped through a foot of snow to the house. Once inside, we reconvened in the kitchen, where Szerain spread out an impressive stack of close to two dozen sketches.

I let out a whistle of appreciation. "Damn, your hand must be about to fall off. These look great!" Even though Rho had only been able to give impressions of the locations, the majority of the sketches were more detailed than I'd expected. Mountains. Rivers.

Landscapes. Trees and roads. A handful weren't quite as precise as the rest, but I had no doubt those were from moments when Rho's attention was more focused on critical stabilization.

"Rho's impressions were clear for the most part," Szerain said, "yet I'm not sure how much this will actually help. Do any of these locations look familiar?"

I shook my head. "It's really hard to tell. Idris? You've traveled the world more than I have. Anything clicking?"

He took his time examining the sketches. "This one *might* be in the Pyrenees, but I'll need to pull up some pics online to compare."

"Ooh, maybe our favorite hacker can help with checking things online." I pulled my phone out and took pics of the sketches. "I know there are vast swaths of this planet that have never been photographed—much less had said photographs uploaded to the internet—but if pics are out there, I bet Paul will be able to find them."

Szerain rubbed his chin. "Like a reverse image search?"

"Essentially." I quickly thumbed in a text to Paul: <We're hunting Earthgate locations. We have sketches of where they'd emerge but nothing more specific. Any chance you could do some kind of reverse image search and help us out?>

It was at least half a minute before a reply came in—which for Paul was like an eternity.

<We're still pretty slammed stabilizing the Between, but send me what you have. If there's any way you could narrow the search location for each gate to something more specific than "Planet Earth" that would be sweet>

<Thanks. btw if Elinor has a free minute, can you have her call me?>

<Sure thing. She's working the machine right now, so may be a while>

<That's cool. Ask her to do video call if possible, and can you make sure Giovanni's with her? I promise it's nothing bad>

<will do>

I sent him the pics of the sketches, then dropped into a chair and relayed Paul's message to the others.

Idris frowned, idly making and dispelling floaters, just like he'd done in the demon realm. "Not sure how we can possibly narrow it down. Apart from the obvious stuff like how palm trees mean it's probably not in Switzerland."

Zakaar let his gaze travel over the sketches. "And Paul is astute enough to factor that in without any assistance from us."

One of Idris's floaters drifted toward me, and I spun out a small glyph of rakkuhr to push it back toward him. "I mean, sure, given a decade or so we could travel the world and try to match stuff up."

Idris made a second floater to flick my glyph back toward me. I met his eyes in challenge, then drew rakkuhr into a giant hammer and squashed his floaters.

He laughed and raised his hands in surrender. "I think you cheated, but I'll give you the win."

Zakaar made a pained noise. "Kara . . . if you could please—" He'd backed up to the counter and now lifted his chin toward the giant rakkuhr hammer.

"Oh, shit, sorry!" I hurried to dispel it, then stared at the now-empty space, pulse quickening. "Maybe we don't have to raise the gates at all. The demahnk can't abide rakkuhr. And Jesral has only a smattering of skill with it, from what I've seen." I turned to Szerain as hope flared, hot and bright. "Would that work? Could that block the channel? Like pouring cement down a hole and *then* putting a brick over it?"

Szerain began to smile. "Rakkuhr in the channel and atop it would absolutely prevent the connection from being made from the demon realm."

Idris let out a whoop. "This could work!"

Szerain chuckled. "Jesral certainly doesn't have sufficient rakkuhr ability to counter any channel block and brick that Kara and I fashion."

I pumped my fist. "Which means we don't have to do ten gate-raising rituals!"

Idris blew out a breath of relief. "Holy shit, we might just be able to pull this off."

We all looked down at the sketches, elation dimming at the reminder of the other giant obstacle we faced.

"Just have to find the damn things," I muttered.

Idris shoved up from the table and yanked the freezer door open. "Fuck it. I know there's a foot of snow outside, but it's time for ice cream."

"Ice cream?"

He pulled two large tubs out and shouldered the freezer door closed. "Yep. When I was a kid my mom always said ice cream was great for freezing out worries." He plopped the tubs onto the table, then retrieved bowls, spoons, and ice cream scoops. "Therefore, we should freeze the fuckers. Kara, do you want chocolate or vanilla? I'd offer you Cream Cheese Cherry, but someone"—he cast a mock-glare at Szerain—"already plowed through it."

Szerain laughed and shrugged with a guilty-as-charged expression.

"Chocolate, of course," I said. "But where'd you get ice cream?"

Szerain pulled a bowl and the tub of vanilla toward him. "Kinsavi got his hands on a restaurant-quality ice cream maker, and of course the cows provided the milk."

Idris slid a bowl of chocolate ice cream to me.

I spooned up a bite, then closed my eyes and sighed in bliss. "Your mother is a very wise woman. This is perfect."

Idris grinned and returned the tubs to the freezer, then sat with his own bowl of chocolate ice cream. We ate in silence for several minutes, worries successfully frozen for the moment.

Eventually, I pushed my empty bowl away and let out a very unladylike belch. "That was fantastic. I think the last ice cream I had was Double Trouble Fudgey Rubble at Ruthie's Smoothies."

"A truly wonderful establishment," Zakaar said, scraping his spoon around his bowl to get the last few drops. "Which, alas, has been supplanted by Kadir's Earthgate."

"Yep. That was back when Jill was still pregnant with Ashava. It was me, her, and Steeev. And we saw Marco Knight in the parking lot . . ." *Holy shit. Holyyyyyy shit.*

Idris peered into my face. "Kara? You're making a very high-pitched squealing sound."

"Sorry," I gasped. "But I just realized Makonite might be able to help us narrow down the locations of the gates."

Just as Cory Crawford podded and became Krawkor, and David Hawkins transformed into Kinsavi, New Orleans Police Detective Marco Knight was now Makonite. And even though his only physical transformation was that rakkuhr now flickered in his eyes, his change had been as deeply profound as the others. A powerful clairvoyant, Marco Knight had been haunted and overwhelmed by what he saw and sensed, often shunned by family and associates for unwelcome revelations. Makonite was still clairvoyant, but now he could control and filter his talent.

I stood, consumed with excitement. "Knight was at Ruthie's Smoothies that day we went there for ice cream, because he was drawn to the location. He'd even gone there once before with Pellini to try and pin down why he felt a pull, with no success."

Szerain tapped his finger on the table. "You think he felt the gate and might be able to feel others."

"It's sure worth a try!" I grabbed my phone, scrolled to his number, and put it on speaker.

He answered on the first ring. "Hey, Kara! I was hoping to hear from you. I called a few days ago and was told you were out of town."

"More like out of planet, but I'm back. Look, I'm here with Idris, Szerain, and Zakaar—"

"What happened with the twelfth?" His tone was oddly conversational. As if he was simply curious instead of concerned.

"Er—" Many months ago, before the valve explosion and the demon incursions, Knight had an overwhelming clairvoyant vision. *The twelfth is a radical game changer*, he'd told me. *Spawned of fierce cunning. Beauty and power exemplified. Beware the twelfth.* And the twelfth, of course, turned out to be Ashava.

"Yeah," he said. "That whole business with the twelfth has been a pressure in the back of my mind for so long that it started to feel like a part of me, y'know? Then it just . . . disappeared."

"Well, that might be because Bryce shot her. Ashava, I mean. And she kinda scattered."

"Okay. Makes sense. Did you need something from me?"

I blinked at his calm acceptance. "Er . . . yeah. Do you remember how you were drawn to Ruthie's Smoothies before the valve exploded and Kadir's Earthgate emerged?"

"Sure do. And you want to know if I'm drawn to any other places?"

Damn he was making this easy for me. "Basically, yes."

"The short answer is 'kind of.' Ever since I unpodded, I've been able to dial my talent down or off, which means I don't get those mega-powerful pulls anymore. I only turn it up when I want to or feel the need. But I gotta tell you, ever since the twelfth vanished from my awareness, I've been dialed up more often."

"And? Do you sense anything?"

"I sense plenty of things, but why don't you tell me what you're looking for?"

I gave him a quick rundown of the whole business with the

Earthgates and our dire need to find the Earth locations before Jesral could. "You sensed Kadir's gate before it emerged, and I'm hoping you can do so again with the others."

"I'm pretty sure I feel something like what I felt before. But it's far away and hard to pinpoint where it's coming from. Like there's more than one signal, which I suppose makes sense as there are multiple gates."

I did a little victory dance. "It definitely makes sense!" Of course, I was assuming that whatever he felt was actually a gate and not something else entirely. Still, this was all we had to go on at the moment. And, considering the gates were part of a network, maybe finding another part of a related network could make it easier for him to "see" the rest. "Are you busy right now?"

He let out a laugh. "What you want me to do?"

I grinned. "Put your entire life on hold for me. Duh."

"Please. That's a given."

I couldn't remember any time I'd simply bantered with him. He sounded *happy*, and I sent a silent thank you to the universe for giving him this gift. "Let's figure out the best way to go about this. Zakaar, would it be possible for him to use a node to get a better sense of where these signals are coming from?"

Zakaar nodded. "It's worth a try. The gates and the valve system are sister networks. Not fully connected, but there are enough points of overlap that it might be possible for Makonite to sense these signals or echoes at a node."

Idris tapped the table. "And if he can indeed sense the direction of the signals, we could map those data points via triangulation. That might narrow down the locations enough to where Paul can either match up the gate location with an image search, or get Makonite close enough to find it directly."

"Yeah," Makonite said. "That could work."

"The plantation node is the most powerful one nearby," Idris said. "Let's start there."

I did a fist pump. "Makonite, can you meet us at the Farouche Plantation at some point today?"

"Give me an hour."

"Deal. See you then." I hung up, then grinned at the others. "Holy shit. I think we have an actual Plan. How crazy is that?"

"I didn't think that was allowed," Szerain said with a snort.

I smiled sweetly at Zakaar. "Wanna teleport Idris and me to the Farouche Plantation in an hour?"

"Not a problem. There are a few things I want to check out there anyway."

"We need supplies," Idris said. "If we're going to be triangulating, then we need a GPS, and compasses, notebook and pens, maps—"

"And snacks!" I added.

"As if we could ever forget snacks."

"Sonny will know where all that stuff is hidden," I said, even as I thumbed in a quick text to him.

Szerain's mouth twitched. "And by 'hidden,' you mean 'put away in an organized fashion.'"

"That's the same thing in my world." My phone buzzed with Sonny's reply. "He says he'll pack bags for us. I'm not sure how I ever got anything done before he came along."

"We should bring the sketches," Idris said. "Easier than trying to look at pics on our phones when trying to verify locations."

"Good point."

Zakaar cleared his throat. "Before we go anywhere, you and Szerain need to design this rakkuhr brick that will keep the demahnk and Jesral from raising the gates."

"Should we go out to the nexus?" I asked.

"Best not," Szerain said. "We don't want the nexus potency to throw anything off."

"That makes sense," I said. "Basement should work, right?"

"Yep. Plenty of room as well. This brick seal will need to be large enough to span the entire footprint of the gate, just to be sure."

I did some quick mental calculations. "Oof. About thirty feet in diameter?"

"That should do it." He pushed up and headed for the basement, and Idris and I followed. Zakaar remained upstairs since rakkuhr caused him a great deal of discomfort.

For the next twenty minutes, Szerain and I experimented with a variety of ways to brick a gate with rakkuhr, then had Idris test our efforts. To our frustration, making an arcane seal as large as we needed meant there were more potential weak spots. And, even though Idris had no skill with rakkuhr, he was consistently able to poke holes in it.

"Would it be possible to interweave normal potency with the rakkuhr?" Idris finally asked. "Like making a polymer. That could provide the strength you need to block the channel and cover the large area, and still have more than enough rakkuhr 'influence' to keep the demahnk or Jesral from being able to get through."

Szerain laughed. "I'm an idiot. I've used combinations for a variety of purposes but never considered using it to increase tensile strength, so to speak."

It took another thirty minutes of experimenting and tweaking to perfect a polymer uberbrick that defied Idris's best attempts to defeat it. Even better, Idris and I could work together to create them, which would hopefully save us time and energy.

I dismantled the prototype. "All right. Let's gear up and get going."

"Y'all have fun," Szerain said. "I'll hold down the fort."

Chapter 41

Idris and I dressed in ordinary, comfortable civilian clothing that wouldn't draw attention, but we also armed ourselves with considerable concealed weaponry, since who knew what we might encounter. Sonny had, of course, come through for us and filled two backpacks with the requested supplies and snacks, as well as a few survival necessities such as first aid kit, water purifying tablets, rain gear, flashlights, hand warmers, phone chargers, and chocolate.

Right before we were about to leave, my phone rang with Elinor's number.

Her worried face popped up on the screen when I answered. "Paul said you had something to tell me? And that Gio should be here with me." He leaned in briefly and waved, looking just as concerned.

"Yes, but I promise it's not bad news." I smiled. "I just thought you should know I have it on unshakable authority that you were absolutely one hundred percent NOT responsible for the cataclysm."

"Wh-what? But I . . . are you sure? Was it indeed Xharbek?"

"Nope. It was the aspect of Vsuhl trapped within the blade." I quickly summarized my conversation with the gimkrah aspect of the Jontari elder Xhan.

By the time I finished, Elinor was all-out bawling, and Giovanni had pulled her into his arms, tears of his own streaming.

"Thank you, Kara," he said as he stroked her back. "This has long haunted her."

I nodded, throat tight as I fought the urge to cry right along with them. Unsuccessfully. "Okay, well, I need to get going. Good luck with everything on your end." I quickly cut the connection and sniffled mightily.

Idris handed me a tissue. I took it, relieved to see his eyes were damp as well. "We're all a bunch of damn softies," I said with a laugh.

He smiled. "The world needs softies."

Zakaar teleported us to the front of the Farouche Plantation, then murmured something about taking care of a few things and vanished again, leaving Idris and me to meander toward the node on our own.

The plantation house hadn't changed much since I'd been out here a few months ago. Still half-burned. Crumbling a bit more, with vines and other vegetation encroaching with mindless determination.

The grounds had undergone a bit of revival since the showdown with the Mraztur. The pond had water in it again, and the charred grass had regrown at some point and was now a normal winter-dead brown.

Idris nodded toward the partially destroyed plantation house. "Not gonna lie, it's pretty nice seeing how much this place has deteriorated."

"Yeah." I didn't need to say anything else. Plantations tended to suck overall due to their horrific association with slavery, but Idris had plenty reason of his own to despise this place. He'd been a captive here, along with his adoptive mother and sister—the latter of whom had been murdered in a brutal ritual. "Feels like a century ago that all the shit went down. Hard to believe it's only been, what, six months? Seven?"

He snorted. "Don't ask me. Time has lost all meaning."

Beyond the ruined house stood the remains of a once lovely gazebo—a raised stone platform that now held eleven broken columns, with a pillar of potency in the center. Nearby, Makonite leaned against his car. I grinned, amused and unsurprised that he'd managed to pass right through the wards and aversions that kept everyone else away from the property.

He pushed off the car. "I think your hunch about using the node might be spot on. I already have a stronger signal, so to speak."

"Is it the same kind of feel you had at Ruthie's Smoothies?"

"Dunno. My perception has shifted since I podded. Like seeing color after only knowing black and white."

We approached the node together. Idris and I stopped at the edge of the platform, but Makonite walked right up and thrust his hand into the column of potency, as if testing the temperature of a swimming pool.

Hand still immersed in the node, he closed his eyes and shifted position around the node, then stopped. "There's something in this direction," he said. I lined my compass up with the direction Makonite faced, and Idris jotted down the reading.

Makonite did this twice more around the node, then withdrew his hand and stepped back. "This might take longer than we thought. I can sense more via the node, but that's the problem."

I made a face. "You mean, now you're picking up signals from farther away as well."

"Exactly. Which is good because it means we should be able to find all the gates. But we'll need to check quite a few nodes to get the best triangulation. And, since there are so many signals—and I'm not really able to judge distance—it's going to be impossible to map out the triangulation on your basic printed map."

Idris muttered a curse. "Because the earth is a sphere, and maps are flat."

"Maybe Paul has an app for that," I said and shot off a quick text explaining the nature of the predicament.

His reply came quickly. <just text gps coordinates and compass readings. Dom is throwing together a script that will do the heavy lifting. Nerds are gonna save the world lol>

I shared the text with the others, who all agreed with the last line.

"There's a node at an industrial park not far from here," Idris said as he sent the readings to Paul.

"Too close to effectively triangulate," Makonite said. "What about other parts of the world?"

"There's one in Oregon," Idris said. "Two in Texas, and another in Colorado."

"And there are fifteen outside of the U.S.," I added, "but I don't know where."

Zakaar had yet to return, so I gave up and called him. "I know you can't tell us where the gates will emerge, but what about nodes?"

"What about them?"

I rolled my eyes. "Their locations. Makonite needs to check nodes that are some distance from each other. He says the warehouse node is too close to this one. That leaves twenty-two other options. You know where they all are, right?"

"Yes, that's not a problem."

"Excellent, how soon—shit!" I startled as Zakaar appeared in front of me.

Makonite grinned—an expression I couldn't remember ever seeing on him.

"Sorry," Zakaar said, clearly not sorry one bit. "I was cleaning up some arcane remnants in the main house that I couldn't take care of before. For best triangulation, we probably want to start with nodes about a quarter or third of the way around the world, then work from there."

"Which are where?"

"There's one in Nepal, another near Ust Ilimsk, Russia—"

"Hey, I've been there!" I said. "Not Nepal but the Russia one. Ust Ilimsk is about two hundred miles south of where the 1908 Tunguska Event happened. Of course there'd be a node there."

"All right, then—"

"WAIT," I yelped. "Ust Ilimsk is in Siberia, and it's the dead of winter, and we are one hundred percent not dressed for that." To be honest, I didn't think it was possible to ever be dressed for Siberia in the middle of winter. "I can hardly be expected to save the world if I freeze to death. And Nepal probably isn't much better."

Idris shrugged. "I have to agree with her about the freezing to death thing."

Zakaar laughed. "Okay, how about Samoa?"

"Ooooh, Southern Hemisphere." I grinned. "Now you're talking!"

A heartbeat later, Zakaar, Makonite, Idris, and I stood on a white sand beach with a view so gorgeous I could only stare in awe for several heartbeats. Morning sun blazed above an azure blue ocean. Dark boulders of volcanic rock extended out in natural jetties, and graceful palms draped over the beach.

I'd been all over the world in the past six months, but never anywhere this beautiful. And it wasn't even the view. There were loads of places on Earth and in the demon realm that were just as gorgeous, if not more so. But somehow this place felt as if it had been created to leech the cares and stress from your very essence.

No question about it: when all this was over, I would absolutely come back to this place, and splash in the ocean, and bake on the sand, and worry about nothing.

I pulled my focus back to the matter at hand. "Where's the node?"

"A short distance up this trail," Zakaar said and led the way into the South Pacific jungle. It had clearly once been a well-tended path, but several months of being left to its own devices during the Demon Wars had taken a toll. Vegetation encroached heavily in several spots, and we were forced to clamber over a few fallen trees, but we managed to push through and eventually came to a gorgeous little pool bounded by more of the same volcanic rock as on the beach. A waterfall tumbled into the side opposite us from at least thirty feet above.

Even Idris heaved a sigh of bliss at the idyllic scene.

"Let me guess," I said. "The node is behind the waterfall."

Zakaar smiled. "I promise it's not quite as cliché as that." He led us around the edge of the pool, then into the woods again, finally arriving at an unassuming cairn about three feet high.

Unassuming, except for the potency that rippled around and through the stones. "That's a node all right," I said.

Makonite placed both hands on the topmost stone. After a moment he shifted around it, just as he had with the plantation node. As he commented on what he sensed, I took readings, Idris took notes, and we forwarded the data to Paul.

<nothing definitive yet>

Zakaar pondered a moment. "We'll do Australia next. South of Birdsville."

In the next breath, the four of us stood in the middle of nowhere. At least it seemed that way. Flat as far as the eye could see. Red-brown dirt. Scattered, scraggly, sun-dried vegetation. And about thirty feet away, in the midst of that middle-of-nowhere, an ordinary patch of earth shimmered with potency.

This time, Makonite simply stood right on top of it, closed his eyes and pivoted, stopping three times to relay what he sensed. Idris read off the GPS coordinates and compass readings, and I texted them directly to Paul.

<getting closer>

Zakaar nodded as if expecting that response. "Madagascar."

The instant shift from bright morning sun to pitch dark night meant it took my eyes several seconds to adjust enough to see we were in a tidy little village of lush vegetable gardens and corrugated tin houses. A slightly larger structure appeared to be some sort of administrative building. All the windows were dark, with no people in sight. A dog emerged from behind a house and let out a sharp bark, but Zakaar glanced in its direction, and the dog quieted and lay down.

A weathered, wooden post in front of the admin building glowed with the arcane. Makonite began the now-familiar process of slowly rotating his way around the node while we texted the readings to Paul. Halfway through, he stopped and pulled his hand back.

"Something wrong?" I whispered.

"Just confusing. I'll see what Zsu thinks."

"What? Who's Zsu?"

Makonite didn't seem to hear me, but Zakaar murmured, "The ilius he merged with during podding."

I took a moment to let that sink in. "I assumed they'd assimilated to make a single entity."

"You're not wrong. Symbiosis, each with their own consciousness, but shared experience and unified mind as well." At my dubious look, he added, "All consensual. Not like being submerged or even like when I was merged within Szerain."

Makonite moved another quarter way around the pole. "Strong sense this way."

Idris texted the readings, then we waited, silent and breathless. Even the dog seemed to be waiting with us.

<new zealand north island> A set of GPS coordinates followed. <not exact location but should be close>

I clamped down on the urge to let out a whoop of victory and settled for giving the dog an excited thumbs up.

Night vanished, and mid-morning light bathed us as we took in the view from the small plateau.

We stood atop a mountain surrounded by even more mountains. Flowering plants and lush vegetation of all colors covered the slopes, and to the north a glittering lake sprawled in a valley. I took a deep breath of crisp air untainted by smoke or destruction, then let it out in a happy sigh.

Makonite strode off to our left about fifty feet down a slight incline, then stopped and spread his arms wide. "It's here."

This time I gave in to the victory whoop and laughed as it echoed around us.

"Let's get started!" Idris crowed, equally elated. With Zakaar's

help we defined the perimeter, then carefully created and an-
chored an uberbrick based on our prototype. The whole process
took us nearly forty-five minutes, but we decided that wasn't too
awful considering the terrain and it being our first time attempt-
ing the process in the field.

Zakaar had remained a fair distance away while I worked
with the rakkuhr and now moved in to test the uberbrick.

"It's good," he announced after several failed attempts to
approach or affect it from afar.

"Whose Earthgate is this?" I asked. "Or rather, whose realm
does this one connect to?"

"Elofir's."

I looked around again, soaking in the beauty. Maybe someday he'd be able to come see it. "One down. Nine to go."

Idris glanced at his watch and grimaced. "Hope the next
ones go faster. We left the compound over three hours ago."

"It'll go faster as we get more data points," Makonite said.

I kept my expression upbeat. "Where to next?"

Zakaar took us to nodes in Brazil and Peru, which yielded coordinates for gates in Uruguay and Kenya—connecting to the
realms of Vahl and Rayst. The nodes themselves didn't take
long to get to, but the Uruguay gate required clambering over
rocky hillsides in the dusk to reach, and then doing more clambering to set the uberbrick.

Kenya's gate had more forgiving terrain, except for being
situated in the middle of a road near Mombasa. It was well past
midnight there, but we were still forced to set powerful aversion
wards to keep at bay the locals roused by our activity.

Nodes in Egypt and Morocco gave Paul enough data to point
us to a gate in Portugal—Vrizaar's—though Zakaar said it was
damaged and almost certainly unusable. Still, we uberbricked
it, just to be sure.

A node in Guatemala revealed Szerain's gate in Jordan. It
also earned me a broken ankle when I lost my footing on a patch
of loose rocks. Thankfully, Zakaar made quick work of healing
it, and Idris and I soon had the Jordan uberbrick in place.

Idris sat heavily on a boulder. "Kara, how long had you been
awake before you returned through the rift?"

"Uh . . . I dunno. Eight hours? Maybe a bit more?"

Idris glowered at me. "You've been awake and on the move

for close to twenty-four hours now. You're dead on your feet, and we can't afford any mistakes in the arcane aspects *or* a more serious injury that might not be so easily healed."

"You *all* need rest," Zakaar said. "With my help, one hour of sleep can be like five. I'll watch over you."

"Done deal," Idris said before I could reply.

"I was going to say yes," I grumbled. "But first, Zakaar, do you know when we need to start worrying about Jesral again?"

His face drew taut. "Soon. I'm monitoring as much as I can, but even with my overwhelming awesomeness, I can't watch everything at once."

"I get that, and trust me I appreciate the hell out of everything you're doing." I rubbed my temples. "Maybe Paul can . . ." I shook my head. "No, he's already running the location searches for the gates *and* stabilizing the interdi—" I broke off as my phone started ringing. "You know it's him," I muttered. "I swear he does this just to fuck with me." I heaved a sigh and hit the answer button.

His grinning face popped up on the screen.

"Paul, do you spy on me constantly?"

He was laughing so hard it took him several seconds to speak. "No, I promise I don't," he finally managed. "But I have a script running that alerts me if you say 'maybe Paul can.' And your expression was priceless."

"I swear, if I didn't love you so much . . ." I left the unspoken threat hanging. An empty threat, to be sure. Like I'd ever fuck with him, Kadir's essence-bond mate or not.

"Yeah yeah yeah. How can I help you?"

"Can you let us know as soon as Jesral is seen anywhere on Earth?"

"You got it." He was all business now. "What about Ssahr, Ilana, Trask, or Mzatal?"

I sighed at the final name on the list, but Paul was right to include him. "Yeah, them as well. Thanks."

"No problem. I'll start a facial recognition bot and—"

"Please . . . *please* don't try and explain it to me. You'll just be wasting your breath."

"You sure? It's pretty cool."

"I don't doubt that for a second. How about you explain the whole thing to me in detail the next time I'm having trouble sleeping."

That cracked him up again. "Once upon a time there were three solid state drives who lived on a server farm . . ."

I dropped my head back and made loud snoring noises. He was still laughing when I ended the call.

"*Now* I'll nap," I said.

I had no memory of falling asleep, but I woke to Zakaar's hand on my shoulder, feeling rested. Idris was already on his feet, and Makonite munched on a protein bar.

Our phones dinged.

<J and Ss and Tr are in Unshoji, Japan>

A muscle worked in Idris's jaw. "That was one of Katashi's strongholds."

I replied with a <thanks>. "Let's get moving."

The Italy node was next, and while Makonite received a few strange looks as he made a slow circle around the Column of Marcus Aurelius, most people seemed to write it off as typical weird tourist behavior.

We'd barely texted the readings when Paul replied: < J et al are gone now. No sign of anyone at that location anymore>

"He wasn't on Earth even half an hour," Idris said with a frown.

Zakaar exhaled. "He most likely scooped up his summoners and other allies and will attempt a gate-raising ritual from the demon realm. The one consolation is that it will take them several hours just to prepare, and far more for the ritual itself."

"This is Jesral's last chance to get a gate," I said. "He's going to pull out all the stops, but we can still beat him."

"Five more gates," Idris said, rolling his neck.

"Five more gates," I agreed. "We can do this."

Several curious sheep at a node in Yorkshire, England made taking readings a bit more challenging, but that led us to a gate in Paris, right in front of Napoleon's tomb. That gate, Jesral's, was also damaged and unusable, which felt like sweet, delicious karma. Still, we uberbricked it, just to be sure, then indulged in a fast breakfast of excellent pastries and espresso before resuming our mission.

We traveled to nodes in Thailand and Oregon, and Paul pointed us to a gate in Sanjay Ghandi National Park in India.

Rhyzkahl's. Nodes in Norway and Colorado gave us the heading for Seretis's gate in Toronto.

We even donned mega-cold weather gear and checked the nodes in Nepal and Ust Ilimsk—though we needn't have bothered for Siberia, which was balmy with strange lavender clouds. Those nodes led us to Amkir's gate in Busan, South Korea. Unfortunately, that one took us over an hour to uberbrick due to a crowd of curious onlookers. Paul reassured us that he had a multitude of bots and scripts that did nothing but scrub our images off the internet, but it was deeply unsettling all the same.

Yet visits to the node in Sapporo and the two in Texas provided no new headings. Nor did the other nodes in the Beaulac area. Moreover, Paul told us there was too much margin of error to get location verification for a good half dozen of the sketches.

"We found and uberbricked nine gates," I said and downed half a cup of espresso in one gulp. By unanimous agreement, we'd returned to Paris for more pastries and caffeine. "Kadir's makes ten and is already secure. The only one missing is Mzatal's. Where the flipping fuck is the last gate?"

Idris pulled the folder of sketches from his backpack. "Here are the ones Paul couldn't positively match up with the other gates." He spread them out and weighed them down with various cups and dishes. A street corner and buildings. A road bordered by trees. A rocky hillside. A meandering river. And several other equally generic views that might or might not have applied to gates already found and bricked.

Makonite shook his head, forehead creased. "I can't figure it out. We've been to every node. Even the damaged gates had an echo."

I stared glumly at the sketches while I pulled apart my *pain au chocolat*. The places in the sketches could be anywhere. I'd once battled Jontari near a road in a remote forest in Luxembourg. A few months ago, I'd chased geckoids alongside a river in Budapest. Hell, for all we knew, the last gate could be in the wooded park across the street from where we were sitting.

"We should return to the compound and regroup," Zakaar said. "Perhaps there's something we've overlooked."

I scrubbed at my face. "You're right. It feels like giving up, but I know we haven't. We're regrouping, like you said."

I finished off my espresso, then looked over at Idris, who was staring glumly into his cup.

"You done with that?"

He extended his cup toward me, then pulled it back at the last instant and gulped the contents down.

"That's just mean," I said, while the others laughed. "I'm gonna remember that."

Chapter 42

The return to my back yard was briefly disorienting as the sun was only slightly farther west than when we'd left, making it feel as if we'd been gone only an hour or so instead of a full day.

It had snowed again, though only a few inches this time. Prikahn growled encouragement as Hrrk and Sammy romped in the drifts, while Bumper and Cake remained flaked out on the nexus, watching the silly dogs with appropriate feline disdain. Prikahn wore a strange leather harness on his chest, but I hadn't the faintest idea what purpose it served. Probably another weird Jontari thing.

The compound's makeshift snow plow slowly made its way up the asphalt drive, piling snow to one side. Amusement cut through my frustration over the failure to find the last Earthgate, as I saw the original plywood-tin contraption attached to the horse farm's tractor had been upgraded to a more durable and plow-shaped piece of metal. Walt's doing, I had zero doubt.

Beyond, a welding torch flashed where the man in question continued to fortify the sally port. It seemed fully repaired and functional to me, but I wasn't going to argue with making it even more robust.

Idris rolled his head on his shoulders. "Dunno about anyone else, but I need a shower and a change of clothes."

"Same," I said. "Makonite, you're welcome to hang out here. I'm sure we can scrounge up clothing in your size."

"I'm good," he said, gaze drifting to the nexus. "Thanks."

"Well, come on in when you're ready to warm up and get a real meal."

"Want a lift to the barracks?" Zakaar asked Idris. At his

grateful nod, Zakaar put a hand on his shoulder, and the two disappeared.

Makonite began a meandering stroll toward the rift and nexus. I watched him for a few seconds then went on inside.

Tessa and Jill were at the kitchen table with paperwork in orderly piles before them. Compound inventory, purchase needs, account balances, and fun stuff like that—all of which I was more than happy to avoid like the plague. But seeing the two of them working on it reminded me that Tessa had owned a successful natural food store for quite some time, which meant she definitely had the business and administrative chops to give Jill valuable help.

"You look beat," Jill told me with a frown.

"More frustrated than anything," I said. "Zakaar gave us some super-sleep, so I'm not physically tired. But we can't find the last Earthgate—and it's Mzatal's, which makes it extra painful. We traveled all over this silly planet, busted our ass and secured all the others, but that last one is being a shy little bitch. It really has Makonite baffled." I pulled out the sketches that maybe possibly showed where the missing gate might be, then gave Jill and Tessa a brief rundown of our adventures thus far.

Tessa's forehead creased as she looked over the sketches. "There's nothing definitive here."

"Yeah, no help. And if Jesral and his lackeys are working on the ritual, we're out of time to stop them." I groaned and massaged the back of my neck. "I mean, whatever destruction Jesral manages with one Earthgate is surely less horrific than with ten—or rather eight, since two aren't functional. But it'll still be pretty awful."

"Go clean up," Tessa said. "You've always done your best thinking in the shower."

"Also, you're riper than a week-old banana," Jill added with a grin.

I snorted and headed down the hall to my room. "Yeah, I can smell myself. That's never good."

My bed was made, which made me grin. Tessa's doing, I knew, because when I was younger, she'd always folded down one corner of the comforter by my pillows, as if to make it just a bit easier to get into bed. It was a tiny little gesture, but one that now made my heart melt.

I was so focused on the comforter that I almost missed the

maroon bundle in the center of the bed and the small piece of folded paper atop it.

Wear this to be even more fierce and amazing than you already are—if such is even possible.

At the bottom was an "H" in elegant script.

Helori. Grinning, I unfolded the bundle to find a set of zrila-made combat fatigues like the ones Idris had worn for the shikvihr, though these were deep maroon with dark copper stitching. Also included were badass boots, sturdy yet soft. The fatigues were not only lovely but exceedingly functional, as closer inspection revealed demon-crafted ballistic padding in all the important areas.

With my mood buoyed by both Tessa's gesture with the comforter and Helori's gift, I cleansed myself of dirt, sweat, and associated stink. Though I didn't gain any brilliant flashes of inspiration regarding the final Earthgate, I did have lovely, kick-ass fatigues and boots to put on that fit like a second skin. Once dressed, I preened in front of my mirror—and of course practiced a few fierce poses.

When I came back out to the kitchen, Szerain and Zakaar had joined Tessa and Jill, and everyone did the *ooh* and *ahh* over my lovely new fatigues. Idris returned, wearing his own blue ones, and gave a wry grin when he saw me. "Guess we'll be looking damn good for the end of the world!"

I laughed. "That's the spirit!"

Tessa let out a mock sigh. "Too bad I no longer have my rainbow-sequined jumpsuit. Now *that's* an outfit for the end of the world."

I snickered. "I just want to state for those gathered that the outfit in question absolutely did exist at one point. And I have to agree about it being a solid end-of-the-world outfit."

"I think I'll stick with the fatigues," Idris said.

"Same! But speaking of outfits, can anyone tell me what the deal is with the harness Prikahn is wearing?"

Jill snorted a laugh. "He carries Hrrk around in it. It's the cutest thing I've ever seen in my life."

I stared at her for several heartbeats while I tried to process that information. "You mean like one of those Baby Björn things? Where the hell did he get one in his *size*?"

"Redd is a Master Saddler. Designed and made it over the course of a couple of days. I don't know what Prikahn gave her in return, but she seemed *very* pleased with her end of the deal."

"Wow. That's amazing on so many different levels." I shifted my attention to Zakaar. "Question: Is it possible we couldn't find the last gate because Jesral's people have already started the ritual?"

"If anything it would be easier to sense through the nodes. A brighter echo."

"Just because we can't find that echo doesn't mean they're *not* trying to raise the damn thing," Idris pointed out.

Szerain scrubbed a hand over his face. "Unfortunately, I have no doubt they are already in the process of raising it."

I poured myself a coffee and loaded it up with even more sugar and cream than usual, wanting the kick and the comfort. Once upon a time, Ryan Kristoff—the overlay construct from when Szerain was submerged—had called it "drinking a candy bar."

Yeah, well, this had more caffeine.

Makonite was still in the back yard, now peering into the rift. He abruptly swept his gaze around the compound, pausing briefly on the house. To my surprise he stepped up onto the nexus—unhindered by wards or aversions—moved to the center and looked down, as if gazing into its heart. A moment later he thrust a hand through his hair in a clear sign of frustration, then jumped off the slab and jogged toward the woods and the pond path.

I tensed as the comms blared the alert tone. *Main Gate to compound. Multiple vehicles approaching. Weapons visible.*

I raced for the front door, fighting down the unpleasant déjà vu of Tessa's arrival, though this time I managed to beat Szerain to the driver's seat of the ATV. He grumbled but climbed up behind me to ride pillion. I was even nice and waited an extra split-second to be sure he had a secure grasp around my waist before taking off down the freshly plowed asphalt drive.

We were nearly to the gate when the comms beeped again. "Stand down," Krawkor said with a laugh. "Code four. Stand down. Kara, you're not going to believe this!"

I stopped the ATV at the gate and leaped off, then gaped at the sight before me. Two large pickup trucks were parked on the highway in front of the sally port, loaded with what looked like all of Alpha Squad. They had on their military issue body armor and helmets over civilian clothing, and were armed to the teeth with shotguns, pistols, rifles, and even crossbows. And every damn one of them was grinning like a maniac. It was as if the Good Ol' Boy Army had descended upon us, and it was glorious.

Scott Glassman waved from the driver's seat of the lead truck while Roma and Hurley hopped out of the back. "Didja miss us?"

"Hell, yes!" I managed when I finally found my voice. "But I thought the squad had been recalled?"

"We were," Roma said. "They told us we were needed elsewhere, then had us sitting on our asses in the barracks." Her eyes narrowed. "I tugged a few strings and found out the recall had Jesral's stench all over it, so . . . we left."

"You *deserted*?" Holy shit.

"No! Deserters are cowards who leave in the heat of battle. We're *insubordinate* and went AWOL because we want to be IN the heat of battle. Big difference." She grinned. "Besides, you need us."

My brain felt half a step behind. "Won't you get court-martialed either way?"

"Not if we save the world!" Hurley put in with a laugh.

Roma gave a fierce nod. "And if we don't save the world, it's not going to matter, right?"

I had to admit, she had a point.

"Our issued weapons were locked in the armory," she said, "but we grabbed our body armor. And Scott practically has a damn armory of his own at his house, plus we have our personal firearms." She grinned. "Sorry we couldn't sneak any of the armored vehicles out."

I laughed and gestured to the rest of Alpha Squad. "You brought the important parts!"

Zakaar and Szerain quickly screened them all to be sure it wasn't a ploy, then we got the squad and trucks inside the protections and proceeded to have hugs all around. Krawkor even came out of the tower to join in the excitement.

"Fuck Jesral!" Scott crowed. The rest of Alpha Squad immediately shouted, "FUCK JESRAL!" right back.

I gave Roma and the others a super-condensed rundown of the conclave hijinks and the Ashava situation, along with where we stood regarding Jesral's plans and the Earthgate search, which of course led to yet another "Fuck Jesral!" rallying cry.

Makonite walked up the driveway toward us, his face a mask of worry. He barely seemed to notice anyone and kept his gaze on the sally port.

"Hey," I said. "You okay?"

His brow furrowed. "I . . . I'm not sure. Your nexus. It used to be elsewhere."

"The confluence?" I said. "Yeah, my grandfather built the house over it. Used to be right beneath the basement—which my grandmother used as her summoning chamber." Over time it had drifted and was currently in my back yard, which is why Mzatal created my nexus in that location.

Makonite gestured toward the sally port. "Long time ago. Longer . . . it was there."

My phone dinged with a text from Paul.

<flows just started going crazy where you are>

I relayed the text to the others, then returned my attention to Makonite, who continued to stare at the sally port.

A bad feeling settled in my gut like an ice-cold hunk of lead. No. He was looking *past* the sally port. At the snow-covered highway. And the line of trees beyond it.

A road and trees.

"Oh, fuck," I breathed.

Idris cursed. "The last Earthgate is at your damn front door?"

"I missed it," Makonite breathed, aghast. "Your nexus. It's so bright and so close to Kadir's gate and the other Beaulac nodes, it threw me off. I never saw this last one."

"It's not your fault," I hurried to reassure him, then raised my voice to a shout. "Everyone get back from the perimeter! Krawkor, sound a retreat! All personnel need to be well within the compound protections immediately! Zakaar, can you please deploy the arcane boulders at the other two sally ports?"

Zakaar nodded and vanished.

Krawkor tapped his sound deck and ordered a retreat that relayed to all comms and the compound speakers.

In the sally port, Walter grabbed the cart that held his welding tanks and equipment and began wheeling it toward the inner gate at an agonizing-to-me slow pace. No way would the stubborn man leave that shit behind either. To my relief, Scott sprinted up and grabbed the cart, then hurried Walter into the compound proper.

I gestured to Idris and Szerain. "We need to uberbrick the Earthgate conduit, stat!"

Szerain grabbed my arm before I could charge out to the highway. "It's too dangerous to block it now. The ritual has already begun."

"He's right," Idris said. "If we try and block it while they have an active ritual, the resulting pressure buildup could cause massive disasters on both worlds. Like shoving a banana in a car's tailpipe."

I cursed, frustrated. "But instead of stalling the car, it blows it up. Then help me get the 'boulder' deployed here."

Fortunately, the arcane barricade was designed to be quickly activated, and in seconds the added protections shimmered into place on and around the sally port.

"It's here," Makonite breathed, expression stricken as he clenched and unclenched his hands.

"All the more reason to get to a safe distance," I told him, ready to drag him away from the perimeter by force. I had a lot of faith in the warding and protections, but I had no idea how they'd be affected by an emerging Earthgate.

In the next instant, the other pod people were there with us, though I never saw them arrive. Krawkor twined a tail around Makonite, steadying him like a hug. Zenra took Makonite's head in her hands and touched her forehead to his, while Kinsavi's hair writhed around all four of them to create a strange cocoon. They remained as a unit for only a handful of seconds before separating. It was almost like a team doing the "1-2-3-BREAK!" thing.

Makonite straightened and gave me a calm nod, clearly centered again. The other pod people stood shoulder to shoulder with him, facing the road.

I instinctively followed their combined gaze, just in time to see Jesral and Ssahr appear on the centerline of the highway.

"Well, shit," I breathed.

Roma barked out orders as squad members and compound security scrambled into position and loaded weapons with shield-buster ammo.

Zakaar appeared next to Idris, murmured something and received a nod. An instant later, the two vanished. What the hell were they up to? Though the demahnk weren't allowed to directly interfere, there'd been plenty of hard bending of that stricture recently, judging by the actions of Ilana and others.

I swept an assessing look over the compound. I definitely didn't need to worry about the competence of the people around me or their willingness to give their all. Every single one understood how much was at stake.

The four Jontari warlords watched from a distance. I knew I

couldn't compel them to help defend the compound. Weyix's honor debt to Jill had been paid by simply being "on call" while we were in the demon realm. Prikahn might fight to protect Hrrk, or if he deemed the threat to the compound would also impact the Jontari. He had Hrrk in the chest carrier now, with the shimmer of powerful wards around it.

Meanwhile, Jesral's triumphant gaze traveled leisurely over the compound. Ssahr stood back from him, motionless. The rakkuhr would hopefully keep Ssahr from stripping our warding, but there were still plenty of ways a godlike being could seriously fuck us over.

I checked my weapons and comms, scrambling to come up with some way to tip the balance in our favor, all the while praying Idris and Zakaar would be back soon. Now that Idris had the full shikvihr, his ability to use floating sigils on Earth would be invaluable.

Sigils. I grabbed Szerain's arm. "You need to consummate your sigil."

He frowned. "Now is hardly the time to—"

"When the fuck *is* the time?" I snapped. "We need every advantage we can get, and the Earthgate is emerging here no matter what. Who knows if it will make any difference, but Nerd Lord Kadir had a burning need to consummate and correct his sigil. At this point, I don't think we can go too wrong by following his lead."

He breathed a curse but laid his hand between my shoulder blades.

Comfortable heat, heavy and clinging, covered my back like warm honey. Dark depths enveloped me but not void-empty. Ordered. Innumerable disparate thoughts, ideas, concepts interspersed with innovation, awe, and inspiration.

The world returned to normal. Or as normal as it could be in this situation. People still loaded weapons and took up defensive positions. Jesral continued to survey the compound and the protections, apparently oblivious to the business with Szerain's sigil. As far as I could tell, barely any time had passed, though I felt as if I'd downloaded a few years' worth of sensations and concepts.

"Thanks, dude," I said and pulled out my phone.

"Anytime," he said with a dry snort.

"Most excellent," Jesral said with a smirk. "Here you all are, gathered before me and awaiting your demise."

"Yeah yeah yeah," I said. "Heard that one before." I didn't

mind his gloating. His pathetic ego demanded it, and it gave us more time to prepare and hopefully find a way through this crap. I shot off a text to Paul. <can we stop the gate from emerging??>

"Is it not an utterly delicious surprise, Kara Gillian, that the final gate is not only on your doorstep but is of Mzatal?"

My phone buzzed, and I made a point of checking the text before acknowledging I'd even heard him.

<no but he and the machine operators have to do the back-door hack to make it his and usable>

I put my phone away and looked toward Jesral as if just realizing he'd spoken. "Hmm? Oh, the Earthgate. Yeah, it'll be extra delicious when it zaps you into next year. I mean, if I were you, I'd be terrified of anything with Mzatal's mark on it."

"I have no reason to fear anything of Mzatal." He gave a sharp laugh. "Oh, how the mighty have fallen."

Szerain smiled. "You're lucky you'll never experience such a fall, Jesral . . . since you'd have to actually *be* mighty in the first place."

"Szerain. Kiraknikahl and failure at, well, everything. How uniquely appropriate you are here to witness a true master orchestrate a *successful* gate-raising ritual."

I rolled my eyes. That was the best jab he could come up with for Szerain? What a loser.

Zakaar reappeared with Idris, both laden with the kind of military grade weapons and ammo Alpha Squad had been forced to leave behind when they went AWOL. The two deposited everything by Roma then disappeared again. I grinned a mighty grin. Apparently teleporting into a military armory didn't count as "direct interference"—or Zakaar Reborn was not as tightly restricted.

Alpha Squad wasted no time arming themselves. Scott grabbed a grenade launcher and slung a bandolier of grenades over his shoulder.

An unsettling buzz started in my bones, one I remembered too well from when Kadir's gate emerged. I braced myself for the wave of nausea that had hit me then, but to my relief, I only felt a wee bit of queasiness. Others weren't as fortunate. Several members of compound security and Alpha Squad looked green around the gills, and I distinctly heard someone retching.

"Bryce," I called out, "is Michael somewhere safe?"

"He's with Turek on the nexus," he said with a grimace. "Flat out refused to go elsewhere."

I winced. In the basement with Jill and Tessa would've been preferable for my peace of mind, but as long as Turek was with him, the nexus was likely just as good.

Potency leaped to Jesral's command, and he began shaping a complex arcane construct, expression damn near giddy. I had zero doubt this was the hack that would give him full control of the gate—whether for travel or for venting potency onto Earth.

I forced myself to cling to hope. We weren't beaten yet. Not by a long shot. Though Jesral and Tsuneo had found a way to replace Dominic with two operators plus Angus as a power booster, if either Jesral flubbed the construct or the remote operators screwed up, the hack wouldn't work, and we'd simply have an impressive road hazard on our hands.

Zakaar and Idris popped in yet again, this time with cases and cases of ammo, along with more ballistic armor. I noted that Idris now wore a blue, open-faced balaclava that matched his fatigues. As soon as he and Zakaar set the ammo down, Idris sprinted to Walter—who was carefully making adjustments to his welding torch—thrust a vest and helmet at him, then ran over to me.

"Why are you giving him armor?" I groaned. "He should be in the basement!"

Idris smiled. "He doesn't want to be in the basement. Said if he's going to die he wants to do it while living. So I gave him body armor. Also, Helori says hi." He handed me a maroon balaclava, then took off to distribute gear to anyone else who needed it.

I sighed, reminding myself that Walter had held his own in the first compound battle, then I shucked my helmet and tugged on the balaclava. The material was supple and comfortable—a bit thinner than normal cold weather gear, but I had no doubt it contained demon-crafted ballistic material that would protect my noggin.

Walter tugged on the helmet and body armor even as Ronda tore up in a UTV laden with giant plastic tubs full of glitter grenade balloons, PVC pipes, and who the hell knew what else. The two immediately began assembling a bizarre contraption that quickly took shape as a giant slingshot. Okay, yeah, Walter was definitely pulling his weight. And, it was possible I'd been acting just a *wee* bit ageist. If I somehow managed to live to his age and had useful skills and experience to offer, I wouldn't want to be stuck in a basement either.

Jesral's cocky grin threatened to split his face in two as he continued to work the arcane. Not even caring if it was a point-less gesture, I pulled my Glock and fired right at his head. Our arcane protections were crafted to allow defenders to fire out while blocking incoming attacks, but Jesral had his own per-sonal shielding. As expected, the round disintegrated in a crim-son pop of sparks a foot away from him. But his grin shifted to a sneer, which told me I'd managed to distract him, even if by only a miniscule amount.

Pleased, I fired again, then again, enjoying the pretty arcane sparks and Jesral's deepening scowl. "Alpha Squad," I called out. "There's your target."

Scott let out a redneck whoop of feral delight and fired off a grenade that exploded a couple of yards from Jesral—plenty close enough to take him out if not for the shielding. Jesral's ex-pression grew tight with concentration as he worked the increas-ingly elaborate construct. A second grenade exploded closer to him, and rounds from high-powered rifles impacted his warding. The shieldbuster rounds weren't robust enough to get through a lord's protections, but just as grains of sand could eventually wear away steel, the attacks eroded Jesral's shields. To my grim de-light, he soon had to devote more focus to reinforcing his protec-tions than creating the construct.

Szerain added relentless javelin-like arcane strikes to the weapon barrage, forcing Jesral to alternate between bursts of weaving the construct and defense. All we needed was for the distractions to precipitate one measly error. Back in high school, I'd taken a programming class where I had to write code to flash "HELLO" on the computer screen. It took me seventeen tries to debug the damn thing, so surely something as complex as hack-ing an *interdimensional portal* would be harder, right?

The air and earth abruptly gave an unsettling shiver. I hol-lered out a cease fire.

"It's here," Szerain murmured.

Chapter 43

The emergence was soundless, which made the entire phenomenon all the more eerie. On either side of Jesral, two crystalline structures grew from nothing to fifteen feet tall, six feet wide, and ten feet apart in the span of a few seconds. Hope surged at the sight of Mzatal's sigil emblazoned clear as day on each giant crystal.

Face twisted into a mask of fiendish concentration, Jesral wove potency into his construct. Strand by strand by—

It flashed bright white and disintegrated into a shower of silvery sparks. My hope crumbled to ash as Mzatal's sigils shimmered and faded, replaced by Jesral's. So much for wishing failure on the replacement hackers.

Jesral stroked a hand down one of the shards. "All other Earthgates shall be mine as well, Kara Gillian. Your precious rakkuhr locks indeed delayed my acquisition, but they cannot deny me." He gave a satisfied exhalation, like a man who'd just finished a perfect steak. "Weep, Kara Gillian, in your defeat."

"Are you shitting me?" I rolled my eyes, even as my gut churned. "Dude, you need to stop watching late-night corny melodramas. 'Weep, in your defeat,'" I mimicked with over-the-top theatrics.

The gate activated, and Vahl stepped through, looking proud and triumphant—a state I knew damn well wasn't deserved or earned.

A wave of furious exasperation crashed through me. "Fucking shit, Vahl," I yelled. "A jellyfish has more goddamn spine than you!"

Jesral barked out a laugh. Vahl's hands tightened into fists as he leveled a fierce gaze upon me. Or as fierce as he could make it, which couldn't hold a candle to Mzatal-fierce. I did an exaggerated jerking-off motion, then made a show of ignoring him, which I knew would piss him off even more.

He stepped to the shard on Jesral's left and refused to look in my direction. Dumbass. Predictable dumbass.

The next person through the gate carried a far more genuine aura of menace and power, even though he wasn't a lord. Angus McDunn, stone-faced and with a MAC-10 slung in ready position across his torso. He took up a position by the other shard, clearly there to play the part of Enforcer. More of Jesral's fucking show—especially considering Angus would have been on Earth only moments before, helping with the Between Machine gate hack. Jesral must have had a demahnk whisk Angus to the demon realm, just so he could stalk through Mzatal's gate—to fucking *return* to Earth—and look all menacing.

I kept an eye on all of them while Szerain and I tapped the nexus and siphoned power into the perimeter protections. "How long do we have before he floods us with potency?" I murmured under my breath to Szerain.

"I'm not sure why he hasn't yet," he replied, brow furrowed.

Jesral swept his gaze over the compound and personnel. "It is, indeed, delightfully fitting for this to become my primary Earth demesne. These trees, gone. Buildings, razed. And I shall pay special heed to the hovel you call home. Every trace must be eradicated so as not to sully the foundation of my new palace."

"The nexus," I hissed. "He dreams of being Lord Emperor of Earth, and he needs the resources of the nexus to pull it off."

Szerain's mouth thinned. "It's a unique and powerful artifact, one he could never hope to create on his own. He won't risk damaging it with a potency flood."

"Never thought I'd be grateful for Jesral's greed and hunger for dominance, but here we are."

A UTV came tearing up with Jill in the driver's seat, and Sonny and Tessa hanging on for dear life. It screeched to a stop not far from me, and all three leaped out. Jill and Sonny were wearing their DIRT-issued fatigues and body armor. Tessa had on jeans and a thick Carhartt jacket with my old body armor strapped over it.

"Tell us what you want us to do," Jill said, a little breathlessly.

"I'm going to assume that if I ask you to stay in the basement, or jump into the rift and take shelter with Dekkak, you'll all tell me to fuck off."

"With great force."

"Fair enough. Jill, you're the best marksman on the whole damn compound, so get with Roma and shoot things."

She gave me a mock salute, then loped to the pile of weapons and grabbed a rifle, loaded it with the expertise born of a zillion hours of practice, then took up the position Roma indicated.

Sonny grinned. "Want me to shoot things, too?"

"Yes, but also use your mojo wherever and however you think would help. Keep our side calm and focused. It's going to get pretty intense."

"On it." He jogged off toward Roma.

I turned to Tessa. "No way I can convince you to stay someplace safe?"

Tessa met my eyes with a steady gaze. "I need to be in this fight."

"I understand." Boy did I ever. I picked up my discarded DIRT helmet and settled it on her head. "Walter's just as stubborn as you, so since neither of you will leave, you're both on slingshot duty."

She grinned, buckled the helmet strap, then headed to where Walter was readying balloons—and what looked like glass Christmas ornaments?

The crystal shards hummed, and a half dozen reyza and four kehza bounded out from between them, forcing Vahl to take an awkward side-step to keep from being bowled over. They leaped into the air as soon as they were clear, roaring in challenge as they tried to tear through our fencing and surrounding protections—hampered not only by the increased warding and Walter's uber-reinforced sally port, but also by a barrage of gunfire.

Unfortunately, it was soon clear they'd learned from past encounters and had beefed up their personal arcane shielding. While our shieldbusters still had more effect than unenhanced rounds, they weren't causing as much damage as we were used to.

A reyza circled above the watchtower, lobbing arcane strikes at the structure. Even with mega-protections covering it, the watchtower shivered with each heavy strike.

Two kehza swooped and dove, firing blast after blast into the ground near the fence, no doubt seeking a way to tunnel under.

Little chance they'd succeed since the warding extended a good distance down, yet it was clear these demons had either been present for, or learned about, the previous attack on the compound and had an actual strategy.

"Focus fire!" Roma shouted. "Reyza on the watchtower!" Krawkor relayed the order over the pertinent comms.

The reyza shrieked as half a dozen soldiers combined their efforts on the single target. Within seconds, the barrage shredded the shielding, and the demon tumbled to the ground and into the ditch, already discorporeating.

A brief cheer went up while Roma continued calling orders to focus on a particular demon at a time.

Makonite lifted his rifle calmly, tracking a slow arc across empty sky before he pulled his trigger—the exact instant a kehza made a sharp turn and crossed paths with the bullet. The kehza screamed as the round miraculously pierced a thin spot in its shielding and severed a tendon in its wing. It flapped awkwardly to the road, where Alpha Squad took it out like the sitting duck it was.

Makonite smiled, eyes glowing with rakkuhr, then raised his rifle and waited for his next target.

Krawkor's fingers danced over his sound deck as he relayed orders and intel. A second reyza bellowed and discorporeated as bullets ripped through his shielding.

Szerain and I continued to draw from the nexus to support the protections and monitor the rest of the perimeter. Two reyza flew toward the horse farm gate, testing and attacking places along the perimeter, seeking a weak spot.

Another kehza joined the tunnel-diggers, increasing the pace and depth of the excavation. Worry curled through me. Could they possibly succeed with such a basic tactic? I turned to Szerain to ask him, then nearly lost my balance as the ground heaved, and a long section of earth beside the road lurched upward. In mere seconds it coalesced into a golem twenty feet high that snatched a kehza out of the air, crushing it between its dirt hands like a mosquito.

I let out a whoop of delight. "Hot damn! Go, Michael!"

The golem dropped the crushed and discorporeating demon and reached for another, but the two remaining kehza darted away to regroup. With a deep rumble, the golem stepped into the excavation then unformed, neatly filling the hole.

The ground rumbled again, but this time it was a thunder of

hooves as the Riders of the Apocalypse came tearing down the drive. Behind them, Lenny drove a UTV with Griz, the demon-killing dog, in the back.

"Boo's on his way," Redd told me. "Had a problem with his mule and said he'd catch up as soon as possible."

"Gotcha. Coordinate with Roma for what to do and where to do it. Relay orders and intel through Krawkor. At the moment we're holding these pricks off, but be ready for anything."

"Always!"

She wheeled her mount toward Roma and Krawkor. I returned my attention to the protections and Jesral.

He was smiling, clearly not bothered by the failure of his demons. Dammit, I hated when he smiled. It was never a good sign.

The crystals hummed again, and more demons poured through.

But these new arrivals were Jontari—large and scarred and adorned with gold. Reyza and kehza and zhurn—nearly two dozen all told.

Last through the gate was a savik, not quite as large as Turek, but wearing more gold than any of the others.

The compound Jontari had stayed uninvolved up until this point, but now they roared challenge, rattling wings and snarling at these newcomers. Except for Prikahn, who leaped into the air and flew toward the house, claws curled around Hrrk in a protective cage. Shit. I'd been counting on the puppy to make him *more* likely to fight, not less.

"Sky Reapers," Szerain said, eyes narrowed. "Not aligned with Dekkak, and known to fight for other clans if suitably compensated."

"Mercenaries then," I said. "But don't all Jontari fucking hate the qaztahl? What the hell did Jesral offer to make them willing to fight on his side?"

He shook his head. "I can't fathom anything that would be worth placing themselves under his direction."

"Yet here they are." I cursed under my breath. The Sky Reapers had to be the allies Jesral mentioned earlier, the ones he said would take care of the rakkuhr-infused uberbricks on the other Earthgates. I could only hope none were working on them at this moment. The only possible spider-thin thread of comfort was that we'd crafted the uberbricks such that it would take even a skilled arcane user a good half hour to undo. Plus, it would take at least another day for Jesral's summoners to prep and do the ritual to raise another gate.

But that simply meant Jesral could win by maintaining this siege, keeping us occupied until he had a second Earthgate under his control—one he had no qualms about using as a potency vent.

The Sky Reapers roared and dove at the compound perimeter, swerving away from the protections at the last second as they peppered the barriers with arcane strikes. The compound defenders responded with force, but these new demons were nimble and quick, making it difficult to focus fire on a single target.

Walter and Tessa slingshotted glitter bombs over the fence, liberally painting the entire area, and successfully bedazzling several zhurn. Tessa shot off one of the Christmas ornament things, yet not before Walter fired up his welding torch and lit what looked like some sort of fuse on it. The globe impacted near a sparkled zhurn, and the viscous contents burst into flame, spattering the demon heavily. The zhurn shrieked and spun out warding to smother the burning gel, but not before it took a fair amount of damage.

Napalm holiday bombs. Hot fucking damn.

The Sky Reapers continued to lob strikes and test the defenses, yet so far they seemed no more likely to break through than Jesral's lord-aligned demons.

All right. A siege it was. The protections were solid and entwined with rakkuhr, which meant that even a demahnk would be unable to strip them and leave us defenseless. We could hold the attackers off, and surely we could come up with a brilliant counter to Jesral's fucked up plots before he gained control of a second gate.

The gold-adorned savik scuttled forward and crouched at the edge of the ditch, directly across from where Szerain and I worked the arcane. It bared its teeth at me, then made a swift outward motion with all four hands.

A too-familiar glowing sun coalesced before the savik, and I stared in pure dread and horror as a ten-foot-tall rift formed. A mere handful of rift-makers in existence, and now there was one right at our fucking door.

I snapped out of my shock as the other end of the rift blazed open fifteen feet above the inner gate of the sally port—well within the compound's protection.

Not a siege.

"Everyone fall back!" I yelled, echoed and amplified by Krawkor, even as Sky Reapers began to dive through the rift on the road and emerge from the one in mid-air.

Jesral laughed as we scrambled to adapt. I prayed that if I had to die in this fucking fight, I'd first get to drive my fist into his face.

Personnel shifted position as Roma barked new orders. The situation was chock full of what-the-fuck with plenty of oh-fuck-oh-fuck on top, but top-notch training and experience reigned, enhanced by Sonny's stay-cool influence.

With the rift open, the lord-aligned demons took to the air, looking puny compared to the Sky Reapers.

Weyix and Dagor screamed challenge and flew to engage the Sky Reapers. Sloosh scuttled through shadows and delivered piercing strikes.

"Thank the gods for clan rivalries," Szerain said as he spun out shields and lobbed attacks. Despite the situation, I barked out a laugh. The compound Jontari would fight these invaders because they hated them more than they hated us.

Prikahn returned, sans Hrrk, and I realized he must have left the pup on the safety of the nexus. He let out a mighty bellow and snapped a good fifteen feet off a massive pine and flung it at a pair of kehza, crushing them. Dagor cast spears of black-red potency, taking out an enemy reyza, while Sloosh and Weyix nimbly evaded attacks and delivered damage.

Makonite and Jill stood back-to-back like a two-headed sniper, while Sonny continued to keep the defenders calm and focused.

Music abruptly blared through the compound speakers, and I burst out laughing as I recognized the ear-wormy majesty of Rednex's "Cotton Eye Joe." But the corny music seemed to affect the Sky Reapers focus, making it worth having that tune stuck in my head for the next week.

It also seemed to annoy Vahl, judging by his deep grimace. Or maybe he simply regretted the life choices that led him to this point.

Either was fine with me.

A zhurn swooped toward Kowal and Ahmed, then shrieked as Kinsavi shot out thick ropes of blue-black hair to foul its wings. It landed heavily, and Zenra darted forward to rake her claws along its back, jumping clear even as Kinsavi released the demon. It leaped into the air, oddly unsteady now, making it an easy mark for Kowal and Ahmed to dispatch.

The music shifted to Chumbawumba's "Tubthumping." Yeah, we might get knocked down, but we'd sure as shit get back up again.

With the help of the compound Jontari, we were holding the attackers off—but only barely. And Jesral knew it. He watched the conflict with amusement. He didn't care if his side took a beating. He was wearing us down and could replenish his own forces from the demon realm. At this point it was simply about how long we could hold out against him.

And what was our end game? Maybe I could have everyone escape through Dekkak's rift? An absolute last resort, to be sure, but at least it would save lives. And surely Mzatal wouldn't allow Jesral to use the nexus.

But Mzatal was so controlled, I couldn't be sure of anything. Plus, we'd be abandoning Earth and leaving billions of people to die. Plus, if I ordered anyone here to retreat through the rift, I'd get a hearty "Fuck You" in response.

Another reyza landed atop the sally port and ripped off one of the newly repaired sections, wringing a cry of dismay from Walter.

The reyza's attention snapped to him, and its lips curled back from vicious teeth as it spied the easy target.

I shouted to Roma, even as I watched the disaster unfold. Eyes wide, Walter held his welding torch before him, as if the measly three-inch flame could do a damn thing against the battle-scarred Jontari. Bullets pinged off the reyza's shielding as he roared and swooped toward Walter, and I could only watch in horror as—

The welding torch became a hellacious flamethrower, and a thirty-foot firehose of chartreuse potency shot forth to bathe the demon in unholy fire. The reyza barely had time to scream before it crashed to the ground and discorporeated.

Walter cut the flame and stared down at the welding torch, then let out a laugh. "Hot damn! I'd forgotten I could do that!"

Oh. My. God. Walter was one of Kadir's kids?!

Roma stared at him in astonishment, then resumed snapping orders.

I pulled myself out of my shock and continued flinging strikes and reinforcing protections. Walter laughed like a kid with a new toy and lobbed chartreuse fireballs.

Another half dozen Sky Reapers bounded out of the gate, and I fought down the growing sense of despair. We'd taken out a good number of the lord-aligned demons and several Sky Reapers, but that hardly mattered when Jesral could keep throwing more and more at us.

I glanced behind me at the sound of pounding hooves and saw Boudreaux tearing up on a mule.

At the sight of Angus he slid off, face a mask of horror and betrayal. "Dad?"

Angus started forward, expression stricken.

Jesral snapped his gaze to Angus. "Return through the gate," he snarled. "*Now.*"

Angus hesitated, eyes never leaving his son.

Fury at the lack of instant obedience suffused Jesral's face. "Obey me," he screamed, "or I will drop your son where he stands then slake my rage on your wife."

Angus gave Boudreaux one last tormented look, then strode between the shards and vanished.

I turned to Boudreaux, expecting to see grief or anger. But instead his expression was smooth stone, his full focus on Jesral. A familiar sensation whispered over me.

Holy shit, was he doing what I thought he was doing?

"Krawkor," I said into my comms, "I need you to put what I'm about to say over the compound speakers so Jesral can hear me, and then do the same for whatever he says in reply."

"Ten-four."

Boudreaux hadn't been the greatest cop, but he'd always excelled at interrogations. I'd learned the reason for this last year, when he questioned me about the whereabouts of his mother. Boudreaux had a talent that made people want to speak the truth and all of it, to basically spill their guts. And he had every ounce of it focused on the demonic lord at our gate.

I faced Lord Weasel Dick and quickly thought out what best to ask. "Hey, Jesral," I called out—in demon, so the attackers could understand. "How'd you get the Sky Reapers to fight for you?"

Jesral curled his lip and—to my relief—instinctively replied in the same language. "They are simple, savage creatures and easily inveigled. I told them I would gift them Mzatal's realm."

Oof. Yeah, I could see them being willing to fight with that as a goal. "That's pretty impressive. And generous!" In my periphery I saw Sonny step up and lay a hand on Boudreaux's shoulder, helping him remain focused.

Jesral let out a bark of laughter. "You are more of a fool than I believed if you think I would truly offer up such a treasure. Mzatal's realm is *mine*! Such would be wasted on these brutish creatures." He waved a hand dismissively. "It was all embarrassingly simple, as they'd clearly never dealt with superior intellects before. And what need have they for such a palace? Besides, I have plans for what is now *my* demesne."

I listened with half an ear while I watched the Sky Reapers react to his ego-driven stream of consciousness. Beside me, Boudreaux was pale and sweating with the intensity of his focus.

The bulk of the Sky Reapers ceased their attacks and shifted to pure defense. A few continued fighting, but I suspected they simply reveled in the thrill of the battle. Even the non-Jontari demons seemed far less invested in putting their all into the conflict.

Vahl frowned as he followed the shift in hostilities. He stepped up to get Jesral's attention, but earned a sharp *Don't bother me!* hand wave for his trouble. Jaw clenched, Vahl retreated to his former position, eyes tracking the Sky Reapers.

". . . and I'll tear out everything precious to him, especially that ridiculous solarium," Jesral continued to blather, talking to hear his own voice, even as the last of the Sky Reapers retreated through the mid-air rift.

"You can stop now," I murmured to Boudreaux. "You saved us all."

He blinked, then blinked again before looking at me, expression glazed.

"You saved us all," I repeated.

He managed a wobbly half-smile. "Egotistical prick."

"Who, Jesral? Me? You?"

He snorted. "All of the above!"

Sonny let out a breath of deep relief and led Boudreaux away to sit and recover.

Jesral looked around, brow furrowing as he finally took note of the shift in hostilities. His body tightened in anger as he rounded on the Sky Reapers. "No! NO! Resume the attack immediately!"

The rift-making savik dropped to all sixes, let out a stream of goopy black excrement that splattered over Jesral, then scuttled between the shards and disappeared. Other Sky Reapers followed.

"You cowards!" Jesral screamed as he wiped futilely at the nasty, sticky mess. "Return at once! Oathbreakers! Deplorable vermin!"

A grizzled reyza mock-lunged at him, causing Weasel Dick-face to take a stumbling step back in reaction. The demon let out a roar of amusement, and bounded through the gate.

Shaking with rage and humiliation, Jesral whirled on Ssahr, who'd stood quiet and still this entire time. "DO something!"

Ssahr inclined his head in acknowledgment, a tiny gesture that left me with a knot of dread.

Well-founded, as mere seconds later Mzatal strode through the gate, hair in a tight braid with zero ornamentation or accent. Ilana remained a step behind and to his right—an almost subservient position for her, though I knew she was in place to monitor and control him.

Expression cold and flat, Mzatal stopped halfway between the crystals and sally port. Ssahr shifted to flank him on the side opposite Ilana.

Mzatal swept his utterly emotionless regard over the compound and its inhabitants, pausing barely a millisecond on me before continuing on.

Jesral stepped forward, face set with new determination and anticipation of our demise. He swept an arm out to encompass the compound protections. "Mzatal, tear down these wards."

Fuck. The demahnk were constrained from that sort of interference, but Jesral ordering a demahnk-controlled Mzatal to do so was apparently an acceptable loophole. And Mzatal was the only lord who could possibly accomplish it.

Hell, who was I kidding. Of course he could do it. It would be like clawing at wet toilet paper, especially considering he had full access to the nexus to draw on.

Mzatal remained motionless for a breathless, agonizing moment, then he lifted his right hand. I tensed, waiting for him to lay us bare and vulnerable.

He flicked a finger, and his braid unraveled, hair suddenly flowing free about him like a glorious extension of his power. Of him.

He met my eyes once again, another millisecond of contact, then turned to face away.

And paused.

Recognition slammed into me. It was *exactly* how he looked in Giovanni's painting.

His pose lasted only an instant. Ilana grabbed his shoulder, Ssahr seized the other, and Trask appeared and put both hands on either side of his head.

"Depart, Mzatal!" Jesral screamed, but the three demahnk and Mzatal were already gone before the words left his mouth.

Pulse hammering, I yanked my phone out and scrolled to the image of the painting. The sigils. They were important. But they weren't real sigils. Were they? No sigils I'd ever seen before. Mzatal had given me a clue, but I didn't know what to do with it. Yet he'd also given me a gift, because now Jesral had no demahnk with him.

Shaking with rage, Jesral rounded on Vahl, shouted at him to stop being useless and to work on the fucking wards.

Expression flat and tight, Vahl moved to the sally port and began unwinding the protections—with as much success as if trying to pull apart a wool blanket hair by hair. Meanwhile Szerain calmly countered his every move and then wound yet more rakkuhr through the existing sigils.

My pulse quickened. I hadn't understood the sigils because they were incomplete.

"Idris!" I sprinted to him. "I need you to make floaters of these sigils." I held my phone out to show him the image. "I know they're not complete. I need to finish them with rakkuhr." Like the uberbrick, but a different kind of polymer.

Idris didn't pause to question. "Hold it steady."

I obeyed, then yelled to Roma. "Keep everyone off me and Idris!"

"Roger that!" she yelled back and barked out orders.

Walter spun out shields of chartreuse. Jill and Makonite shifted to cover Idris and me.

Eyes on the phone screen, Idris sketched out floaters that shimmered blue in a ring around me. As soon as he finished the last one, I shoved the phone into my pocket, reached deep into my intuition as I'd practiced with Xhan, and started filling in the gaps with rakkuhr. As I completed each sigil, it flared and settled into a fierce, bright gold.

My heart pounded a staccato. Mzatal had sacrificed himself to give me this clue. Had planned countless steps ahead so Gio would create the painting.

I finished the last sigil then, obeying some unknown instinct, ignited the ring, just as I would the shikvihr. The sigils began to spin, faster and faster until they were an unbroken ring of gold and sapphire around me. The ring flared with near-blinding brilliance, then contracted in the blink of an eye and disappeared into me. I gasped as heat flared in my chest, but it faded an instant later.

Idris's eyes widened. "Kara! Are you all right?"

I held up a finger while I got my breath back. "I'm good," I finally managed. Then raised my voice a bit and said, "*Maybe Paul can* get Elinor to help with what I'm about to do." I sure hoped he still had the script running that alerted him any time I said those three words. "Right now I need to get to the gate." I bared my teeth in a feral grin. "I need to get to Jesral. And I need him to think he's won."

"Jesral's never going to believe you're surrendering," Jill said with a frown.

"You're right about that." My gaze went to Prikahn as he—almost lazily—delivered a strike against a non-Jontari demon. "Jesral won't know the difference between Sky Reapers and our resident warlords."

My phone dinged with a text from Paul. <Elinor's on the machine and ready>

I texted a quick <thx> then quickly laid out my—admittedly insane—plan to the others.

Idris grimaced. Jill sighed. "I really hate this plan," she said, "but I get why you have to do it."

Roma didn't look very pleased either, but she didn't argue. "As soon as you're ready, I'll have everyone pretend to surrender."

Jill strode to Prikahn and spoke quietly to him. She had a way with the compound Jontari that none of the rest of us had managed.

Prikahn abruptly let out a roar and batted Jill aside, sending her flying. At least that's what it looked like to anyone who didn't know Jill and her gymnastics skills.

He bounded to me, seized me by my upper arms and flew toward Jesral while I struggled—though not hard enough to risk him dropping me. Below, Alpha Squad began laying down weapons and raising hands in surrender.

Prikahn dumped me not very gently in front of Jesral—who'd managed to potency-burn the savik shit away. I made sure to collapse into a crumpled kneeling position, even as I pressed my hands flat on the asphalt, feeling the resonance of the Earthgate deep in my bones. I quickly activated the construct from the painting and felt Elinor's contribution via Kadir's Between Machine, reached inside the very core of the gate and made the needed changes. The very clever hacks.

"I . . . I can't believe you beat us," I gasped. Damn, I wished I could squeeze out some convincing tears. I looked up, contorting my face into what I hoped was an expression of fear and misery. I must have been close enough, because Jesral was lapping it up.

"Get used to being on your knees before me, little chekkunden," he laughed, sneering.

"Please don't hurt my people," I begged, delighted I could make my voice quaver. The resonance of the gate made a subtle shift that I noticed only because I was looking for it, expecting it. I cast my gaze around as if seeking an escape. Watched as the sigil on the shards changed. To mine.

Jesral was oblivious, too deeply involved in his gloating. "Oh, yes, do continue begging. You need the practice, for I see a great deal of it in your future."

I shifted one foot beneath me. "Please . . ." I met his eyes and began to laugh. "Please . . . go fuck yourself."

I activated the gate as I surged to my feet, tackled him around the thighs, and forcibly evicted his ass from Earth.

Chapter 44

I landed heavily on top of Jesral, making sure to drive my elbow into his groin. Lord or not, he was still enough of a human male that it bought me a few seconds of advantage. For good measure I lifted up then came down hard again, then slugged him in the jaw and wrapped him in rakkuhr, just for kicks.

I rolled off and backed away so I could take stock of my surroundings. It had been bright midday at the compound, but here it was dim and foreboding. Not nighttime, but with a sky clouded and shrouded by black clouds. Definitely Mzatal's realm, though. Ahead and to my right, the damaged palace hugged the cliffside above the sea, its windows shattered on all sides. The basalt column speared into the air a few hundred yards directly before me, and a dozen feet to its left, the land fell away at a forty-five degree angle—a rocky slope I'd lugged bricks up when I first started my training with Mzatal. Beyond the slope had once stood a thick swath of forest that was now reduced to charred stumps, like a field of reaching, blackened fingers. Farther away, beyond the ravine at the other end of the palace, the white trunks of the grove glimmered in stark contrast to the grim surroundings.

All else was char and ash. No grass. No vegetation.

My gaze rose to the rubble-strewn rooftop garden of the palace. Mzatal stood at the very edge, still as a statue, hands stiff at his sides, and his hair braided and bound again. Even from this distance, I felt our eyes meet—for a mere whisper of an instant—before he slid his gaze away. He was locked down again, the controls on him tighter than ever before, the consequence of his brief rebellion and self-sacrifice that gave me the key to saving Earth.

As if in confirmation, Ssahr, Ilana, Trask, and Dima stepped forward to flank him.

The Earthgate—*my* Earthgate!—hummed as Alpha Squad poured through, followed by the Riders on their mounts, and Griz. Part of the settings I'd tweaked had included allowing all compound personnel full access.

Zakaar appeared with Szerain a couple of yards from me. Farther away from the gate, Vahl arrived with his ptarl, Korlis, who immediately vanished.

I snickered as I realized I'd managed to strand Vahl on Earth when I changed the gate, which meant he'd been forced to ask his ptarl to come get him. *"Um, dad? I . . . I kinda need a ride home."*

A number of humans emerged from the palace and started running our way. Tsuneo and other summoners, but also a dozen or so people in paramilitary gear. So Jesral had himself some mercenaries. Made sense that he didn't use them at the compound since they had no chance of getting through the protections, nor did they have any heavy weaponry.

I frowned at the sight of Angus near the palace door, giving the summoners and soldiers a pat on the back or a shoulder squeeze of encouragement as they went by. Pretty clear he was still firmly Team Jesral. I could only hope Boudreaux never saw any of that.

Jesral shook free of the bindings and scrambled to his feet, face twisted with fury as he hurled an arcane strike at me. I snapped up a shield just in time, but before I could gather a counterstrike, Szerain lobbed a ball of rakkuhr at Jesral that ensnared him in clinging tendrils and sent him staggering.

"Kara," Szerain said. "Go complete the shikvihr."

I looked at the foreboding thirty-foot, jet-black column, then back to him. "Are you shitting me? Now?!"

"This battle is only going to get worse, and we need every advantage. *You* need every advantage." His eyes flicked to where Mzatal stood motionless on the ledge. None of us knew what he was watching or waiting for, but I couldn't imagine it would be anything fun. "Go! I'll culminate it as soon as you're finished."

I gulped down more stupid arguments and took off in a hard run toward the column. Just over a year ago, Mzatal had told me, "You *will* be able to dance the shikvihr even though the world breaks apart beneath your feet." He'd always had faith in me, confident I'd reach this point, that I'd complete the full shik-vihr initiation.

And because of his faith and trust in me, I'd come to believe it.

But, just like Idris, I'd always . . . *always* . . . assumed Mzatal would be the one to culminate it for me.

It doesn't matter who culminates it, I told myself fiercely, and pushed down the thick knot of grief. *I'm still doing it for him, and for everyone who helped me reach this point, and for all the people and entities fighting to save two worlds.*

I skidded to a stop at the base of the column, placed my hands on the dark storm-grey surface of the polished basalt, and murmured to it, asking it to reveal the stairs so I could ascend and begin.

Nothing. What the hell? I'd asked the column for stairs several months ago when I was seeking the gimkrah, and it had obliged quite readily.

I removed my hands from the column, counted to five, then tried again.

Still no stairs.

I thought furiously, then groaned and changed my request to a simple, "Please supply me with a way to climb to the top."

To my relief—and dismay—the surface rippled and shifted. My first introduction to the column and shikvihr had included watching Mzatal ascend, but instead of nice handy steps, the column had created a constantly shifting pattern of ridges and outcroppings.

Which is what it gave me now. Apparently it knew I was here for the whole shebang.

I stepped back a pace and observed the ebb and flow of the protrusions. A corner of my brain yammered at me to get my ass in gear because, y'know, a war was going on around me. But I shushed it and let myself watch for another dozen heartbeats. Then another.

Yep, there was a pattern to it. A complex one, but there nonetheless. I rolled my neck on my shoulders and silently thanked everyone who'd helped me get into top shape over the past year. Because, damn, I was going to need it.

I grabbed an outcropping with my right hand and immediately pushed off a ridge with my left foot to propel me up enough to reach another handhold. A half second's pause, then I reached again, pushed with my other foot. Ascended a bit more. I breathed, deep and even, feeling the rhythm now. Reach, pull, push, shift. I could do this.

I missed a ridge with my foot and slithered down half a dozen feet, gouging a cut into my left palm on the way. I cursed and started up again. Reach, pull, push, shift, slide, reach. Reach, pull, push—

An arcane blast hit an inch away from my right hand. I lost my hold and fell all the way to the ground, landing flat on my back, impact driving the breath out of my lungs.

Above me, lightning flashed in and around roiling purple-black clouds, and the tingle of grove activation signaled the arrival of more lords. Rhyzkahl. Vrizaar. Amkir.

I sucked in an agonizing breath. *C'mon, Kara, get up. Get UP!*

I rolled to my belly then staggered to my feet, ribs and back throbbing like a bass drum as I faced the column again. The complex rhythmic dance of ridges continued in its syncopation, like that piece Michael was playing the other day. A fusion of melodies and beats.

I grabbed the first handhold, humming Michael's catchy and crazy tune under my breath. Reach. Grab. Push. Pull. Push and push, then pull-pull-pause.

Another blast struck the column above me, throwing off my rhythm and causing me to miss a hold, but this time I managed to catch myself before falling. Heart pounding, I pressed my cheek against the cool basalt, allowing myself five full seconds to pygah and get my act together. There . . . the rhythm still pulsed and flowed. I hadn't lost it, and that was the most important thing right now.

I lunged for a handhold and resumed my climb.

Reach. Grab. Push. And then I clambered onto the top, arms and legs trembling from the effort. The flat surface was about five feet across, its center marked by a two-foot-wide perfect circle of the blackest black of the void. Much like the first time I'd been here, the darkness sucked at me, promising certain horrific doom, primed for the shikvihr initiation. The knowledge that it was a psychological ploy shaved off only a thin slice of its distracting effect. As if standing on the narrow rim around the void circle while demons and humans fought on all sides weren't distraction enough. As an extra-special bonus, a storm blossomed to the east, violet lightning arcing through sickly green clouds that presaged fire rain, and in the distant north a mountain spewed lava. Not far from the base of the column, Rhyzkahl, Elofir, Vrizaar, and Amkir danced their own shikvihrs.

That was all the rest I could afford myself. I found my focus and began the first ring.

As I traced the third sigil, the column trembled hard. I dropped into a crouch beside the accursed blackness, abruptly reminded of Mzatal's comment when he'd first demonstrated the shikvihr for me. "This was without the distractions that accompany the final trial," he'd said with his usual slight smile. Somehow I doubted that a full-out war typically raged during shikvihr initiations so, apparently, the column supplied plenty of its own distractions, threats, and perils. Great. I was lucky enough to get hammered from multiple fronts.

I extended my awareness as I completed the first three rings. An enemy reyza screamed defiance and dove at me, forcing me to drop flat to avoid being knocked off. My hand missed the basalt rim and plunged into the nightmare maw of the void. My mind clamped shut, and my body froze in a rictus of sheer panic. *I'm going to die. I'm going to die!*

No. Not here. Not now. I drew on the intense mental and physical training of the last year, compelled myself to breathe, to pygah. *Mental games, nothing more. I can do this.*

Through sheer force of will, I yanked my arm free of the darkness, shaken, but not beaten.

I'd barely scrambled upright when a bullet winged by, close enough for me to feel the breeze of its passage, followed immediately by another that punched my ribs, stopped from penetrating by whatever ballistic material the zrila had built into the fatigues. I crouched again—carefully—while I caught my breath and waited for the hard ache of the bullet to fade a bit. This was some serious bullshit. I was willing to bet the late, great, shikvihr all-star Calvus Atilia hadn't been forced to deal with fucking *guns*.

Yeah, well, fuck Calvus Atilia. I still had resources, and a shitload of motivation. I drew power from the grove to reinforce my physical shielding. Just in time, as another bullet arced away from its through-my-neck trajectory.

Okay, Kara, how about we get this shit over with? Just because I was doing the big horking shikvihr initiation didn't mean I couldn't make it what I needed it to be. A foundation, yes. But right now I also needed a mighty fortress for protection and defense.

The fourth and fifth rings flowed out of me as I dodged, parried, blocked, or simply kept my balance. By the seventh, I danced around the rim with sheer brute force and elegance, tracing sigils like a madwoman. I had no bandwidth to spare for the battle raging on the ground and in the air around me, but peripherally I caught the radiance of many lords' shikvihrs as fire rain swept closer.

The eighth. Then the ninth. At some point during the tenth, white hot pain blossomed in my side, but whatever caused it didn't drop me, and so I kept going.

I finished the tenth and swept my gaze around the column, noting Kadir, Paul, and even Rayst had joined the lords' shikvihr party. Mzatal hadn't moved from the ledge. I was bleeding from a number of wounds, but nothing seemed life-threatening. With lordy insight cranked up to a billion, it was time to finish this bullshit.

I pulled more grove power and began the eleventh ring. The column swayed, the void chittered promises of torment, more projectiles found their mark.

I sketched the final sigil, reassessed and tweaked each ring, then ignited the entire series. The column stilled, and the psychological shenanigans of the void faded to nothingness.

"Holy shit." I croaked out a laugh. "Szerain! Come culminate this thing!"

No reply. I scanned the battle, and my heart sank at the sight of Szerain engaged in an intense arcane firefight with Jesral.

No way could he disengage to reach me. And the other allied lords were all battling not only flesh and blood enemies, but also an anomaly that had opened like a glowy, glitching beachball near the base of the palace cliff. A sick pit filled my stomach. I couldn't leave the pattern to fight, then come back when a lord was free.

All this work . . . for nothing. No, less than nothing. An utter waste of time, when I could have been fighting.

Shaking with a vile concoction of frustration and despair, I turned to descend and rejoin the battle.

And ran right into a woman standing atop the column with me.

I shrieked and backpedaled, my foot landing on empty air beyond the edge of the column. My arms windmilled futilely as

I began to fall, but she grabbed my shirt and hauled me back to solid footing.

I stared at the young woman before me. Mid-twenties or so with auburn hair that fell past her shoulders. Wearing jeans and a plain blue t-shirt. Face familiar, but . . .

She grinned, and recognition clicked in.

"You're back," I said stupidly.

Ashava laughed. "Yes. I'm back."

"And you can culminate this for me!"

"No." She gave a low laugh and placed her hand on my shoulder, warm and radiating subtle power. "You're not finished. You need one more ring."

"But I did eleven already, and—*ohhhh!*"

I gave her a quick hug, using that precious second to convey my love and gratitude and relief, and also to remind myself of all that she was as well as everything I stood for.

Then I danced the actualization of myself, of Ashava, of the lords. Of our Ekiri lineage and human heritage.

One final ring.

It flowed from my hands, not in individual sigils, but as an outpouring of my essence, a shimmering stream of jewel-toned potency. I guided it around the other rings and deftly sealed its circle, sensing the rightness of completion. The twelfth ring.

Foundation. Protection. Fierce cunning. Beauty and power exemplified.

It sang to me in soft, clear tones that uplifted my spirits and replaced dogged determination with hope and promise and a passionate vigor I'd forgotten I could feel.

I sensed more than saw Rhyzkahl tip his head up to behold this wonder. Then felt him call forth his own twelfth ring, followed by Elofir and the other lords.

Ashava gave a nod of approval, and I waited for her to culminate the pattern. But she merely smiled and gestured to my shikvihr.

My beautiful, *complete* shikvihr. My heart leaped, and as if I'd done it a thousand times, I swiftly linked the sigils of the first eleven rings and attuned their vibration to that of the twelfth. A heartbeat later, I ignited the whole.

Gentle power that matched my energy, my essence—*me*—suffused every cell. As I received it, the pattern dimmed and faded away. A part of me.

"Go," I said. "Help the others deal with that anomaly. But

damn, I'm really glad you're back." I sucked in a breath. "Wait! Does your mother know you're back?"

Ashava laughed. "Yes! I went to her first. She'd find a way to ground me for a thousand years if I hadn't!"

"You're not wrong," I said with a grin.

She pulled me into a fierce embrace. When she released me, she vanished, and I was on the ground at the base of the column, my wounds healed.

Chapter 45

I took stock of my surroundings, extending my senses to see where everything stood. And whoa, those senses had definitely kicked into high gear.

Dark violet lightning forked overhead as Szerain and Jesral battled grimly with blades and arcane a dozen yards from the Earthgate. Between the column and the palace, Alpha Squad took on demons and clusters of mercenaries, and the bodies of several mercs flared as they discorporeated. Meanwhile the Riders rampaged through Jesral's summoners and shikvihrs, doing everything possible to disrupt their support of the sharp-faced lord. Tessa stood with Walter and his welding rig, crafting shields and protections with skill and confidence while Walter did his chartreuse flamethrower trick and took out more demons. Both looked happy and fierce.

Out of the corner of my eye, I saw Angus grab Redd's leg in an effort to pull her off her mount, but she managed to wheel the mule and twist free, sending him scrambling back to avoid the hooves. Makonite and Jill crouched back-to-back and resumed their sniper roles, while Zenra darted through the melee to tend wounded, and Kinsavi tangled enemy demons and humans alike with his hair. Elsewhere, a bald woman with shimmering red skin passed near the mercs and left melted weapons in her wake, while a man with dead-white eyes turned in a circle, slowing enemies within a fifteen-foot radius to half their normal speed. More pod people—no doubt the ones Pellini had mentioned when he said Kadir was tracking them to be sure they were where they needed to be.

Well, this was certainly it.

Near the sea cliffs, Dagor and Prikahn battled a trio of Sky Reaper zhurn, which surprised me. Not because they were fighting, but that apparently my "full access for compound personnel" setting on the gate included the Jontari warlords. They'd probably be horrified to learn they were now honorary members of the hu-beast's Compound Clan.

The Sky Reapers themselves seemed to be fighting for the sheer brutal joy of battle, as well as their continued desire to overtake Mzatal's realm. Meanwhile, the bear-sized Griz seemed to be having the time of his life finishing off wounded enemy demons.

A quick assessment of Szerain and Jesral told me the former was holding his own for the moment—which was good because there were other hot spots that needed my help far more urgently.

I spun out webs of arcane and grove potency to tangle the wings of a lord-aligned kehza before it could rake Hurley with its claws. Spears of rakkuhr took out the front legs of a spider-like graa poised to leap on Abercrombie and Blauser. Yet I was too far away to reach Chu and one of the Riders before a Sky Reaper zhurn slashed claws across their throats and they discorporeated.

They still have a chance to return to Earth through the void! I told myself fiercely, even as tears stung my eyes. I dashed them away and refocused on the living.

Scott, Petrev, and Hines were engaged in a battle with a handful of mercenaries while Vahl maintained arcane shielding around the mercs. Vahl's face was set in a scowl, but not one of determination. He mostly looked as if he just wanted to get the fuck out of there. I readied a strike, then decided there was a better way to deal with this.

"Vahl!" I yelled, using the arcane to be sure he heard me. "You're better than this! Do the right thing this time—not what you think will make the other lords accept you. I know you don't actually believe any of Jesral's crap. And *you* know he'll never share glory. He's using you!"

Vahl stared at me, then frowned and flicked a glance toward Jesral. Fed the fuck up, I let my anger show and thrust my hand toward the base of the column, where the other lords worked to control the anomaly and the fire rain. "They're busting their asses to save *everything*. Now get *your* goddamn ass over there and help them!"

His expression cleared as if he'd finally accepted something critical. He gave me a single nod and sprinted toward the circle of lords.

I stared down the mercs and casually tossed a ball of potency up and down in my hand like a tennis ball. "Surrender right now, and I'll get you a ride back to Earth."

They were not stupid soldiers of fortune, and they quickly complied. Zakaar popped in, gathered them close, and then they were gone. Knowing him, he'd drop them someplace perfectly safe, but a helluva long hike from civilization.

Though I didn't really need to look with my physical eyes, I glanced toward Mzatal, a foreboding presence on the ledge. I clenched my left hand, feeling the ring press against my other fingers, then returned my focus to the battle around me.

Angus seized Blauser's bicep and yanked her off balance but retreated right before I could blast him or she could deliver a knee-destroying kick. He met my eyes for a split second then pivoted and stalked over to where Tsuneo and Jesral's other summoners were laying support. Angus put a hand on Tsuneo's shoulder, murmured something lost in the overall din, then gave his shoulder a squeeze before moving on. Tsuneo frowned at his back then redid a support sigil, scowled and dispelled it, then sketched it again.

A dozen yards behind me, Roma let out a curse. I spun to see her doing the tap-rack-ready to clear a jam on her pistol with no success. A Sky Reaper kehza roared and dove at her as she tried again to clear the jam. Face set in grim focus, she jerked the pistol up and sighted down the barrel, even as I drew potency for a strike.

Click

The kehza shrieked and tumbled out of the sky.

Except the gun hadn't fired. I was positive of that. And my arcane strike never left my hands.

Roma stared at her gun, then at the kehza writhing on the ground, wrapped in arcane tendrils of . . .

"Holy shit!" I cried out as I registered the chartreuse potency crawling over the demon. "You're a Kadir Kid, too?!"

Roma gave me a baffled look, then her eyes widened as if old memories had just flooded in. She barked out a laugh. "God-dammit! He looked so familiar when I first saw him out on the road with you. Now I know why!"

Holy fucking shit. The Pellini Patrol really was going to save the world.

Ugly lightning spiderwebbed through the sky. A tremor shook the ground, and a section of the palace wall collapsed, sending people scrambling.

Past the column, Giovanni and Elinor danced a shikvihr together, flowing together in perfect harmony. Though he had no arcane talent, his movements emphasized and enhanced hers, even including lifting her at times as if they were a pair of ice skaters. It made little logical sense, yet Elinor's shikvihr shone bright and vibrant, thrumming with fierce power.

Angus stalked through the shifting battles, eyes scanning, tracking Jesral's location and our forces. He still carried the MAC-10, but I had yet to see him fire a single shot, seemingly more interested in sheer intimidation than anything else. I suspected he was holding himself back from more violence because Boudreaux was in the vicinity. Not that the two were anywhere near each other. Angus seemed to take pains to be out of his son's sight whenever possible.

Over by the Earthgate, I felt Szerain falter—just for a millisecond, but enough to tell me it was time to jump into that fray.

I took off at a sprint toward the two lords, drawing from my culminated twelve-ring shikvihr and the grove to ready a devastating strike on Jesral. It wouldn't stop him as long as he held Xhan, but even a slight chink in his protections would surely give Szerain some advantage.

Szerain met my eyes and gave a microscopic headshake, then pointedly dropped his gaze to my right hand. I stumbled to a stop and held my power in check. Was he telling me to strike at Jesral? Was I supposed to wait for his signal? How was I supposed to interpret any of that?

He lifted Vsuhl over his head. I had no idea what his plan was, but power thrummed eagerly in my control, and I stood poised to follow his lead.

Szerain exhaled . . . and sent the blade away.

"No!" I took a staggering step forward, shocked to my core as Szerain stood before Jesral, unarmed. Unprotected. What the hell was he doing? He wasn't even drawing power to himself. Why? Why would he give up like that?

Jesral let out a cry of triumph and delivered an arcane blast that sent Szerain sprawling. Not a killing strike, though. No way would he dispatch Szerain so cleanly. He had other plans. With a swift gesture, he raised a barrier of potency around them that pushed me back a good dozen feet, sent Xhan away, then seized Szerain by the hair and hauled him to his knees.

"Now to submerge you so deeply you will *never* claw your way free." His lips pulled back from his teeth in a feral snarl as he set his hands on either side of Szerain's head. Agonized, I battered at the wall of potency, struggling to find some chink, some weak spot. Angus stepped up to the far side of the potency barrier, eyes on Jesral and face impassive.

Szerain jerked and let out a tortured moan. To my horror, his face began to shift. Change. Resolve into features that were once so familiar to me. Features of a man I'd come to care for deeply. Ryan Kristoff. The man I'd come to love, but who had never truly existed.

I called grove power and rakkuhr to me, delivered strike after strike at the barrier to no avail. Why . . . why would Szerain send Vsuhl away? He had to have known Jesral would submerge him given the opportunity, make him suffer in the worst way possible. Why sacrifice himself when the battle was far from won or lost?

Szerain/Ryan met my eyes, and his gaze once again dropped to my right hand. Comprehension hit me with a visceral jolt. Then Szerain disappeared and it was only Ryan, blinking in confusion like a man waking up.

Jesral laughed and shoved him harshly away, dropped the arcane barrier, then sneered at me. "Your pet qaztahl is gone now."

He gestured in my direction, gloating triumph in every inch of his bearing. "Angus, drain her to a husk. And fucking do it right this time, or Catherine will pay the price."

I pointedly looked off to where Boudreaux and the rest of the Riders battled Jesral's demons, then returned my full attention to Jesral.

Angus didn't follow my gaze. I had a feeling he knew exactly where his son was. But would it make a difference when Jesral held his wife hostage?

He began a slow advance in my direction, and I braced myself, called more power. I couldn't let him touch me. That was the most important thing.

Angus abruptly pivoted and seized Jesral in a headlock.

Struggling, Jesral let out a howl of rage, then bright white potency flashed from him like an exploding transformer. Angus screamed in agony and flew back several feet to crumple in a heap. I heard Boudreaux yell, "Dad!" and in my periphery saw him wheel his mule our way.

Sick horror filled me at the sight of Angus lying unmoving, his clothing charred and melted, and burns covering most of his torso. I sent out a mental plea. *Ashava! Help Angus!*

A whisper of acknowledgment, and then she was there beside him, seconds before Boudreaux slid off his mount and fell to his knees beside the only father he'd ever known.

And just like that, all of Angus's actions during the battle clicked into place. While Jesral was distracted, he'd been doing little acts of subversion. Touching Redd and Blauser and any others he could to give them a boost, and doing the opposite to Jesral's summoners and mercenaries.

There was nothing I could do for Angus except take advantage of the incredible sacrifice he'd just made for me. He'd only had a few seconds of contact with Jesral, but even merely dulling the edge of Jesral's power gave me some small edge.

I ruthlessly cleared my mind and breathed. Focused. Extended.

Jesral made a show of straightening his clothing before turning to face me. "Your worthless lord writhes in suppressed torment even now. I look forward to keeping him on a collar and leash to kneel at my feet. And as for you, I'll finish what Rhyzkahl started. You'll be my weapon with no will of your own." His smile grew as he stalked in my direction. "And Earth will be mine."

This fucking prick. I locked eyes with him and lifted my right hand over my head.

He stuttered to a stop, eyes wide in shock as Vsuhl coalesced in my grasp. But he recovered quickly and called Xhan to him.

"You stupid woman," he sneered as he resumed his advance. "Who the fuck do you think you are? You cannot stand against me, blade to blade."

Vsuhl's hilt warmed against my palm. "You're right, Jesral," I said, tone placid. Conversational. "I cannot, in fact, stand against you, blade to blade." I let the smile grow on my face, enjoyed the confusion in his eyes when I raised my left hand. "I suppose I'll have to remedy that."

He jerked and dropped his eyes to where he held Xhan clenched in his fist. "No. That's not possible!" Disbelief coiled with shock on his face. He tightened his grip on the blade until the tendons stood out on his hand and the skin grew taut over his knuckles.

The voices of Vsuhl and Xhan rose in harmonic majesty, joined distantly by Khatur. The blade song wound through me, familiar and invigorating.

"I was able to call Vsuhl because it knows me," I said. "I was its bearer for a time." I started a slow walk toward him. "But you forgot something very important. Xhan knows me as well."

His gaze dropped to my torso as if he could see the sigils beneath my demon fatigues. "No." Horror mingled with comprehension as he realized the truth: Xhan had carved every single one of them.

"That's right," I purred. "Xhan and I have an *intimate* history."

Jesral let out a cry of horrified disbelief as the blade vanished from his grasp. For an instant he could only stare at his empty hand, then his gaze traveled to me as if reluctant, unwilling to accept the evidence of his own eyes, yet unable to deny the truth as Xhan appeared in my possession. He stood unmoving, fear beginning to shadow through the utter denial and confusion on his face.

"Who the fuck do I think I am?" I smiled a vicious little smile as I closed the distance. "I'm Kara Fucking Gillian. And Xhan likes me better."

Jesral stared at the blades, all trace of arrogance gone, replaced by utter bewilderment. He couldn't comprehend that he might lose. Would lose.

"Sucks to be you, fuckface," I said and drove both blades into his chest. It wasn't the most elegant of catchy murder zingers, but Jesral didn't deserve anything fancy.

His breath froze in his throat, and he shuddered. His eyes went wide and sought mine in desperation as he finally, truly, recognized his defeat. A violent spasm wracked his body, and his mouth worked.

The blade song crescendoed to a predatory scream of slaughter and bloodlust as the light left his eyes.

I yanked Xhan and Vsuhl free, and Jesral's legs buckled as if the blades had been the only thing keeping him upright. The instant his body collapsed, white roots burst from the soil to wrap over and around him like a living shroud. I felt the whisper touch of Rho as the roots drew him down into the soil, and understood.

Jesral had gone terribly astray, but he was still a child of the Ekiri, and Rho would take care of his remains.

I sent the blades away then pelted over to Angus. Boudreaux cradled him in his arms while Ashava fought to heal what she could of the devastating injuries. Angus clung to consciousness, mouth working as he struggled to breathe. Vines emerged and twined loosely around him, amethyst leaves shimmering. Angus took a slightly easier breath, but I felt Rho's touch, and Ashava met my eyes. I didn't have to read minds to know his injuries were beyond healing. Right now all she and Rho could do was ease pain and give him a bit more time.

He needs to know his wife is safe, I thought at Ashava.

She nodded, touched Boudreaux's shoulder, then vanished. More vines twined about Angus. A few seconds later, Ashava reappeared with Catherine beside her.

Catherine cried out in anguish and grabbed Boudreaux's hand, then dropped to her knees beside Angus.

"He saved us all," I told them. "He drained just enough from Jesral that I was able to call the essence blade from him."

Catherine looked up at me, tears streaming. "Jesral is dead? You killed him?"

"Yes."

She gave a fierce nod.

Angus looked up at his wife and son, managed a faint smile through the vicious burns on his face. "Tried . . . to make things right," he wheezed. "Too many wrongs . . . but had to try. Love you both."

"Love you, Dad," Boudreaux choked out.

Angus's eyes sought mine. "Don't . . . don't let me die here. Not here."

My brow puckered in confusion. "But you'd have a chance to recorporeate—"

"No." A shudder of pain went through him. "I . . . I want to go home . . . be with my wife and son. It's . . . time. I'm ready."

Boudreaux lowered his head, eyes streaming, but didn't protest his father's decision.

I touched Ashava's arm, silently asked her to take them back to Earth. The vines retreated with a whisper of sound.

An instant later all four vanished.

I looked around, relieved to see that Alpha Squad and the Riders were making sure Jesral's remaining forces knew their side had lost. The majority of them were being smart by laying down weapons and surrendering. The allied Jontari were helping convince the rest. What few Sky Reapers remained were already departing through rifts.

Szerain . . . no, *Ryan*. He was conscious and sitting up, blinking around him in confusion. He focused on me with some difficulty as I ran over to him. "Kara? What the hell? Where are we? What's going on?"

I crouched beside him. "Demon realm. We won," I said. "We beat the bad guys and saved the world."

He grinned. "Was there ever any doubt?"

"Pfft. As if!" I smiled. "But now it's time to go."

Ryan looked around, expression turning wistful. "Guess that's right." He exhaled. "We had a good run, huh?"

"We did." I smiled even as the tears spilled over. "The best. I'll never forget any of it. Or you."

"It's goodbye then," he said, exhaling. But he seemed accepting, as if a core part of him, of the Ryan overlay, knew he wasn't real.

"It's okay," I said, telling myself as much as him. "Goodbye, Ryan." I leaned in and gave him a gentle kiss.

He returned it just as gently, then touched my cheek. "Goodbye, Kara."

I sat back on my heels, watched as Ryan's features shifted, faded, once again became Szerain.

"Well done," he murmured, voice trembling in reaction to the trauma of submersion. He wiped tears from my face, then pulled me into a hug. I held him close, giving him all the comfort I could, in awe of his incredible bravery to willingly submit himself to that torment again.

A shimmer of . . . *something* passed through me, drawing my gaze up to the ledge where Mzatal had remained still and watching this entire time.

I clambered to my feet and gave Szerain a hand up, all while keeping my focus on Mzatal. It was as if the entire world held its breath.

Even from this distance, I felt him meet my eyes.

Then he stepped off the balcony into open air.

I couldn't hold back the shriek of horror. Was suicide his final move? The ultimate way to cheat Ilana and Ssahr of their weapon?

But my horror turned to a different kind of shock as his body changed, shifted before even a full second had passed.

And a midnight-black dragon the size of a 747 swooped upward.

"Huh," Szerain said. "I did not see that coming."

The Mzatal dragon let out a roar that shook the ground, then dove toward us.

Chapter 46

The dragon dove, wingtip carving a furrow into the ground as people and demons scattered. The lords rallied and hammered him with a myriad of brutal attacks, but nothing penetrated. He soared high and circled the column, as if peering into the depths of the void at the center of the basalt pillar, then came around for another pass, scattering sigils and shattering support structures.

Lightning spewed from his jaws, striking the ground with a concussive force that sent lords and humans flying. I threw myself flat to avoid being pelted by dirt and debris, then rolled to my back and flung potency spears at the dragon's belly as he passed over. I might as well have been tossing marshmallows for all the good it did. Yet so far he didn't seem to be trying to kill anyone. But why not? What was his goal?

I scrambled up, ears ringing. A number of people moaned on the ground, but no one appeared to be seriously hurt. Rayst, Vrizaar, and Ashava already worked to heal injuries.

Once again, the dragon climbed high and circled the column.

"Roma! Get Alpha Squad back to the compound. This is a shitshow."

Roma gave me a cool stare. "Go fuck yourself."

"Goddammit, you don't understand!"

She stepped up to me. "I do. We all do. We're not leaving." Behind her, the rest of Alpha shouted unanimous and emphatic agreement. Farther back, Tessa and Walter wore equally mulish expressions. To my surprise, Pellini stood with them, entire bearing one of calm determination. I hadn't seen him arrive, but I wasn't going to complain.

"Fine." Honestly, I'd pretty much expected this response but had to try anyway. "Stay back from the lords and arcane users. They'll likely be his focus."

"Duly noted." She hefted her rifle, then set chartreuse potency writhing along the stock. "Good thing we have ranged weapons."

I limped back to the front lines, such as they were, and tried again to reach Mzatal through that hairline crack in his prison, struggled to widen it, find him, the real him. Save him.

Nothing.

"We need to combine our attacks," I told Szerain. "Right now it's like kids throwing pebbles. Everyone needs to focus on one spot."

"Where? What spot?" he said, scowling as he wiped a smear of dirt and blood from his face. "Do you see any missing scales like Smaug?"

"Who the hell is Smaug? Never mind, I'm sure it's some nerdy thing, and no, I don't see any missing scales. How about we all try for his eyes." Surely that was a vulnerable target?

"Worth a try." Szerain glanced up as Mzatal circled the column again, then he jogged to the other lords and passed on the instructions. I relayed the same to Roma and Alpha Squad.

Idris stood shoulder to shoulder with me while the lords, including Ashava, took a stand not far away. Spread out a fair distance behind us, Alpha Squad readied firearms. Mzatal roared and stooped in a hard dive. I flung a spear of rakkuhr at his slit-pupiled eye . . . right before his wing caught us and sent everyone flying.

I landed hard and remembered to roll, dragged in a gasping breath as soon as I came to a stop. Agony knifed through my left shoulder, and moans and screams of pain surrounded me. I struggled to press up far enough to take stock. He'd scattered us as if we were toy soldiers on a game table. Twisted limbs and bleeding gashes. Someone—Abercrombie?—discorporeated. Fuck. Fuck-fuckfuck.

Zakaar crouched and placed a hand on my shoulder. Warmth flowed through it, and the searing pain faded. He helped me to my feet, and I looked up at the dragon. He was back to circling the column, peering into its depths with two fully functional eyes. So much for that being a weak spot.

"What is his obsession with the damn column?" I cried out in frustration. "It feels like he's just toying with us. What the hell is he waiting for?" I'd been in the column once before but couldn't think of anything I'd seen that would have a demahnk-controlled Mzatal-dragon so hyper-focused.

Zakaar went very still. A heartbeat later Helori appeared beside him, along with Greeyer and Fiar—Vrizaar's ptarl. And they all looked really fucking grim.

"What the *fuck* have you lot done now?" I snarled.

"It was millennia ago," Zakaar said. "We never thought it would . . . *could* ever come to this—"

"I don't want excuses! Give me some actual facts, right fucking now."

He took my hand, and awareness flooded in. Of the column. Of its history. Of what was hidden deep in its darkest depths.

A doomsday device, for lack of a better term. A reset button that tapped into the core of the planet. That awful chittering void that promised death and doom? Yeah, it wasn't lying.

The demahnk Ekiri had created it long long ago, after they screwed up and made kids. They of course had fully expected to succeed with this lord relocation venture from Earth to the demon realm—after all, they were the Ekiri! Still, they knew there was always that exceedingly slim chance of failure, in which case they'd need to wipe the slate clean in order for them to rejoin the collective.

But they built a failsafe into the device: none of the demahnk could activate this world-ending device. Only the eldest of their children could do so. Mzatal.

Years and centuries and millennia passed. Mzatal learned the true nature of what the column held and began building protections and additional failsafes into it, making it far more than a mere container for a bomb—because simply deactivating or destroying the device was beyond even his power. As time went by, he continued to adjust and tweak those protections, adding and fine-tuning, even as he planned ahead, knowing there might come a day when some might wish to use it.

"Well," I finally said. "That's . . . a thing." As much as I wanted to, I just didn't have it in me to be mad at Zakaar and Helori and the others for not mentioning this sooner. After all, it had been placed literally thousands of years ago, and I figured even eternal beings could have brain farts. Plus, they surely NEVER thought things would reach this level of desperation. Besides, what good would anger do me now? "Basically, if Mzatal reaches it, we'll all be destroyed. And Earth as well, right? Since the two worlds are linked?"

Helori gave me a single nod.

The enemy demahnk didn't give a fuck about any of that. Mzatal was a tool and nothing more.

An incredibly powerful tool.

Mzatal had circled the column over and over, that deeply buried seed of his Self giving me the hint that the danger lay there. But why do so if there was no way to stop him?

Which meant there was indeed a way to stop him.

A chill swept through me.

The heart of darkness devours all.

Part of Mzatal's message to me before Idris's shikvihr. He was referring to the doomsday device, not the shikvihr initiation on the column. The line before had been, *Failure is imminent, short of the ultimate triumph.*

He didn't mean my failure, not with the hints he'd given, both with the message and his current focus on the column. No, he was telling me the failure would be his—and the Mraztur demahnk's. Here at the heart of darkness.

I hadn't given up hope by any means, but knowing there truly was a potential path through this disaster was a much-needed boost.

I gathered everyone close and filled them in on the doomsday device. After the shock and fury settled, we abandoned any tactic that involved attacking with force—as clearly, that was pretty damn futile. It was Scott Glassman who suggested making a net.

"A big one made of magic and woo woo," he said. "I mean, I've seen you arcane types do webbing and snares. Can you do that on a bigger scale?"

We arcane types looked at each other.

"Yes," Rhyzkahl said. "Between all the lords, plus two summoners with the full shikvihr, we can construct a dragon-sized net."

We separated, then spun out thick ropes of potency, flung them to the next person, wove them, reinforced. Formed shields and protections. Readied.

The Mzatal-dragon roared and came at us again. More aggressive this time, no doubt pressured by Ilana and her ilk to fucking get on with it already. Still, he only raked the area nearby with lightning, sending an eye-stinging wave of ozone over us. They controlled him, but he wasn't *theirs.*

"Now!" Rhyzkahl ordered. Together, we deployed the giant

arcane net, drew it taut around the dragon. He roared in rage and thrashed to the ground while we held on grimly, channeling everything we had into the cables, binding his wings close to his body.

Mzatal grew still, breath hissing through teeth as long as my torso. We hurried to anchor the net, reinforce it, add more and more until we could barely see the dragon beneath the arcane.

A slit-pupiled eye tracked to me, and I felt *him* for a bare instant.

"Oh, shit."

The world went white as potency lightning incinerated the net as easily as if it had been cotton thread. An instant later a blast wave sent me tumbling, even as Mzatal leaped into flight with a triumphant roar.

I stared up at the sky, fighting back despair, then pushed up to sit. Beside me, Amkir grimaced and cradled an obviously broken arm.

"I really thought that would work," he said, then looked my way with a frown. "Can you feel anything at all through your bond?"

Grief threatened to smother me. "I've been trying. I can't reach him." I took a shuddering breath. I couldn't reach him. Couldn't widen that hairline crack. Couldn't turn him away from this mutual destruction. "We've tried everything. Ilana and Ssahr and the others are going to fucking win." Hell, we were only holding him off because he was letting us.

Ashava wiped blood and sweat from her face, eyes dim and exhausted. "Not . . . everything."

"What? What haven't we tried?" I demanded.

She hesitated. "There is still one weapon at your disposal." Her eyes dropped to my torso. Beneath the demon armor, a tingle swept through the sigil scars.

Rowan.

I felt myself blanch. "Are you shitting me?"

"Kara, I can't think of anything else. It might defeat him."

Might. "You're not even sure it'll work?"

"I . . . don't know if it's enough."

I took a moment to pygah. It might not be enough. But what we were doing now certainly wasn't enough. "Will I still be me?" The words came out in a croak.

"I don't know." She bit her lower lip. For an instant I saw the uncertain little girl within the confident and powerful woman, and I was reminded that despite her incredible abilities, she was still half human and very young. "I'm sorry."

Strangely enough, her honest answer settled a good measure of the What The Fuck screaming through me.

Basically, I'd be volunteering for what would likely be a suicide mission. Or, worse than death, if my Self was subsumed by the Rowan construct, and I maintained even a flicker of awareness. True submersion, and one that I could never escape.

As if second guessing herself, Ashava placed her hand on my arm. "Kara," she said emphatically, "we may still prevail. No one's fate is set and sealed."

I looked up. The dragon circled high above, breathing lightning as if for funsies. Delaying the demands of the demahnk? Taunting? Waiting for us to make a move? Or perhaps simply getting ready to make an unstoppable strike on us. Or, worse, on the column.

An odd peace settled over me. This was one hundred percent my choice. No one would force me. No one would fault me if I refused. If I stopped being me, at least I'd go out trying. But hell, we'd all gone into this absolutely ready to give our lives to stop the Mraztur demahnk. Many already had.

This was just a different flavor of sacrifice.

I clambered to my feet. "I've decided."

"Are you sure?"

I opened so she could feel my complete acceptance. But still I spoke the words.

"Yes. I'm sure."

She took two steps to close the distance between us, threw her arms around me in a fierce hug, then released me. We were on top of the column now, wind shrieking and lightning slicing and the heart of darkness gibbering.

Mzatal roared above, sound penetrating to my core. He couldn't hold back much longer.

"Ready?" she asked.

Despite the thudding of my heart, I couldn't help but laugh. "Let's do this shit."

Ashava lightly touched the middle of my forehead with her index finger.

I let out a choked cry as sensation like pure cleansing fire raced through the sigils. Not pain. Not burning. But an unadulterated sense of the lords. Kadir and Szerain had already consummated their sigils, adjusting them to reflect their true and current selves, and now the rest shifted, adapted, elevated and unified by my total and willing acceptance. They became an intrinsic and essential part of me, and in doing so created the quintessential expression of my potential. Timeless in the universe, among the stars and galaxies. Free. Whole. *Me*.

I drew in a breath of rebirth and dropped to a crouch, the fierce sensations settling into my being as thoughts caught up to experience. I was still Kara. Still very *very* Kara. Yet the definition of Kara Gillian had expanded. I was everything I was before, and so much more. I was . . . complete. Ultimate.

"Well, this is pretty fucking cool," I murmured, then grinned. Oh, yeah, I was definitely still Kara who loved a good f-bomb.

Testing, I extended my senses. Holy shit, I was aware of, well, *all* of it. The people, the lords, the demons. In Dekkak's chamber, Michael sat cross-legged with Hrrk cradled in his lap, face a mask of concentration. I sensed that Prikahn had encouraged him to go through the rift to protect the pup and himself. I stretched farther, testing. The Between shimmered with shifting light. On Earth, Tandon and Bryce organized security personnel to assess and repair defenses, to be ready in the event of another attack. On my porch, Boo and Catherine wept in each other's arms while Lenny sat beside them and did his best to offer comfort.

Plenty of time to explore all of the potential later. I turned my attention to the column beneath me.

Oh yeah, if Mzatal reached that, everything was fucked. Now I understood the full nature of what it held and what he'd done to safeguard it. Several months ago, I'd entered its depths and found summoner Rasha Hassan Jalal al-Khouri in a dimensional pocket, sketching sigil after sigil.

I now knew she'd been working with Mzatal, layering in a final crucial firewall at his behest: He could only activate the doomsday device if Rowan existed—fully realized and aware and having come to it of their own volition. Not the abomination the Mraztur would have wrought.

It was the ultimate failsafe. He could only try to destroy the world if there was someone who could stop him.

Well, that someone sure as fuck existed now. And I wasn't going to wait for Mzatal to come to me.

Wings sprouted from my shoulder blades. Kickass warrior angel wings of fierce red and gold.

For the barest instant, I considered reaching into the column to disarm the device, nullifying the demahnk's plan in a single swift action. But no. Even that oh-so-brief access would give Mzatal the opening he needed to trigger the device.

My gaze locked onto the circling dragon, then I let out a battle cry and leaped into the air.

Mzatal dove at me the instant I took flight. Now that I existed as Rowan, he could indeed flip that final switch, which meant the battle was truly on.

He folded his wings, arrowed toward the column. I body slammed him out of the way, using the considerable power at my disposal. I still had control of the arcane and the grove power. Could still call rakkuhr to me. All an intrinsic part of my very being now.

And I was *really* good at it.

The dragon tumbled and landed awkwardly, gouging deep furrows in the ground. I quickly raised shields of power between him and the people and demons. His other attacks had seemed more geared toward chaos and mayhem than murder, but everything had shifted now. Those prior sorties had been to draw me out, show me what the stakes were, give me the opportunity to make the choice. To stop him.

I wrapped him in cables of arcane, a hundred times stronger than the net we'd tried earlier. Bound his wings and limbs and jaw.

No more testing. No more feints. This was war.

A deep growl rumbled in his throat, his eyes intense upon me. An instant later blue-white power flashed from him, weakening the cables enough for him to break free and spring into flight.

He climbed, higher and higher, while I maneuvered to stay between him and the column. He wheeled toward Alpha Squad with a roar that shook the ground.

I appeared between him and the squad—allowed myself an instant of *Holy shit! I can fucking teleport!*—then blasted him hundreds of feet back into the air.

I teleported to hover before him, then immediately darted aside to evade a blast of lightning. Again he breathed lightning at me, but when I blipped away, I was startled to find yet more aimed at the precise spot where I reappeared.

The reaching forks of electricity slowed to a crawl, and I let out a shaky laugh at this discovery of yet another neat Rowan trick. Time itself hadn't changed, but my perception of it had, which allowed me to take control of the energy and redirect it into the charred wasteland.

But the experience was eye-opening, and a gut-wrenching reality check. Mzatal had always been formidable, powerful, able to assess countless probabilities and plan and react accordingly—and becoming a dragon had clearly not blunted any aspect of that ability.

I allowed my perception to return to normal and delivered a devastating blast of combined potency at him, then returned to my position above the column. The force of my attack sent him hurtling back, yet still he recovered, eyes narrowed, arcane crackling around his jaws.

I hovered above the column as he climbed high above me. Higher and higher yet.

My gaze followed his upward progress. I couldn't save him. I couldn't beat him without destroying him. And I couldn't spare him. Not with literally *everything* at stake. Billions of lives. Dreams. Hopes. Loves.

It was an awful, gut-wrenching realization. Tears tracked down my face as I looked up at that fierce and beautiful and oh-so-deadly creature. I knew what I had to do. For everyone. And for him. He was a slave to the Mraztur demahnk, and I would NOT leave him to that fate.

As if in response to my epiphany, the lightning scar that wove through his sigil on my chest flared with stinging heat. An affirmation—gut wrenching but undeniable.

I appeared directly before him, stroked his cheek with a feather-light arcane touch. The dragon bared his teeth, and I felt the hair-thin crack in the barriers around his essence widen by the tiniest, infinitesimal amount. A single concept flowed through me: Together.

The truth of it could not be denied. *Together we can do anything.*

I opened up enough for even the demahnk-controlled aspect to see . . . to *feel* my love. Though I was resolved in my course of action, I allowed it to sense a whisper of uncertainty within me, hesitation. What would hopefully appear as weakness.

Together we baited the demahnk.

Together we offered all to save the worlds.

I let my love for him shine until I glowed with it. Then I retreated, just enough to look as if I wouldn't commit. Couldn't.

Mzatal let out a roar that thundered across the landscape and dove toward the heart of darkness.

I teleported to the column top, ready and waiting when the lightning came. Embraced it, reshaped it into a supernova column of power and directed every bit of it at that hair-thin crack around his essence.

It burned through the crack, through his core, through his essence.

Burned away his fetters and the controls holding him, backlashed hard and vicious through the ones who held those fetters.

And for a millionth of a second, I felt his caress . . .

Approval

Love

Sorrow

Joy

And then he went nova.

I threw a shield over everyone on the ground to protect them from the blast, yet let it pass through me—a brilliant nebula of coruscating colors across the spectrum.

Felt the faintest final touch of him.

Then it was gone.

He was gone.

Chapter 47

No time to grieve. First things first. I reached into the column and deactivated the doomsday device, detached it from the heart of the world, and scattered its elements to the farthest reaches of the universe.

That done, I lifted my hand and called Khatur to me. It leaped into my possession as if it had been waiting. I welcomed the blade, promised it wouldn't have to wait much longer now, then sent it away again until the time for restoration.

Ilana and Trask and Ssahr had fled. But there was nowhere they could hide from me, and I'd deal with them soon enough.

I dispelled the shield protecting everyone below, then descended to the ground.

Ashava threw her arms around me, and I hugged her close as we spoke and shared without words. Triumph and grief and crushing loss and stunning victory. She understood, and I loved her for it.

After a moment, I released her and gave her a crooked smile. Then Szerain came and embraced me, and right on his heels, Idris. They, too, understood what this victory had cost me. Everyone did.

"Give me a moment," I said quietly, then I closed my eyes, touched the void, sought the essences of all who'd died in this battle and were now making their uncertain journeys back to Earth. Too many. Our people and Jesral's. Even the three mules who'd perished. With gentle nudges I set them on their way, guided them home, took away chance. Once the last made it through, I did the same for the demons slain on Earth, helping them return to their home world.

With that addressed, I turned my focus to the next and most pressing priority.

"It's time to set the elders free," I said, then backed away and opened a twenty-foot-tall rift.

Dekkak emerged and took a position a dozen feet before me. "You are prepared to fulfill our pact, Kara Gillian?"

I stood tall, felt the blades and all three gimkrahs on the fringe of my consciousness. "I am."

Seretis, Bubba, and Gurgaz stepped through the rift, each carrying a gimkrah.

Lord. Human. Demon.

Michael followed behind them, carefully cradling Hrrk, and I grinned as Prikahn bounded over to retrieve his puppy.

Without a word, Seretis, Bubba, and Gurgaz set the three gimkrahs before me. The heart of each crystal orb shifted from deep maroon to pulsing blood red.

I called Khatur to my hand, set the tip of the blade into the topmost rune of their gimkrah. Rakkuhr snaked from the orb to entwine the blade and hold it in place. I did the same with the Xhan and Vsuhl blades and their respective gimkrahs, then took a step back. Blade song rose anew, joined this time by deep bass vibrations from the orbs, hauntingly beautiful, tragic—and exultant. The unexpected resonance of Mzatal shimmered through me for a bare instant, bringing a wave of grief I almost failed to quash. It wasn't him, merely the lingering shadow of his hand in the making of these prisons.

I beckoned to Lord, Human, and Demon. Each moved forward and took hold of the blade hilt before them, waited.

Dekkak gave me a grave nod then backed away. A lot. I suddenly remembered the massive manacles and chains of makkas I'd seen within the column when I recovered the master gimkrah. Xhan hadn't seemed all that large in his gimkrah, but then again, that was more of a virtual setting.

Out of an abundance of caution, I retreated as well. A lot.

"Let's do this," I said, then disintegrated the makkas bands with a thought—and perhaps a showy flick of my fingers.

Lord, Human, and Demon drove the blades into the crystals, deep into those pulsing hearts, then scrambled back to stand by Dekkak.

Light blazed, radiant and fierce, and deep tones beyond

hearing shook the ground. A hot, dry wind whipped in a vortex around us, carrying sparks of rakkuhr. A roar like a thousand lions engulfed us then faded to silence.

The air stilled, and the world settled. Before me were three enormous demons, larger than Dekkak. I already knew Xhan's true luhrek form, though seeing him full-size made him all the more impressive. He carried himself with fierce intensity, no longer merely a gracious and mellow philosopher and teacher, but the full embodiment of all aspects of his essence, with an aura of breathtaking presence and potency.

Khatur was a zhurn, with crimson eyes glowing like a forge, her hide the deep black of the void, and each wing as long as a school bus. To my everlasting shock, Vsuhl was a zrila—demons I'd only ever known as small, scuttling tailors and weavers. The one before me now was epically massive, with a head as big as my entire body, and skin of deep indigo and magenta. They bared their teeth in greeting—pointy teeth as long as my arm.

I gave all a deep bow of respect. Xhan lowered his head and peered at me. "You are fresh and new, Kara Gillian."

"Much has transpired, honored Xhan."

Dekkak stepped before the elders and gripped an appendage of each in turn, ending with Khatur. "Kara Gillian told a tale of betrayal and sacrifice. Did she speak truth?"

Khatur's voice rumbled like a mountain rockslide. "Kara Gillian spoke truth. And we, the three, have reconciled amongst ourselves. We take a moment now to commune."

The three settled facing one another and went still as statues.

Dekkak spread her wings wide and bellowed in triumph and jubilation. "Kara Gillian, our agreement is fulfilled, your honor unblemished."

Seretis beamed, face full of pride. "Well done, my dear."

Dekkak angled a clawed hand toward him. "Qaztahl, we must address your standing, for you were never in the terms of the pact with Kara Gillian."

"Indeed, Imperator. My bargain is my own, and I will continue to live by it."

She bent low, her face in front of his, breath stirring his hair. "Much has changed. Perspectives. Perceptions. Perspicuity. You have acted with honor and courage worthy of the Jontari. I release you from your oath of bondage. You are free."

He inclined his head to her. "As I have ever been, honored one. May we move forward together in harmony."

Bryce swept Seretis up in a bearhug the instant Dekkak returned her attention to me.

"What of the kiraknikahl?" she growled. "The Ekiri and the demahnk."

"Trust me," I said with a fierce smile. "I haven't forgotten about that lot."

First things first. Taking Seretis and Bryce with me, I teleported to the top of the column. Chittering void no longer, merely a smooth, unbroken surface. We held each other's hands, three points of a triangle. Aided by his bond with Bryce, I drew in the *feel* of Seretis, then flung a billion seeking tendrils into the universe to call his sire Lannists's scattered essence home. A tiny prismatic speck appeared within our triangle. Then another. More gathered, faster and faster, as if drawn by ever-increasing gravity. Soon the aggregation was as large as a beachball, flashing crystalline colors.

I welcomed Lannist, helped him coalesce into his human form. He gave me a brilliant smile, then pulled Seretis into a fierce embrace. No longer ptarl-bonded but still acknowledging and treasuring the paternal link.

Lannist released Seretis and turned to Bryce, embraced him too, murmured gratitude and appreciation, then faced me again. I smiled and returned all three to the ground below.

Time to deal with the others.

I reached out again, this time to all of the Ekiri demahnk. Ilana. Trask. Fiar. Greeyer. Zakaar. Helori. Dima. Korlis. Lannist. Ssahr.

The worlds are still breaking. Your fuckups must be rectified. You may either remain and help or rejoin the collective. I conveyed the message without words, in an instant outside of time.

Zakaar and Helori joined me atop the column. A swirl of amethyst leaves indicated Rho's full support and presence.

Below, Greeyer appeared by Elofir, wrapped him in an embrace, then kissed him on the cheek, stepped back and disappeared to await banishment.

Fiar did the same with Vrizaar—held him close for several heartbeats, then placed a gentle kiss on his forehead and was gone.

Lannist remained steadfast beside Seretis.

I didn't expect any of the other demahnk to show themselves, not after everything they'd done or had supported. But to my surprise, Dima teleported to Amkir, took his hand and brought it to her forehead, as if asking forgiveness. Emotion twisted his face as he gave a quick jerky nod, then he threw his arms around her. They remained like that for several heartbeats before Dima stepped back, cupped his cheek with her hand and gave him a soft, sad smile. Then she vanished.

I took a moment to center myself and get my eyes to stop stinging. Yeah, I was a mega-powerful being now, but still the same old sappy Kara.

Breathing deeply, I extended, linking together Helori, Zakaar, and Rho, then added the Jontari elders and Dekkak, the lords, the humans and demons below, the pod people, Kadir's Kids on both worlds, and myself to form an indomitable and glorious gestalt. Reached farther and linked in the human companions, everyone still at the compound, and the other summoners and practitioners on Earth. More connections, more links, on and on, until both worlds stood poised and ready.

With the gestalt at my control, I reached to the Ekiri pavilions, dove deep into that infinite space at their heart and sought the collective. Made contact. Connected. Then evicted the banished demahnk, yeeting them toward the heart of the Ekiri collective with the command to never *ever* return.

Xharbek! I called, found him distant and still very much scattered. Teeth gritted, I gathered him, relishing the thought of sending him away forever. But my anticipated angry vengeance failed to manifest. Instead, empathy spawned compassion. My now broader perspective understood his suffering and the subsequent madness brought on by being abandoned by his kind. I finished gathering him and sent him to the collective. *Go home. Do better.*

But I wasn't finished with the Ekiri. In this moment, I was fucking eternal, I was the goddamn universe, and I had their attention, whether they liked it or not.

Though I didn't use words, my message and warning to them was clear. *The worlds of the universe are not your playgrounds. Stop fucking with emerging and existing civilizations.*

I showed them the stark truth of how badly their "observation" had fucked things up, and how close their interference and arrogance came to destroying two worlds and countless billions of lives.

I showed them the destruction, the torment, the needless suffering they'd wrought. I showed them the cruel subjugation of the lords—their children.

And then I gathered the full power of the incredible gestalt and sent the entire Ekiri collective hurtling to the most remote point in the universe I could find, far from any life whatsoever.

I left them with one, final, thundering message:

I'm watching you.

Slowly, I released the gestalt, carefully disengaging the parts from the whole, while gently ensuring the experience would feel to most of the humans on Earth like little more than a peculiar dream.

Only the three Jontari elders remained in union with me. "Now to seal the way," I told them.

Once more I reached to the pavilions—reached to the core of each one, the conduit that allowed the Ekiri access and, with the help of the elders, cauterized those conduits with devastating blasts of rakkuhr, ensuring the Ekiri could never return by that means.

I released the rakkuhr, returned to the ground below, and thanked the elders. The pavilions still held the Ekiri resonance, which was vital for Lannist, Zakaar, Helori, and Rho. Enough remained to sustain and provide comfort for them for several million years.

Zakaar held me close for a moment, returned to Szerain and embraced him, then finally moved to Rhyzkahl, took his hands, and gave him a dazzling smile.

"I am very proud of you," he said, then laughed when Rhyzkahl pulled him into a fierce hug. After a moment, Rhyzkahl stepped back, face shining with joy and peace, though his eyes were suspiciously damp.

Zakaar's body fragmented into a million points of light, like mist struck by a sunbeam, then dissipated in a flash of pure beauty. A gentle rain began to fall, and a rainbow arced across the sky over the column—the most magnificent rainbow I'd ever seen.

Helori stepped to me and kissed my cheek. "Beautiful lady."

I grinned. "My mad syraza."

He laughed, kissed me again, then approached Kadir and placed a hand on his cheek. They remained still and silent for a long moment, then Kadir took a deep breath and nodded, entire posture easing ever so slightly. A wisp of something that might have been a true smile touched his mouth. I didn't know what had passed between them, but Paul wore an ear-to-ear grin.

Helori took two steps back, flared like a mini-sun before turning into coruscating sparkles and vanishing.

Idris's brow puckered. "What happened to them?"

"Helori's merging with the Between space for reinforcement and support," I said. "Kind of like how Rho merged with the core of the demon realm to stabilize it. And Zakaar is . . . well, not sure exactly how to describe it, but he's becoming part of the water systems—oceans and rivers and lakes and waterways on both worlds, for overall substructure, foundation, and connection. Basically, they're going to get shit fixed up and keep it that way."

Those within hearing range murmured in awe.

"Lannist," I said as I beckoned Ashava over. "Would you be willing to take this one under your wing, and help her learn everything she needs to know about her abilities, especially being an unfettered lord?"

Lannist inclined his head. "It would be my absolute pleasure, Kara Gillian."

Ashava sucked in a gasp of delight, eyes wide with *Oh, yes, please!* She spun to look at Jill with naked hope on her face.

Jill laughed. "You don't actually need my permission, you know. But, yes. Go. Learn. Kick ass. Come back every now and then."

Ashava gave her mother a squeeze, then did a happy little boogie.

"Speaking of unfettered," I said, sweeping my gaze over the lords. "This is long overdue."

I closed my eyes, pulled in a deep breath, then exhaled it to create a soft breeze that fluttered over and through the lords, stripping away the dross and chains and barriers and mega-governors as it passed.

Amkir let out an exultant shout, startling everyone, then shifted fluidly into a snow-white mountain lion.

The others looked perplexed then awed then jubilant as long-suppressed memories flooded in.

Rhyzkahl stood very still, then bared his teeth as a large sand-colored wolf—though the imposing image was spoiled somewhat when Squig soared down to perch on his head.

Elofir transformed into a badass mountain gorilla and beat his chest in thunderous percussion. Vrizaar became an enormous spiral-horned Kudu with a shimmering gold hide. Not to be out-done, Rayst dropped to all fours as a fifteen-foot crocodile with glittering green scales.

Vahl stretched his arms out wide then crouched to become a jackal with iridescent midnight-blue fur.

Ashava cheered, delighted as the lords tapped into long-forgotten abilities.

Paul cocked his head at Kadir with an unmistakable *Well? What are you waiting for?* expression. Kadir laughed—startling everyone—then leaped into the air as a cerulean and gold Phoenix, with Fillion a heartbeat behind.

Seretis eyed the others then shifted into a unicorn, deep crimson from horn to tail.

And finally, Szerain took a deep breath, stretched his arms out wide, and an instant later a cobalt and copper griffin took to the skies.

I nudged Ashava. "What are you waiting for? Go play!"

She giggled like a schoolgirl and vaulted into the air, shifting into a silver dragon—quite a bit larger than the one she'd been after the valve explosion.

I snickered as I noticed Paul filming the antics with his shielded phone. Yeah, this definitely needed to be recorded for posterity.

Idris came over to stand beside me. "They look happy," he said. "About damn time."

"Yeah. About damn time."

Eventually the lords transformed back to their human forms, though still and forever unfettered and free. Rayst and Seretis embraced, but like good friends, and I knew that what was past was truly in the past for them.

Ashava gave Jill, Bryce, and me long hugs, then she and Lannist vanished to go learn more about . . . everything.

I delivered everyone else home then raised the rest of the undamaged Earthgates and set reasonable restrictions on their usage.

Now it was time to help both worlds get back on their feet.

Chapter 48

The café smelled delightfully of chocolate and coffee and luscious baked items, reminding me in all the right ways of Grounds For Arrest, which had reopened just last week, across the street from the newly rebuilt Beaulac PD. I'd been present for the dedication of both, along with Boudreaux, Pellini, and Krawkor—who was Major Krawkor now and headed the PD dispatch and communication division. Boudreaux continued to run the horse farm, along with his mom and Lenny. Walter stayed on as handyman and caretaker, and Redd had stuck around, too, though she and Boo insisted they were just very good friends. Pellini was now the director of an organization that provided aid to disadvantaged parents, making sure their children had a solid start in those formative years. He also had ties to the Child Find League—the organization founded long ago by J.M. Farouche to track down missing children—which had seen an influx of anonymous, and consistently credible, tips, thanks to Paul and Kadir.

In the year and a half since the end of all hostilities between the worlds, Kinsavi had opened more cafés around the country, all named with clever coffee-related puns, such as The Business Grind, and Espresso-ly For You. As things continued to settle down across the planet, his business picked up nicely. Kinsavi was adamant that his company would be a supportive and positive place to work. He not only encouraged the employees to unionize, but also offered a living wage, a great bonus system, excellent benefits, generous vacation and leave policies, and a compassionate view toward working with employees' personal schedules, family lives, and physical limitations. As a result, he had many hundreds of loyal and happy employees, and his profits skyrocketed—which he put right back into the business in the form of higher wages and increased benefits.

Which meant that other popular coffee shop chains had little choice but to adopt similar policies or suffer. Terrific ripple effects that kept on going.

I kicked back in Latte For Class—one of his locations near Georgia Tech—as I ate a chocolate donut and drank my coffee. Heavily sugared and creamed, of course. There was no chance I'd be recognized as Kara Gillian, since it was simple enough for me to shift my features and alter my skin tone and hair to whatever best served my needs. Right now I wanted to pass as a typical grad student, which meant I looked to be in my early twenties, with hair in a semi-neat ponytail, and otherwise nondescript.

A few tables away, a thirty-something woman tapped away at her keyboard, brow puckered. I waited until she paused and leaned back, rubbing her eyes, then I picked up my mug and plate and started toward the place to deposit dirty dishes.

As I passed her table, I made a show of letting my gaze drift casually onto her screen, then stopped and backed up.

"Oh wow . . . you're working on atmospheric carbon capture?" I shook my head and gave a rueful smile. "Sorry, not usually nosy like that. It's just, I literally had a conversation yesterday about how some special rock could lower the cost of a major aspect."

She offered up a polite smile. "Yes, one of the main roadblocks has always been the cost of the materials for an effective solvent."

"Right. That's what this materials science grad student was telling me. She believes a certain demon realm mineral could be the solution, but she can't get permission to go to the demon realm without a more cohesive proposal. No one's been willing to work with her on it without more data—which she can't get without going there." I snorted, gave a wry smile. "Poor lady's caught in a loop." Much like the roadblocks Dr. Aniyah Tayler—the woman before me—had encountered in her own research. And while travel between Earth and the demon realm was possible with the Earthgates, there were still careful restrictions on their use—managed by me, Idris, the lords, and Jontari—to avoid the kind of problems unlimited access could and would cause.

Dr. Tayler's gaze sharpened with interest. "Don't suppose you happened to catch her name?"

I made a show of racking my brain. "Umm . . . Kami some-thing. Kami Nomura? I think that was it. She was my seatmate on a flight to L.A. Said she was a grad student at Cal Tech."

Dr. Tayler scribbled the name down, clearly trying to control the flare of hope. "Thanks. I'll have to see if I can get in touch with her."

I gave a perky grin. "Cool! I sure hope that works out!"

I put my dishes in the bin and left the café, aware that Dr. Tayler had found contact info for Ms. Nomura and was already drafting an email.

I replayed similar scenarios numerous times, putting scientists together who could fill in missing pieces. Or making sure certain research papers didn't die in obscurity. Or ensuring ridiculous bureaucracy didn't keep people from obtaining or continuing their education. I didn't solve problems or give answers. I simply . . . lubricated the process.

Other times I made obstacles. Like when the translation system at a big global summit ceased to work in the middle of a deeply stupid speech filled with racist dog-whistles and dangerous misinformation. And somehow it wasn't recorded either. Huh. Go figure.

Meanwhile, some of the more hate-filled politicians—who didn't actually believe the vile shit they spewed but used it as leverage for power and profit—had inexplicable mechanical issues that made them terribly late to rallies. Or technical issues that plagued their websites and social media. And for the ones with shady fund-raising, who targeted the elderly and made it look as if they were only making a one-time donation—which was actually every month or, in at least one horrific case, every week—I made sure that any withdrawal after that first donation was miraculously returned by the bank. If someone wanted to donate to a candidate, it wasn't my place to stop them. But I made sure they weren't getting fucked over.

In the first weeks after the battle at the column, I returned to the beach in Samoa every other day or so. Jewel-toned leaves and a white trunk now glimmered among the palms, and the sparkle of the Between teased the edges of my vision.

I'd wade in the ocean, lie on the sand, soak in the beauty, and commune with Zakaar. Though I could commune with him in any body of water, this place felt special. I would let my consciousness drift, seeking. Always hoping for the faintest whisper or feel of Mzatal.

After a while, I started coming only every couple of weeks. Then months.

Then years.

The end of all demonic incursions became known as The Entente, and marked the beginning of informal relations between the two worlds. Idris had gained a great deal of respect in diplomatic circles, known to be the man to consult in reference to demon/human relations, as well as anything regarding access to the demon realm.

He was also in high demand in another area. A handsome, fit, intelligent, successful, and clearly powerful young man, barely a day went by when Idris wasn't the subject of fierce speculation and online gossip about his love life, preferences, and plans for the future. The only reason he wasn't constantly stalked by paparazzi and drones was because he dealt with any invasion of his privacy by frying intrusive tech with potency.

As far as the majority of the world knew, he never dated. However, I and a very select handful of other people knew he'd been very discreetly seeing Nandi Chola, the former DIRT summoner from Capetown. I liked Nandi tremendously, and they seemed quite happy together. Fortunately both were sensible and centered, well aware they were young and that this was the first time either had been in anything resembling a serious relationship, and they had no intention of rushing into anything.

"You look happy," I told Idris after the two had been dating for a little over a year.

He grinned. "That's all you're going to say?"

I laughed. "Fine. I like her."

"Yeah. I do too."

The elders returned to watch over their rakkuhr reservoirs, bringing the wisdom of restraint to the flourishing Jontari. They eased the potency imbalances between the worlds and developed ways to tap core rakkuhr without reliance on dangerous overabundance. It had taken ten thousand years for the Ekiri presence in the demon realm to inadvertently drain Earth's natural potency, and it would take that long to rebalance—time enough for humans to re-adapt to a world where "magic" was real.

* * *

Adrift without Mzatal, Dakdak began spending more and more time on Earth, especially at the horse farm. The ilius seemed to enjoy accompanying Lenny on his rounds as he checked on the animals, and thus I was unsurprised a year later when I sensed a very interesting shift in their friendship.

Catherine was naturally shocked out of her mind when she found Lenny collapsed in a stall and covered in red goo. But I'd already given Pellini a heads up, and he reassured her that podding was a natural and safe process, as long as Lenny and the goo were left undisturbed. Sure enough, a couple of weeks later, Brulen emerged from his pod with a very fine sheen of silver-black fur covering his body, and purple sclera, along with an unerring sense of exactly what ailed his animal patients.

The lords began making regular visits to Earth. Unfettered now, they'd regained the ability to teleport—though they still had to use the Earthgates to travel between the worlds.

They'd also regained suppressed memories from thousands of years ago, memories of their lives before they'd been ripped away from families and loved ones and everything they'd ever known. As expected, this was traumatic and a source of true grief.

I'd once seen a vision of Rhyzkahl with two young sons. Because of the actions of the demahnk Ekiri, he would never know what became of them, or if the boys had even lived long enough to have families of their own.

Other lords experienced different flavors of loss. Amkir wasn't even a teen yet when he'd been taken away from what was now Belarus, and absolutely nothing remained there of what he'd known. He wandered Minsk for weeks, visited museums and consulted historians in the hopes of finding some reference or relic, anything that could tie his memories to the present that existed now. While the historians had been thrilled beyond belief to record his first-hand experiences, they'd been unable to satisfy his desire for a tangible connection.

Yet now that the lords no longer had to focus their entire lives around keeping the demon realm stable, they had the freedom to do more for their self-fulfillment, and even for sheer enjoyment. To my undying relief, Rayst, Vahl, Amkir, and Rhyzkahl all began seeing well-vetted therapists—*firmly* encouraged to do so by various human companions. Elofir made frequent visits to Earth, enchanted by the California Redwoods, delighted by Sagano Bamboo Forest in Japan, and in absolute awe of the hundred-million-year-old Daintree Rainforest in Australia. Vrizaar sailed to every continent, and Rhyzkahl developed a surprising interest in Broadway theater. Never would have imagined that happening, until I realized the lords had literally been without that sort of entertainment *their entire lives*. In fact, all the lords save Kadir became huge movie and TV buffs, pestering Szerain and their companions for advice on what to watch next.

And, to my utter joy, delight, and relief, Tessa and Rhyzkahl formed an essence bond, which greatly eased my worry for both of them.

Fuzzykins went to live with Eilahn in the demon realm, where the cat was pampered and spoiled and coddled and cooed over. Fuzzykins was, of course, quite pleased with this arrangement.

Jekki and his mate Faruk traveled to a variety of places on Earth but spent much of their time at my house, where Jill, Bryce, and several others still lived. During one of their excursions to Germany, an extremely foolish pair of humans attempted to capture the two faas in the hopes of selling them to a collector.

It went badly for the humans, as Rhyzkahl, Amkir, and Vrizaar appeared and showed them the error of their ways. Idris made sure the attempted demon-napping—and lordy response—was well-publicized, so opportunists would think twice before targeting passive demons.

Turek developed a liking for K-pop music, especially the group DK-Demonz, so I repaid my honor debt by buying him front row tickets and backstage passes to one of their concerts. Turek was deeply pleased, but DK-Demonz was over-the-moon *thrilled*—and even pulled him onstage for one of their numbers. To absolutely everyone's delight, the six-legged demon flawlessly kept up with the group's complex choreography and became an instant internet sensation.

With Mzatal gone, the reyza Gestamar split his time between exploring various aspects of Earth and arcane research with the Jontari. Kehlirik—the very first reyza I ever summoned—ended up as friend and counselor to Idris, and had all the buttery *papcahn* he could ever want.

Some six months after The Entente, I attended Paul and Dominic's wedding, held on a plateau in Dekkak's realm. Kadir was

Paul's best man, and I was Dom's best woman. Ashava even took a break from her travels with Lannist to be there. It was a small ceremony, but all the people who mattered were present. Except one, of course.

Afterward, Ashava came and sat beside me on the ledge where I was watching the brilliant orange and purple sunset. Her hand found mine, and I gave it a squeeze.

"I can't feel Mzatal anywhere," she said after a moment. "Lannist and I . . . we've tried to find him. I'm so sorry."

"I know." I exhaled. That hair-thin connection had vanished when I destroyed the dragon, and there'd been no trace of it since. "But thank you for looking for him."

She sighed and rested her head on my shoulder. "Don't you dare tell me you'll be okay."

I couldn't help but chuckle at that. "All right, I'll be excellent."

"You already are."

Paul and Dom founded Fillion Entertainment, a game development company that not only went on to make absolute gobs of money—which they used to fund absolute gobs of social services—but also had rock-hard policies about diversity and workplace harassment. They refused to put their employees through the sixty-to-eighty-hour "crunch" weeks near the end of projects that many other companies did, or indulge any of the other ugly practices that were common in much of the game industry—which meant they were able to attract and keep the best and the brightest, and nurture the ones not far behind. Plus, when fans started harassing developers for failing to make games exactly how they wanted them—or for any other reason—the management stepped in with full support of the game devs. And since Paul was literally a god of the internet, anything hateful or threatening simply . . . went away, as did the authors' social media accounts.

Fillion Entertainment hired Giovanni to do most of the art for their promo materials, which made him hugely popular and wildly successful. Elinor became the company's art director, after demonstrating a real aptitude for that side of the business.

A year after The Entente, Elinor gave birth to a baby girl, who they named Szera.

After wishing Elinor and Gio the best of everything, I dropped in to visit Jill and Bryce.

They were reading on the front porch, reminiscent of a couple who'd been married for decades, when in fact they'd decided not to bother with the whole getting married thing. It wasn't as if they needed it to be sure of their commitment to each other.

They smiled and waved as I strolled up the driveway, like I was a neighbor popping by for a chat, and not at all as if they hadn't seen me since Paul and Dom's wedding. But once I made it up the steps, Jill greeted me with a big hug, then Bryce had to have his turn.

Once he released me, I plopped into one of the rocking chairs. "Y'all have been busy," I said with a grin. "The place doesn't look like a compound anymore."

Jill smiled. "It's a relief, isn't it? We've been doing our best to turn it back into a real home again. No more sally ports and defensive perimeters. I didn't figure you'd mind, though let the record show that I *did* try to reach you and get your permission."

"Yeah, sorry about that. I've been putting out a lot of little fires here and there." And keeping to myself. "But you don't need to ask my permission . . . since the house and Forty are yours. Officially. In your name and legal and everything. Oh, and Boudreaux now owns the horse farm."

Jill's mouth dropped open. "Huh?"

"I don't exactly need a house anymore. And I know you'll take really good care of the place."

Jill exchanged a look with Bryce, then grinned. "That's even more awesome, because we have an idea about what to do with the Forty."

Bryce leaned forward. "We want to turn it into a shelter and retreat for troubled teens and runaways. All the facilities are right there and ready to go, and a bunch of the former compound guards and members of Alpha Squad have said they'd love to be involved, assist with vocational training, and be support staff. Hell, Roma, Tandon, and several others have already been living here and helping out."

"Boudreaux has talked about having the horse farm be part of the program," Jill added. "He's always had a soft spot for kids. And Pellini said he'd like to get his organization involved as well."

"That sounds absolutely fantastic," I said, then laughed. "And you have experience, since you had the ultimate troubled teen."

Jill grinned. "Did I ever! Luckily she's far better now."

I set the chair into a gentle rock. "You know, you could make some changes to the house, too."

"Yep, we've already turned the basement into a kind of rec room and—"

"Pool table soon," Bryce coughed.

Jill laughed. "Yes, we'll get a pool table!"

"And the conference room is back to being a dining room," Bryce added.

"That's terrific," I said. "You could even convert the office into something. I dunno, maybe a nursery?"

Jill snorted. "I don't think that's going to be . . ." Her mouth formed an O. "Wait."

Bryce jerked upright. "Are you shitting me?"

"No, that office could totally be converted—" I ducked as Jill winged a coaster at me. "Okay, yes, you're pregnant. Jeez, so violent!"

But Bryce had already hauled Jill to her feet, holding her close while tears streamed down his cheeks. "Oh my god. Are you okay with this? We've been using protection and never talked about the possibility—"

"Yes, yes," she laugh-cried. "I'm very very okay with this." She looked back at me. "I can't be very far along, right?"

"Only a few weeks or so." I grinned, really enjoying this. "A boy," I added, because I knew she'd want to know.

Eight months later, I returned for the birth—which was fortunately far less eventful than Ashava's. Jill commented afterward that she very much preferred the kind of delivery where the baby simply teleported itself out of the mother.

Bryce was a total weepy, gooey mess as he held his son for the first time.

"We're naming him Zack," Jill told me with a weary but brilliant smile. "When he's a little older, we'll take him to the river to meet his namesake."

I gazed down at little Zack. "He'll be thrilled."

Two and a half years later, I returned to the compound when I felt Jill and Bryce's panic.

"We can't find Zack anywhere!" Jill told me, wringing her hands. "Somehow he managed to open the front door. Everyone has turned out to search."

I took hold of Jill and Bryce and teleported them to the back yard, just as Dekkak emerged from the rift with the giggling toddler tucked under one arm. Bryce sagged in relief, and Jill darted forward to take her wayward son and lavish thanks and apologies on Dekkak. The imperator merely rumbled, clearly more amused than anything.

"Guess we need a taller fence around the rift," Bryce said.

Little Zack became a regular visitor to the Jontari realm and to Uncle Bubba—who became "Unkaba" to Zack, and then also to the demons. Unkaba *adored* Zack's visits and delighted in showing him everything there was to see and teaching him the joy of making things.

On his fourth Christmas, Zack gave his parents a very clever articulated wooden fish.

Two months later, Idris and Nandi married in a very private ceremony in Rhyzkahl's demesne.

By the time he turned six, Zack was damn near fluent in demon—perhaps aided by how much his parents had been exposed to the arcane, as well as his frequent opportunities to speak the language. His Christmas present to Jill and Bryce that year was a wooden reyza with wings that flapped if you turned a crank.

Eight years, three months, and twenty-one days after The Entente, I realized I'd done enough. Nothing specific I could point to as a reason, except for the unerring sense that humanity and the demons and the lords could take it from here. Any further interference or nudges on my part would be too much, and I had the Ekiri as a shining example of What Not To Do.

I returned to the beach and waded in the gentle surf. Smiled as sparkling azure swirled around my legs and I felt the always welcome presence of Zakaar.

After a short communion, I went up to the white sand and lay back, closed my eyes. Over the past several years, I'd often pondered what I would do or where I would go once I was finished here. I'd always known there would indeed be a finish, a stopping point. But my options were as limitless as the universe. Now it was time to explore. I'd no doubt return for visits now and then—after all, there were people here who I loved and who loved me. Plus, I looked forward to seeing what the humans and lords and demons would do with themselves next. It felt a bit like sending a kid out into the world, except I was the one who'd be going off into the unknown.

I let the sun warm me as I considered my myriad options.

A whisper drifted through my consciousness. I opened my eyes to a sky dark with dusk, half the sun already below the horizon.

A shadow flickered oh-so-briefly across the sun.

No, not a shadow. Something emerging from the water.

I inhaled deeply and stood, absently brushing off sand as I walked to the surf's edge.

"You're late," I called out.

Mzatal grinned—*grinned!*—as he strode to the shore, gloriously nude except for the ring on his left hand. His hair flowed past his knees around him, adhering deliciously about his body.

He caught me up in an embrace. "And you have been most patient, zharkat."

"I just hope you're worth the wait," I said with a laugh, then took his left hand and cocked an eyebrow. "I thought you destroyed this."

He chuckled low. "Simple sleight of hand. I would never relinquish it to Ilana. A dimensional pocket kept it safe."

"Clever!"

He dipped his head to mine and proceeded to show me the many other ways he could be clever.

We lay on the beach, limbs loosely twined around each other. A gibbous moon looked down on us from a sky packed with stars.

"What shall we do first?"

"Anything we desire."

Epilogue

Darcy set her coffee on the side table, safely away from keyboard and paperwork, and took her seat in the command center. It was three a.m. in California, but that time didn't matter, except to her sleep cycle. Right now the only time anyone cared about was the one on the mission clock. The first manned mission to Mars had left Earth almost seven months ago, and they had 2.26 days to go until it arrived at its destination.

She leaned back and called up footage from the various rovers. There were nine on Mars now, though four were no longer functional. Sadly, the newest and most sophisticated rover, *Perspective,* was among the ones who'd stopped working properly. It continued to send images—but of the exact same stretch of landscape, and was completely unresponsive to every effort to shift it. Stuck, or glitched, the result was the same.

In the dozen-plus years since The Entente, funding for science and exploration had experienced a huge uptick, with terrific leaps in technology as a result. The amount of time it took to get from Earth to Mars hadn't changed much, but everything from life-support systems and camera resolution to better tech for transmitting data had improved dramatically.

This meant the footage from the newer rovers was stunningly clear. Darcy gazed at *Perspective's* unchanging feed and let out a pleased sigh. A landscape of reds and browns and yellows, breathtaking instead of boring—a view that never grew old to her. Still, it was a shame they couldn't turn the rover to obtain from-the-ground footage of the arrival of the manned ship. None of the other rovers were anywhere near the landing site, though a couple of them might be able to pick up a very distant entry burn. And, of course, there'd be imagery from the ship itself as well as various satellites.

Perspective's feed abruptly went black. Darcy leaned forward as a spear of true grief went through her. Dammit, this poor rover may have been stuck, but to have it totally crap out right before the landing seemed deeply unfair to the little robot dude.

The image flickered and returned, but the barren and beautiful Mars landscape was gone, replaced by . . .

It took Darcy several seconds to process what she was seeing, vaguely aware of a growing buzz of shocked and excited conversation around her. For a heart-stopping moment she thought the feed had been hacked. Except the background was still clearly Mars.

But in the foreground, two people filled the screen, wreathed in smiles and waving like maniacs. No protective gear, no space suits, no breathing apparatus.

Then her brain engaged, even as she heard the murmured names spread through the room. Kara Gillian, who'd dropped out of sight half a decade ago. Beside her was a tall man with Asian features, silver-grey eyes, and long unbound black hair.

Mzatal, the demonic lord straight out of a legend.

The two stepped apart to reveal an easel holding a large sheet of poster board. Big block letters written in marker, the words surrounded by stickers of spacemen and planets and stars, like you'd find in a first-grade classroom.

Darcy burst out laughing. Around her, people began cheering and clapping. Especially as it sank in that *Perspective* was working again. In fact, *all* the rovers were working, even the ones from decades ago.

Grinning, Kara and Mzatal put their hands together to form a heart.

Then they were gone, leaving the schoolroom easel with its posterboard sign:

WELCOME TO MARS!!!!!

* * *

In loving memory of my dad, Walter Harrison Rowland

Glossary

The Demonic Lords (Qaztahl) And Their Demahnk Ptarl

Amkir | *Dima*

Ashava | *None*

Elofir | *Greeyer*

Jesral | *Ssahr*

Kadir | *Helori, estranged*

Mzatal | *Ilana*

Rayst | *Trask*

Rhyzkahl | *None (formerly Zakaar)*

Seretis | *None (formerly Lannist, now scattered)*

Szerain | *Zakaar (formerly Xharbek, now scattered)*

Vahl | *Korlis*

Vrizaar | *Fiar*

Characters

Amkir *demonic lord*: Light olive complexion, short dark hair. Unsmiling. Known for his temper.

Ashava *demonic lord*: Daughter of Jill Faciane and the demahnk Zakaar (Zack Garner). The only free and unfettered demonic lord (a *qaztehl*).

Bayliss, Elinor *summoner*: born in the 17th century. Trained in the demon realm with Mzatal, Rhyzkahl, and Szerain. Killed by Szerain during a ritual that precipitated the Cataclysm. A part of her essence was attached to Kara's. Giovanni's lovemate.

Boudreaux, Marcel: (early 30s) Head of DIRT 1st Cavalry Unit. Ex-Beaulac PD detective, partnered with Vince Pellini. Former jockey for J.M. Farouche. Small and wiry. Nickname of "Boo" to those in the horse world.

Bikturk *demon, reyza*: Jontari. Nicknamed "Big Turd" by Kara. Killed by Mzatal with essence blades in Ust-Ilimsk, Russia.

Brewster, Lenny: (late 60s) Veterinarian and barn manager for the DIRT 1st Cavalry Unit. Hale, sharp-minded, and soft-spoken. Lanky black man.

Cantrell, Lilith: Compound security team. Tech expert.

Cleland, Michelle: (24) Physics major turned drug addict and prostitute on Earth. Taken to the demon realm by Rhyzkahl after the Symbol Man ritual. Flourished with Vahl as she recovered from addiction and trauma. Beloved of Elofir and resides in his realm.

Crawford, Cory: (early 40s) Compound communications specialist. Ex-Sergeant with Beaulac PD. Lost his right leg while trying to clear jail cells during the PD valve explosion. Podded and became Krawkor. Skin a brilliant and shifting canvas of colors. Three prehensile tails.

Dakdak *demon, ilius*: Associated with Mzatal.

Dekkak *demon, reyza*: Jontari. Warlord and imperator. More than three thousand years old. Made pact with Kara.

Dima *Ekiri demahnk*: Ptarl and parent of Amkir.

Dominic (see Gilroy, Dominic)

Eilahn *demon, syraza*: Multiethnic beautiful in human form. Former bodyguard of Kara. Adores holiday decorations and her cat, Fuzzykins.

Elinor (see Bayliss, Elinor)

Elofir *demonic lord*: Beloved of Michelle Cleland. Enjoys the quiet of his wooded realm. Short, sandy-blond hair. Slim, athletic build. Calm, gentle, deeply caring. Pacifist by nature.

Engen, Nils: (early 20s) Compound security team. Medic.

Faciane, Jill: (30ish) Kara's best friend. Compound manager. Smart and sarcastic. Mother of Ashava. Former crime scene tech. Former gymnast who'd been favored to make the Olympic team before a bad fall. Red hair, blue eyes, petite, athletic.

Fiar *Ekiri demahnk***:** Ptarl and parent of Vrizaar.

Gestamar *demon, reyza***:** Mzatal (essence bound). One of the oldest lord-aligned reyza. Sense of humor and scary, all at the same time.

Gilroy, Dominic: (26) Paul's boyfriend. Highly skilled computer engineer. Has a doctorate in Physics. Kidnapped by Jesral to create the Between Machine. Rescued (in a roundabout way) by Paul and Kadir.

Giovanni (see Racchelli, Giovanni)

Glassman, Scott: (late 30s) Corporal of DIRT Alpha Squad. Ex-Sergeant and patrol training officer for Beaulac PD. Acts like a hick, but savvy. Stout, bald, ruddy complexion.

Greeyer *Ekiri demahnk***:** Ptarl and parent of Elofir.

Greitz, Ronda: (mid 30s) Compound security team. Mechanic and engineering specialist.

Gurgaz *demon, unique***:** a.k.a. Slugthing. Jontari. Associated with Dekkak.

Hawkins, David: In charge of the compound commissary and mess hall. Former owner of the Grounds for Arrest coffee shop. Podded and became Kinsavi. Now has deep indigo skin, silver eyes, and long hair that he can control.

Helori *Ekiri demahnk***:** Estranged ptarl and parent of Kadir. Spurned by Kadir. Prefers human form to the "elder syraza" form. Often associates with Mzatal. Proven ally of Kara.

Hernandez, Sonny a.k.a. Jose Luis Hernandez: (mid 30s) Kara's aide de camp. Former coerced hitman and kidnapper. Best friend of Bryce. Has an enhanced talent for calming people. Previously caretaker for Zakaar.

Idris (see Palatino, Idris)

Ilana *Ekiri demahnk***:** Ptarl and parent of Mzatal. Influential. In league with Ssahr (and, formerly, Xharbek).

Jekki *demon, faas***:** Mzatal. Spry and energetic personal attendant of Mzatal. Loves to cook.

Jesral *demonic lord***:** Kara's current archenemy. Slim, brown hair, keen gaze, impeccably styled and graceful. Smiling, outwardly friendly. Slick, cold, and calculating.

Jill (see Faciane, Jill)

Kadir *demonic lord***:** Perceived as cold, psychopathic, chaotic, vicious. Protective of children and innocents. Ruthless to any he deems deserving of punishment. Utterly brilliant. Lives slightly "out of phase" with the rest of the demon realm. Essence bond: Paul Ortiz. Tall, slender, blond, androgynous.

Kehlirik *demon, reyza***:** Associated with Rhyzkahl. Often summoned by Kara. Skilled with wards. Loves popcorn and human books.

Kellum, Jordan: (mid 30s) Compound security team. 5'4". Former world-class powerlifter.

Khatur *demon, Jontari elder***:** Imprisoned by Mzatal within gimrah and essence blade. Blade held by Mzatal.

Korlis *Ekiri demahnk***:** Ptarl of Vahl.

Knight, Marco: (mid 30s) Detective for the New Orleans PD. Clairvoyant or similarly gifted. Podded and became Makonite. Red rakkuhr now flickers in his eyes.

Lannist *Ekiri demahnk***:** Scattered by the Ekiri collective for divulging forbidden information to Kara. Parent and former ptarl of Seretis.

Lenny (see Brewster, Lenny)

McDunn, Angus: (mid 50s) Works for Jesral, who holds his wife, Catherine McDunn, hostage. Has the ability to enhance or diminish abilities, especially those related to the arcane. Stepfather to Boudreaux. Lost a young son over twenty years ago to abduction and murder. Broad-shouldered, big and stocky. Red and grey hair.

McDunn, Catherine: (early 50s) Ex-head trainer for Farouche's thoroughbreds. Wife of Angus McDunn and mother of Boudreaux. Captive of Jesral.

Michael (see (Moran, Michael)

Michelle (see Cleland, Michelle)

Moran, Michael: (early 20s) Suffered a traumatic brain injury at the age of twelve. Brilliant pianist. Has the ability to form golems out of dirt. Can sometimes clairvoyantly see the lords' locations.

Mzatal *demonic lord***:** Zharkat of Kara. Eldest of the lords. Powerful and focused. Creator of the essence blades. Tall and elegant, keen silver-grey eyes, Asian features, very long jet-black hair worn in a braid. Wields the blade Khatur. Essence bonds: *Gestamar* (reyza), *Dakdak* (ilius), Kara.

Nguyen, David: (late 20s) Compound security team. Arborist and experienced tree cutter.

Olson, Rupert: (early 60s) Senator with an education agenda.

Ortiz, Paul: (22) Computer genius. Uses potency flows in tandem with computer networks to find information and accomplish hacker tasks. Can tap into pretty much any audio/video/internet feed. Like a brother to Bryce. Hispanic. Essence bond with Kadir.

Oshiro, Tsuneo *summoner***:** (late 20s) Jesral's prime summoner. Has a tattoo of his sigil.

Paul (See Ortiz, Paul)

Pazhel, Tessa *summoner***:** (late 40s) Kara's aunt and former mentor. Student of Katashi. Mother of Idris Palatino. Raised Kara from age eleven. Worked closely with Katashi. Possibly betrayed Kara to serve Katashi's interests. Frizzy blond hair and eclectic fashion sense.

Palatino, Idris *summoner***:** (20) DIRT Arcane Specialist. Student of Mzatal. Kara's cousin. Son of Tessa and Rhyzkahl. Gifted summoner. Adopted as a baby, and then again as a young teen after his first adoptive parents were killed. Innocence stripped by the Mraztur. Forced to watch his sister be ritually tortured and murdered. Killed Isumo Katashi.

Pellini, Vincent: (early 40s) Trained and mentored in the arcane by Kadir. Works in tandem with Kara and Kadir. Former detective for the Beaulac PD as a partner and best friend to Boudreaux. Black hair, dark eyes, mustache, not as out of shape as he used to be.

Racchelli, Giovanni: 17th century associate and art student of Szerain. Named by Gestamar as one of Szerain's favorite humans. Elinor's lover. Died young but returned to Earth not long ago.

Rasha Hassan Jalal Al-Khouri *summoner***:** (80s) One of Katashi's first students. Came out of summoning retirement to work with Mzatal in the demon realm.

Rayst *demonic lord***:** Partner of Seretis. Considerate, but not a pushover. Pays attention to the dynamics between others. Swarthy. Stocky build but moves with grace.

Rho *transformed Ekiri***:** Parent of Szerain. Merged with the demon realm planet core to stabilize it after the collapse of the Earthgates three thousand years ago. Manifests as the sentient white-trunked groves.

Rhyzkahl *demonic lord***:** Seductive and charming. Betrayed and tortured Kara in a failed ritual to create a weaponized summoner (Rowan) and raise an Earthgate. Exiled from the demon realm by Mzatal and imprisoned beside the nexus in Kara's back yard for a time. Earned a measure of redemption. Long white-blond hair, ice-blue eyes, tall, muscled, utterly beautiful.

Roma, Debbie: DIRT Sergeant. Alpha Squad leader.

Ronda (see Greitz, Ronda)

Roper, Dennis: (early 40s) Compound security team. Skilled in logistics and planning.

Scott (see Glassman, Scott)

Seretis *demonic lord***:** Prisoner of Dekkak. Partner of Rayst. Loves being around humans and has gone to extreme lengths to protect humans in the demon realm from other lords. Protected Kara from Dekkak. Chiseled cheekbones and shoulder-length dark, wavy hair, reminiscent of a Spanish soap opera star. Bisexual. Essence bond: Bryce Taggart.

Sonny (see Hernandez, Sonny)

Ssahr *Ekiri demahnk***:** Ptarl and parent of Jesral. In league with Ilana (and, formerly, Xharbek.)

Suarez, Bubba: (early 40s) Voluntary hostage of Dekkak as part of Kara's pact. Compound security team. Construction specialist. General handyman.

Szerain *demonic lord***:** Brilliant artist. Smart and inquisitive and very patient when his plans call for it. Is called a kiraknikahl—oathbreaker. Diminished, submerged, and exiled to Earth as Ryan Kristoff but now free. Terrified of being resubmerged. Newly ptarl bound to Zakaar. Bears the essence blade Vsuhl. Essence bond: *Turek* (savik).

Taggart, Bryce *(formerly Thatcher)***:** (40ish) Head of compound security. Ex-hitman. Has essence bond with Seretis. Was once Paul Ortiz's bodyguard and considers him like a younger brother.

Tandon, Sharini: (late 30s) Compound security team. Military experience. Black belts in Krav Maga and Danzan Ryū.

Tessa (see Pazhel, Tessa)

Trask *Ekiri demahnk***:** Ptarl and parent of Rayst.

Turek *demon, savik***:** Ancient demon. Has known Szerain for thousands of years, and they share an essence bond.

Tsuneo (see Oshiro, Tsuneo)

Vahl *demonic lord***:** Tends toward rash decisions that cause him to be indebted to other lords. Has a smoldering sexiness. Tall, black, and just the right amount of muscle.

Vsuhl *demon, Jontari elder***:** Imprisoned by Mzatal within gimkrah and essence blade. Blade held by Szerain.

Vrizaar *demonic lord***:** As cautious and prudent as Vahl isn't when it comes to dealings with the other lords, but not so staid that he doesn't enjoy the thrill of adventure. Loves to sail. Dark-skinned, bald, with a goatee and no mustache. Dresses like a biblical king, with gold and jewels just shy of gaudy.

Watson, Chet: (mid 50s) Compound security team. Gunsmith and firearms expert.

Xhan *demon, Jontari elder***:** Imprisoned by Mzatal within gimkrah and essence blade. Blade held by Mzatal (and, formerly, Rhyzkahl.)

Xharbek *Ekiri demahnk***:** Scattered by Mzatal. Ex-ptarl of

Szerain. Was ringleader of the demahnk who were willing to sacrifice Earth and humans in order to return to the Ekiri collective.

Zakaar *Ekiri demahnk***:** Parent and former ptarl of Rhyzkahl. a.k.a. FBI Agent Zack Garner. Sire of Ashava. Thought by the demahnk to be scattered but is sequestered within Szerain and in hiding. New ptarl bond with Szerain.

Zeno, Rania: Primary medic at the compound. Former Emergency Room NP with over fifteen years of experience. First encountered by Kara at Fed Central shortly after Rania podded and became Zenra. Human in appearance except with a cat's hind legs and tail. Is able to make medical assessments via her claws.

Animals

Griz: Caucasian Shepherd Dog. Two-hundred-pound demon-killing dog of DIRT's First Cavalry Unit.

Copper to Gold: Thoroughbred stallion owned by Boudreaux. Stellar career ended by a track accident with Boudreaux as jockey.

Fuzzykins: Eilahn's calico manx cat. Mother of Bumper, Squig, Granger, Fillion, Dire, Cake.

Sammy: Pellini's chocolate Labrador retriever. Goofy and lovable.

Squig: Winged cat with furry green scales, and tail covered with needle-spikes.

Fillion: Winged cat with metallic-silver fur.

Demon Words

Chak: Hot beverage without an Earth equivalent.

Chekkunden: Derogatory. Rough translation: *honorless scum*.

Dahn: No.

Ekiri collective: A non-corporeal, immortal race of telepathic beings who entertained themselves by traveling to various worlds to "enlighten" emerging species before moving on to a new destination.

Jhivral: A true plea. Not the casually polite usage of "please" in English.

Jontari: Demons who do not associate directly with the demonic lords. The vast majority of the demon population. Cities and enclaves are far from the palaces of the lords.

Kiraknikahl: Oathbreaker.

Kri: Yes.

Ptarl bond: Mental connection between Ekiri demahnk and their lord offspring. Can be used for control.

Pygah: An arcane sigil used for calm, focus, and centering. A foundational teaching for summoners (though Kara was not taught it until she met Mzatal). Most effective when traced as a floating sigil but may be done mentally.

Qaztahl: A demonic lord, or the demonic lords as a group.

Qaztehl: An unfettered, unmanipulated demonic lord. Ashava is the only one.

Rakkuhr: Core potency of both Earth and the demon realm. Overabundant in the demon realm. Toxic to Ekiri demahnk.

Shikvihr: Rough translation: *potency of the eleven.* An eleven-circle ritual that offers a power base and foundation to other rituals. Enhances a summoner or lord's abilities. Completing the shikvihr initiation—mastery of all eleven rings—gives a summoner the ability to trace floating sigils on Earth, along with other advantageous perks.

Tah sesekur dih lahn: Rough translation: *I understand and feel for/with you.*

Yaghir tahn: Forgive me (sincere).

Zharkat: Beloved.

Terms

Anomaly: A tear in the dimensional fabric. Various causes. Effects can be catastrophic. Repairs can be made by demahnk, demonic lords, and (for small anomalies) syraza.

Blade (verb): To stab a being with an essence blade. With rare exceptions, results in permanent death and a scattering or consumption of the target's essence. The body of one killed by an essence blade will not discorporate.

The cataclysm: Demon realm disaster that began in the 17th century and lasted nearly a century, with effects still felt to this day. Earthquakes, floods, fire rain, and rifts in the dimensional fabric. Caused by a ritual performed by Szerain and Elinor.

The Child Find League: Non-profit organization founded two decades past by J.M. Farouche to help find missing children. Impressive track record.

The compound: Kara's original house and property plus newly acquired land and development. Militarized for the Demon War.

Conclave: An annual meeting of all qaztahl where global issues are addressed and plexus schedules for the upcoming year are confirmed. Outward hostility is frowned upon. Intrigue is rife.

Demon realm and demon language: The world of the demons and demonic lords. The demon language has never been fully mastered by a human because of the verbal complexity and telepathic component. The same sound may have a multitude of different meanings depending on the telepathic pattern behind it. The demon word for their world is heavily telepathic and contains seventeen syllables.

Demahnk: The Ekiri parents to the lords. Can take on demon and human forms. Their favored demon form looks like a large syraza with ridges on the torso and skull. Sometimes called "Elder syraza." Each demahnk is (or once was) ptarl-bound to a lord. The lords are half demahnk, half human.

Demonic lord: Human-demahnk hybrid. Able to monitor, maintain, and influence the potency flows of the demon realm. Has the ability to read and manipulate thoughts of humans.

DIRT: Acronym for Demonic Incursion Retaliation and Tactics. Special units on the front lines of rift formation and suppression of invading demons. Kara Gillian is DIRT's Arcane Commander.

DNN: Demon News Network. Television network devoted to coverage of rifts and demon activity.

Earthgate: One of eleven gateways between the Earth and demon realm. Defunct for thousands of years.

Eleven: A significant number in the demon realm in rituals, architecture, and managing potency. Also, the number of demonic lords (before Ashava).

Discorporeate: The immediate dissolution and disappearance of the physical form after death when the death occurs on the non-home world. A demon that dies on Earth will discorporeate with a chance of resurrecting in the demon realm, and the same goes for a human who dies in the demon realm. Death caused by an essence blade precludes discorporeation.

Essence blades: Three daggers created by Mzatal as artifacts of power. *Khatur*, *Xhan*, and *Vsuhl*.

Faas *demon type*: Resembles a six-legged furry lizard with a body approximately three feet long and a sinuous tail at least twice that length. Bright blue and purple, jewel-toned iridescent fur, brilliant golden eyes slitted like a reptile's.

Federal Command Center a.k.a. Fed Central: Beaulac Ground Zero headquarters for DHS, NSA, CIA, and other national agencies, with the FBI Arcane Investigations task force taking the lead. Located in what used to be the Southern Louisiana Heart Hospital, now converted into a secure compound.

Geckoids *demon animal*: "Like fox-sized geckos on an insane amount of steroids." Bright red and yellow skin. Potentially invasive. Intelligence akin to that of a dog.

Graa *demon type*: Spider-like with wings like roaches and heads like crabs. Can have anywhere from four to eight multi-jointed legs that end in strange hands that consist of a thumb and two fingers, each tipped with curved claws.

Ground Zero: The Beaulac PD parking lot and immediate surroundings. Relates to the valve explosion and its resulting destruction and arcane activity.

Groves: Clusters of white-trunked trees that form a network of organic teleportation nodes, with one in each realm of the eleven lords and a dozen or so more scattered around the planet. Animate and sentient, a.k.a. Rho. Kara has a unique relationship with the groves. Teleportation can only be activated by a lord, demahnk, or Kara.

Ilius *demon type*: A coil of smoke and teeth and shifting colors. Feeds on animal essence.

Kehza *demon type*: Human-sized, winged, face like a Chinese dragon, skin of iridescent red and purple, and plenty of sharp teeth and claws. Can tell if a human has the ability to be a summoner.

Kzak *demon type*: Vicious, black, and dog-like. Rows of teeth and sinuous movement.

Lord headache: Excruciating head pain triggered by thoughts of topics deemed off limits by the demahnk.

Luhrek *demon type*: Resembling a cross between a goat and a dog with the hindquarters of a lion. Often a good source for unusual or esoteric information.

Manipulation: The altering of memories or controlling of actions through telepathic means. Utilized by demonic lords and demahnk.

Mehnta *demon type*: Appearing like a human female with long flowing hair, segmented wings like a beetle's, clawed hands and feet, and dozens of snake-like strands coming out of their mouths.

Mutagen: Specialized rakkuhr that can cause mutations. Overflow at ground zero.

Mraztur: Derogatory demon word used by Kara and her allies to refer to the demonic lords who once unified against her personal interests and those of Earth. Formerly, Rhyzkahl, Jesral, Amkir, and Kadir. Rough translation (per Seretis): motherfucking asshole dickwad defilers.

Nexus: A confluence of potency streams harnessed as a focal point of power in each lord's realm. Universally marked in the demon realm by a platform of stone, wood, or crystal surrounded by eleven columns. Foundation for the most powerful rituals. Mzatal and Kara created a basic nexus in Kara's back yard. Mzatal later amplified its power by creating a "super-shikvihr" on it, and then by anchoring Rhyzkahl to its perimeter.

Nyssor *demon type*: Looks almost exactly like a human child, often beautiful with angelic faces. Features a little *too* perfect, and eyes a little too large and having sideways-slit pupils. Hundreds of sharp teeth. Many humans find them creepy.

Plexus: The chamber in each lord's realm where the arcane potency flows of the planet can be monitored, manipulated, and adjusted by a demonic lord. Kara's rough translation: *a demonic lord's man-cave*.

Ptarl: The demahnk counselor and advisor to a demonic lord.

Ratos *demon animal***:** Akin to a large sewer rat, but with sharp, brown-black scales instead of fur. Low intelligence. Potentially invasive.

Reyza *demon type***:** At least three meters tall, leathery wings, long sinuous tail, skin the color of burnished copper, horns, clawed hands, bestial face, and curved fangs.

Rift: A Jontari-created opening in the dimensional fabric, often manifesting on Earth in the form of surface crevices that span anywhere from a few inches to hundreds of feet in length. Jontari can form and use them to travel between the demon realm and Earth, or from point to point on either world.

Rowan: As yet enigmatic personality that Rhyzkahl intended to overlay on Kara. Demonstrated arrogance and sense of invulnerability. Seems to be familiar with Szerain.

Savik *demon type***:** Immature savik: two-foot-long dog-lizard kind of thing with six legs. Mature savik: Over seven feet tall, reptilian with dark and smooth bellies, and translucent glittery scales elsewhere. Head like a cross between a wolf and a crocodile.

SkeeterCheater: Graphene-enhanced netting capable of physically entangling and holding a demon. Relatively immune to their arcane attempts to break free. Used to cover or partially cover rifts to slow demon arrivals. Exorbitantly expensive to produce.

Syraza *demon type***:** Slender, almost birdlike, long and graceful limbs. Pearlescent white skin, hairless. Large and slanted violet eyes in a delicate, almost human, face. Wings that look as fragile as tissue paper but most assuredly are not. Shapeshifter.

Valve: An arcane conduit between the demon realm and Earth that acts as a potency pressure valve to help stabilize the demon realm.

Zhurn *demon type*: Black, oily, shifting darkness. Winged. Burning red eyes. Voice like a blast furnace. Sharp claws.

Zrila *demon type*: About the size of a bobcat, looks like a six-legged newt with skin that shifts in hues of red and blue. Head like a hairless koala. Brilliant artisans who make the majority of the clothing and textiles in the demon realm.

Jim C. Hines

Janitors of the Post-Apocalypse

"Jim Hines is one of the funniest, and most fun, writers in our genre! *Terminal Alliance* skewers science fiction tropes and takes on a wild romp through an original universe." —Tobias S. Buckell,
author of the Xenowealth series

"A solid premise, an expansive universe, a compelling history, a strong and varied cast of characters, pulse-pounding action, and a galactic crisis with high stakes. The fact that it's funny is icing on a rich and delicious cake. Clever, and should appeal to fans of Douglas Adams and John Scalzi."
—*Booklist*

Terminal Alliance
978-0-7564-1275-3

Terminal Uprising
978-0-7564-1278-4

Terminal Peace
978-0-7564-1280-7

www.dawbooks.com

Christopher Ruocchio

The Sun Eater Saga

"Epic science fiction at its most genuinely epic. Ruocchio has made something fascinating here, and I can't wait to see what he does next." —James S.A. Corey

"Space opera fans will savor the rich details of Ruocchio's far-future debut, which sets the scene for a complicated series.... Readers who like a slow-building story with a strong character focus will find everything they're looking for in this series opener." —*Publishers Weekly*

"Although stretched across a vast array of planets, the story line is often more focused on the intimate than on the expanse, giving it a wonderful emotional punch. This wow book is a must for fans of Pierce Brown and Patrick Rothfuss." —*Library Journal*

EMPIRE OF SILENCE   978-0-7564-1301-9
HOWLING DARK   978-0-7564-1304-0
DEMON IN WHITE   978-0-7564-1307-1
KINGDOMS OF DEATH   978-0-7564-1310-1
ASHES OF MAN   978-0-7564-1660-7

www.dawbooks.com

DAW 218

Tanya Huff
The Peacekeeper Novels

"Huff weaves a fast-paced thriller bristling with treachery and intrigue. Fans of military science fiction will enjoy this tense adventure and its intricately constructed setting."
—*Publishers Weekly*

"Anyone who has read any of Huff's previous books featuring Kerr . . . knows of her amazing ability to combine action, plot, and character into a wonderful melange that makes her books a joy to read."
—*Seattle Post-Intelligencer*

AN ANCIENT PEACE
978-0-7564-1130-5

A PEACE DIVIDED
978-0-7564-1151-0

THE PRIVILEGE OF PEACE
978-0-7564-1154-1

To Order Call: 1-800-788-6262
www.dawbooks.com

Suzanne Palmer
The Finder Chronicles

"A breakneck-paced and action-packed science-fiction adventure featuring an endearing con artist whose current mission to retrieve a stolen spaceship ignites a war.... A nonstop SF thrill ride until the very last page."   —*Kirkus*

"Fergus Ferguson makes an excellent lead in this fast-paced hard-sf repo adventure set in space opera's sweeping scale and balanced on the heart of one very finely wrought character. Suzanne Palmer's writing is delightful."

—Fran Wilde, author of the Bone Universe trilogy

Finder
978-0-7564-1635-5

Driving the Deep
978-0-7564-1694-2

The Scavenger Door
978-0-7564-1807-6

www.dawbooks.com

DAW 219